GATEWAY TO HEAVEN

Also by Sheldon Vanauken

A Severe Mercy (1977)

Gateway to Heaven

SHELDON VANAUKEN

Illustrations by author

Harper & Row, Publishers

San Francisco

Cambridge
Hagerstown
Philadelphia
New York

1817

London
Mexico City
São Paulo
Sydney

ACKNOWLEDGMENTS

The poems quoted in part in the Journey to Hawaii are "Waikiki" and "Tiare Tahiti," which may be found in *Rupert Brooke: The Complete Poems,* published by Messrs Sidgwick & Jackson, London, 1932.

The lines from T. S. Eliot's "Burnt Norton" in *Four Quartets,* copyright 1943 by T. S. Eliot and copyright © 1971 by Esme Valerie Eliot, are used with the permission of Messrs Faber & Faber, Ltd, London, and Harcourt Brace Jovanovich, Inc., New York.

The author expresses his deep gratitude to those who read the book in manuscript for their insights and criticism, with special gratitude and love to Lady Frances of Elk Hill.

FIRST EDITION

Designed by Jim Mennick

Library of Congress Cataloging in Publication Data

Vanauken, Sheldon.
    Gateway to Heaven.

    I. Title.
Pz4.V2177Gat   1980   [PS3572.A418]   811'.54   79–3600
ISBN 0–06–068822-X

80 81 82 83 84 10 9 8 7 6 5 4 3 2 1

To S, nonetheless: for her winged vision.

What might have been and what has been
Point to one end, which is always present.
Footfalls echo in the memory
Down the passage that we did not take
Towards the door we never opened
Into the rose garden.

—T. S. ELIOT, *"Burnt Norton"*

Contents

Author's Note

Gateway to Heaven is a work of fiction. A story created in the imagination. Neither Mary's character and personality nor her experiences are modelled upon those of anybody I have ever known. Nor are Richard's. Mary's poems are what the Mary who lives only in these pages—a Mary, be it remembered, who is more *girl* than woman— would have written. Similarly, the other characters are imagined and no reference to anyone else is intended. Often it seemed best to locate certain adventures in places—hotels or harbours, caves or coves, dining places or dancing places—that were wholly imagined. Finally let it be said that, quite apart from being a love story, this book is conceived to be a tale of high romance, which may loosely be taken to imply ladies fair and knights on quest and roast dragon for dinner.

WIND SONG
(Mary sings it)

Listen, the wind!
April-morning wind,
Wind blowing the Maytime in.
Listen, Wind!
Blow to me!
Blow the walls down!
Break the dark house!

Across my paned window, the eye of the wind,
The gulls like splinters of light sweep down
The bright sky, and girls like flowers of the wind,
Hair blowing, skirts flying, go lightly below.
Oh girlhood is a desperate glory!
And joy is a girl in a blue April breeze,
Bare-foot, wind-blown, and free! My cry
Is a bell ringing down the wind,
A gull falling down the sky.

I'll break out or die! Burst out like a fury,
Leaving only a girl-shaped hole in the wall!
And run, run lightly away in the wind,
Winged in the dancing wind and free!

Oh, God!—these choking tears! Oh, God!—
This time, this time,
This terrible will might tear down the walls!
They stand. —What else shall I do today?

Oh, Wind, blow! Tear the dark house!
Blow the walls down! Blow
My hair into wings, and let me run,
With you, Wind, soft and joyous, around me,
Under a blue April sky into May.

I would go as the wind goes—a girl
Blown by the wind, as light as a drift
Of cloud, as gay as a flurry of joy,
The wind's winged girl, beloved of
The wind, blown lightly along and away,
Wild-crying in the lift and the soaring
Of wings in the wind. Oh, Wind!
Wind, my lover, blowing the Maytime in!
Blow the walls down!

Journey to the Crossroads

Dearest Mary,

Will you ever read this? I do not know of course, but I am driven to write to you. Because I do not know, because of the thing that has happened, I've called this letter Journey to the Crossroads—the crossroads of our life together. It is very right so to do: we have always called our travels journeys, haven't we? Journeys to somewhere and implicitly from somewhere. And a journey, strictly speaking, is something that happens in a day, like our little Journey to Tintern Abbey from Greyfell. Today I haven't moved out of the house, and yet I have journeyed from bright morning to night, from happiness and well-being to darkness and pain. From the straight road ahead to the crossroads. All since the post came.

Although you may never be able to read this, I picture you reading it: your sea-blue eyes—the blue of the ocean off-soundings—searching the words for meanings. Writing the letter is, perhaps, an act of faith—faith that you will, some time, read it.

Or am I only writing to keep pain at bay? To reduce it to a word instead of the thing itself? Helpless pain, for I cannot grapple with the cause of pain. All my thoughts turn to you, Mary, just as a compass needle must seek the north. But I cannot rush to your side: it is forbidden. I cannot reach for the telephone. I cannot even send this letter. One whole month—less six hours now—must creep by before I shall know. There is nothing I can do. I cannot act. Yet perhaps, after all, I *am* acting: this writing is act. Futile it may be, yet disciplined act. A faintly encouraging thought.

The letter came six hours ago. I strode to the door, blithely whistling. And then the pain began. You don't need me to tell you of pain, Mary, do you? You have known so much pain in your life. And you will know, if you are able to be conscious of me at all, of my pain. But can you know of the element of terror and shocked amazement in it? I am mazed, Mary dear.

But I have a month, a month of silence and unknowing, to find my way out of the maze, if I can. To try to come to terms with catastrophe. To try to see the real meaning of that entity called Richard and Mary. And perhaps the meaning of God, a loving God, who let it happen. Couldn't He have stopped it? But perhaps He doesn't care. Perhaps He does care, though. Jesus, who was God become man, would care. He would have sad eyes, looking at Mary and me. Yes. He would care. Perhaps He will help. I must pray, though perhaps this whole day has been a prayer. But, apart from praying, how do I sort this thing out?

How does one begin? I am Richard Vallance—Val to you, Mary— and you are my wife. Are you aware of that, Mary—that you are wife, that I am husband? And we are over here in New England from Old England for a year. I took a year's leave from Worcester College, Oxford, and we turned Greyfell, our house in Oxfordshire, over to friends so that I might teach history here at Holywell College, where seven or eight years ago I was an undergraduate. But Maryland—a house called Redrock by a slow tidal river on the Eastern Shore—is my childhood home. Here at Holywell we are occupying a pleasant old house on the edge of the campus. But Mary is not at home—a fortnight ago she went down to Georgetown to visit her father—and perhaps she will never be able to come home again.

The letter came six, almost seven now, hours ago. And the shell of silence closed round me. I think I've never known such agony. A slight late snow is falling, making the silence more silent with the soft, somehow ominous, silence of the snow. April is the cruelest month, Eliot says, and so it looks like being for me. Yet I think of the lilacs at Redrock and Greyfell, and the lilacs in Virginia.

Now, here's my plan. I almost smile, albeit wanly, at those words. Remember that great cartoon, Mary? The two naked men, fettered wrist and ankle, feet not even touching the floor, in a windowless, doorless cell, the stone walls sweeping up hundreds of feet to a steel grating: and one of the chaps was turning his head towards the other man with a big grin and saying, "Now, here's my plan!" The spirit of man, in both senses. Come the end of the world, some chap, I expect, will be saying that to some other fellow. And here I am, saying it on our own doomsday.

I do, in fact, have a plan. Since I must not go to Georgetown, since there's no direct action I can take, I will do the one thing I can do: I will think, I will look for meaning—instead of allowing my mind to run around in circles like a rat inside my skull, as it has been doing. I can't look at the thing itself—not yet. And the future is hidden. I only know that the road, the old road that we intended to travel with light hearts, has been crossed by another road, the dire road. But I'm an historian: I can look at the past. If I look steadily enough, contemplating cause and effect, perhaps I shall see some light through the present darkness.

It will be, at least, a kind of action. Fortunately I have the materials: our journal. Your journal, really, Mary, for you were so much more faithful in keeping it than I—and that's what I want, above all: your words. There is where I may find understanding. What I shall do is type the whole thing up, perhaps omitting or minimizing my entries, adding my comments at the ends of journeys—we only kept the journal on our journeys. Our gay journeys to France and the Greek Isles and Hawaii, remember, love? But you delved into the remoter past in the course of those journeys, didn't you? Of course our whole happy time together has been rather less than a decade.

What I shall do is teach my classes and come straight back here to my study to be alone, to write and think. And when I have finished with the journals, I'll write some account of the present year—our journey to Holywell—and add my final comments based on the whole study. And hope that you will be able to read it, Mary. I shall have plenty of time this month, for I shan't need much sleep. I'm not at all certain that I *can* sleep anyhow.

"Don't worry things," my father said once when I was a boy. We were walking back to Redrock along the river, just coming onto the lawns, and the hound puppy was worrying a stick. Dad grinned and said: "When you have a problem, Son, that seems too big for you, and there's nothing you can do for the moment, don't worry it. Let it alone until you can act." It was good advice, made for today. I'll take it.

Very well. I shall begin, begin with the beginning of the journal in another April, four years ago, in 1964. But no, even before that, I'll begin with your poem, my darling: "Wind Song." That's the key to you, perhaps the key to everything, including my love for you. If you *do* read this, Mary, know that now, on this darkest of days with darkness ahead, sitting here with the quiet snow descending, I love you, dear. I think I shall never love anyone else. You are my gateway to heaven.

Yours,
Val

Journey to Provence

In the English Channel under a grey sky flecked with patches of blue, a ferry boat is wallowing towards Dover where a long queue of motionless cars awaits its arrival.

About midway in the queue is a small blue two-seater with top down despite the chilly breeze. The man at the wheel is smoking a pipe with a contemplative look on his face: it is a strong face with a look of quietness, distinguished by a straight nose and level grey eyes. The girl on his left has short hair of a lighter brown than his. Her head is bent, for she is writing in a notebook on her knee. When she lifts her gaze for a moment to glance with a little smile at her companion, her eyes are as blue as the Mediterranean to which the car and its passengers are bound.

"What are you writing, Mary?" says the driver. "A poem? A deathless poem called 'Queuing Up at Dover' or 'Where Now the Bloody Ferry'?"

"Not at all," I say, for I am the scribbler, Mary Vallance by name. "Deathless and dignified prose. I have, in fact, just composed the first gripping paragraph of the account of our journey to Provence, in which I pointed out that you had a contemplative look on your face whilst waiting for the ferry. Would you care to say for the record what you were contemplating?"

"Food," says the man with a grin—that is, Richard Vallance, my still quite new (and first) (and only) husband, says. "A noble vista of lunch. Or a chocolate bar."

4

"Well," I say, "you may as well contemplate the lunch since we haven't got either one. Hush up now. The Muse is about to dictate another paragraph."

Richard grins and hushes, and I scribble away in my special shorthand. As I've said, I am Mary, wife of this fine Richard, also known as Val, and I'm twenty years old—or, to be quite truthful, I shall be twenty in three more days, on Friday, the twenty-fourth of April, 1964. Richard is five years older than me and much wiser, except now and then. And we are about to have a holiday in the south of France.

We have already been together now—together with certainty, though Richard was not certain of my certainty—for almost three years, for Wingsday was in May. That was when we knew at last that what we had hoped for so hard—hoped for, prayed for, longed for—the passing of the dark shadow that had lain across my life, had come true. That is what we call *wings:* the lifting of that dark shadow. Wings to suggest the soaring up of a freed bird. And on Wingsday I was freed: I stepped, literally stepped, into life. I stepped, I walked, I strode, with Richard smiling beside me.

Later on that same day, the day I was winged, we were in Virginia where the first red roses were blooming, and we drove to our special mountain meadow at what is locally called the Gateway to Heaven, where the sunrise or the moonrise can be seen between two mountains— a meadow which has been for us the gateway to heaven in all truth. Once, earlier, in that meadow I had made a little joke, not very funny, asking Richard sort of lightly what he would give for the wings. He looked at me a long moment and then just whispered, "I'd give me!" And with someone like Richard, as I knew at that moment, such words mean for ever. He came into the shadow with me; he would have dwelt there. So now on Wingsday, when we were full of joy at the passing of the shadow, looking at the rose in the neck of the winebottle as on that earlier day, I said: "Somehow, love, you made me winged." And you—I mean, Richard—took my hand and murmured, "May will always come for me with a flutter of wings."

Well, in June of that year Richard was graduated from Holywell College in New England; and in the autumn, after our summer of winged joy, I went back there with him—I who had never been to any school, only tutors, went off to college like any other girl. Our plan was that Richard would do an M.A.—and he did, in fact, get deep into his subject, which was England's Royal Navy, or, at any rate, the use of sea power prior to 1600—while I went to college as a special student. But we didn't stay there long, after all, only a semester; and then we came on to Oxford, where mediaeval and early modern sea power expanded into an enormous D.Phil. thesis.

I speak of those days as though we were already married or at least living in sin together; but we weren't, for Richard resolutely refused. I had been too shut off from life, he said: I must have a chance to experience things and look about. Besides, he said, what I felt for him might just be gratitude, mightn't it? I knew perfectly well that it wasn't just gratitude, but he continued to be resolute.

So I lived with a girl named Katie at Holywell and saw Richard when I could, which was quite a lot; and when he came on to Oxford I did too, matriculating at Lady Margaret Hall. Thanks to my father's insistence on my being taught Greek practically in the cradle, and being now in his beloved Oxford, where he had been at Trinity, I read Greats, as the combination of classics and philosophy that has been said to be the severest university course in the world is called. In view of that severity, I should probably not be taking a journey to Provence in the vac and shall pay for it later, I expect. But Richard, at least, is in a lull now, for his mighty tome on sea power is completed and bound, possibly in oaken boards, and sent off to the Examiners; and he knows from Roger Denby, a friend of his in college—Richard's in Worcester—who knows one of the Examiners, that they are quite enthusiastic (in a restrained Oxonian way, of course) about the sea-tome. Moreover, the *viva voce* or orals can't be set before June. So we immediately became very blithe, or at least Richard did, and I caught blitheness from him.

"Mary," says Richard. "The Bentley ahead of us in the queue has started its engine. And cars are coming from up there. The ferry's in."

"Let's not leap to conclusions," I say. "It's probably the head of the queue going home, having been told that the ferry has sunk. —Oh, we're going!"

A half hour later we are in the Channel, choppy as usual. The breeze is mild and chilly at once—mild with chilly edges—and the sky has become a pale, pure blue.

Richard, sitting beside me in a deck chair, remarks, "I feel a bit headachy."

I immediately picture him in hospital, dreadfully pale, dying, with nuns standing round with pitiful faces. Of course I'm rather given to dire imaginings where my only husband is concerned. In order to preserve him, I say tenderly, "Would you like half my croissant?" We had bought two from the steward earlier.

"Yes," he says. "If you're sure you don't want it." He takes it and

6

eats it in two bites and then becomes absorbed in a science-fiction book, *The Day of the Triffids.*

I look hungrily at the waves, wishing I had my half-croissant back or perhaps a whole one. Then, looking out at the waves, I am reminded of crossing the ocean long ago, before wings, with Daddy in the *Queen Mary.* We were on our way to see Mummy's family in Gloucestershire, though Mummy was dead by then.

Richard gets up, saying, "I think I'll walk about." He looks inquiringly at me, but I shake my head. I have an impulse to tell him not to fall overboard, but it occurs to me that he probably already intends not to. Still, I picture him in the waves, swimming strongly for England.

On the other side of me is a young Frenchman, and he now—the competition being gone—endeavours successively to lend me a magazine and a probably vile French cigarette. I refuse, giving him my Smile #1, Archaic and Remote. Richard by the rail is watching with his Smile #2, Mild Amusement—though once, not long after wings, before I became a worldly woman, my little encounters with men caused him to smile Smile #4-b, Genuine Hilarity (Repressed). That was because, after my Dark Ages, when I'd had no experience with men at all, except Daddy and Richard, such things caused me fright and awe—awe that they could be happening to me.

Anyway, now that the Frenchman is rebuffed, I can get on with my writing, and if the ferry sinks in the Channel I shall insert these pages in a winebottle and throw it overboard. Years later it will be washed up in the Hebrides, and people will know that I was faithful to Richard when a French moustache tried to take me away from him. But since the Hebrideans will hardly consider the moustache to have had a fair show and will mention that he was only a Frenchman after all, I will say that there were others.

Richard himself said that I must have more experience with men. I told him I loved him and, besides, I didn't know what to say to any men but him. And he said I must just think up something to say to them and become sure through experience. So I met some boys at Holywell mixers and went out with one or two, not without fear and trembling. And I did think of some things to say, particularly No. And then at Oxford there were others, but I continued to love Richard in every way the best.

And then there was Peter—Peter Shirley of Magdalen College and of Yorkshire, the North Riding. This is a good time, this Channel-crossing, poised between England and Europe, to write about Peter, whom I really liked a lot and still do. He was thoroughly English with fair hair and fine blue eyes and a sort of happy way of talking. He was also humorous and witty as well as being, quite genuinely, an English gentleman, courtesy and breeding in all he did. Above all, he had that surest mark of a gentleman, according to my father: a sort of largeness of spirit, carelessly generous of all that he had and was. One day he would be Sir Peter, Bart. He, too, was reading Greats, which is how I came to know him. We both came out of the Schools after a lecture that November, and the rain was pouring down. I was just deciding that I should have to wait it out, having no umbrella; and then I heard his pleasant voice.

"I say," he said. "Would you care to share an umbrella? It's quite a big one. I'm going towards Carfax." I didn't know then that he was in Magdalen, which is in the other direction.

So I said, "Thank you very much. I'd like to."

We talked a bit about the lecture as we walked along the High—we'd both been to the same one, which is how I learned that we were both reading Greats. Then he suggested that we go into the Mitre and have our tea; and I said, again, that I should like to.

It was very pleasant, there by the fire. I don't remember what we talked about—books and Oxford and, a little, about the North Riding and his horse; he loved hunting. It came out, somehow, that he knew and liked Richard—some club they were both in—although he didn't of course know that there was anything special between Richard and me. To tell him there was would not be the openness to other men that Richard insisted on. I remember that at the next table to Peter and me there was a fresh-faced family with a country and county look, obviously up from the shires to see their son. I remember also thinking that Peter had a first-rate mind as well as his charming, merry grin. At one point he talked about architecture, both classical and gothic, with a range of knowledge and appreciation that I couldn't match, though I resolved that I would immediately read lots of books on the subject. Oh, yes, we also discovered, Peter and I, that we both liked Vaughan and Yeats and Browning, and could often complete each other's quotations. In the end we left the Mitre, after two orders of toast and lots of cups of tea, as almost old friends.

Well, after that we kept seeing each other here and there, and I liked him a lot. He asked me to tea one day in his rooms at Magdalen: from his window I could see a deer wandering about in the park. And he came to LMH—Lady Margaret—for tea and crumpets, and I had Richard, too; it was apparent that there was a strong friendship between them.

There never was a nicer chap than Peter or one more fun to do things with. Once he borrowed a car and we drove out to Minster Lovell to explore that rather haunting ruin—the great house of the Lovells on the River Windrush, I mean, not the church. And then we dined at the nearby Swan, and Peter was witty and funny and gay, all at once. But much as I liked him and enjoyed being with him, I was a little worried. I was doing what Richard had said I should do, going about with a man, and a very attractive one, too. But I didn't feel any inloveness for him, as I did for Richard. Still, how could I be sure that I shouldn't come to feel it? Besides, Peter didn't show any signs of being in love with me. It was just that I was afraid he might be, and it would be awful to hurt him. But maybe I would be in love with him later: if I were going to be open-minded and really find out, I had to go on. I really did love him, in a way: the shape of his head, his beautiful blue eyes and slow smile and his nice clean smell. And I thought a little bit about how it might be, married to him. He had told me enough by now of the big old country house in Yorkshire, with half of it closed off because of the lack of servants—and showed me pictures of it, too—so that I could sort of imagine living there. That part, living in the country, would be just what I should want. And Peter, subtle and sensitive and—well, just so good, so decent, would be a grand companion. But—a companion? There has to be something more than that: some sort of magic, a spark or a flame. As there was, I thought, with Richard. Maybe it would come though. Maybe a flame would suddenly spring up, far greater than anything with Richard. I didn't believe it, but I would give it every chance. So I continued to go about with him, but I tried in little ways to suggest that I wasn't in love.

And then in late May of the second Summer Term of our Oxford years, with the may trees in bloom, I went with Peter to the Magdalen Commemoration Ball with a champagne breakfast to follow in a punt at dawn, if the weather held fine. I was a little hesitant about going—after all, I had never been to a big formal dance in my life; actually, I had only been even walking for two years. But Richard said of course I should go, if I wanted to. So I went. And it was gay and lovely.

After the ball we took to a punt, as other couples were doing. And Peter proposed to me that night—or that morning, rather.

The birds were singing, singing birds everywhere, and the sun was shining in a long slant across the meadows along the Cherwell, and Magdalen's grey tower was far astern. I was wearing the long dress I had bought for the Commem, all shimmering pale yellow. It was a gown I had fallen in love with on sight, because it reminded me of the loveliest dream of all my shadowed childhood. In the dream I was in a dress of that same pale yellow and I was standing—standing!—in front of a looking glass while the sun shone down through green branches and into the window, and I was straight as a young tree. I was thinking about that dream as the rising sun shone through green branches and Peter poled us peacefully along, not far from the riverbank where a water rat was just getting up. Perhaps it was Ratty from *The Wind in the Willows,* calling to Mole to hurry up.

Then Peter shipped the pole and let the punt drift into the bank. He sat down, smiling at me while all the birds in Oxfordshire sang round us. He opened the champers with a pop that caused at least one bird to miss a note, and we drank to the morning and the bird on the bough. Then we ate our breakfast with more champagne, talking a little of the Commem but mostly just being companionably still, smiling at each other. When the breakfast was eaten, he poured the last of the champagne—just two glasses full.

He raised his to his lips, smiling at me, and said, "This is a morning like the North Riding. I wish we could go there; I want you to see it very much. You'd love it, I think. In fact . . . well, in fact, I've often thought of . . . you know, taking you there." He paused for a moment, looking at me steadily, not smiling. And then he said gently, "I love you, Mary. I've never loved anyone so much." He swallowed hard, and I saw that his hand was trembling a little. He said, "Will you marry me? Mary —will you?"

Something in me was trembling a little, too. A thought flickered through my mind: so this is the way it happens! I looked at him, the steady blue eyes intent upon mine; I noticed that his bow tie was slightly askew. I thought, almost objectively, for a flashing instant of this scene: the sun and shadow of the river, me in the yellow gown, Peter's fair hair in a bar of sunshine, Peter asking me so gently, waiting so courteously— Peter, so dear. But something frantic was nudging at my thought: Richard. Richard whom I loved so thrillingly, whom I was in love with. I wanted to say Yes to Peter just because all this was so beautiful and he so sweet, but—it was Richard I loved. I knew that in this instant for always.

But, oh dear God! How could I bear to say No, how could I hurt him so?

"Peter," I said. "Peter, I am so sorry. I like you, you know I do, but —but don't you know I'm not in love with you? Why, only three days ago, when we were having tea in your rooms with Trevor and Elizabeth, I said I hoped we'd be friends always—that you were like the brother I never had? And before that, too, I said I wanted us to be friends, just friends, remember? Peter, dear, I wish—well, I wish I didn't have to say No . . ."

"Oh, I know," he said. "You've played fair, played fair all along. It was just—oh, you look so lovely sitting there! And the morning reminding me of home and all. And I thought—oh, I thought that p-perhaps things had, oh, you know, changed." He looked at me sadly, and then managed a little grin. "Forget I said it, Mary."

"No, Peter," I said. "I'll never forget it—never. I'm incredibly grateful. Truly! And you are very dear to me. But, Peter—I don't think we should go on seeing each other, do you?"

"That's why I asked you to forget it," he said. "Please! Let it be as before. Just think of me as being carried away by all those dances and all the champers for breakfast, don't you know. Come on, now—friends?" And he held his hand out with a grin.

So I took it, feeling very fond of him, and murmured, "Friends— always."

He took the pole and then laid it down again.

"Mary," he said. "It's Val, isn't it?"

"Yes, Peter," I said. "It's Val."

"Shouldn't you have told me?" he said gently. "If you knew . . . ?"

"But, Peter," I said, "you always agreed that we were just friends; and you never showed any signs of being in love with me."

"I know," he said. "But, still . . . if you knew . . ."

"Listen, Peter," I said. "It's only right that you should know how it all was. Do you remember that afternoon in the Magdalen Deer Park when I told you what life was like for me in what I call my Dark Ages? Before the healing I call wings? It was then, in my Dark Ages, that I fell in love with Richard, and he, he says, with me. But, after wings, he thought—well, he thought that what I felt might be just gratitude. After all, I had never known a boy, except him—never been out with one, never danced—nothing. So he said I'd have to know other men, in order to be sure. And Peter, dear, in all that time between our walking down the High in the rain to the Mitre up to now, the Commem and this punt, I have been . . . well, open to loving you, you know. I just didn't. I mean, I love you but I'm not *in* love with you. I think I'm made to love one person—and it was Richard who was there. Maybe if I had known you then it would have been different."

"I'm glad you told me that," said Peter. "I mean, about being open to loving me."

"Yes, Peter," I said. "I'm glad you know. And I'll tell you one more thing. It was not until this morning that I was absolutely certain. Peter, dear, if it weren't that Richard already lived in me, I think I'd have said Yes this morning. I like you enormously."

"Thank you, Mary," he said, a little unsteadily, and he immediately stood up and began to pole the punt back to Magdalen Bridge. After a few minutes he said, "Val is my friend—there isn't a finer chap in this university. I'm glad it's Val if . . . well, I mean, blessings on you both." He gave me a grin, and gave the bottom of the river a mighty poke.

We parted at Magdalen Bridge, and I told him not to come back to Lady Margaret with me. "Right you are," he said. Then he leaned down and kissed me on the cheek, and I kissed his cheek. He managed another grin. "Goodbye, old thing," he said. "Cheerio!" He turned and strode into college, and I went down the High, wearing my long yellow gown in the bright morning.

And there I saw Val in his black gown just going into the Schools, and I ran up to him, calling, "Val! Richard!"

And you said, "Mary! You're crying!" You said later that, in that moment, you had a frightful pang of fear that I was in love with Peter. But you merely said kindly, "Here! Wipe your eyes, and let's go into the Botanic Gardens and you shall tell me all."

So there in the lovely gardens under a tree with the morning sunlight streaming down I told him all. When I told him of my instant of knowing, there in the punt, that it was he, Richard, that I loved for ever, he gave a long sigh; and then we suddenly kissed each other with such passion that it left us both shaken. Fortunately nobody else was about so early in the morning, except for one old gentleman who pretended not to notice. Then Richard confessed that he had, for a long time, been terrified that I was going to fall in love with Peter—"I thought, how could you help it, he's such a splendid chap?" And he had thought that he wouldn't be able to bear it if I did, yet he was determined not to breathe a word about his fears until I had, certainly, made my own choice. I felt like weeping again for all Richard's fears as well as for poor Peter, too.

Then Richard said, "Mary, I don't think that any more experience with other men is necessary, do you? How would you like to have a second proposal in the same morning?"

"Oh!" I said. "Why, Val!" He was grinning and looking tender at the same time. I pulled myself together. "It doesn't seem quite decent, somehow," I said. "But, er, I'd like it very much, please, sir."

"Will you, Mary?" he said, not grinning. "I've loved you all my life, I think."

"Yes," I said. "I will. I've always known, always . . . ever since Winebottle Mountain. Always known where the Gateway to Heaven was." I paused, and added, "I'm so glad you proposed to me in this dress!"

He laughed. "Spoken like a true woman, love!" Then he kissed me. "When?" he said.

"Now," I said. "At once." I thought afterwards that I said it rather like a Prime Minister laying down an ultimatum: Her Majesty's Government require that France agree at once . . .

Anyhow, Richard said, "Right! The sooner the better."

That is how we came to our wedding day still in Maytime, a quiet little wedding in the chapel of St Mary Magdalen church without a bridal party, though Daddy flew over to give me away; and, to my immense astonishment and joy, Val, after a long talk with him, announced that Peter was to be his best man.

And that is the story of Peter and my testing, of the Proposal in the Punt and the Proposal in the Gardens. It is why I'm so certain that Richard is the man for me.

I feel a hand on my knee and look up, ready to rebuff Frenchmen, but it is my love, Richard. "France is getting close," he says. "What are you writing?"

I close my notebook. "I have just written a concise history of our life," I say, "full of drama and, er, passion. You can read it later."

We stroll about the decks until it is time to return to the *Broom,* which is the name of our car because of the sound it makes: b-r-r-o-o-o-m. There is a bump and some yelling. We have arrived. A few minutes later we have presented passports and been waved through the barrier and are driving down a long street parallel to the waterfront.

I remark gently that it is interesting that in France it has long been the curious custom to drive on the right side of the road.

"Mon dieu!" says Richard, swerving swiftly over. A *gendarme* removes his unblown whistle from his mouth and addresses a remark to himself, probably about *les Anglais.* I offer him Smile #3, Radiant, Every Tooth.

Once into the country the *Broom* speeds south, Richard swerving me out to tell him whether we can pass. After about a hundred kilometers we pause at a restaurant for lunch.

A waitress with tired but tender eyes in her wrinkled face comes up. I smile at her and she smiles back. Then Richard and I pool our knowledge to order in French.

Then he sits back, smiles, and says, "At last!"

I think how fine he looks with his broad shoulders, his smiling mouth, and his level gaze. "At last—what?" I say. "At last France? Or at last food?"

"Well, both," he says. "Only a croissant since dawn."

"A croissant and a half," I say. "Because of your headache."

"Noble Mary!" he says. "Maybe I meant, at last a winged wife with a noble nature. It's still a bit incredible—wings, I mean. I watch you sometimes, and you look—jumping about, you know—as though you'd never had anything wrong except a stubbed toe."

There is a little tranquil pause. Then I say, "I remember, too. All those years of . . . of deadness. Then you and wings—both miracles. Oh, Val! I praise life—and the dear God—every hour. I just don't want to bore you with a joyful yelp every few minutes."

"Oh, you wouldn't bore me," he says. "Go ahead and, er, yelp. Are you quite sure that's the precise word you want?"

"Cry the paean, then!" I say. I emit a sound designed to be a paean, which, in fact, sounds like a banshee. A man with a brown moustache at a nearby table eyes me with considerable wariness. Not unreasonably, his face wears an expression of the liveliest apprehension. "That was a paean," I say to Richard.

"Oh," he says. "Was it? —There's something else. Before wings, even when you were happy and laughing, there was something sort of serious and sedate underneath. It's only since wings that you've developed all this craziness and bone-deep lightheartedness."

"I've thought about that myself," I say. "I think it's this: the soul and the body interact. No matter how gay and frisky my soul potentially was, I couldn't be that way in that broken body . . . which I couldn't ever, ever, quite forget. I mean, I am a whole, not just soul or self or whatever."

"I'm sure that's true," says Richard. "There's an odd contradiction in you, though."

"Not at all," I say. "Still, what?"

"A very understandable one," you say. "You're twenty—and one minute you talk seriously and well, as though you were twenty-eight; and the next you act like a sixteen-year-old. Of course it's all that agony of soul. And all the books."

"And Daddy's company," I say. "He's a pretty wise man. And my tutor, Miss Williamson, who loved poetry so. Not to mention you! As for the alleged sixteenishness, remember I'm about three in terms of frisking about."

"Oh, I know, love," he says. "Don't think of changing."

"One thing about all that's happened," I say. "It does make me feel that *anything* is possible if you sort of believe hard it is. Just to go into a shop and try on a dress and *walk* out wearing it . . . or skip out! If I can do that, I can be Prime Minister or go to the moon or command a regiment—*any*thing!"

"Most anything," says Richard. "I'm not quite able—not yet, anyway—to imagine you as a Guards Colonel. You do have to look the part, you see. Remember that interaction of soul and body."

"Oh ye of little faith!" I say. I push up the neck of my turtleneck pullover, sit up very tall, and twirl an imaginary moustache. "Charge!" I say in a gravelly voice. "Charge for the guns! Forward the Greys!" I wave my knife like a sabre.

Richard grins. Then I notice a look of active hostility on the face of the moustache at the nearby table. I turn my colonel-look on him, ready for the last stand of the Greys; but he averts his gaze.

"That moustache thinks I'm imitating my betters," I say. "Hiss! —What's happened to our omelettes, do you think?"

The headwaiter comes towards us purposefully, and I think that perhaps he is going to arrest me for being a colonel; but he merely wants Val to move the *Broom.* Richard disappears.

I look at the moustache out of the corner of my eye, feeling slightly more vulnerable with Val gone. The moustache is regarding me with a look of perplexity mingled with revulsion mingled with an awareness of my femaleness. It is the look he might give to a not-unattractive green female Martian who might prove dangerous. I take my notebook out and scribble in it. While I am scribbling the *salade* arrives.

Richard returns and we eat the *salade.* Still no omelette.

"I have written a poem to that disapproving moustache at the next table," I say.

"Let's hear it," says Richard with a grin.

"It's called 'Brave Moustache'," I say, and read.

> In mood contemplative and queasy
> Men think being Female can't be easy:
> Unfree, of course, the sex that's second,
> In limbo till we're lordly beckoned.
> And though they're glad that *we* are women,
> They're gladder still that they are him in
> A world where if one would prevail
> It's such a help to be a male.

"The Lady-with-a-sting," says Richard. "Actually, very neat. Especially that rhyme with 'women'. Is that going to be the end?"

"I expect so," I say. "Where does one go from there? It's all based on his expression. —Oh, good. Here are the omelettes, at last."

After we have eaten a few mouthfuls, Richard says, "Going back to your spirited rendition of the Guards Colonel, don't you feel that there might be a few problems when it came to commanding men? For instance, that American soldier who followed you back to Lady Margaret —what about *him, mon colonel?*"

"Ahem," I say. "Well, that was pretty awful. The street was so dark and deserted, and he was so close and muttering in a sort of scary way. Thank God the bobby rode up and grabbed him. Still, even colonels can be cut off and beleaguered, can't they. And, after all, my trusty men—the bobby—did for him. 'Ha, ha!' I said like a perfect lydy as he was carried off."

"A wonder, you are!" says Richard. "What about ladies with hubris?"

We pay for lunch and depart, I giving the moustache a last stern look.

Richard writes of the arrival in Provence

It is dusk, two days later, and we are approaching Nîmes, where we plan to spend the night. Mary is driving, but she is slightly pale; she was sick last night and threw up into the bidet. We had been warned of the 'Southern Sickness', caused by either the water or salad greens, and were not excessively alarmed. Our journey has been notable only for Chartres Cathedral and its glorious glowing glass, especially the spendour of the western rose and the haunting quality of the pilgrimage window of *Notre Dame de la Belle Verrière.*

We are driving along a narrow road, and suddenly a huge arch looms ahead. I can see its top is crumbling even in the fading light. The car lights disclose carved battle scenes of Romans fighting barbarians. We pause to look, and I notice a fire burning off to the right, across the fields.

"Look," I say. "It's the camp of the Tenth Legion. The men are gathered round the fire, and the Aquilifer is polishing the Eagle."

Mary says the *Broom* has slipped through a crack in time. Then we drive on, not long afterwards arriving in Nîmes. We look briefly at the Maison Carée, the perfect little Greco-Roman temple, and then, postponing a better look until morning, go on to a hotel.

There we are told with a shrug and a *non* that they have not even one little room. We argue in bad French, and the manager arrives to say no in English. But would the monsieur like him to call the Hotel Paris?

The monsieur desires him to do so. He does: no room. He calls the Inn of the Coq Rouge: no room. There is, one must comprehend, the convention of the wine growers.

"But, monsieur," says Mary. "What are we to do? We have come all the way from England, and we are so tired. . . . Can't you help us?"

"Oh, well played!" I murmur. Then as the manager shrugs, I say aloud, "And this lady has been ill. You will perceive how pale she is."

The manager looks concerned, and Mary sways a little and looks forlorn. I take her arm delicately.

The man says, "Perhaps madame would like to sit down?" He looks alarmed. He pictures the English lady being sick in his lobby, dying perhaps—who can know about *les femmes?* Mary allows herself to be led to a chair. The man says to wait óne little minute and he will consult. We hear rapid French through the doorway. I murmur that we could drive on to Arles or even back to Avignon.

The man returns, beaming. At the Abbey of St Michael travellers may stay. And it is very close, not four kilometers, and the good fathers will have a *petit* repast waiting. Will monsieur and madame go there? They will be *enchanté* with the abbey.

We shall, we say; and he gives us complicated directions, to which we listen somewhat despairingly. We drive off into the dark night; there is supposed to be a moon, but it is behind clouds. We turn and turn again and the road ascends. Trees are thick, and the muted b-r-o-o-o-m of the *Broom* echoes from a rock wall. Something scuttles across the road, and Mary cries, "A bear!" I remark that it was no bigger than a rat. "A small *French* bear," she says. We round a bend and the trees thin.

"Good God!" I remark, rather precisely. Three massive crosses, upon which hang with appalling realism the figures of the crucified, bathed in light, loom before us. We feel rather shaken. Then we arrive at a gate and are met by a black-gowned figure.

The old monk, who is the guest master, gives us bread and soup and wine, telling us something of the history of the seven-hundred-year-old abbey, and then shows us to our room.

Mary resumes the narrative, writing of bells and pearls—and a cliff

I awaken in Richard's arms to the clamour of great bells, ringing for mattins or lauds. A cheerful sound. Bright sunlight and a breeze pour into the open window.

Suddenly Richard says, "Mary! Happy birthday! Happy birthday!"

"Oh!" I say. "My birthday! The bells are ringing for me!" The bells stop. "Oh, very well!" I add. "They are *not* ringing for me! Still, let us thank Him for whom the bells ring . . . thank Him for morning and love and life. And wings!"

"Thank Him indeed!" says Richard. He reaches behind him to the table.

"Me, too," I say, meaning a cigarette.

At that moment something icy-cold slithers suddenly down between my breasts. I jump spasmodically and utter a squeak.

Richard laughs and says, "Sorry! I didn't mean to do that."

I fish about down my front and feel linked roundnesses and cry, even before the light confirms it, "Pearls! Oh, Val! Pearls for morning—my favourite!"

"Truth, too," he says, "according to Bacon. Morning truth." He kisses me.

We sit up and I hold the pearls in the light. Richard takes them and slides off my pajama top and lays the pearls against my breast. I look down at his strong hand and my breast and the pearls glowing there, and my heart almost stops with a surge of joy at being alive and in love and a winged girl. Richard knows and kisses me again.

Then we spring up and, just as Richard is kicking off his pajama pants, he glances out the window and cries, "Look, Mary!" The wall of the abbey is continuous with a sheer cliff. We look down to remote vineyards and silvery olive groves. After a moment, he says, "Good thing that only eagles overlook this window if you're going to lean out without any pajama tops. The monks would have heart failure."

"I care not!" I say, thinking sinful thoughts about tempting monks to their doom. "Anyhow, an ancient Minoan would think I was very well dressed."

"Few ancient Minoans about," he observes justly.

"It's not as though I had *ugly* breasts," I say. "Besides, you have no pants on."

"No," he says. "And I'm not hanging my bottom out of the window, am I?"

We dress, I in a blue denim skirt, and go down for coffee and croissants, wishing as always for a proper English breakfast. Then, taking jackets and bathing suits, we drive away in the *Broom,* having agreed to return to the abbey and go to lauds next morning.

At Nîmes we look more carefully at the Maison Carée and then drive on in a northerly direction, eventually turning off on a smaller road that follows a rushing river. We round a curve and suddenly, there ahead, stern and faultless against the sky, are the triple tiers of arches of the great Roman aqueduct, the Pont du Gard.

"Good lord!" says Richard. "I had no idea it was so big. It's immense!"

Immense it is, each tier of arches on the shoulders of the one below, leaving room on the lower tier for the roadway to cross the Gard. More than all the temples, more even than the Colosseum, this work stands for the grandeur of Rome.

We drive across and follow the road up and then park in order to walk over to the water channel itself; it is big enough to walk through. Then we climb up on top of it and walk out a way. It's about as wide as a paved walk, with occasional gaping holes down into the water channel. The ground below drops away; the River Gard is far below. There is empty air all around us. My enthusiasm for this venture wanes, but Richard strolls casually on and I follow. There are two young men far out in the middle. I glance down and refrain from doing so again. A breeze is blowing, and I find that I am leaning into it as though I were afraid—as I am!—that it might blow me off. There is a strong gust. It does not blow me off, but it catches my full skirt and blows it up in my face. I utter a despairing yelp, convinced that I am about to teeter over the edge. I see my broken body in the Gard, sightless eyes staring at the sky and Richard alone for ever, weeping. I claw at my skirt. It descends and I clutch it firmly to me.

Richard is heartlessly laughing, and I briefly consider pushing him over.

"Never," he says, "never in all the time I have known you have you shrieked like that."

"How can you laugh, you pig?" I say. "I almost fell off and died." I think with nostalgia of hands and knees as a way of getting some place.

"Well," he says. "I expect we've come far enough, don't you? Let's go find the sea." He turns around, nodding to the two young men who are now coming back, grinning at me. I turn, too, with careful alacrity, and we go back.

In the *Broom* again we decide to go into Avignon and see the Palace of the Popes, and as we drive Richard fills in a little of the background of the fourteenth-century "Babylonian Captivity" of the Church when the Popes were under French control and lived at Avignon. "And in the end," he adds, "there were *two* popes, one here and one in Rome, and nobody knew which was the rightful one. The scandal paved the way for Wycliffe and Luther and the Reformation."

"Was that when St Joan of Arc was burned?" I say.

"No," he says. "She was a bit after the two popes."

"Oh!" I say. "I just remembered. Roger Denby and Molly stopped at Winchester Cathedral last month—and, you know, it was a bishop who's buried there who was involved with the trial of Joan—"

"Beaufort," says Richard. "Branch of the Tudors. Ahem!"

"They're bound to make you an Oxford don!" I say. "Anyhow, if the stone eyes of Beaufort's effigy were to open, right there in his own cathedral, do you know what he would see? —A shining little statue of Joan in her armour. The Dean must have a sense of humour. English fair play."

By now we are in Avignon. We park near the centre and head for the Palais des Papes on foot.

"The men here certainly stare, don't they?" I mutter. We have just passed several men on a street corner who stared at me, unblinking, like snakes; and I can feel them staring at my back. "Damn them!" I say. "I'd like to shoot ammonia into their eyes."

"Ignore them," says Richard easily. "They just like to look at beautiful things."

"Grrr!" I say. "Things is right! I'm being looked at as a thing. —Oh, Val! My billfold! I left it lying on the seat of the car. I've got to go back and get it."

"I'll come with you," he says.

"No, go on," I say. "Find out what to see at the Palais. I'll catch you up there, okay?"

I start briskly back. I again approach the coldly staring, snake-eyed men. Suddenly, unable to resist, I make a horrible, snarling, slit-eyed, teeth-bared face and then, instantly, recompose my features. The men look shocked—like cobras, perhaps, who have just seen a mongoose. "Aha!" I mutter. "Mary the Mongoose."

Then I whirl into a shop. I have not, in fact, left my billfold in the *Broom,* but I did see something in the shop window. Now I look more closely and am enchanted and pay over beaucoup francs, brushing aside thoughts of budgets, and emerge with a small parcel in my handbag.

When I approach the snake-men, I look straight at them, like a mongoose about to dine, and—to my amused delight—they look uneasy and avert their eyes.

The Palais turns out to be a rather sombre fourteenth-century building, and we don't find much of interest. I tell Richard about the mongoose and the snake-men, and he barks with laughter, startling some tourists.

Leaving the dead popes, we stroll beneath the plane trees down to the River Rhône where there is a centuries-old ruined or unfinished bridge, the old Pont d'Avignon in the nursery rhyme. It is at least a couple of centuries older than the Palais and very peaceful-looking. We wander out and sit on the end, gazing at the current. Another couple are also sitting there, a couple of yards away.

"Nice," says Richard. "The sun feels good. What shall we do with the rest of the day? A swim in the Mediterranean?"

"Oh, yes!" I say. "Certainly we must bathe in the Med! And then find a place to dine—I wish we knew a really nice place, beautiful and quiet, don't you?"

As Richard agrees, I notice that the other couple are talking rapidly, and then they stand up and move towards us. Both are dark-haired, perhaps about twenty-eight.

"Forgive, please?" says the woman in a soft, low voice. "We could not help hearing. You are *Anglaises, non?* And the strangers in Avignon?" We nod. She continues: "You say a place that is *attractif* and has the quiet, *n'est-ce-pas?*" Again we nod, smiling in response to her smile. *"Très bien!"* she says. "There is such a place. And there is the dinner. You would like that, *non?"*

"Oh, yes!" I say, judging the place by her most favourably. "Very much."

She looks pleased. Then she hands me a small card. "It is La Verrière Bleue," she says. "It is on the card, 78, Rue Jeanne d'Arc. It is what you call the—the club. And we should be happy to welcome the friends from England. Say to them at the door that Jean and Pauline invite you. I am Pauline and he is Jean—he has no Engleesh." A radiant smile lights up Jean's thin, serious-looking features, and he flaps his hand helplessly.

Richard smiles at Pauline, liking her, and says, "We shall come if we possibly can. Shall we see you all there? I am Richard, by the way, and this is Mary."

"Très bien," says Pauline. "Yes, we shall come also. We must go now. Please come. Now *au 'voir."* They trot off with a friendly wave.

"How nice!" I say. "We make a wish, and a fairy godmother appears and grants it. People can be so nice!"

"Some people," says Richard. "And some of course *not* nice. Don't forget the folk who like to anticipate God's wrath by creating little hells on earth. There are still people who would like to burn a witch on weekends. Or a lesbian for lent. Don't forget Joan."

"I'm afraid so," I say, picturing me looking bravely out of the flames like St Joan. At that moment my cigarette burns my fingers and I drop it rapidly along with the notion of Death in the Flames. "Anyhow," I add, "we are going to this place of the Blue Glass, aren't we? What do you suppose that means? Chartres Cathedral, South?"

"Or blue wine glasses, maybe," says Richard. "I liked Pauline and Jean, didn't you? Certainly we ought to go and have a look. An Adventure. What is it your father says about the white bird of Adventure?"

"Just that it flies high in the sky," I say. "Invisible. And it only descends to people who are infinitely receptive and welcoming to it."

"I must say you weren't very receptive to the adventurous way your skirt blew up on the Pont du Gard," says Richard. "Notice, by the bye, that both that and this were *ponts*. Perhaps the bird likes bridges."

"Well," I say. "It's almost Wingsday—that was a day of adventure! Don't you think spring is the most adventurous time of year?"

There is a little silence. I listen to the Rhône gurgling against the ancient bridge. It is very peaceful. After awhile we talk of this country round—popes and knights and lords and, before that, Imperial Rome and Greece. Marseilles had been a Greek city-state.

"Looking back," I say, "it's all legions and knights charging under the Flame of Gold. But there must have been others, sitting in the sun by the river. Maybe they're what's important. The castles go back to dust, but *we* through Christ are eternal."

"Dear Mary!" Richard says. "You make me immortal."

I reach in my bag for my purchase. "Happy Wingsday in advance!" I say.

"Crafty Mary!" he says, unwrapping. "I *thought* that billfold thing was jolly odd." And then, "Oh, beautiful! Exquisite!"

It is a tiny figurine of a man and a maid in old ivory, carved with delicate precision. A slender nude girl, her hair in a bun at the nape of her neck, faces a broad-shouldered young man, who seems about to draw her close with his extended arm.

"I think the original is Greek, about third century B.C.," I say. "And this, I bet, was done on commission for some great lord or lady. —The man looks just like you!"

"So this is why your mind was on the past," he says, smiling, holding it up. "Actually, she is very like you—hips and back. And your look on that tiny face—wistful and mischievous at once. When we're old and grey, I'll look at this, and for me you'll be always and only a girl. Thank you, darling, for our love in ivory."

We put it in my bag and arise. Richard extends his arm like the ivory figure. "The moment of arrested motion," he says. Then he pulls me close. We kiss with sudden passion—my knees are weak—while the river swirls and gurgles round the bridge.

Some while later the deep blue of the Mediterranean spreads before us, and as we drive along its edge we talk of all the vessels, from Greek triremes to grey warships of the Royal Navy, whose keels have traced their brief disappearing wakes across its surface. Or sunk into those blue depths.

We find a bath-house and are soon in the sea ourselves. I throw a ball of seaweed.

"Woof!" says Richard, spitting sand, marvelling perhaps at the perfidy of lovers. "This is the end of you, Missy." I flee but he pursues with great bounds. I accept fatalistically a justified spank. He says, "Pax? Let's climb up there."

He points to a cliff or bluff about as high as a house, and up we go like monkeys, slowing as it becomes steeper. Then he pulls me over the edge. A ripping sound.

"Oh, lord!" I say. "There goes my suit!" I examine it. It's ripped from the navel to about as far down as it can be, and it gapes widely. *"Now* what do I do?" I say. I draw up my knees, which causes a further ripping sound. "I'm really going to look like that ivory girl in a minute."

"Dear, dear, dear!" says Richard laughing. "This *is* a problem."

"Don't laugh!" I say. "This is awful! I'll have to stay up here until dark."

A group of teenage boys comes along the beach. They see us and point, and then run towards the cliff with the obvious intention of climbing up.

"Oh, Val!" I say. "Do something!" Then I add, "Oh, dear God! They're going to come right up here!"

Richard guffaws and says, "You can lie on your stomach, can't you?"

"Richard Vallance!" I say frantically. "Throw stones at them or something!"

A man's voice calls sternly in French. The boys descend. It is the scoutmaster.

"You see?" says Richard. "All things pass. Now I'll go down and get you a robe."

"But—but, Val!" I say. "You can't just leave me up here alone. What if someone comes up?"

"I'll have to," he says heartlessly. "Just remember how you used to long to sit on a cliff winged. Sitting on a cliff and running in a meadow

—those were your dreams. Now, you see, one of them comes true."

"This wasn't the way I planned it," I mutter as he goes over the edge.

He climbs down, smiles up at me, and goes off with his long stride.

A man comes down the beach. He sees me and waves. I do not wave back. I gaze stonily out to sea. I attempt to convey that I am perhaps in mourning: out there somewhere my husband perished in the waves. He walks on. I breathe again. I think about life and the bird of adventure. Then I think about food. A cheeseburger, perhaps. I see you returning.

You shout, "Why don't you come down like that? There's no one near, and you can't climb in a robe."

"All right," I say.

"Keep your front to the cliff," you add, unnecessarily.

I turn over on hands and knees and back over and descend slowly. There are further ripping sounds with every move. I am about a third of the way down when I feel an alarming looseness: the bottom of my bathing suit has given way altogether, and it is now two flaps over either hipbone. I look around. Val is laughing so hard that he can scarcely stand. A boat is cutting along near the shore. I moan and hurry. I picture the boat driving up on the beach and men leaping out.

I reach the bottom, jumping the last few feet. Richard wraps the robe around me, still gurgling with laughter. "Bare bottoms on the beach!" he says. "Distinguished Lady Margaret scholar descends a cliff! Oh for a camera! What a photograph for the common rooms!"

"I'm thinking of taking the veil," I say darkly. "Then you'll be sorry. You don't know what I went through. First I nearly fall off the Pont du Gard, and now this."

Richard chuckles.

"Don't laugh," I say. "You're not supposed to laugh at your wife when she's in trouble." I grin myself. "And just after I give you a beautiful present, too. You serpent, you!"

"Serpent I may be," says Richard. "But a smiling serpent."

"How sharper than a child's tooth is a thankless serpent!" I say. "As some great man put it."

We dress with as much care as possible, Richard donning coat and tie; and then we drive back to Avignon, the sun setting on the way and a full moon rising. After a little bother we find the Rue Jeanne d'Arc and Number 78. There is no sign over the door, but as we look two nicely dressed couples come along and enter. We follow.

A cheeful-looking man comes up to us with an inquiring face and addresses us politely and rapidly in French. We have no idea what he is saying. He pauses, tilting his head slightly. We are to speak.

"Anglaises," says Richard sturdily. "Richard and Mary. Invitation: Pauline and—and—"

"Jean," I say.

"Oh," says the man, and smiles and nods. He gestures to us to follow. We are in. We follow him into a larger room with little tables, candlelit, along the walls. At the end of the room a woman plays the piano softly. But what seizes our attention and makes us gasp is the ceiling.

The whole ceiling is deep-blue stained glass. It glows like some wonderful translucent roof of lapis lazuli—obviously there is light falling upon it from above. But the impression is of infinite depths, a twilight-blue vastness. Here and there, we later notice, flecks of glowing red. La Verrière Bleue.

Our guide has paused, smiling, while we stood entranced. Now he leads us to one of the small tables for two. Two tables away we see Jean and Pauline, who smile and wave. The people at the table next to ours, a tall fair man with a well-rounded red-headed girl, also smile, and we surmise they've been told of our encounter with Pauline and Jean.

A waitress comes with menus and the remark that she can speak, a little, the English. We order chicken-in-wine and wine to drink and settle back to look at the heaven-blue above. So much does it seem a marvellous night or twilight sky that we almost feel a little night breeze blowing among the tables. We are delighted at the chance that brought us here.

"You know," says Richard, "this place really is a masterpiece. What a splendid idea it is to design a room—a drawing-room or a dining-room— around some single great beauty, like this ceiling or a view of a garden or perhaps a fountain. Everything else can be very simple, subordinated to that one perfection."

"Oh, I agree," I say. "What is so great here is their thinking up their own masterpiece."

Our dinner arrives, and it is delicious. As we finish, we notice that the pianist has been joined by a man with a violin. The music is soft, never too loud for conversation. But it becomes a little livelier, and we see Jean and Pauline rise, along with another couple across the room, to dance.

"Oh, Val!" I say. "Dancing under that blue heaven!"

"Up, lady!" he says, rising and stretching out a hand, and we dance.

When the music stops we see that our coffee has come, and we resume our seats. A little later, when the music begins again, Richard says he will ask Pauline to dance; and a moment later Jean comes over and bows and smiles, and I dance with him. I try to convey how grateful we are to have been invited to this place, and he seems pleased.

Mindful of the long drive back to the abbey, we pay for our dinner and depart a bit before ten. In the car Richard says, "I didn't have a chance to tell you, but Pauline says that she and Jean have a big house with lots of room and she wanted us to come and stay with them. But I thought we should go back to the abbey tonight, since we said we would. Anyhow our things are there."

In our room, we set our alarm clock to get us up for lauds. As we undress, we hear a strange wild cry out in the night and switch the light off and peer out into the moon-silvered night but see nothing. Richard says it must have been a bird.

"Or a departing soul," I say, with a slight shudder. We continue undressing by moonlight.

"A day of blue immensities," Richard murmurs. "This and the Med and the blue glass."

"Also," I murmur, "our walk into the blue sky on the Pont du Gard."

"Good lord!" he says. "Seems a week ago. It's been a right full day, hasn't it?"

"Beginning with bells and pearls," I say. "Don't they sound interesting together? Bells and pearls. Oh, look at the figurine in the moonlight." We both look at the little ivory figures on the table, for ever in love, for ever young. "Oh little ivory lover!" I murmur. "Never canst thou kiss . . . yet do not grieve . . . 'For ever wilt thou love, and she be fair.' "

"Mmmm," says Richard. Then, softly, "But we can. I love you, Mary."

We look at each other in the moonlight for a timeless moment. A small breeze brushes our nude bodies, and I let it blow me to him. Our bodies press warmly together, and we kiss deeply. Then, never parting, we are in our bed in the soft Provençal night. There is a deep indrawn breath from us both in the same instant, and sighs, mingling with the night wind.

Mary continues the account with a luncheon and its aftermath
The alarum buzzes. Flicking it off, I open an eye to the morning. On the wall, bathed in sunshine, is the crucifix. I open the other eye as a gesture of respect. It occurs to me that I am a girl, formerly Mary Ann Hubert and now, delightfully, Mary Vallance; and that this strong arm

about me is that of my fine Richard. Simultaneously it occurs to me that I am winged. Even after three years, this morning thought can and does send a little thrill down my spine. I am fully awake. I recall all the happenings of yesterday and the vague plans for today. It occurs to me that I need a new bathing suit. We are going to lauds. It is good to be awake, and the morning is good. Approximately three seconds have passed since I opened the first eye.

I attempt to slide out of Richard's encircling arm. He attempts to keep me by tightening the arm; and he also buzzes, indicating disapproval. I kiss his cheek, and he relaxes. I take his hand and, still holding it, slide out and move my pillow to where I was. I release the hand. He seizes the pillow and holds that.

I go to the washbowl to make instant coffee in water tumblers. While the water runs, getting hot, I inspect my face in the looking glass. Under tousled light-brown hair, I see a face that appears to be mostly two large round dark-blue eyes. There is also a narrow nose and a slightly too wide mouth. I think the chin is firm. The face appears to me to be a very feminine face, as it does to Richard—when his eyes are open of course—and he, as well as the departed Peter, has called it pretty, also. It does not, at the moment, look pretty to me, although it does look girlish, I think. On the whole I feel friendly towards it. I try experimentally narrowing my rather too-round eyes to see if I look like a mysterious femme fatal or anything, but I merely look sleepy.

I stir the coffee and take it over and wake you with the word that we must be ready and dressed in twenty minutes. You say, "Pooh!" though whether it indicates disbelief or resolve or simply a commentary on life I do not know. Then you spring up and vanish.

A few minutes later, I with a scarf over my head for courtesy, we enter the Abbey Church of St Michael. There are a few other people there, servants of the abbey or village folk. We kneel and pray. As always my thanks are first for the healing—the wings—and then for the miracle of love. A door opens in the choir and the monks, chanting the Latin of the plainsong, enter. It seems a wonderful way to say good morning to the holy ones. The sun streams through the stained glass and falls gently, in reds and golds, upon us all. Then it is over and we go out. An old white-haired monk stands by the door, and he gives us a happy smile but does not speak.

"Mary," says Richard over our coffee and croissants, "I looked around at you once during the service; and for a moment, with your head covered and bent and a ray of gold falling upon you, I saw you as a nun. Gave me a bit of a shock. Don't become a nun!"

"No fear!" I say. "Too wicked." After a moment, I add, "Anyhow, for me, the Way of Negation—shutting out all that is not God—doesn't seem the way that I should go. It is the Way of Affirmation—affirming all things, beauty, poetry, animals, all the loves, life itself maybe, as of God and therefore holy—that seems right to me."

"Oh, quite," says Richard. "For me, also. Only, one must remain aware and, er, affirm. If one can remember to say 'Blessed be He' with love when one sees the cow in the meadow or the smile that makes a wrinkled face beautiful, like that monk by the door—"

Another monk comes up and says, *"Bonjour!* There is the telephone for you." He smiles at us, and leads the way to a small telephone room. It is Pauline, and she is inviting us to a luncheon party, Richard says, and we are to bring our cases and stay as long as we like. He also learns that she and Jean own La Verrière Bleue.

"No wonder it's so nice," I say. "Or no wonder they're so nice. Whichever. Anyhow, this'll be fun, I bet. —Two things we ought to do this morning. Check our mail, and get me a new bathing suit—run-proof, if possible."

Richard chuckles. "I'll never forget it, never. You coming down, looking round at that boat and howling to yourself. I bet it's already renamed *Leaping Demoiselle.*"

We find the Guest Master and pay him, with something over for the Poor Box, and drive to Arles, which we'd given as a forwarding address. There is one letter from Oxford addressed to us both. "From Roger Denby," I announce as I return to the car.

"Oh, lord!" says Richard. "Hope nothing's gone wrong with the thesis. Read it!"

As he heads out the Avignon road, I say, "Be calm! Tactful Roger! The very first sentence is: 'All's well with the Sea-tome!' Oh, and your *viva*'s on June 3rd."

"Ah," says Richard. "Very good. Well, read it."

I read of the small news from Oxford, including the weather; then— good news, indeed—of the healing of the quarrel between Roger and his fire-breathing Highlander wife, Molly. But the big news, he said, was what Peter Shirley had heard about: a Captain Denis Easter of the schooner *Windrush,* who wanted to recruit about a dozen people for a two-month, share-expenses cruise to the Aegean Isles, starting in mid-June. Peter had seen photographs of the vessel, and said that both the yacht and the skipper were impressive. " 'Peter told Easter about you two being sailors, and, although sea experience isn't necessary, it would be helpful. Molly and I will go if you two will. Think! Yo, ho, ho!' "

"Good lord!" says Richard, shaken out of his usual calm. "What a way to explore the Greek islands! Fantastic! Shall we do it?"

"Wow! We've got to do it!" I say. "And listen, Val—remember your mother's last letter? About the little legacy from your Great-Aunt Lucy? That'll more than do it, I bet. Not that Daddy wouldn't give it to us if I asked him. He'd do anything to help me make up for my Dark Ages. Anyway, he thinks that freedom from the grind of money worries is one of the best things a parent can give. No puritan work-ethic for Daddy."

"Well, bless Aunt Lucy!" says Richard. "And your father, too. Let's send a telegram to Roger as soon as we get to Avignon. No doubt of it —this was made for us. What perfect timing, just after the thesis and *viva*. If all goes well with it!"

"Val," I say. "Listen. If we get to do this—well, doesn't it scare you a bit, our being so lucky, everything working out so beautifully?"

"Not at all," he says stoutly. "No one could say you'd had precisely a fortunate life, half-dead, missing almost everything. I have sort of a theory of compensation. Or do I mean balance? Anyway, you're eligible, so to speak, for a lot of quite incredible good luck, while the gods make it up to you. And I'm just hanging onto your coat tails."

"Maybe so," I say. "I do hope so! Actually, I've just thought of something else. It's partly what one reaches for, isn't it? Lots of people, even if they had Great-Aunt Lucy's legacy, would be too cowardly or too unadventurous to go off on a schooner. They wouldn't even think of it. They'd spend it on a new car or a huge TV set for second-hand life or a monstrous caravan-trailer to do what they call getting back to nature in. I think people sort of create their lives by what they reach for."

"Hmmm," says Richard. "Interesting idea. Doesn't Browning say something along those lines?"

"Not exactly," I say. "He says, 'Ah, but a man's reach should exceed his grasp,/Or what's a Heaven for?' He means, reach for the highest or best."

"Quite right," says Richard. "But your theory is sort of implicit in the Browning line, isn't it? I mean, if we reach for the highest and best things, including beauty—and including God—we'd be creating our life by what we reach for, whether we got it, exactly, or not. Wouldn't we?"

"That's true," I say. "A classical archeologist, for instance. He may never find the statue by Pheidias he dreams of, but by trying to he makes a jolly interesting life. Or think of painters and poets: maybe they don't quite reach their vision of perfect beauty, but by reaching for it they sort of live with it. Or monks . . ."

"It's a great theory," says Richard. "We'll have to talk about it some more. But to come back to the practical: we are going to have to cut this trip short, aren't we? Get back to Oxford and meet Captain Easter and check it all out."

"Oh, that's all right," I say. "We ought to be back for May Morning anyhow—in a punt! And this voyage—we'll never have a chance like this again. Never!"

"Let's see, now," says Richard. "If we are going to get to Oxford on the thirtieth, we're going to have to leave here day after tomorrow, aren't we?"

"Oh, Val!" I say. "I'm *so* excited about this!" I bounce up and down on the *Broom*'s seat. "What a wonderful, perfect way to see Hellas . . . sailing the wine-dark sea, walking where the great white oleanders grow! Oh, oh, oh! Let's start now! Right this minute!"

"Don't be silly!" you say, laughing and excited yourself. "Don't you want to see Pauline and Jean?"

"Of course I do!" I say. "But it's all so lovely! Life is beautiful!" I scoot over to you and plant a hasty kiss on your cheek, causing you to swerve violently.

The car behind hoots its horn. I scoot back to my side and sink down till the top of my head is not visible from behind and utter small plaintive squeaks.

After two minutes of penitence, during which Richard maintains a heroic silence about the wreck we might have had, I burst out singing, "Rocked in the cradle of the deep . . ." Richard joins in and we enter Avignon singing lustily, to the astonishment of a few strollers. A car overtakes us and a girl, having seen our GB plate, sticks her head out and cries, *"Vive les Anglais!"* We wave.

The first thing we do is to send a telegram, carefully printed, to Roger, saying: YOU AND MOLLY HOORAY STOP ANCHORS DEFINITELY AWEIGH STOP RETURNING MAY MORNING STOP HOORAY.

And the second thing is to go into a women's-wear shop. We search for bathing suits but get sidetracked at dresses, or I do. But it is Richard that finds it. "Mary," he says, pointing to a medium-blue frock with darker blue trim. "Would this fit you? You've got to try it on. It looks like you."

Nothing loath, I do so, and it is a perfect fit, although the skirt is a bit shorter than I am used to. I twirl about and the fullness of the skirt bells around me.

"Bluebell!" says Richard. "Perfect! With your eyes. Get it."

"Right," I say. "I ain't saying no to this frock. But what we *ought* to be buying, matey, is bell-bottoms for swabbing decks. Ho! Man the mizzen tops'l braces!"

"Keelhaul that man!" he says sternly. "Um, what's a brace?"

"I dunno," I say. "Drink? After you splice the main brace—a noggin of rum—maybe you go on to the tops'l brace, then the topgallant and on up to the royals and skys'ls, getting higher and higher."

We move on to bathing suits. I try on a red one while Richard sits and smokes, leafing through a French *Vogue* with a slightly disdainful expression on his face.

When I emerge in the red suit and a pleased smile, he says, "No! Not with your skin."

My smile vanishes, for I had pictured myself a flame on the beaches. I go back and emerge in a dark blue one with bits of red here and there and a new smile, the salesgirl trailing behind.

Richard grins at me. "Good!" he says. "Very good. La Verrière Bleue."

Pleased at the thought, I'm about to say so, when the black-haired salesgirl says, "La Verrière Bleue? *Vous*—you go *la, non?*" She smiles.

We nod, and Richard says, *"Oui, mademoiselle—avec Pauline et Jean."*

"Ah," she says. *"Très bien. Avec mes amies."* She adds, *"Très jolie,"* nodding at my suit.

Again we nod, and I indicate that I shall have it. I return to the booth to strip it off, she following as before. As I hand it to her, standing there in panties only, she gives me a speculative look and says, *"Oui—très jolie!"*

Slightly taken aback, I wonder if this is normal French politeness. *"Merci,"* I say and add hastily with a nod towards the door, *"Wrappez, s'il vous plait!"* I wonder whether there is such a word as 'wrappez' in French, but she goes off, smiling.

I come out wearing the Bluebell Frock, and as we pay her, she says, *"Moi, je suis Jacqueline."*

Later in the car, as Richard drives towards the river, I tell him about the remark in the fitting room. He grins and says, "It's your fatal charm, I expect."

We find the house of Pauline and Jean—it is noon, by now—and Pauline meets us at the door with, "Ah, *voila!* I am so glad to see you." She leads the way upstairs and out upon a roomy verandah with trees all around and glimpses of the river. The verandah is edged by a wooden railing—white pickets and dark rail—and above it an orange-and-white striped awning over all, its scalloped border moving in the breeze. In the centre there is a rather small table laden with fruit and platters of pâté and cheese as well as a great many graceful wine bottles, mostly without labels. At the table or leaning against the railing are at least a dozen people. Everyone looks up as we enter, and a tall young man with his hands on the rail behind him pauses in what he is saying to two or three others.

Pauline says, in English, "Here are Richard and Mary." She repeats it in French. Everyone smiles at us. Jean waves from the corner. Pauline says to us, "I have told them how we met, and they will make themselves known to you a little at the time." She hands us each a glass of wine and says, "Now, you must take what you wish from the table. We are all so glad that you are here." A bell rings somewhere, and she says, "You will excuse me, *s'il vous plaît?*" She hurries into the house towards the stair.

"Val," I say. "Look!" And there in the corner with a merry smile is Jacqueline.

"She probably quit work at twelve," says Richard.

"My God!" says a voice. "Look who's here!" A tall dark girl is standing in the doorway looking at Richard.

"Rozica!" says Richard, looking startled. He says to me in a low voice: "Remember? The Hindu girl who came to Holywell from Cambridge my senior year? She was gone when you were there the following year."

Rozica comes quickly towards us. I have the impression that her slender legs twinkle under her as she walks. She has a white kerchief on her black hair, giving her a rakish look, and she has a caste mark on her creamy skin. I remember Richard telling me how he had been quite bowled over by Rozica in the beginning of his senior year—a fierce passion that lasted for a fortnight or more without ever being communicated to its object. Looking at her, I feel a combination of smugness and uneasiness. What if the passion were to flare up again?

"Well, Richard!" says Rozica. "So you are here! You know, I used to wonder about you back at Holywell—the way you looked at me sometimes! Was I imagining it? And Jim Sutherland used to tell me about all the letters you got from Mary Somebody."

Richard looks slightly disconcerted, but he replies steadily enough, "Imagination plays tricks on us all, doesn't it? Allow me to present my wife—that same Mary. We are at Oxford now, and Mary is reading Greats."

"Ah, the Other Place!" says Rozica with a grin. "Hello, Mary. And you two are *still* together after all these years? Incredible!"

"Not at all," says Richard. "Permanently together! And what about you, Roz? Are you married?"

"Nothing is permanent," she says with a grin. "Certainly Jim Sutherland wasn't. Anyhow, come along over here and tell me all that has been happening. You'll excuse us, won't you, Mary?"

"No, come along," says Richard; but I do not.

I wander off and spread pâté on some crusty bread and go to the other end of the porch. The river is to my left, and through the trees I glimpse little boats on it. Richard is sitting with his back to the table and to me, and Roz is leaning down, facing him, with her elbow on the railing and her round chin in her hand. On the table are long beautiful bunches of grapes as well as the long crusty loaves and clear shining bottles. Two girls are sitting at the table with another woman behind leaning on their chairs, all talking animatedly. The tall young man is still leaning against the railing: he looks a bit unhappy and seems to be waiting for something. Jean is calling something to Pauline. I think how much I like the scene—the people's faces and the colours of frocks and the grapes and loaves and bottles, with the sunlight striking in, and the trees beyond.

A soft hand touches my arm, and I look round to see Jacqueline. She, too, is very pretty, with eyes as black as Rozica's—so black, indeed, that iris and pupil are one—and she has long black lashes.

She points downward towards the river, and I see the corner of a garden with bright flowers. "Go," she says. "Go? See?"

I glance at Richard, but he and Rozica are still deep in talk, so I say, "Okay. Oui, Jacqueline."

She turns and leads the way into the house and down the stairs and out into the back garden. It is lovely. There are bright beds of flowers stretching away towards the river with occasional trees and a winding path. There are, also—what seem charming to me—two round beehives.

Jacqueline puts her arm through mine, and, though I do not quite like it there, I do not want to hurt her by withdrawing it. Then I think that, after all, it is sort of friendly and nice. We stroll towards the Rhône. I look back at the house but see only a gable and green leaves. Jacqueline points to flowers and smiles, and I smile back. We come to a bench, and she points to it, and we sit down. The sun soaks into our skin, warm and languorous. The balmiest of breezes blows into our faces. A bird sings somewhere near, and I can hear a faint humming of the bees in their hives. I feel almost drowsy.

Jacqueline's hand on the bench is touching mine. She murmurs something in her soft voice. I feel affectionate towards her. Flower scents are borne by the breeze. I close my eyes for a moment.

Suddenly I find myself caught in Jacqueline's arms, and her red mouth comes down on mine. For an instant of time I am overwhelmed— the warm sensuous sunlight, the sound of the bees, the scent she wears, and the warm soft lips. I give a little shiver. I am unresisting, drifting in a bubble of time. Her little tongue—as red as her lips, I think fleetingly —enters my mouth. The sensual overcomes the sensuous. It has all happened in a micro-instant.

I wrench free, suddenly, violently, and spring up. We stare at each other. I feel my heart beating. This is the first time that I have ever been kissed by any girl, except for Mercia in my childhood. I am angry and shocked and confused. I am swept by a great tide of love for Richard.

"Non!" I say firmly. *"Non,* Jacqueline, *non!* Absolutely *non! J'aime Richard! Richard seulement. Vous comprenez?"*

Jacqueline shrugs, but her hand makes a little placating wave.

I look at her, remembering the moment, wishing I had the French to say more, to say, perhaps—sorry.

"Sorry," I say. I offer her a little smile. "Sorry! *Au revoir."*

She looks forlorn, alone there on the bench in the sunshine, her black eyes looking up at me, so I bend and give her cheek a little pat. Then I walk away towards the house, leaving her there in the sunlight.

A phrase from somewhere comes into my mind and I mutter, "An adventure of the flesh, that's what it was. Sex alone as if it were the whole thing. Like—like a book with a handsome leather binding and nothing printed inside. Or, anyhow, nothing read. Some people maybe have whole libraries like that—just bindings. Nothing to remember except the animal skin that covers them. Still—for people that can't read . . ."

As I come out onto the verandah again, alone, Jean looks up from the table with a friendly and almost approving grin. It comes to me suddenly that Jacqueline's little ways must be known and he has guessed what happened and what my coming in alone signifies. I give him a slightly wry grin back.

Pauline comes up, smiling with that same hint of approval. With her is the rather tall, fair man who was with the redhead at the table next to ours at La Verrière Bleue. He has an open face and wide smile. A camera case is slung from his shoulder.

"Marie," she says. "This is Lewees from Marieland in America. And this is Marie, of whom we have told you." She trots away.

"Hullo!" I say. "Lewis, is it? And Maryland, right? I was brought up in Georgetown, and Richard, my husband, comes from the Eastern Shore."

"Right," he says. "Lewis Hughes. And you're Mary Vallance. Hi! Let's sit down, shall we?"

We sit down at the table, and I pour us some wine and take a small bunch of grapes. Richard and that Rozica, I notice, are still talking animatedly.

"We're practically neighbours," says Lewis. "Baltimore's my home town. Grew up there and went to college there—which is where I met Beulah. She's that redhead I was with last night. She's from Toronto. We got married right after college and headed for New York."

"What was in New York?" I said. "I mean, opportunity and all that, of course, but what sort?"

"Oh," he says, gesturing towards his camera case, "I thought maybe Pauline had told you. Photography is my thing, always has been. I probably took a photograph of my parents' pleased expressions when I took my first step out of the cradle. And Beulah is a painter, a very good one. That's why she's not here today: couldn't bear to miss the light. You'll meet her tonight."

"Good!" I say. "And what are you doing in Provence? Photographing?"

"Right," he says. "I'm doing a sort of photographic essay on Provençal life. While Beulah paints it. I have a sort of commission from Life, and we're hoping to combine our efforts: two kinds of seeing, you know."

"Yes, splendid," I say. "If you could add a poem or two about Provence, it would be still another way of seeing, wouldn't it? The more different visions there are, the more people can be shown, don't you think?"

"I do, indeed," he says with that wide smile. "I can see we must talk some more. I've said virtually those same words often. But you haven't told me what you and—and Richard, is it? are doing in Provence?"

"Oh, wandering about," I say. "Soaking up a bit of sun. We're at Oxford—not the one on the Choptank in Maryland, I may add—and we thought we'd get away for a few days."

"A fascinating place to be, I imagine," he says. "I've seen it briefly— the dreaming spires. I'd like to stay there and photograph it. But, speaking of photographs, excuse me, will you? I'm supposed to take some photographs of this luncheon, and people look like going."

He jumps up, and he and Pauline shepherd people back from the door and into various groupings for the photographs. Then Lewis gives me a wave and disappears. I sit there a moment, thinking about multiple visions, watching people depart. Then I look round for Richard, and he is walking towards me. Rozica is nowhere to be seen.

"Hullo," I say. "Where's Roz?"

"Gone," he says. "Gone to Paris. Wait a bit and I'll tell you all about it. Who was the man you were just talking to—the camera man?"

"Lewis Hughes," I say. "From your own state of Maryland. Baltimore. His wife, Beulah, the redhead we saw last night, is a painter; and we were talking about the multiple visions of painter and poet and photographer."

"The musician's too, of course," says Richard. There is silence for a moment. I notice that we are alone on the verandah, though voices float up from below. It is suddenly very peaceful sitting here.

I glance at Richard and he is glancing at me. We simultaneously say, in identical tones: "I've got something to tell you." We laugh. And kiss each other.

Then I say, "All right. Tell."

"Rozica," you say. "She wanted me to go to Paris with her."

"What?" I say. "Us? Paris?"

"No, *me!*" says Richard. "She wanted me to leave you here and go with her."

"Oh, that brown viper!" I say. "That serpent! What happened?"

"I didn't go," you say.

"Didn't you?" I say.

"No," you say. "It was like this. We talked a lot about Holywell, of course. And a bit about Oxford and Cambridge. And the curious thing that came out is that when I was having that fortnight's spasm of attraction to her—"

"Spasm of lust!" I interject.

"Lust, then," you say. "Anyway, at that very time, she said, she couldn't get her mind off *me* in spite of the affair she was having with Sutherland."

"You told her about the, er, spasm?" I say.

"Not at the time," he says. "But I told her now—why not? We laughed about it. She's really an interesting woman and has thought a lot. One of her deepest beliefs is in living for the moment, seizing the moment. Whatever you feel, do it. Stay with someone as long as you feel attracted, then move on. That's all love is, to her."

"Empty bindings," I say.

"What?" says Richard.

"Never mind," I say. "Tell you later. Go on."

"Well," he says. "She kept saying how much we had in common, though I had some reservations about that. She was impressed, I think, by the fact of our mutual spasms back there in the fall of my senior year. I was a bit impressed myself, because I had never dreamt that it was at all mutual. And I was enjoying our talk. And then, quite suddenly, she sort of leaned over and breathed in my ear, 'Richard, Richard. This is one of those moments. I know it! Come with me, Richard! Don't think about tomorrow. Come with me to Paris . . .' And she took my hand and just said, 'Please come!' "

"Heavens!" I say. "Go *on!* What did you say? What did you feel?"

"Just for an instant," you say, "I felt a wave of that old desire. Sort of weak in the knees. Almost breathless—just for a moment . . ."

"Oh, Val!" I murmur sadly.

"Be still, silly girl!" he says. "I didn't go, did I? Do you know what happened? I looked away and saw you—oh, Mary! You've been so damned appealing all day in that blue dress that I can hardly stand it!" He gives me a passionate look that is very restorative. He continues: "I told her I was in love with you, and I told her we were building a love —and a marriage—to last. She said it was impossible. And I said, 'Of course it's impossible for those who don't *do* anything. Listen, Roz, it doesn't just last for ever by itself: you're right about that. But Mary and I think marriage is something we create—by sharing, by steady loving, by giving each other the gift of our vows to lean on.' Roz said it would be great if it could be done, but she'd have to see it to believe it. And—and she went, that's all. —So, my lady, what have you to tell?"

"About Jacqueline," I say. A much simpler story. Still, when I tell how, for a single instant, I was sort of carried away, he murmurs sadly, "Oh, Mary!" Then we both catch the echo of my earlier, "Oh, Val!" and laugh weakly. Then I tell him the rest: the great tide of love for him.

We are both suddenly happy. We kiss each other fiercely at first, then deeply.

"Mary!" he whispers intensely. "I love you with all my heart, mind, and body."

"So do I love you," I say. "Everything in me connects up to the corresponding thing in you."

We look at each other in silence. I am aware of birds twittering in the trees.

"Every day we live," I say, "we seem to go deeper—more things to connect up."

"Right you are," he says. "That's the totality of love. All the connections. Some people, even married ones, have only a few connections, maybe only one. But love is *not* just the Dark Gods in the Blood—Sex. That's not even the main thing, though it's part of the wholeness. A marriage without wholeness has no health in it. Same word, you know—whole, health. Sex alone is not wholeness—so not healthiness."

"People who think it's the only thing," I say, "they're tone-deaf people at a concert thinking that the beat of the drums is all."

"That's the animal side of us," he says. "But we're spirit, too. If you deify the animal, it's a little squat African god in the bedroom."

"Unless you put it there to laugh at," I say. "Sex *is* sort of funny—naked bodies writhing about. Fun, of course—fun *and* funny. But no god or solemn mystery."

"I've just had a thought," he says. "If one makes sexual desire the only thing, it's the way to ensure—absolutely ensure—that *no* relationship will last. Each new attractive woman—or man—seems to promise the . . . the unfolding of the ultimate sexual mystery. Of course the promise is not kept because there is no ultimate sexual mystery. The physical alone is . . . well, if you've seen one, you've seen them all. The mystery of this one vanishes, so you turn to the next. It's spirit or soul that is mystery."

"All the same," I say, "I'm having some, er, impulses along those lines." I spring up and kiss him. There is a little sound. It is Pauline. She looks apologetic and tender, but I feel myself to be blushing.

She says, "Do not be embarrassed, Mary. It is good, love."

"Yes," says Richard. "It truly is." We smile at one another.

She suggests, then, that we get our cases and she will show us our room. It is an airy, high-ceiled corner room, with Renoir prints on the wall and lacy white curtains moving at the open windows. I hang up some dresses while Richard unwraps the ivory figurine and sets it by a bowl of orange flowers on a small oval table covered by a blue cloth. The sun shining through the river window falls upon it.

Pauline exclaims with pleasure and then calls Jean. They are astonished when we say it was bought in Avignon, and Pauline says, "It is beautiful. And we are so glad you have it to remember our Avignon."

Richard and I help with the after-party debris. A maid is in the kitchen washing up, so it is mainly carrying things down from the verandah. Pauline remarks that Lewis and Beulah will come to dinner, and then says that she and Jean will have a little nap. We are to be at home—to walk in the garden or to nap, also.

Richard says, after she has gone out, that he's about ready for a nap, after getting up at dawn for lauds—and after all the wine and pâté.

"Not to mention Fighting off Temptation!" I say. "Virtue takes it out of you!"

Smiling, we go along to our room and take off our outer clothing. Richard says, "Let's take everything off."

"Ah, lust!" I say. "That's sweet." I peel my slip off. We sit, naked, on the edge of the bed, looking at the figurine and the orange flowers in the sunlight. The house is very still, and distant laughter from the river only makes it more still.

"The sunlight carries blessing," I say, stroking your hair.

"Isn't that from something," you say, running your fingers up and down my back.

"Yes, 'Patterns,' " I say with a small shiver. "Love-making in the garden with her heavy-booted lover: 'Underneath her gown was the softness of a woman . . .' "

"Like this," you say, suddenly taking me into your arms, holding me almost fiercely, kissing my mouth. "Oh, lord, Mary!" you breathe. "My dear love!"

Our passion meets and mingles. Once there is a ghost of laughter in the room, once a little moan. . . .

An indefinite while later there is a knock at the door; and trustful Richard, without waking, says, "Come in." Jean comes in, smiling to see me peering forth between Richard's shoulder and ear, and sets down two cups of coffee. I chuckle and wake Richard.

Bathed and dressed, I in the Bluebell Frock again—this is its day—we enter the little Empire drawing-room where four faces turn towards us. I introduce Richard and Lewis, and Lewis presents us to the round-faced girl we'd seen him with last night, his wife, Beulah, once of Toronto. She has merry eyes and dark red—auburn—hair, and her fingers have paint stains on them, which, for some reason, I like.

Pauline wishes to know whether we will have an apéritif—sherry or pernod—and Richard and I as one say, "Sherry, please!" Everyone smiles at our single voice.

Conversation begins with Avignon and moves on to include all this sunny land of Provence. Lewis has with him some of his splendid photographs, including to my delight some of the luncheon party, one showing Richard at his most magnificent. Other photographs show Provençal villages and rural scenes, including coastal ones.

Suddenly Richard exclaims. "Mary, look. Isn't this your cliff?"

Beulah picks that up. "Why does Mary have a cliff? Not everybody has a cliff. There is a story here."

I attempt to divert attention by commenting warmly upon a photograph of a church, but Richard, the hound, is grinning broadly, and everyone is looking at him expectantly. He then tells with verve the tale of my descent, to the accompaniment of much laughter, ending up with, "But no one came along except a boat full of wide-eyed men who would certainly have driven onto the rocks if there had been any."

"Ah," says Pauline. "Mary the Siren, luring vessels to their doom."

"I'm not listening to any of this," I say, grinning. "Still, I should like to point out that the Sirens lured in a more dignified way."

"Perhaps we shall find out about that in the schooner *Windrush,*" says Richard.

This, naturally, leads to an account of our projected voyage to the Greek Isles, after which Richard says with sudden enthusiasm, after Pauline has said how she'd like to visit Greece, "Why don't you all come, too?"

But Pauline says that she and Jean have guests coming in mid-June, something that has been long planned; and Lewis and Beulah say they mustn't let themselves think of it because they still have much painting and photographing to do in Provence, though they wish they could come. They tell us about their work, and ask about Oxford.

Richard and I hold forth in turns about the "sweet city of the dreaming spires", and Richard tells something about his Sea-tome, as we call it, mentioning a poem of mine on a ship's figurehead that he means to include.

The servant comes to the door, and Pauline says, "The dinner, it is ready. Perhaps after we dine Mary will say a poem for us."

In the wainscotted dining-room, Pauline and Jean sit at opposite ends of the table. I sit on Pauline's right with Lewis beside me, next to Jean, perhaps because his French is good. Richard is at Jean's right and Beulah across from me. It is an odd arrangement, the women at one end, the men at the other, but an interesting one to look at; and of course we are all intimately together. There is white wine in our tall stemmed glasses, and candles burn on the table and sideboard.

Pauline says, "Jean will ask the blessing of *le bon Dieu.*" Jean crosses himself and murmurs the grace.

Then we smile at each other and eat the fish course before us. Pauline says something to Beulah, who smiles merrily. Jean is saying something to Lewis in French. Richard looks at me happily and winks. I think how I love him and attempt to convey this truth by wrinkling my nose at him. Perhaps I succeed.

For a moment I am just seeing: the table, the still candle flames, and the figures in candlelight. Jean's dark thin face has high cheek bones and deep-set eyes; he looks serious, intense, then suddenly his face lights up with humour. Richard and Lewis smile, too. Lewis, I think, ought to be English with his fairness and outdoor look. His arm sketches something in the air, and Jean counters with a quick gesture, more angular and more swift. Richard shakes his head, smiling, and the others turn towards him. He speaks, his face alight with intelligence, and the others listen, leaning towards him. Lewis speaks rapidly, perhaps translating. I look across at Beulah's rather bosomy figure in her pale green gown, just as she turns her green eyes towards Richard and asks him a question: her auburn hair is lovely in the candlelight.

Suddenly I become aware that Pauline is watching me gravely, her heart-shaped face soft and glowing. She stretches out a slender arm and puts her small hand on mine for a moment. I see little blue veins through the thin skin. Her dark eyes seem to contain some question.

"You are very still, *ma petite Marie*," she says in her soft voice. "Are you being the poet, then?"

"I don't know what I'm being," I say. "A pair of eyes, perhaps. Seeing beauty. And love, too. Love and beauty—that sounds like the poet, doesn't it? Or the painter. Or the theologian, if he's really concerned with *Theos*. But you, Pauline . . . you see, too. I know you do."

She gives me an indescribably happy look.

I say, "Why do you call me 'little' Mary? I'm a good two inches taller than you."

"It is right, I think," she says. "It is because you are so happy, so gay, so full of the *joie de vivre*, so young, so the *jeune fille*, almost the little girl. I have not known anyone ever who had—oh, how shall I say?—who had such a . . . a fire, yes, such an inner fire of joy. It is as though you loved being alive, loved being in your body, not just taking it all for granted."

"Oh, Pauline!" I say, putting my hand in turn upon her arm. "You *are* one who sees, aren't you? You look so deep—and so lovingly."

"I know that you love your splendid Val, little Marie, as I love my Jean," she says. "And I know you are the poet. But this puzzles me, a little. You have somehow seen so deep and yet you are so young. So gay, and yet the eyes that see and the . . . the thinking. Have you been hurt? Have you known the pain? And the darkness? A very black darkness? And after the darkness . . . have you found heaven?"

"Oh, heavens, Pauline!" I say, almost whispering. "No one ever has seen so deeply as you. All you have seen is the truth—all! Listen,

Pauline, I will tell you what it was . . . in a poem I wrote. Pauline, dear, this is the darkness . . . listen." I almost whisper it to her:

DESPAIR

Oh God! nails tear my hands and feet,
  The water I weep for is denied:
My pain and loneliness complete,
  My womanhood is crucified.

God's Son knew why He had to die,
  His pain by purpose purified;
But I, Eve's daughter, know not why
  My womanhood is crucified.

Harsh wooden arms alone embrace
  Their naked unconsenting bride:
While this strange love holds me in place,
  My womanhood is crucified.

The last line is barely audible. As my voice trails away, there is silence between us for a moment. No one else is noticing. Pauline looks at me without speaking. Her eyes are full of tears. Then she says quietly, "I knew: the girl and the woman, yes?"

"Yes, Pauline," I say. "You knew. All you have seen, you have seen truly. More so than anyone has ever done. I don't know how you could have. It was all so long ago: I was only sixteen when I wrote it. You have the greatest wisdom there is, Pauline—the wisdom of the heart."

"It is the loving," she says. "Perhaps it is of God."

"It is!" I say. "It must be. I'll tell you the whole story one day, but you know the essentials already. I was terribly crippled, and no one saw any hope. All I had were books and, as you said, 'the thinking'. And then the gateway to heaven. Oh, you know. You know! . . . Pauline, will you be my friend? Our friend. I want that very much."

"Yes," she says, with that happy look. "You do not speak that lightly, nor do I. Yes, *ma petite,* let us be friends, we two, we four, on our journey in this world."

"Always, then, Pauline," I say, picking up my wine glass and holding it towards her. She picks up hers, and they touch with the clear note of a tiny bell.

I glance about again; no one is paying attention to us: they are engaged in an animated discussion. I turn back to Pauline and say more lightly, "Here we have just pledged eternal friendship, and I do not even know your last name!"

"Oh," she says. "That is so. We are Verrière—we were both Verrière even before we married, for we are cousins. We played together when we were little ones . . . and we stayed together always."

During our conversation the dinner has been finished, the wine glasses emptied and filled again, and again.

Beulah is saying to Richard: ". . . and the light. The quality of the light. That, in a way, is what my painting is all about."

"It's just as true, in a different way, of photography," says Lewis from across the table, and he speaks to Jean in French, who nods. Meanwhile Richard gives me a look that tells me that he, at least, has noticed my absorption in Pauline and wants to know about it.

Then Pauline looks about, gathering us up, and we arise and return to the drawing-room, where there is coffee as well as cognac and liqueurs. Pauline moves towards the piano, as does Jean. "We shall play for you a little," she says simply, and Jean takes out a violin and tunes it. Then they play.

I am struck by the way Jean's dark, restless face becomes still and intense, almost anguished. There are candles here, too, and soft shaded lamps, all reflected in the many mirrors. They play without music, merging from one thing into another, sometimes only a fragment of something, or some brief motif. Jean stands very straight in his dark clothes, with Pauline's delicate figure in dove grey beside him. The candles pick out gleams from the mahogany of the piano and the lighter wood of the violin. The music soars and is by turns gay and sad and tranquil. Once Richard and I catch a singing motif from Brahms that we love, and we look deep into each other's eyes. Everyone is very still, listening. Time stops and there is only the music, although music, like a poem, moves in time. Then, suddenly, it is over and the room is still.

Someone whispers. "Oh, lovely!" like a sigh.

Pauline rises and, as Jean puts his violin away, she says, "Now, Marie, you will read or say the poem?"

"Yes, Pauline," I say, knowing that tonight it is very right for me to do so. "Val," I add. "I thought 'Wind Song'. Would that be the one, do you think?"

"Yes, yes," he says. "That's certainly the one." He looks round. "Perhaps I should tell you all," he says in a louder voice, "that this poem that Mary will read—'Wind Song' is its name—is a poem she wrote in what she calls her Dark Ages, when she was so crippled that she couldn't even stand, let alone walk—or run. That is the meaning of the dark walls in the poem."

"I might say, too," I say, "that when I wrote 'Wind Song' back then,

I didn't have any reason to suppose that I should ever be . . . well, like this—able to run and walk. But it's a poem about running in the wind. Sometimes I think that . . . well, that I'm still back there, you know, just dreaming a dream of Oxford and Provence. If so, then all of you, even Val, are people of the dream . . . and I'll wake and hardly remember. Although"—I grin at Richard—"he seems pretty real, doesn't he? Still, maybe this is a different dimension, a parallel world, you know. Parallel lives. And perhaps there are thin places where we half-glimpse one of the parallel worlds. So, you see, in one dimension I'm not healed and have no Val, and I'm just glimpsing this one where—well, here I am."

"Maybe I'm pretty lonely in that other one," says Richard. "I prefer this one. Anyway . . . read it, Mary."

"All right," I say. I have already taken it out of the pocket of my notebook, and I stand where Jean stood by the piano, conscious of being able to stand, conscious too of the Bluebell Frock . . . standing in this bright little drawing-room in France with friendly faces turned up towards me. I read in a low voice.

WIND SONG

Listen, the wind!
April-morning wind,
Wind blowing the Maytime in.
Listen, Wind!
Blow to me!
Blow the walls down!
Break the dark house!

Across my paned window, the eye of the wind,
The gulls like splinters of light sweep down
The bright sky, and girls like flowers of the wind,
Hair blowing, skirts flying, go lightly below.
Oh girlhood is a desperate glory!
And joy is a girl in a blue April breeze,
Bare-foot, wind-blown, and free! My cry
Is a bell ringing down the wind,
A gull falling down the sky.

I'll break out or die! Burst out like a fury,
Leaving only a girl-shaped hole in the wall!
And run, run lightly away in the wind,
Winged in the dancing wind and free!

Oh, God!—these choking tears! Oh, God!—
This time, this time,

44

This terrible will might tear down the walls!
They stand. —What else shall I do today?

Oh, Wind, blow! Tear the dark house!
Blow the walls down! Blow
My hair into wings, and let me run,
With you, Wind, soft and joyous, around me,
Under a blue April sky into May.

I would go as the wind goes—a girl
Blown by the wind, as light as a drift
Of cloud, as gay as a flurry of joy,
The wind's winged girl, beloved of
The wind, blown lightly along and away,
Wild-crying in the lift and the soaring
Of wings in the wind. Oh, Wind!
Wind, my lover, blowing the Maytime in!
Blow the walls down!

When I have read the last words—"Blow the walls down!"—I just stand there a moment. The silence is like that which followed the music. There is a little sigh from someone. Richard and I look at each other for an instant, and then I look at Pauline, whose eyes are soft and understanding.

She says, "The last lines—they are like a chant. It is beautiful. Will you come over here and read it slowly, by the one line, so that I may translate to my Jean?"

As I go across the room to sit beside Pauline, I hear Lewis say to Richard, "I think girlhood is a desperate glory to her, isn't it?"

After Pauline and I have finished saying "Wind Song" to Jean, and he has reached out and patted my hand, Pauline says to me, "If you will send me a copy of it—the one at dinner, too—I shall try to make French poems, if you permit. Marie, *ma petite,* I understand what I saw in you more now—that despair, that longing, and then the great joy. And from the pain there comes the poet, *n'est-ce-pas?*"

"Yes, Pauline," I say. "Truly. You see truly. And I'll send you the poems, as you say. Now, would it be good to persuade Val—Richard, you know—to read a poem, too? I have one of his in my notebook pocket."

"Oh, yes!" she says. "That would be so good—a completion, yes?"

Richard is persuaded to stand where I stood and read. "This poem," he says, "is just a little one. I wrote it one afternoon in Bagley Wood near Oxford when we were there with some friends. I should remind you that Lothlorien is the elven wood in Tolkien's wonderful *Lord of the Rings.*" He reads in a deep, dreaming voice.

G R A S S

> Still the deep wood
>> Lost and enchanted
>>> The green-gold glade
>
> Eleven singing
>> Remotely heard
>>> Notes reach and fade
>
> Lothlorien now
>> Sunlight pools
>>> Upon the shade

His voice fades away, like the elven singing. I think that his slow deep voice might have been that of the elven king. The room is silent for a moment. Then, as I had done, he reads his poem slowly to Pauline and she translates to Jean.

"Beulah," I say. "Pauline and Jean have given us their music; Val and I, poems; and Lewis has interpreted Provence in photographs. Now, for us all to know one another in the truest way, through the arts, we need to see your vision of light, as you said at dinner. When do we see your paintings?"

"Oh, yes!" she says. "I want you to. I was just thinking about it—how perfect it is that we should all have a way of speaking deeply to all of us . . . each of us giving the others a vision of reality."

"It's the Great Dance!" I say. "Did you ever hear that? A name for heaven, where we each contribute the notes or the steps in the Dance that are uniquely ours—like, maybe, your vision of the light."

"C. S. Lewis," says Beulah. "Oh, he was at Oxford, wasn't he? A great image."

"Right," I say. "He died last year. Same day as President Kennedy. Val and I heard him speak a couple of times. We've read most of his books."

"So have we," says Beulah. "Actually, one of my paintings is of Narnia—the *Dawn Treader* just as she sails. Anyway, if you will come to our house—just beyond Nîmes—you shall see the Provence paintings." She looks about. Then she says, "Would dancing be nice? La Verrière Bleue? Maybe it's this talk of the Great Dance."

There is general gaiety at the thought, followed by a bustle of trips to the lavatory and the collection of wraps. Then out into the moon-haunted Provençal night.

We all go in the Hughes' big American car, Richard and I in front with Lewis; and a short time later we are ensconced at three small tables. Richard and I are overwhelmed all over again by the great glowing blue of the ceiling.

I tell him about my talk with Pauline—he had noticed that we were deep in talk—and he tells me how much he likes Jean. "At one point," he says, "we were actually talking in bad Latin. Let's dance, shall we?"

As we dance, I am overcome by bliss—our new friends, poetry, music, love, everything. I half-expect to go limp and be carried off with a beatific smile on my face.

"Mary, dear," Richard murmurs, "you are dancing like a wind-blown feather tonight."

During the evening, with interchanges between the tables and of dancing partners, a picnic is planned for the morrow after seeing Beulah's paintings.

Not long before leaving, I say to Richard, "Hasn't it been a fine day —all the way from lauds at the abbey to now? It's like a story."

"Not enough drama for a story," says Richard. "Too happy."

"No drama!" I exclaim. "What about the Two Wicked Seducers! Trying to steal you—that serpent! Anyway—drama!"

"But we weren't seduced," he says. "In a story we should both have been seduced and broken each other's heart—although, come to think of it, if we had *both* been seduced, there'd have been no hearts to break. What a letdown! Anyway, having been seduced, we should have sunk by stages and ended up crazed hollow-eyed wrecks. What a story!"

"What's wrong with happiness?" I say. "I *like* happy stories. Like ours."

"They're nice to live, anyway," he says. "Of course, one can't count on our story staying happy to the end. We can't know till we read the last page, can we?"

"I'm not quite sure," I say. "Maybe you can, somehow. At least, the happiness we have had is eternal. —Oh, looks like we're going."

Richard writes of the walled city

Next morning we pack the four of us in the *Broom*—Pauline on Jean's lap and Mary in the cuddy behind—and pausing briefly in Nîmes to arrange about future mail, drive to the red-roofed Provençal farmhouse that the Hughes have rented. They are sitting on the doorstep when we drive in.

Coffee in hand, we go up to the room that Beulah is using as studio. Paintings are scattered about, and she, seemingly taller in this place, gives us freedom to look with a gesture that seems to say Here I am, or Here is my vision. I am struck by the glowing colours and clear atmosphere, and remember her remarks about the light. It occurs to me that, having seen these paintings, I shall never see Provence itself in quite the same way. I think of a post-Cezanne Renoir. We thank her and she glows.

Our forward journey is less cramped, even though there are six of us in the Hughes's big car. We are going to the walled crusader city of St Louis, Aigues-Mortes, so we drive south through the interesting, rather flat countryside. When we arrive, we find a picnic spot outside the city. Pauline and Jean, who have been here many times, sink down with books. Lewis and Beulah contemplate the city; indeed, Beulah has chosen the picnic spot for her painting of Aigues-Mortes. Mary and I walk round the walls with Lewis and then, leaving him, go down into the city to visit the church.

We enter and kneel for a few moments in prayer—a courtesy, if nothing else, in the place of our courteous Lord. Then we wander about. There are only a few people in the church. I pause to look at an inscription, while Mary wanders on.

Then she comes hurrying back. "Come quickly!" she says. "I want you to see those two women—oh, dear, they've gone."

"What was it?" I say. "What about them?"

"Oh, I don't know," she says. "One of them, a rather dark woman with a strong nose—no one I've ever seen in my life, I'm sure—looked at me almost as though she half-knew me. She smiled a little as though she were about to speak. And then the other one came up and distracted her. The other one looked a bit like you. And now they've both gone."

"Well," I say, "maybe you did meet the dark lady somewhere."

"The Dark Lady," says Mary. "That's the name for her. Dark Female, anyway. No, I positively never saw her before."

"Why are you so impressed by her, then?" I say.

"Because she sort of knew *me*," says Mary. "Maybe I know her in another life."

"Reincarnation?" I say. "Isn't that heresy or something?"

"Not reincarnation," says Mary. "Another dimension. Another me in a parallel world is a friend of hers . . . maybe. It may not be a true friendship, though."

"Nut," I say, with a grin, and Mary smiles, too. "You *are* a nut," I add fondly. "You and your parallel worlds." I think how dear Mary is, not least because of her fantastic speculations. "Anyway, they've gone back to their world."

We explore the city awhile longer and then go back to the picnic and eat a lot, after which I, at least, full of wine and pâté and cheese, have a small nap in the grass. Then, after some general chat, the lengthening shadows suggest that we should start back. At the farmhouse there are farewells to Lewis and Beulah, who promise to visit us in Oxford.

Packed back in the *Broom,* we and Pauline and Jean drive on towards Avignon. As we approach, a huge full moon is rising more or less ahead of us, and we enter the city in moonlight. I suggest that we go back to the old bridge where we first met.

There is silence for awhile, with the moon-silvered Rhône swirling beneath us. Then Pauline says, "The May Morning you go back to, is it, then, a festival?"

"More of a custom," I say. I explain how at Magdalen College they celebrate the May with a Latin madrigal sung by little boys from the top of their tall tower, after which the bells ring out, ringing-in the May. "Mary and I," I add, "will be in a punt in the river below. And when the bells ring, we'll drift off for a picnic breakfast."

"It is charming!" says Pauline. "The way May should be greeted." She tells Jean.

"We wish you were coming, too," says Mary. "These days in Avignon have been so lovely, thanks to you all. Val and I will never forget them."

"We, also, shall not forget," says Pauline. "We wish that you did not have to go."

"Sometimes," says Mary, "when a perfect day ends, I think that, well, at least, we've had this, and it can't be taken away. It's not just the bombs waiting or even a world that thinks tanks or labour parades are the way to greet the Maytime; it's also just being alive: we live with danger."

"Yes, it is so," says Pauline, after murmuring to Jean. "But the danger of living is good, too, if one is—is remembering of it . . . is aware—that is it—aware. The danger makes better . . ."

"Enhances?" I murmur.

"Yes," she says. "Thank you. Being aware of the danger of the living enhances the days. In the peril, we find the beauty, the joy. And the love made more dear. And then we are the more grateful, for it is the gift, the gift of *le bon Dieu.* It is true, is it not, *ma petite?* The gift of *le bon Dieu?*"

"Oh, yes, yes," says Mary. "Exactly right. The gift of our loving God."

"Blessed be He!" I say. Then, after a pause, I add: "The idea would not find favour among our more earnest and humourless reformers, but it is my radical notion that we add more to the sum of happiness in the world by *being* happy than by making ourselves and everyone else miserable working for causes."

"Yay!" says Mary softly. "I'll vote for you. Especially for husband."

"It is so," says Pauline. "It is to accept the gift of *le bon Dieu.*"

A stillness follows, broken only by the swish and gurgle of the moon-silvered river. I look down to the face of Mary, white in the moonlight. I kiss her lips.

The Study, Holywell, April, 1968—Richard

It seems a shame to come back from that gay journey to Provence to the dire present, but I said I would comment at the end of each journey. I do not know that I have any very profound comment to make here. I have been deeply moved by the journey, by the journey as a testament of love. I find myself wishing that old Peter Shirley were here, instead of far away in Yorkshire. If ever I needed a friend, a real friend, it is now. He'd come if I cabled him to. But, no—not yet. It's odd: every now and then as I sit here typing I fancy I hear your light step in the other room, Mary. Once I thought I heard your little laugh on the doorstep. That time, I confess, I made it to the doorway in about three bounds. No you. No raven, either, croaking "Nevermore!" God be thanked for that, at least. And I must say that more than once as I've read through Provence I've felt tears burning in my eyes. One such time was when you read "Wind Song" at Pauline and Jean's. I was much moved at the time, and the moment came back with extraordinary vividness: I heard your low, soft voice, saying those loved lines. The poem is indeed the key to your soul. Perhaps, somehow, to the present situation: I keep thinking that it may be. Another thing that struck me forcibly was your words about the Way of Affirmation that day after lauds. And I thought a good deal about that strange encounter of yours with the 'Dark Female' in the church at Aigues-Mortes. Reading about it now, it seemed as though it might be in some way significant. And of course that day of the luncheon party and Roz and Jacqueline—odd, to say the least. If this were a novel, every incident would be significant, bearing on the predestined end. But this is the haphazardness of life. Things without the least significance are cheek-by-jowl with things of the deepest significance—if only I knew. But I don't. Not yet anyway. So, onwards.

Journey to Sea

The long slanting light of a summer evening in England falls upon Oxford, river-girt and old, touching the grey stone uprush of half a hundred towers and spires with gold. Not far from the centre of the ancient city, the light falls upon the roof and chimney pots of a house near the corner of Beaumont and St John's and streams through the open westerly windows of a flat named by some long-gone scholar 'Attica' by reason of its being on the top floor. There the light bathes an ivory figurine of a tall youth and slender maiden. It also falls upon a young man who is seated, contemplating the carving, and upon a girl-sized girl who is pouring out tea from a brown pot and adding milk from a brown jug. They have just returned to Attica from a walk and feeding the ducks in the gardens of Worcester College, which is at the end of Beaumont St. Somewhere, perhaps at St Mary the Virgin, bells are change-ringing, and the sound drifts through the open windows with a subdued gaiety. Closer at hand, sparrows are twittering under the eaves.

The seated man, who is named Richard, sips his tea and says, "Queen Mary's blend? —I thought so. It is definitely the best. I hope we've packed enough for the cruise."

The girl, who is named Mary, comes over and seats herself. This girl is me, the writer of logbooks of journeys—or journals of journeys. "Yes," I say. "I'm sure we have. I about cleaned out Twinings. We shall have tea, even if we're becalmed for months. We also, thanks to my wise forethought, have deck shoes, sunburn cream, sunglasses, and much else.

The question is, what have I failed to forethink of?"

It will already have become evident to the discerning reader—that is, us, when we are old and grey—that we are about to go a-voyaging; and, indeed, this venture was foreshadowed in our previous logbook of our short journey to Provence. Tomorrow, Sunday, the fourteenth of June, 1964, we shall travel up to London and join the crew of the schooner-yacht *Windrush*, sailing for the Mediterranean and the Isles of Hellas. We are very excited about it, though Richard pretends not to be. For the last month and a half, ever since we returned from Provence—or ever since Captain Denis Easter came to Oxford a few days later and signed us on—we as well as Roger and Molly Denby have been getting ready for this new journey to sea.

We have also of course been getting Richard ready for his *viva voce* examination—the oral defense of his enormous D.Phil. thesis on sea-power in England. I say we, but my contribution, apart from keeping him fed and in clean shirts, has mainly been worrying in private and lending moral support in public, which he can return when I come to my far-worse Schools. Anyhow, the *viva* has been over now for a week and a half. Richard looked awfully noble and learned, albeit rather pale, in his cap and gown on the Doomsday. Of course, I practically had to hold him up walking over to Jesus, where the *viva* helpfully was—helpfully in the sense of being so close. He might not have been able to walk farther. Perhaps he will cut my head off for saying all these things.

And then, after all, the *viva* was nothing, he said, once he got into it. I expect that was because he looked so learned and knew all the answers. And though the Examiners are not supposed to say whether one has passed, one of them, who had heard of our forthcoming cruise, said kindly to the other one that he thought that Mr Vallance need not worry unduly whilst sailing the seas, and the other one nodded and gave Richard a grin.

When Richard came out springily, I was waiting, for I had spent the whole *viva* slinking nervously about the Jesus quads, except once going into Duckers to buy a beautiful pair of walking shoes to stop me worrying. I also muttered a number of prayers for Richard. Then he appeared, and we both became incredibly light-hearted. We rushed back to Attica and Richard got out of his sub-fusc, and then we caught a bus to Wolvercote and the Trout, where we sat on the terrace by the Isis and had brown ale and sandwiches, tossing the crumbs to the swans, and looking across the river to the one still-standing building of Godstow Nunnery where some farmer keeps his hay. Richard kept taking long breaths of freedom, as well as long draughts of brown ale, as though he was relaxing muscle by muscle and nerve by nerve.

Then we crossed the river by the bridge and took the towpath towards the distant spires of Oxford. It was a beautiful smiling afternoon, and we were both very happy and in love with each other and with all Oxfordshire. Once a couple of the Queen's swans flew over us, and we were astonished at the wind-whistle through their pinions. Why does a swan make such a whistle when an owl is silent as a ghost? Halfway in to Oxford we sat down under a tree and talked and dreamed awhile, watching the river flow by and the occasional boat.

A little farther on we turned off to the tiny village of Binsey, where we had just time to have another pint of brown ale before the Perch shut for the afternoon. When we came out, we went on along the main (and only) street to the end, and then down a long lane, lined with great beeches, to the little Binsey church, St Margaret's, which has a holy well where some miracle took place in the Middle Ages. We went in and knelt down to offer our prayers to our sustaining God.

After the prayer we sat there for a few minutes, and I remembered that I had my old prayerbook in my bag, and took it out so that it might have a link with this day and this church. I don't normally carry it about. I slipped down onto my knees again and opened it at random and prayed a prayer: it was the third Collect in Mattins—for grace, for defence. And then for the millionth time, I looked at the faded inscription in the front: "To darling Mary from her loving Mother." It touched me, as always. I could scarcely remember her—the loving English voice (not that I thought of it as English then but only as Mummy's) and the sense of someone beautiful holding me—but I remembered the awful emptiness of the world without her, after the Disaster that killed her and left me twisted. I wondered once again whether some hint of foreknowing had caused her to give me the Prayerbook when I was far too little to appreciate it. Now, though, I was very glad, for it seemed important to hang on to every link with her. I held the book up for Richard, across the aisle, to see and know what I was thinking.

Then we arose and went back into the sunshine and tossed a couple of pennies into the holy well, and I at least wished a wish for a happy voyage. The path led among the graves, and as we left the churchyard we said hullo to a brown cow that was looking over the wall. We went back through Binsey to the river and eventually crossed it and came to Oxford again over the vast expanse of Port Meadow, hearing the distant bells ringing, as well as a lark's song. It was a lovely walk.

The next day, early, we caught a train to North Wales for several days of stiff climbing on Cader Idris—the chair of Idris, whoever he was

—in order to get in shape for the voyage. We stayed in a comfortable farmhouse, and every day took mutton sandwiches and a bottle of cider and went climbing, sometimes accompanied by a cheerful black border collie from the farm. We scrambled up steep, dangerous screes, leaped from boulder to boulder in the mountain's saddle, and once went up a rock face where we practically hung by our fingernails. Often we would fling ourselves down on the soft springy turf amongst the heather and gorse, with the odd sheep or two grazing nearby, and look down the mountain at the great sweep of the Barmouth estuary or perhaps at the farmhouse, looking like a toy, that was our temporary home. Perhaps the tiny farmwife would walk across the yard, with a black dot that was the collie puppy bounding beside her.

It was a fine and bracing few days, though once we had a small, spirited quarrel over nothing more than my calling him Doctor Vallance after he had asked me not to. That was only the beginning, of course, after which we said unkind things. I shan't record them because we should look such asses, as we were. But we soon caught ourselves and kissed and made up, and each of us took all the blame. He said I could call him doctor if I wanted to and I said I never would. In the loving aftermath, scrambling down the mountain, I said:

"It's a good thing for you, Vallance, that you admitted you were wrong, for, if I turn out to be Second Mate of *Windrush,* I was going to clap you in irons."

And Richard replied, "It's also a good thing, Mate Vallance, that you admitted *you* were wrong, for I was planning to lead a mutiny, sword in hand, and Take the Ship. Then where would you be?—walking the plank, that's where. Or condemned to the galley."

The next day we came back to Oxford to get ready for the cruise—

"What are you writing, Mary?" says Richard. It is about half an hour since the initial cups of Queen Mary's blend. "You are looking amused."

"So I am," I say. "I'm writing about you as d-o-c-t-o-r and as a mutineer named Black Val. It's the beginning of our new logbook. Listen." And I read you what I've written so far.

"Well," you say with a laugh, "it won't come to mutiny if our officers are very, very kind. I'm glad by the way, that you've put in more about Oxford. Nice description. We really ought to keep a journal when we're *not* journeying, too."

"How can we when we spend so much time on the books?" I say. "Listen, Val. I want to ask you something. You've heard or read the Journey to Provence—the parts I wrote—and you know that I haven't got every one of your immortal utterances verbatim, though a lot are, of course. Anyhow, what do you think about the you in the logbooks?"

"Very true," he says. "I think your characterization of me is terribly accurate. I felt very much at home in everything I did or said. You do know me pretty well."

I laugh and, scribbling rapidly, say, "If I don't, my love, who does? But I'm glad you think so. And these words I do have verbatim. Just in case you some day deny that you were ever like that. If you ever do, then, when I publish my memoirs, I'll turn you into a man with a forked beard or something."

"Not likely!" says Richard with a grin. "There's no doubt of it, I *am* very like that—what you see. As a matter of fact, this is a very appropriate conversation, for I have a surprise for you. A day in our lives, not in Provence, that *I* wrote. What do you think of that? Aha!"

"Good lord!" I say. "When have you had time to write it?"

"Ohhh—not here," he says. "About three years ago, less a few months."

"Back at Holywell?" I cry. "And you kept it secret all this time? But why? That was wicked: the act of a—a serpent! Why haven't you read it to me? Why, why?"

"Because I couldn't, that's why," says Richard. "It was lost. I wrote it, a day I thought should be remembered . . . wrote it to be a surprise for you. And then I couldn't find it. I searched everywhere, inch by inch, and finally I decided that it must, somehow, have got thrown into the fireplace and burnt."

"Why didn't you rewrite it?" I say. "Or did you?"

"No," he says. "I meant to. But then we got caught up in the rush of getting ready to go to Oxford in time for Hilary Term in February—all we could think of was Oxford, and you spending half your time on the telephone to your father about you going. And 'the day' kept getting further and further away. Finally I decided that I just couldn't write it again. And then three weeks ago, getting ready for the *viva,* I was going through all sorts of books. And there, on page thirty-eight of Mahan's *Sea-Power*—stuck there, with jam probably—was the lost day. Actually, I've consulted that book dozens of times since Holywell; God knows I had trouble enough getting a copy. But, plainly, I didn't consult page thirty-eight. So now we have it again."

"Oh, that's fantastic!" I say.

"Especially my *using* the book all the time and still not finding it," he says. "Anyway, I thought that, after all this time, I'd wait a little longer till the *viva* was over and a good moment came along. So—now. Right?"

"Right!" I say. "Wow! Journey to the past! Read it! Read it!"

"Do you want to guess what special day it was?" says Richard smiling. His grey eyes are twinkling and he looks pleased. "Is there any more tea?" he adds.

I pour out more tea and add more hot water to the pot to stretch it—never let the leaves get dry, Jolly used to say. As I pour out, I think back to the days at Holywell College in New England. We were only there one semester—together, that is—although Richard had been there for four years before that and had been graduated the June before, just after wings. Now he was back to do an M.A. And I who had never been to any college, or school either—just my Miss Williamson and some special tutors and, of course, Daddy, who was a university in himself—came joyously back with Richard as a special student. I wanted us to be married, but he was refusing because, he said, I was so young—actually I was seventeen! and *very* mature—and because I had to see whether I should fall in love with some other man. Of course I knew I wouldn't. Anyway, I roomed with a girl Richard knew and liked named Kate West. She and I found a little flat that we called 'Dormers' because of its dormer windows, although the name had a private meaning for me because I had always longed to live in a girls' dorm in a college like a regular person, and Dormers was a girls' dorm in little. And Richard, despite himself, couldn't stay away, and came to see us all the time, much to my joy. Also, he had had his mail sent there because of an earlier plan to live there himself, so that gave him an excuse.

And then he had won a Crown Scholarship to Oxford, a brilliant accomplishment since there are only twenty for the whole world. At first he thought he'd go in the following October, but then the thought of getting started at Oxford months earlier, and even more, the thought of all the material on sea-power in the Bodleian Library caused him to reconsider. Meanwhile—almost instantly, in fact—I had determined that if he went, I would, too, somehow. So I had entered into consultation with Daddy, who had wanted me to go to Oxford even before Holywell —even before wings, actually, for he thought I could manage tutorials in a wheelchair. That's why he had had me taught Greek and Latin almost in the cradle. His only regret was that I couldn't be in his old college, Trinity. So Daddy had entered into the plan with enthusiasm, and with the help of some people he knew at Oxford it was all arranged. So I announced to Richard that whither he went, if he did, I, too, went. And, fortunately, after all this arranging, he won the Crown Scholarship. And off we went with a rush in January.

I wonder whether the special day that Richard wrote about was our first day at Holywell that fall, when we sat on the grass on what he called ever after Marymount, although it was only about twenty feet high; or whether it was my first nervous day of classes; or my first even-more-nervous date with a boy I had met at a Holywell mixer. Then, suddenly, I know what the day is.

"Val," I say. "I know. The day we drove in the Berkshires. Right?"

"Wrong!" he says. "That was a beautiful day, though. I wish we had written an account of it. Guess again."

"Before I do," I say, "what do you remember about that day in the Berkshires?"

"Everything," he says modestly. "Ummm. Let me see. I was driving back from town in Frank's sports car. It was a wonderful Indian Summer day. And I suddenly had such an overwhelming feeling of loving closeness to you that I actually said 'Hi!' out loud."

"You never told me that!" I say with a pleased smile, scribbling rapidly in my special shorthand. "I was probably sending out loving thoughts from Dormers. So, anyhow—you rushed over and got me and said Down with Work. And rang up Frank. Then what?"

"Then we drove," you say. "And we just drove on and on, taking some of the back roads in the country that I knew about, and got up in the Berkshires. It was mild and the sky was a clear powder blue with marvellous billowing clouds slowly making their way across it. And the clean white bark of the birch trees stood out from the darker background of the woods. —Are you sure you want all this?"

"Heavens!" I say. "I certainly do. I thought I remembered it, but not with that kind of vividness. Go on. I'm writing it down."

"Okay," you say. You are silent for a moment and then go on in a dreamy voice: "We were driving by the birch woods. Right. Well, we drive silently through the hills, stopping at one point out of sight of all civilization . . . we stop and listen to the silence. To the resting earth. Our hearts are lifted up by the beauty around us. We look at each other without speaking—do you remember? We didn't say anything. I took your hand, and I thought, 'I love you, Mary.' I didn't say it, because I was being restrained in those days, a little. But I thought you knew. Anyway, you rested your head on my shoulder, and we just stayed like that for a small eternity." Richard's slow voice stops, and he opens his eyes and grins. "How's that?" he says.

"Heavens!" I say, moved. "You've never described anything like that in your whole life. Almost poetry. And how can you remember it like that?"

"I just do," he says. "One of those days one remembers when the ones all around are forgotten. I remember a bit more—shall I go on?"

"Oh, yes, do!" I say. "All of it. I'm back there now."

"Right," he says. "Well—I start the car again and we drive on through the hills, stopping at some little place for big bowls of clam chowder and, I think, swordfish steak about dark. Then homeward in a gay mood under a gibbous moon, making up legends for villages we go through. Once we think we see a ghost in a graveyard—"

"We *did* see a ghost!" I say. "It waved its arms!"

"All right," he says with a chuckle. "Anyhow, that's all. When we got to your flat we were worn out from laughing so much. Katie was out somewhere, and we had mugs of coffee with thick cream. A wonderful day—just happiness. And Mary, one thing I kept thinking all that day was that you were going to be the perfect life's companion."

"Dear Val!" I say, springing up and kissing him. We hold each other for a moment. Then I say, "Oh, darling, look—the moon!" In the direction of Richard's college, Worcester, a young crescent moon rides in the serene evening sky.

We resume our seats as I say, "Oxford can be so lovely sometimes—lovely tonight. —I give up on what day it was. Not the day we went to Yale? —Well, read it."

"This is a wintertime story," he says. "Remember, snow in the birch woods?"

"That was when Katie was playing the 'Toy Symphony' all the time," I say with a laugh. "It was always tinkling through the rooms—remember?" I feel the teapot. "Still hot. More?" I fill our cups and add milk.

"Now," says Richard. "I haven't reread this. The bits where I wasn't present are from things you told me. Probably not very good, but, well—here goes."

Mary at Dormers

The early morning sun slanted across the room to a girl curled up in a big armchair with a book and a cup of coffee steaming beside her. There was a faint tap on the door, and she sprang up, smiling, to open it.

"Good morning, funny-face," said Richard, kissing her on the cheek.

"Good morning," said Mary. "Have you come to sweep me away and marry me? No, alas, one does not call the bride 'funny-face'. What, then?"

"I came," he said grinning, "to ask whether you wanted to learn to skate, as you've often said you did. The pond is frozen hard. This afternoon?"

"Oh, good!" said Mary in the hurried light voice she used when excited. "But let's go when no one's around: I'll fall down. I know I will."

"You'll be fine," he said. "There'll be masses of people who won't know any more than you do. Listen, I'm off to class. Be back by noon and we'll get you some skates."

He was gone, feet descending the stairs, and Mary went in to wake Katie.

"Ka-a-a-tie! Time to get u-u-p!" she sang. She looked down at the tangled mass of fair hair that was all of Katie that could be seen. "Ka-a-a-tie!"

There was a stir beneath the covers. A wrist with a watch moved towards the mound of hair. Presumably something peered out. A small voice said, "Okay."

Nothing else happened. "C'mon, Katie!" said Mary. "Here's coffee!"

The covers flipped suddenly back, and the hair said, "Oh boy!" She was awake.

As the two girls ate toast, Mary told Katie of the skating plans and promised to wait till she got out of class. Then they clattered down the stairs together and ran off in different directions.

When Mary returned shortly after eleven, the postman was at the door. One letter, for Richard, bore the return address of Her Majesty's Ambassador in Washington. With a cry, Mary flew up the stairs and cast herself on her bed, on the point of tearing it open. Then she checked herself. She knew it contained the fateful news of whether Richard was to be a Crown Scholar at Oxford. He should be there when it was opened.

"Heavens!" she muttered. She held it up to the light, but it was totally opaque. Then, virtuously, she put it in the middle of the bed and went into the other room to study. Five minutes later she came back to make sure it was still there.

Finally she heard the front door open and Richard's firm, light tread on the stair. "Quick!" she cried from the landing. "The scholarship letter! Come quick!"

Richard came in, his face grave, while Mary pranced about, crying, "Open it!"

"Mary!" he said. "Calm down. I've got to prepare myself." He sat down and held the letter a long moment. Then with a decisive stroke he ripped it open.

Together they read: "Dear Mr Vallance, I have great pleasure in informing you . . ."

There was a shout of joy from both of them. Then a wild dance about the room. Then the rest of the letter. No mistake: Richard had the scholarship.

"Oh, Richard!" said Mary. "Remember, before wings, we used to talk so gaily about how we'd go to Oxford winged? I didn't believe it, but it was so lovely to pretend that I'd be well and we'd go. And now it's all coming true . . ."

Richard looked down at her. The sea-blue eyes were big with tears. Richard thought of his self-imposed restraints—and threw them away, for the moment. He kissed her deeply. She sobbed and hugged him.

"Mary," he said and paused. "Mary, this wouldn't mean a tenth as much to me if you weren't going—you know that, don't you?" He kissed her still more deeply.

Then, the moment having passed, they went down to buy Mary some skates.

Katie arrived at Dormers as Richard and Mary were looking with pleased eyes at half the contents of the shops on Leaf Lane—skirts, pullovers, a jacket, and of course the skates. They told her the news. Then Richard ran off to his own room to get his skates, and the girls prepared to set off to meet him.

A small crisis developed at their front door when a dog endeavoured to lead his pet lady up the steps in order to bite Mary. Meanwhile the lady said soothingly, "Don't bark! It's just two girls—two nice girls." Finally he led the lady away.

At the pond, while Katie glided effortlessly about, Mary, on Richard's arm, was taking her first timid steps on the ice. "Try a step or two," said Richard. "Try to glide a bit on each skate. That's right! Keep hold of my arm."

"Dear lord, yes!" muttered Mary. "Nothing could make me let go!" Then there was a mournful howl that signalled her first fall. Bravely, she continued to try and eventually began to get the feel of it. "Hey, look!" she cried. "I'm really doing it. Look at me! Brave Mary!"

Finally a halt was called. Again Richard swung by his room, and Mary and Katie trudged on towards Dormers just at sunset. The last light threw a rosy tint over the snow and over their already rosy faces. They climbed the steps to Dormers with a sense of well-being despite their tiredness. Pausing only to throw off coats and scarves and for Katie to start the "Toy Symphony," they threw themselves on the floor, talking with tired gaiety in the warmth of girls' friendship.

Richard arrived and joined them on the floor. When Katie went to turn on the oven, he murmured, "Oxford!" with all the dreaming spires in his voice, giving her a hug.

The story ends and Richard's voice ceases. He lays the last page on the table by the figurine. Oxford re-forms itself around us. The western sky is quite dark now, the last of the twilight having faded off the west and the young moon set. I hear the brisk sound of heels on the pavement as someone goes along St John's Street. The change-ringing has ended long since, but somewhere a silvery bell strikes the hour. Before it is done, we hear the deep bomm-bomm-bomm of Great Tom at Christ Church, and all the other bells of Oxford strike. And tomorrow we shall be sailing from London, outward bound for who knows what adventure. We are aware of past and future at once, all in this quiet Oxford present.

" 'Oxford!' " I say. "How nice that that was almost the last word. Thank you, Val dear, for my long-delayed 'surprise'." I reach across the table and take his hand. "I think it's almost better hearing it like this in Oxford, don't you?"

"Yes," he says. "I certainly do. Much more meaningful. What did you think of it? Or, rather, what did you think of the portrayal of us— apart from our being maybe a bit mushy. Of course we *were* sort of mushy, in a nice way; but I think that the writing itself was too sentimental, probably."

"Maybe," I say. "But I wouldn't have it changed. That just makes it more touching, at least to me. One thing I noticed was that you were a bit more big-brotherish in those days. Not in steering clear of letting me know you loved me—how could I not know?—but in being protective. Very understandable, of course. Also, you have a way of looking at things—for instance, in your Berkshire memories—that is different from me, though I can't say what it is. You show me things, things that I've seen myself, in a slightly different light. A revealing light. Together we see more than either one of us alone could see."

"Isn't that just what marriage is?" he says. "The combined vision? It's rather like one's having two eyes, looking at something, say a distant tree, each eye seeing it from a slightly different angle—which, by the way, is how we see depth. Or judge distance. Same thing with marriage: two views, filtered through two personalities, being combined. Of course, some couples never reach a combined view: they see double."

"Oh, yes!" I say. "That's exactly it! Neither view right or wrong, just a part of a wholeness. Together, only together, we see depth. This is fascinating! You see as a man, slightly differently; I as a woman. But, also, I as someone who—well, had my Dark Ages . . . crippled. You, someone strong and confident . . . who sort of reached down and lifted

62

me up, bless you. And—and—where am I?—oh, I know: our different studies. They go into the combined vision, don't they?"

"Exactly," says Richard. "But the key thing is combining them into one vision. After all, the two eyes see *one* tree—unless you're drunk."

"In a true marriage, then," I murmur, "each must share their vision of things. If that Day you wrote had really been lost, if we hadn't talked of the Berkshires, I'd never have seen those things through your eyes. Doesn't it seem a long time ago: you speeding about like a happy panther arranging our night flight to England, and both of us so much in love, though you tried not to admit it. But I knew—after all, you'd said back in the summer of wings that our love was the most perfect thing you'd known."

"So it was—and is," he says. "And I remember something else I said then that might have, er, given you a clue: 'In all the world of women I've never met any other girl that I've felt such an affinity for.' Remember? Still true, too." He gets up and comes round and kisses the top of my head. "Let's walk down to the corner."

We go down the stairs and out into the night, walking down Beaumont, past the Ashmolean, pausing at the corner and looking at the shadowy mass of Balliol College and, off to the right, the dark tower of St Mary Magdalen. There is still a faint twilight. Oxford with her memories of a thousand years seems bathed in peace.

As we come into Attica again, Richard says, "It'll be fine tomorrow, I predict."

"Ah," I say. "The call of the running tide." I yawn.

"To bed!" he says. "Sleepy little girl!"

Richard writes of the sailing of the schooner WINDRUSH

The fast up train from the west is flashing through the outer reaches of London. In one compartment sit four people with their kit scattered about. We had had from the train windows a last glimpse of Oxford with her towers and spires reaching up to the morning sky, and then our thoughts looked forward towards the tall masts.

The four people are of course Mary and I and Roger and Molly Denby. Roger is now a Fellow of Worcester College in Modern History. While he can be very crisp indeed, his brown eyes are humorous behind his spectacles, and he can be the merriest of companions. He is the son of a country doctor in Kent. Molly, who was Molly MacDonald, is a true Highlander from an incredibly remote village. She has orange-red hair, moves with a shy wild grace, and is capable of fiery outbursts of temper during which her speech becomes virtually unintelligible owing to an access of Gaelic and a stammer. She came to Oxford after doing an M.A. in physics at Edinburgh; and she spends her time doing mysterious things with cloud chambers in the Labs. She and Roger are much in love, despite a foolish and violent quarrel a couple of months ago.

At the moment she is saying to Mary, "Weel, lassie, we'll soon be awa' on Captain Easter's wee vessel."

"Not so wee," I say. "She's almost a hundred feet long!"

"The Queen Elizabeth is mair what I'm accustomed to think of in terms of spacious accommodations and stabeelity," says Molly with dignity.

"Don't mention stability!" says Roger. "I feel seasick already."

"Don't worry, mate," I say. "Schooners don't roll—just heel over and stay there."

"Heel over and sink," says Roger. "I can see it now. The ship breaking up in a gale. The Captain shouting, 'Man the boats!'—if there *are* boats. People saying, 'Where's old Roger?' Denby still standing bravely at the wheel as the ship goes down through miles of dark green water. Fishes going by. Denby gone."

"Come off it!" I say. —"Look! Paddington!"

In the vast echoing reaches of Paddington Station, where one half expects to see the hurrying figures of Holmes and Watson, Roger skilfully snares a taxi out of the very jaws, as it were, of an imposing dowager, who gives us a vindictive look.

"We've made that bonnie mistress vurry unhappy," says Molly. "Happen she'll turn out to be the mate o' *Windrush*."

"Happen we'll jump ship if she does," says Mary.

The taxi swings through Trafalgar Square where the great lions stare benignly out at us, and we wonder whether Nelson atop his column can see the masts of *Windrush*.

When the taxi draws up at the designated dock, we pick up our gear and walk through part of a warehouse. Emerging onto the pier proper, we instantly see the tall masts and the schooner herself, moored alongside with her stern towards us and her long bowsprit pointing out into the Thames. On the stern, in white letters against the deep blue of the hull is the word WINDRUSH, and in smaller letters below, LONDON. A blue flag with a white centre flutters from the rigging, and I remark, "That flag's the Blue Peter. Means the ship's about to get underway."

Mary says, "Listen, everybody. Daddy used to keelhaul people who wore hard heels on his deck. We'd best take off our shoes."

A gangplank stretches down from the wharf to the glistening deck aft. Forward are white deckhouses. There are two women in the cockpit with their backs to us, one slightly plump with auburn hair and a slender one with dark brown hair. Then a rather tall young man with a familiar face and an amiable grin comes up through the deckhouse companionway, sees us and waves.

"Lewis!" Mary and I say together; and Mary adds, "Beulah, too! But they said they couldn't!"

Shoes in hand, we file aboard as Beulah, the one with auburn hair, cries, "Mary! Val! How wonderful to see you!" Her round face is wreathed in smiles and her green eyes sparkle.

Lewis says, "We just kept thinking, we're losing the chance of a lifetime—and we got so much done in Provence that we telegraphed to the Captain. And here we are!"

The dark haired woman, slim and poised, says, "I'm Shelley—Shelley Easter. Mate, Chief Engineer, what-have-you. Welcome aboard. The skipper'll be here in a few minutes, I expect."

There are introductions all around, and we remind Roger and Molly of our meeting Lewis and Beulah Hughes, photographer and painter, respectively, in Provence. Roger comments that it should be a well-recorded voyage. Beulah says that Jean and Pauline sent us their love.

I am seated atop the deckhouse facing aft, and I see three more people emerge from the warehouse. One of them is the skipper, Captain Denis Easter, whom we met in May when he returned to Oxford. He is tall—four or five inches over six feet—broad-shouldered and powerful. With his tawny hair, bright in the sunlight, he looks like a Viking. He wears blue jeans and a white shirt with the sleeves rolled up, displaying strong sun-tanned forearms. He sings out in a pleasant, carrying baritone: *"Windrush,* ahoy!"

As every head in the cockpit swings round, I glance at the skipper's two female companions. One is a girl whom I mentally classify as slinky. She has a bored expression on her face, along with a good deal of eye makeup. Then I look at the other woman with a sense of shock.

"Val!" says Mary in an intense whisper. "He's got that snake Rozica with him!" She looks dismayed.

"Good lord!" I say. "How on earth did *she* get here!" It occurs to me that Roz, despite her effort to lure me off to Paris, can be a very jolly companion. Mary is not, perhaps, thinking along the same lines.

"Val!" she hisses fiercely. "She's going to spoil everything! Maybe I should send for Jacqueline!"

"Stop that!" I say with a grin. "Ain't nothin' to worry about! It'll be all right, darling."

"Stop!" says Captain Easter without raising his voice but with astonishing firmness. Mary looks wildly around as though she were feeling beleaguered. But the Captain is speaking to the girl with Rozica who has forged ahead and is clattering down the gangway in her heels. "Miss Linton, the first rule is: No hard shoes on the deck. Rubber shoes or bare feet."

Rozica, who had been about to start down the gangway, grins amiably, says "Sorry!" and takes off her shoes. But Linton, who has paused halfway down, now takes three more steps, two of them on the deck, seats herself and kicks off her shoes. The Captain's mouth tightens, but he comes aboard without saying more.

Again there is a flurry of introductions and greetings and a good many people all talking at once. Roz explains that she had come from Paris to London to stay with Pam Linton, who had been at school with her, and they had heard about the cruise and decided to join it. She looks at me as she speaks, and I hear a faint hiss from Mary.

When there seems to be a slight lull in the talk, the Captain says, "The other two won't be here for awhile. Perhaps this is a good time to look over the schooner. Let's begin here. This sunken area, here behind the deckhouse, is the cockpit—the centre of the ship's life. Under the blue seats all around are stowed the life jackets—*remember it!* That affair with the compass in it is called the binnacle. Just aft is the wheel and wheelbox. Whoever's at the helm sits straddling it. On aft is the after deck with the hatch to the lazerette—a stowage place—in the middle. Those round deckplates are for filling our tanks. The after end of the ship is called the stern, of course; and you'll notice that we say 'after deck' but the *direction* is 'aft'—one goes aft." He grins. "All this will be second nature in a day or two."

He turns and points forward. "Now," he says. "Forward. The two deckhouses, naturally, are called the forward deckhouse and the after deckhouse. The masts, though, are the foremast and the main. If there were a third one, aft, it would be the mizzen."

He then points out the step or shelf at the forward end of the cockpit and says that the engine is under it; and he identifies the combination of small door and sliding hatch leading down into the deckhouse as the companionway. He leads the way through it and down the ladder, after remarking that the right side of the boat as one looks forward is the starboard side and the left, the port side. At the bottom of the ladder we crowd round, except for Lewis and Beulah who had an earlier introduction to the mysteries. The skipper points out the chart desk and wireless to port and an oilskin locker to starboard. Just forward of these, we push through a curtain and enter the roomy main saloon, its length running from side to side, or athwartship, of the vessel.

In it there is a long table, also running athwartship, covered with a blue baize cloth. In addition to its dozen chairs, there are built-in red-covered seats along the sides of the ship—that is, the ends of the saloon. Above them are ports, two on a side, with little blue-and-white curtains, and these throw shimmering water reflections on the ceiling, which features a big skylight over the table. There are sailing prints mounted on the paneled walls or bulkheads. On the starboard side forward, instead of a full bulkhead, there is a polished oaken counter, with the galley visible beyond it. Opposite, on the port side, we learn, is galley storage—the pantry. Here, then, in saloon and galley, is the other centre of ship's life.

We go round the table and forward, past the foot of the mighty mainmast. A short corridor leads forward with stateroom and locker doors opening off.

"These are the staterooms," the skipper says. "Two people each in most of them. This first one on the starboard side is mine and Shelley's; and Roger and Molly Denby, the first to sign on, to port. Going forward —you'll have to duck a bit here, no headroom between the houses." As we duck and straighten up again, he says, "We're under the forward house now. And the room to starboard is Richard and Mary Vallance. Lewis and Beulah Hughes are to port; and Rozica and, er, Pam Linton forward of them. The other two will be in the two very small rooms on the starboard side." He opens the door at the end of the passage to show us a compact compartment containing the water closet and washstand and a tiny shower stall. He shows us how to pump the water closet, and says the whole compartment is called the heads. He also tells us to conserve water in every way possible, especially in the shower by turning it off while we soap ourselves and turning it back on for a quick rinse.

The tour now completed, we go to our rooms. Mary and I find ours neatly compact. It has one port and a small round skylight as well. There is, I am pleased to see, one fairly wide berth, with a board that can be slid up, when necessary, to keep us in. There are lockers under the berth as well as a built-in chest of drawers and looking glass. There is also a small bookshelf with a bar to hold the books in.

"Not precisely spacious," I say. "Not bad, though. Let's get our kit and stow it."

We do so, learning from the skipper that we can hang our shore clothes and stow our empty cases in the starboard locker between the houses. We shift into blue jeans, Mary's sawed-off ones. I put on a blue shirt and roll up the sleeves, and Mary puts on a light-weight, short-sleeved blue pullover. And our deck shoes. Mary remarks that with our tan from climbing in Wales we look quite sailor-like. Just as we finish stowing everything away in our once-again ship-shape cabin, a buzzer that we had not noticed buzzes sharply.

"We're wanted, I think," I say. "Let's go."

We make our way aft, ducking under the low overhead, and in the saloon we see the Captain at the starboard end of the table and some of the others drawing up chairs. Shelley and Beulah are filling coffee cups, and there are platters of sandwiches.

A voice from one of the transom seats under the portholes says, "Hi!"

"Betsy!" cries Mary, looking as though her mind had suddenly been shattered. "Betsy! This can't be happening!" She runs round and flings her arms about the beaming Betsy.

"I knew you all were here," says Betsy, as I too hug her, "so I'm not so surprised."

I know that Mary is being transported back to those long, anxious days in hospital, wondering whether, unbelievably, she was going to be able to walk. Betsy, getting over a back operation, had shared the room, and she and Mary had passed the long hours making up stories for each other. The unbearable waiting—unbearable for Mary, at least—had become bearable owing to Betsy's cheerful presence. But they had not seen each other from that time to this.

"—with my father, on business," Betsy is saying. "And I came to Oxford to surprise you, but you were in France. But I met Roger—on your steps, actually. And he and Molly told me about the cruise, and why didn't I come, too? So I talked to Captain Easter, and told everybody to say nothing, and went on to Norway with my father—and here I am!"

This breathless speech is just over, and Mary is saying, "Well! You surprised us all right! Good heavens! But what a wonderful surprise!" I glance up just as another surprise, a tall, fair-haired young man, steps into the saloon.

He looks about, quietly, his blue eyes smiling. His eyes meet mine and we grin at each other, just as Mary says in a high squeak, "Peter!"

Peter Shirley it is, Peter of the North Riding and Magdalen College, Peter who had loved Mary and then, gallantly, been my best man, Peter whom I counted as just about my dearest friend.

"Hullo, Val, old chap," he says, shaking hands. "Hullo, Mary dear. Did they tell you I was coming?"

"Not they," I say, looking at Roger, who grins. "Why aren't you in Yorkshire tending to the horses and hounds as you said?"

"Well," he says. "I always wanted to run off to sea—when I was about ten. So when Roger rang up to tell me about the ship and all the charming company"—he smiles at Mary who smiles happily back—"I decided that I wasn't going to be left out."

"I couldn't be gladder!" I say. "I didn't dream you could come, or I'd have rung you again myself."

The Captain's deep carrying voice says, "Will everyone please sit down now?"

Everyone finds a chair, and the saloon becomes quiet. I hear the lapping of water against the hull and the distant roar of London.

"Welcome aboard the yacht *Windrush!*" says the Captain. "We'll be getting underway in a bit more than an hour, and there are some things to arrange first. I suggest that we eat now, and then I'll have a few things to say."

He reaches for a sandwich, as do other people, and the babble of talk breaks out again.

I hear Betsy saying, "I wonder whether we'll have real adventures on this voyage?"

"Do you want to?" says Mary.

"Oh, yes!" says Betsy; and Beulah says, "I do, too. Not sinking, though."

"Then we'll have adventures!" says Mary firmly. She tells them about her father's great white bird of adventure that only comes down to those who welcome it.

The skipper says, "I like that! I'd like to meet your father."

"He'd like to meet you," says Mary. "I told him about you. He's a sailor, too, both Navy and yachts. Only our schooner is about a third the size of *Windrush.*"

"And you sailed with him?" says the Captain. "Richard said you'd both had some experience sailing on the Norfolk Broads and in the States."

"Yes," says Mary. "Sort of. My father used to take me out whenever he could. I couldn't do much, you know—I was crippled—but I loved it, and I could steer. And I learned a bit about piloting and seamanship."

"Tell me about the luff," says the skipper.

"Well," says Mary. "You are luffing when you come up into the wind. But I expect you mean the other luff, the leading edge of the sail —the little quiver in the luff that tells you when the sail is drawing right and 'asleep'. Not flapping."

"Good!" he says. "You do know something about it, Mary. How about you, Richard? Or is it Val?"

"Either way," says Richard. "Most people say Val—it's shorter. And I would have known that about the luff. Anyhow, I've sailed a good deal. I grew up on the tidal rivers and creeks of the Eastern Shore of Maryland, on Chesapeake Bay. When I was a boy I was in boats almost as much as on land."

"Ah," says the skipper. "That's the way I grew up, too—in Devonshire. The Bristol Channel, you know. A good way to grow up, too. Well, which of you is the better seaman?"

"Mary knows more—" I begin, just as she says, "Val is!"

The Captain smiles.

Mary says, "I might know a little more about navigation, but Val is really much more at home in boats."

"Well," says the skipper, "you two are the only ones, apart from Shelley and me, who know anything at all. Unless—?" He looks at Peter.

"I rowed for Oxford," says Peter with a grin. "But that's about the extent of it. Not very useful unless we take to the boats."

"Doesn't exactly qualify you as an old salt," says the Captain. "Anyhow, I'm jolly glad you two, Mary and Val, are aboard. Val, suppose you start out as second mate, and Mary can be third. The idea is for you to take a watch—you can do it together. Either Shelley or I will be with you at first. And you'll have to help teach the others. Even more important—both of you—keep an eye on the others and keep them from doing anything foolish, like getting themselves knocked overboard by the booms. Right?" We nod, and he adds, "Good!"

He looks around the table and sees that everyone is finished, then he tinkles his spoon against a cup. As people look up at him, he says: "As I said earlier, there are a number of things that need to be explained. We'll be getting underway when the tide has reached the flood— dropping down the river with the ebb. And you will all have duties. Even though everyone is paying expenses, everyone must do his share of the ship's work. There can be no shirking at all. There are a dozen of us, and we shall be divided up into three watches of four people each. These watches will go in turn—four hours on watch, eight hours off. Every morning, weather permitting, the decks will be swabbed down and the below-decks areas cleaned: this will be an all-hands job, except for the people on watch who are steering or doing some other necessary task. The watches change at eight bells—which means at midnight, four A.M., eight, noon, four, and eight. Each of the four-hour watches is marked off in bells every half hour. Thus 12:30 is one bell, one o'clock two bells, and so on to four o'clock, which is eight bells." He pauses and looks about. Most people look as though they are following, though Roger is counting something on his fingers.

The Captain continues: "Under this arrangement everybody would have the same watches every day, which would be rather tiresome. To avoid that repetition, we do what is called 'dogging' the four-to-eight watch in the afternoon, which means dividing into two two-hour watches, called the first and second dog watches. When you hit one or the other of these, your time on watch is shortened. You'll soon get used to all this. As for cooking and meals, the oncoming watch will get the meal and eat before coming on watch, and then the off-going watch will eat and wash up. Unless—" he looks hopefully around— "unless a couple of people want to volunteer to take over the galley and be free of all watch-standing. And be able to sleep all night." Again he looks round the table, but no one volunteers.

"Ah, well. Later, perhaps," he says. "Now, a very important matter— discipline! This is a pleasure cruise and I hope we'll all be friends—but legitimate orders *must* be obeyed. Sometimes instantly! The safety of the ship—and your lives!—may depend on it. I am the Captain of this vessel, and I and the officers *must* be obeyed without argument when we are underway. I want this to be clearly understood. We are not playing a game. Shelley, here, is first officer or first mate; and I have appointed Richard Vallance and Mary Vallance to be second and third mates, respectively. They all speak with my authority."

Betsy looks at Mary who smiles, and then—thinking perhaps of the skipper's grave voice—looks severe.

The skipper goes on: "I don't want to burden you with unnecessary formality, but all the same, I'll ask you to call me Captain or Skipper when we're aboard. Ashore, make it Denis, if you will. Similarly, the officer of the watch—*when* on watch—will be addressed as First or Second or Third on any matter concerning the ship or the watch. And when an order is given, please reply, 'Aye, aye.' That, in the age-old language of the sea—a perfectly legitimate language, by the way—means *both* that you understand and will obey. Learn the sea-terms for everything as soon as you can. The officers will help.

"One thing more, now, and the speech will be over. Second, you will have the Third on your watch, at least for the moment. Will you also take Betsy Bohun and Peter Shirley. On my watch I shall have Roger and Molly Denby and Pam Linton. The others will be on the First's watch."

"I say!" says Pam. "Can't Roz and I be on the same watch?"

"Sorry, Pam," says the skipper. "This is best for now. Stick it for a bit, and we'll change about in a few days."

"Captain," says Shelley. "Tell them about the buzzer."

"Ah, right you are!" he says. "The buzzer! In every cabin. One buzz is a reminder of a meal. Two longish buzzes mean a conference in the saloon. Not so important, those. *But* when it goes continually in short, sharp buzzes, it means *emergency!* All hands! All hands on deck! It might be fire or collision or storm. Night or day I want everyone on deck in *one minute flat.* Come as you are. Show them, First!"

Shelley goes to the companionway button. Suddenly the saloon is filled with short, sharp, snarling buzzes.

"Like that!" says the Captain. *"Jump!* Well, that's all. Remember what I said about not wasting water. Oh, yes—be careful about too much sun. It can be very bad at sea because of reflected glare. Now—let's make everything ready for getting underway. Those of you who haven't got out of your shore clothes, do so. And then come on deck."

As the others begin to move away, he says, "Val, Mary. Wait a minute." We look at him. He says, "Since you two are the only ones, apart from Shelley and me, who know a sheet from a halyard, you'll have special responsibilities when we are getting underway or anchoring or coming alongside of anything. Mary, suppose you take station forward as a regular thing: cope with the forward lines or anchor as well as the jib and foresail, calling on others for help as needed. And Val, after lines— and the mainsail. Shelley will help Mary if she's not tied up with the engine. And both of you, watch that nobody gets fouled in the bight of a line. Clear?"

"Aye, aye," I say, and Mary, who has started to say Okay, manages, "O-aye!"

The skipper grins and so do we, and we go topside. Shelley is tinkering with the engine controls. Her dark hair is in a knot on the top of her head, and she is wearing a dark-red shirt. "Know anything about diesel engines?" she says.

"Not a thing!" says Mary, and I shake my head.

"Oh, well," says Shelley with a rueful grin. "Looks like I'm chief-and-only engineer, as always."

Other people pop out on deck, the girls in colourful and abbreviated costumes.

The skipper comes back along the wharf and comes aboard. Shelley hauls down the Blue Peter. A couple of dock workers draw up the gangplank and others go to the bollards. There are a couple of subdued whistles for the feminine part of our crew. The engine catches and settles down to a steady rumble.

The Captain shouts, "We'll cast off in ten minutes. Third, remember you'll be casting off the forward line when I give the word."

"Aye, aye!" says Mary, going forward. "Betsy, mind you get your feet out of the way—that line could snake you overboard!"

"Okay," says Betsy and draws her bare feet under her.

"Stand by the foresail halyards!" calls the Captain, as Shelley also goes forward.

"Aye, aye!" cries Mary, going to the halyards. Shelley and Lewis take the throat halyard and Mary and Betsy the peak.

"Up fore!" orders the Captain, and they hoist away. Up goes the heavy gaff followed by the canvas, and the boom swings out to port in the light westerly breeze. As the people forward secure the halyards to the belaying pins at the foot of the foremast, I tell Roger and Peter and others to be ready to hoist the great mains'l.

"Up main!" commands the Captain. "Set the jib!" I see Mary spring to the jib halyards up forward, and the triangular jib goes up with a rush. Meanwhile five or six of us hoist the mains'l, and I say sharply, "Pam! Mind your head! Watch the boom!" She ducks and the boom swings out to port. We belay the main halyards.

Men are standing by the bollards on the wharf, and about ten others are watching.

"Cast off forward!" shouts the Captain.

Mary cries, "Aye, aye!" and with Lewis's help lifts off the heavy loop of line, and the men drag it in. The bow swings out. I stand by the after line.

"Cast off aft!" says the skipper. "Stand by the sheets!"

As I cast the mooring line into the Thames and jump to the main sheet, Shelley engages the engine.

"Lewis!" I hear Mary say. "Stand by this jib sheet—this line, here—and haul it in till the sail doesn't flap when the word is given." She moves to the fores'l sheet.

Windrush glides forward, the skipper at the helm. "Sheet in!" shouts the Captain, and we haul in the lines controlling the angle of the sails. In the same instant that the giant mains'l fills, Shelley yanks a white cord, and a small ball at the main peak breaks into the Red Ensign and streams out.

It has been a good performance, especially for an untrained crew. And as the vessel, all dark blue and white, moves majestically forward over the calm waters, the men on the receding wharf give a hearty cheer, and one cries, "Good luck, chaps!"

We move out into the Pool of London and head downriver. On the portside is the Tower of London, grim and magnificent. Every eye is fixed upon it until we pass beneath Tower Bridge. Soon thereafter we are passing the St Katherine Docks and on ahead are the Isle of Dogs and the Limehouse Reach. Since it is Sunday, the river traffic is comparatively light. One of Her Majesty's frigates is lying alongside the jetty at the entrance to the docks, the white ensign snapping at her stern: sailors crowd the rail as the schooner goes by.

A long low launch of the river police shoots up to us on a parallel course. The men aboard look us over. Captain Easter waves, and one of the men shouts, "Where are you bound, Captain?"

"Cleared today for the Med," says the skipper.

The officer, a grizzled, kindly looking man, doesn't reply for a moment. For a moment his eye rests upon Mary and Betsy and Molly sitting in a row on the forward house, and Peter murmurs to me, "I expect he'd like to take them home and tuck them in, all in a row, and read *Winnie the Pooh* to them."

But the man merely says, "Thank you. Good luck!" The launch sheers off.

We proceed steadily down the river under both power and sail, occasionally adjusting the sheets, especially in the great U round the Isle of Dogs, passing the endless docks of this mightiest of ports. Finally we pass Tilbury to port, just as one of the great "Strath" liners of the P. & O. Lines is coming in. London lies behind us now.

The westerly breeze freshens, and the skipper, still at the helm, cuts out the engine as we come round to a more northerly heading on the port tack. The sails are sheeted in, and the schooner heels a bit to starboard and begins to slip through the small waves with a silent ease— only a whisper of water along the hull.

"Ah," I say to Mary, having come forward to sheet in the foresail. "This is what I love. No engine. Just that hiss of water. It's going to be a great voyage."

"Knock on wood!" says Mary. I knock. "It's a sea thing, knocking on wood. Did you know that? In wooden ships. Tells the demons you're only kidding."

"Wooden ships and iron men," I say.

"Iron women, too," says Roz with a laugh. I look at her standing there, her blouse flattened against her by the breeze. Perhaps "flattened" isn't the word. Anyhow, I do not get the impression of an iron woman. Perhaps she hadn't intended me to.

Mary whispers to Betsy, "Iron maiden, more likely." This is a bit obscure, but it is not a friendly remark. Mary is not about to forget Roz's attempted piracy.

At this moment the Captain shouts, "All hands! Lay aft for high tea on deck!"

We go aft, where Shelley is fatiguing a great bowl of salad, just as Beulah pops up the companionway crying, "Chicken à la Thames." We realise that we're starving.

When the meal is done, I say to Mary, "Come on, let's wash up, since we didn't help with the cooking." As we wash, we marvel that so many friends should be aboard, though actually it is merely that we recruited Lewis and Beulah, and the Denbys recruited Peter and Betsy. Peter's idea in the first place of course. Roz is the real surprise.

By the time we come topside again, twilight is coming on and the breeze has dropped to a whisper. A sliver of moon is in the sky. The Essex shore is close in to port, and the coast of Kent is far away. Nobody is talking much. Finally the Captain quietly tells Shelley and Mary to stand by the anchor. Then he puts the helm hard over, cautioning people to mind the swinging booms. *Windrush* comes slowly up, and the anchor splashes down. The sails are dropped and secured. The anchor lamp is lit.

"It will be as well to have daylight for the Estuary and passing the Goodwin Sands," says the skipper. "And a good night's sleep the first night. All hands at four."

For awhile in the brightly lit saloon there is animated talk of Greece, and some people play cards at one end of the table. Beulah tells Mary and me small news of our Provence friends, and says that the paintings she did in May and early June had come off so well that she was willing to come away. After awhile I go up on deck, Mary and Betsy following; and then, a few minutes later, Betsy yawns and disappears towards her tiny cabin—she and Peter have adjacent cabins not more than half the size of the others. Mary and I stay on deck a little longer, looking down at the reflections of the ship's lights in the water. The ship seems a little world of its own. Overhead there are stars, and the dark masts swing across them like pointers.

Mary resumes the narrative, writing of the first day at sea
Buzz-buzz, buzz-buzz-buzz! I swim rapidly up from sleep, picturing

enormous steel bows smashing through the yacht and cutting Richard in two while the green ocean comes flooding in. The Captain shouts down the passageway: "Ten minutes! All hands on deck for getting underway! On deck in ten minutes!"

We yank on our clothes, adding pullovers, and run up on deck. The sails go up, though there's little breeze; and the engine rumbles into life.

"Anchor's aweigh, Captain!" I cry. He acknowledges and steers out into the river.

"Your watch on deck, please, Second," he says to Richard. Nearly everybody else goes back to bed except our watch and the skipper. The breeze freshens. "Ah," says the skipper. "Turn of the tide. Breeze always picks up." He switches off the engine. Then he says, "Mary, will you take the helm?"

I do so and swing the schooner a bit to get the feel of her and of the wheel. The skipper explains to Peter and Betsy about steering and the set of the sails. They take short tricks at the wheel, then Richard takes it awhile, relinquishing it to me.

"Third, ma'am!" says Betsy, with a small giggle. "May I go downstairs—I mean, below—and make coffee, please, ma'am?"

Peter and the Captain chuckle, and I say sternly, "Permission granted. Lots of cream."

"Aye, aye, ma'am!" says Betsy in a little-girl voice and disappears below.

When she re-emerges, the Captain takes his and one for Richard who has gone up forward. The two of them stand there easily, both seamen, both tall and splendid, though Richard is not as tall as the Viking skipper.

Betsy says in her soft Virginian voice, "Did you all notice who wasn't on deck for getting underway? I wonder if the Captain noticed?"

"Pam?" said Peter. "He noticed. Good officers always notice. When I was coming out of my cabin, I heard Pam say, 'Don't be silly!' I don't think she likes getting up."

Beulah's red head appears in the companionway. "Couldn't go back to sleep," she says. "It's all too exciting. So I've come up to help keelhaul somebody."

I think, with regret, of the passing of that fine old custom, for it seems to me that it would be a just thing to keelhaul Roz for attempting to steal Richard.

The skipper calls, "Third, mind that fishing boat ahead!"

"Aye, aye," I say. "I'm steering to clear him." It is a rowboat with a single man in it. He waves as we swish by, and we wave back.

Time passes and we begin to meet the surge and swell of the sea. Breakfast is made and eaten, and our watch, being relieved, washes up. Then All Hands for cleaning up the ship. I notice that Pam, although at breakfast, is not present, but Roz is.

The skipper speaks to her and I overhear the end, as I come aft to polish the binnacle: "—and tell her it's an *order.*" Rozica disappears and returns eventually with a sulky Pam. The skipper is at the helm, and since I am using brass polish on the binnacle, I overhear, willingly.

"Captain," Pam begins. "I want a different room. Ours is right by the heads, and someone is pumping all the time." Good tactics, I think, but very weak.

"Miss Linton," says the Captain. "Where were you at getting underway?"

"I was tired," says Pam. "I'm used to sleeping late."

"And where were you when All Hands was called half an hour ago?"

"I went back to bed," she says defiantly. "Since I had been waked up so many times. I'm paying for this cruise. You can't make me do these ridiculous things. So there!"

The Captain looks at her for a long moment, then he says mildly, "I'm sorry about your stateroom, Miss Linton. It's the same for Betsy, you know. Others are near the galley. It's just possible you'd sleep better if you did your share of the work. But in some quite wakeful moment, do read the Agreement you signed. You are paying, yes, but not to be a passenger. Only a fraction as much." Then he looks at Pam again. I should not care to be looked at so.

"Now, Miss Linton!" he says, and his voice, without being raised, is suddenly inflexible with command. "This is a vessel on the high seas, and I am the Captain. The law, do you understand. Withdraw from the cruise, if you like, when we reach port—but that's days away. Now we are at sea. Stay in your berth again when the All Hands goes, and you may be wakened with a bucket of sea water. Think it over, Pam."

She turns away sullenly and goes forward, where she and Roz talk.

During the forenoon watch the Captain and Shelley instruct everyone in the art of sailing and steering; and in the afternoon there are other lessons, including the tying of the important reef knot and bowline. Beulah, with Lewis as assistant, volunteers to take over the galley, with a little assistance from time to time, though they affirm their wish to learn all about sailoring, too. They do so mainly in order to have the morning and afternoon light for pictures. The watch bill is slightly revised, both Pam and Roz going on the skipper's watch and Roger and Molly on the mate's.

By nightfall there are twelve tired people aboard *Windrush,* but the Third—me—has the First Night Watch. Richard has said it's my turn—one of us must be *the* watch officer of any given watch. We therefore eat hurriedly and go topside, where Shelley gives us the course. We are in the English Channel, out of sight of land. There is nothing to see anywhere but waves and setting sun and the quarter-moon.

Nobody feels like talking. I sing to myself about how Henry Martyn turned robber all on the salt sea to maintain his two brothers and he. I fall silent.

"Sing some more," says Richard. "I love it when you sing."

"Sing winged songs," says Betsy.

I sing "Mary Hamilton" and a song from *Camelot,* not very loudly, and lapse into silence again. After awhile I relieve Richard at the wheel. Darkness comes on and we switch on the running lights, green to starboard and red to port, as well as a dim lamp in the binnacle. Peter calls back that there is a light off the port bow, and I turn over the helm to Richard while I examine it through the binoculars. It is the masthead light of a steamer, and through the glasses I can see the red glimmer of her port light as well. I use the bearing compass—a small, liquid-bowl hand compass that can be sighted across—at intervals and determine that the steamer is on a steadily changing bearing, meaning that we are not on a collision course with it.

"Betsy, love," I say. "Will you find Captain Easter—he said he'd be on the starboard transom in the saloon, if he's asleep—and tell him that there's a ship broad on the port bow, distance several miles, on a changing bearing? Broad on the port bow; changing bearing."

"Sure," she says. "I mean, aye, aye." She departs.

"Well done!" says Richard. "You do that sort of thing more efficiently than me."

Captain Easter returns with Betsy. He checks that the running lights are lit and says, "Good!" He also looks at the steamer, more distant than before and now almost abeam. Then he says, "You handled that just right, Mary—first getting the facts and then sending to notify me. Good show!"

"Daddy was in the Navy," I say. "And he always said that that was the way to do it."

"It is," he says. "Now, listen, Third—and you, too, Second—I always sleep on the saloon transom underway. Lee side. And I want to be called if you sight anything at all—*anything!* Understood? Or if the weather changes or becomes threatening. In case of doubt, *call* me. Clear?"

"Aye, aye!" say Richard and I together, followed a second later by

Betsy. There is also an "Aye, aye" from Peter up forward, who has heard.

"Now," says the Captain. "Your handling of the sighting, Mary, without being told how to do it, and your remembering the running lights without being told that, make me feel that you can handle a watch by yourself. And I also feel that Richard with his almost instinctive seamanship can. Either of you: certainly both together. How do you both feel about it?"

"I feel that we can cope, Captain," says Richard. "Or, at least, know when to call you." I say I think so, too.

"Very good!" he says. "Very helpful, too. You can't imagine how difficult a cruise like this is when no one, except Shelley and me, knows anything. Keep alert, all of you. Wake me and Roz and Pam about quarter to midnight. One of you might put some coffee or chocolate on a bit before that. Remember: call me if there's *anything!* Good night." He drops below.

I turn the wheel over to Betsy, showing her how to steer by compass. We trim the sails a bit. Then Peter comes aft to take the wheel. It soon becomes apparent to Richard and me that he has a natural aptitude for it —a horseman's hands, perhaps. Looking at him sitting lightly there astraddle the wheel box, as he might sit his hunter, his fine face dimly visible in the glow from the binnacle, I think—and eventually say—how glad I am that he is on this ship with us. He asks me about Betsy—she has gone forward to be lookout—and I tell him about Betsy's country background in Virginia and how she, too, loves horses, and the way we amused each other in hospital. Peter listens with interest and pricks up his ears when I speak of her love for horses, but he continues to steer the schooner deftly. Then Richard takes the wheel, and Peter goes forward again and sits with Betsy on the forward deckhouse. I imagine that they are talking about horses.

The hours wear on. We keep alert and stare about. The wind is steady on the beam, and there is no trouble in holding our course. *Windrush* is at her best on a reach, that is, sailing with the wind abeam. The ship's clock in the saloon strikes the bells of the watch every half hour, sounding, I think, like a big-ship bell at a distance . . . five bells . . . six . . . The ocean is dark, the moon has set, and there are clouds in the east. There are occasional creaks in the rigging aloft and the constant swish-swish of the waves under the forefoot and along the sides. I see Richard's face ghostly when he leans forward to the binnacle. We go on into rushing darkness.

Ding-ding, ding-ding, ding-ding, ding. Seven bells.

"Betsy!" I call. "Would you like to make some hot chocolate?"

She does so, and we all four sit in the cockpit and drink some. Then I ask Richard to wake the skipper and Pam and "your friend, Roz." I think he is probably grinning in the darkness at that. He goes, and when he returns says that the Captain woke instantly.

The Captain relieves me. Pam is five minutes late, but she comes. The skipper merely says, in her hearing, "Call Pam five minutes earlier next time."

We say good night and go below, through the dimly lighted saloon, aslant with the heel of the schooner. We separate with quiet good nights.

Mary continues with an account of the first storm at sea

Next day we have the forenoon watch, eight to twelve, which is again instruction. Reefing is explained—how the sails are lowered a little until the reef points, which are bits of line run through eyelets in the sail and knotted on both sides to keep them there permanently, can be tied around the booms, thus literally shortening sail. The foresail is reefed, and the reef shaken out, and then reefed again for practice. The mysteries of the compass are gone into, as well as the points of bearing in relation to one's own ship—dead ahead, fine on the starboard bow, broad on the starboard bow, abeam, broad on the starboard quarter . . . astern . . . and up the port side. Coming about is explained, including backing the jib, and the procedure is illustrated. The dangers of gybing are explained but not illustrated, since a gybe, especially an uncontrolled one—getting onto the other tack by heading downwind so that the heavy booms swing across the ship with hurricane speed—can mean death to the unwary or masts torn out. So the forenoon passes, and the Second's watch is relieved.

After lunch I linger in the saloon, where Roger is reading and Molly apparently calculating something. I write in this logbook, and read what Richard wrote about getting underway. Then I go topside in search of him, since he hasn't come down to the saloon to find me. On deck I notice with sudden gloom that Richard is in close talk with Rozica up on the forward house. I remember how attracted to her Richard had been at Holywell, and how Roz had tried to steal him away to Paris when we were in Provence. She is, I think, a dangerous woman, and I think that she is going to try again. I picture Richard leaping along after Roz on a Greek isle and me crying in vain, Come back! and then being turned into a swallow or something in the usual way by a pitying Zeus.

Roz is lounging on the deckhouse with a sort of easy grace, and I see her white teeth as she smiles at something Richard has said. Her creamy brown throat looks strong and graceful above the open neck of her white shirt. I wish I could turn her into a sea gull. Or perhaps a brown fish.

I notice that Pam, who should be on watch, is nowhere in sight, and I say to the skipper, "Where's Pam?"

"That one says she's seasick now," says the Captain, not very sympathetically. "But she ate her lunch."

"Oh," I say. "Want me to take her place?"

"No, thank you, Mary," says the Captain. "Roz and Richard are on deck."

"I noticed," I say. I look at Richard and Rozica again and don't like it. It occurs to me that Richard hasn't even noticed that I'm on deck—absorbed in that brown girl. I go gloomily below and forward to our room, where I curl sadly up on our berth and go to sleep.

I wake up and hear one bell. Half past four, first dog watch—an hour and a half till we go on for the second dog. I decide sleepily to look for Richard. I open the door just as the door of Lewis and Beulah's room across the passageway swings open with the roll of the ship. For one awful instant, I see Richard and Rozica locked in each other's arms, too lost in each other to see me. The door swings shut with a bang.

I stare blankly at the now-closed door across the passage. I can't seem to breathe. A terrible shudder goes through me. I manage to shut our door and lock it. I am shaking all over. Richard and Roz. I hadn't really believed it possible before, despite my thoughts—I know that now, having seen the reality. I collapse on the bunk and cry soundlessly. Someone tries the door and goes away.

"Oh, God! Oh, God, where are you?" I whisper. "I can't fight this—this physical thing! Brown girls! And she *is* attractive, and she and Val were at Holywell together. Who knows what really went on? Oh dear God! Everything is ruined—the cruise, our love, everything!" Sobs stop the whisper, but not my thoughts. The world lies around me in ruins. I think about the books that say men are polygamous. Like dogs. Always running after some bitch. Bitch is *right!* Bitch, bitch! Damn her! Then I think how I am trapped in this boat with someone who doesn't love me. There's no escape . . . except death. I picture me drifting along in the ocean, drowned, with seaweed in my hair, and Richard and Roz in each other's arms on the deckhouse, not caring. I feel utterly despairing and cry very hard. The pillow is soaked.

After awhile I realise that even in the midst of utter tragedy I have to go to the heads. I peer out of the door and, still crying, run into the heads and return. I know that our love is ended, everything is destroyed. Nothing is left. I decide that I shall say nothing to you, just be remote

and impersonal on watch and sleep in the saloon. I shall change my
clothes—my shirt is soaked with tears—and go and be forward lookout
on our watch. I take my clothes off and hurl them into a corner and get
out fresh shorts, when, suddenly, I am overcome again and sit on the
bed naked and cry. I feel tears falling on my breast. In the night I will
go into the ocean and be dead.

The door opens and Richard is there.

"Mary!" he says. "Good God!"

I cover my face with my arms and continue to cry wildly.

He shuts the door quickly and stands over me and says, "Mary! Mary,
darling!"

It is the dear voice, but it is mine no more. Never anymore. I sob,
choking and gasping.

"Mary! Stop it! Tell me!" you say. "What is it? —Oh, of course!
Listen! Listen, Mary!"

I say, sobbing, "I know you . . . love her." I sob wildly. "It's . . . all
right . . . you—you . . . always . . ." I can't go on. I'm shaking all over.
Somewhere, in some corner of my head, something is commenting,
truthfully, that I am getting a bit out of hand. I ignore it.

You try to put your arms around me. I fight you off. I hit you,
sobbing. You say, "Mary, dear, listen! Please, listen! Mary! . . . Mary!
Listen! Stop crying and just listen! Mary!" You take my hands. I wrench
them away, choking, my eyes tight shut.

Suddenly there is an explosion—my head has blown up. You have
slapped me hard. Perhaps I am dead?

I open my eyes and see you through a blur of tears.

"You hit me," I state forlornly.

"Oh, Mary! you darling fool!" you say, torn between impulses to
laugh and to howl like a dog. "Now, will you *please* listen? I'm sorry I
had to slap you but—hysterics, you know. Will you listen?"

"Yes," I say. "I will listen." I pluck uselessly at the coverlet with a
vague thought that my tragic dignity is diminished by nakedness. Still,
perhaps not.

"Here!" you say, handing me a lighted cigarette. "Now, listen! You
saw Roz and me in there, didn't you?" You hook a thumb towards the
passage, and I nod desolately. "Now! You didn't see one thing more
than I might have seen when you let that Jacqueline kiss you—and that
didn't mean *any*thing, did it? One kiss, and not my doing—just chance
the door should swing that instant. Here's what happened. Up on deck
she got to telling me her problems with Pam—what a mistake she'd
made to persuade Pam to come. Then we came below to go to our

cabins, and she said, "I forgot one thing I wanted to tell you, Val. Come in here a minute; they're on watch. So I did. She said she'd been thinking about what I said in France—about us building a lasting marriage. And she said, again, how much she and I had in common. Then she said in a low voice, 'And with you, Richard, I think I might find such a love.' Before I knew it, she was kissing me."

"But, Val!" I say. "You were kissing her back! I could tell! Oh!" Fresh tears roll down my cheeks and drip, cold, onto my breast. I can feel one, wet and cold, on my nipple, and I have a fleeting wish for a small muscle that would twitch it off.

"Mary, *dear!*" you say. "You promised to listen. So, listen! Roz is not a bad sort, and she is attractive. But that first-wave attraction of Holywell days is gone. Quite gone. That's the danger time, always—that first wave. Anyway, I like Roz, but I *love* you. I pushed her away instantly and told her it was no good. *Never* could she get me to leave you—and if she did, it would just prove that real love *didn't* exist."

"What did she say?" I ask with a renewed appreciation of life.

"She said she was sorry—you know, 'Sor-ry!' with that little lilt. And then she said, 'You know, Val, you are convincing me. I shan't do this again. I almost . . . don't want to. But do let's be friends. Please?' And I said, 'Right. Friends—only.' And that was *all*. But, Mary—"

"Don't say it, Val!" I say. "I know. Trust? . . . Yes, I read your mind, maybe. I remember. We said a life of fear about love would ruin it. And you said that with each other's commitment to lean on, we could trust. And I—I didn't! Please forgive me. I'm a—a serpent!"

"Mary, you silly darling!" you say. "Of course I do. Partly my fault anyway for not being more alert. I don't blame you—what you thought you saw would seem proof—but, darling, we've both got to remember this." You lean down and kiss me hard. Then you drop down on one knee and kiss the tear-wet nipple of my starboard breast.

I murmur happily, "I'm unbalanced!" So you kiss the portside one.

"Come on," you say. "It's twenty to six—almost time to relieve the watch. Wash your face and get dressed. I'll go on up."

My glance in the looking glass appalls me. My eyes are as red as a stoat's and puffy, and one cheek is decidedly pinker than the other. I do what I can with cold water and a dab of powder.

Then I run up to the cockpit, where Richard is at the helm. I try to keep the pink side of my face to seaward. Even so, Betsy, the see-all, is looking at me. I announce that I'm going aloft. Richard looks slightly alarmed but says nothing. The yacht is steady on a broad reach, the booms far out to port. I go to the starboard ratlines of the mainmast and clamber up to the gaff, the schooner's heel to port making it quite easy. There I wrap an arm about the mast as it swings across the sky. The deck below looks small, and everybody is looking up.

I think about what happened. I am astonished that I came so near hysterics, thanking Richard in my mind for having the sense to slap me. But mainly I think about commitment, resolving with all my strength to remember it and to trust. I look down at the yacht's fine bow rising to meet the waves and think of marriage as a ship. Trust and keeping faith makes that ship seaworthy. I say a prayer for Richard and our ship.

Glancing down, I see the skipper come up on deck. He glances about, perhaps wondering whether to demote me as a faithless watchkeeper. Then he glances up.

He laughs. "That's what I call keeping a sharp lookout," he says to Richard and then calls up to me, "Aloft there! Do you see anything?"

"A gull," I cry. "Gull broad on the starboard bow."

Richard thinks, he tells me later, that I sound rather like a gull myself, my cry carried down the wind. He is also slightly afraid I shall fall off.

The Captain laughs again and sits down, stretching out his legs and putting his elbows on the cockpit coaming. He and Peter are talking, with Richard putting in a word now and then. I can't hear very well, though Peter is saying something about a hunt breakfast. I see Betsy go below, probably to fetch tea. I decide to descend and help her and hear what everybody is saying.

Rozica is in the main saloon reading as I go towards the galley. She glances up, and I smile sweetly at her. Betsy and I return to the cockpit with tea mugs.

Betsy sips hers and looks at the sea. "It's the patterns of foam on the waves," she says. "Always different. Saying something if only I could read it."

"Aren't the swells rather larger than they were?" says Peter. "The wind isn't any stronger though."

"There's a bit of weather somewhere," says the skipper. "The glass is falling and the breeze is backing."

"I thought something might be building up," says Richard.

"What does that mean—backing?" asks Peter.

"Normally," says the Captain, "the breeze veers, which means it hauls round or shifts in a clockwise direction. In the northern hemisphere, anyhow. A north wind veers to nor'east and then to east. But when it backs, it goes counterclockwise. We had a nor'east breeze, and now it's a bit west of north. Backing usually indicates a disturbance somewhere. Also, as I said, the barometer is falling. And—do you see those low-lying clouds to the west that the sun is going down behind? A high sunset—we may get a bit of breeze."

"A storm at sea?" says Betsy. "I'm not sure I'd like that."

I glance at Richard, thinking of our own recent storm at sea, rain and thunder and lightning. He knows and grins at me.

"Nothing serious, I expect," replies the skipper easily, yawning and stretching his strong arms along the coaming.

Shelley and Molly come up to join us, Shelley sitting close beside Denis—the Captain, that is. Her dark hair is done up in a knot on the very top of her head, as usual, and her delicate features are alive with interest as she says, "For heaven's sake, what is all this about the Place of the Blue Glass? Roger was telling me about your trip, and the place sounds magical."

"It is, indeed!" says Richard. "La Verrière Bleue. The whole ceiling is deep-blue stained glass with light above it. It's like dining—or dancing —under a perfect twilight sky."

"Or inside a sapphire!" I say. "Or with the blue Mediterranean upside down over your head."

The Captain says, "That last comparison isn't quite so appealing to a sailor."

Everybody chuckles. Then Shelley sighs and says plaintively, "I want to see it."

The skipper smiles tenderly at her and says, "We'll go there one day, my darling." I contemplate this new human side of the Captain. Shelley pats his leg.

Pam's face appears in the companionway. Rozica follows, saying, "Hullo-ullo, everybody!" She looks at me and says, "Hullo, Third! Looks like you're doing a good job." She gives me a friendly smile. I think about that.

"Time to relieve," says the Captain. "Second, I relieve you."

"You have the ship," says Richard formally. "Watch, let's dine." We go below, followed by Shelley who serves two plates, for herself and the skipper, and disappears. All but the watch on deck draw up to the table, including Lewis and Beulah. It is a merry meal, mainly because Beulah's in a clowning mood. But there's a bit of serious talk, too, about the differences between the painter's eye and the photographer's. I interject a word about the poet's eye: condensed and vivid words to re-create the image.

After dinner, I write about this day in the journal, then give it to Richard to read. Once he gives a huge shout of laughter, causing everybody to look round and say "What?" But, to my relief, he merely shakes his head, grinning. Then we go to bed.

Mary continues the journal with another storm

I awaken in the dark. Richard is holding me so tightly that I can hardly breathe. I think that the motion of the schooner is more violent than it has ever been. There are creaks and groans from the timbers. The bow goes up and up, and descends with a crash. You hold me even tighter, and I consider how it will be going through life from now on with a left breast shaped like a pancake. The clock in the saloon goes ding-ding, ding-ding, ding. Five bells. I know somehow that I've slept more than an hour, so it's not ten-thirty but two-thirty. There is the smash of a wave hitting the quarter, and I feel sure that some of it came aboard. Somewhere, in one of the cabins or in the saloon, something has come adrift and rolls back and forth, banging into bulkheads. I suspect it's a coffee mug.

Buzz-buzz, buzz-buzz-buzz, buzz-buzz! It is the all-hands alarum. Richard jumps violently and wakes at once, as though he'd been expecting the alarum in his sleep. The buzzer sounds again, urgently. We spring up, grab our clothes, and go.

I say urgently, "Don't let go of something for a second!"

"Don't you!" he says. "A death grip!"

There is a crash and a shrill feminine yelp in the passage behind us. Someone has fallen. Others are crowding behind us, and we warn them about hanging on.

We emerge into black darkness, wind, and rain. The Captain shouts, "Got to get the main and jib off her! Shelley and Roz have gone to the jib. Val! Mary! Drop the peak of the main!"

As we scramble towards the peak halyards, I hear the skipper shout to Lewis and Peter to get onto the throat halyards. The peak drops, spilling the wind, the sail bellying and flapping. I can feel that the schooner is eased, a little. We are soaked by spray. The throat begins to drop, and we pay out line on the peak.

There are cries from forward, but the rush of wind and the smash of waves make it impossible to hear. There is a crash of solid water hitting. Richard grabs the belaying-pin rack, and also Betsy's arm. I grab the boom itself. Some of the wave sweeps over us, wrenching at us. There is a violent metallic banging aft.

Suddenly the gaff comes down with a rush, and a great bulge of heavy wet canvas hits me an almost stunning blow, knocking me off my feet. I clutch at nothingness and feel myself rolling off the deckhouse towards the sea. "Val!" I cry, knowing that no one can save me. Then a powerful arm is about my waist. Richard has leaped in the dark for the mainmast shrouds—if he had missed he would have gone straight into the sea—and seized them and me simultaneously. Nothing less than instant thinking and perfect co-ordination and reckless courage could have saved me. And perhaps his almost instinctive at-homeness with boats and the sea. I do not of course know at that moment what he did or how, only that I am saved. No one else knows either except the Captain, who had been able to see one dark shape rolling into the storm-churned ocean and the hazardous leap of another. The whole episode has taken no more than three seconds.

"I'm all right," I cry to Richard, although my heart is pounding hard. "We've got to secure the main."

"Right!" he says; and we claw our way back to the sail, helping to lash the gaff to the boom. Others are doing the same farther aft, where the boom-end has been secured in its crutch. We claw at the wildly flapping canvas. The banging aft continues, heavy and dangerous-sounding. We finally succeed in gathering the bulk of the mainsail and lashing it and the gaff to the boom.

Shelley has just shouted, "Jib secured!" when Richard shouts, "Main secured, Captain!"

"Tie a reef in the fore!" the Captain shouts.

"Aye, aye," say several voices.

There is another struggle in the darkness during which I hear Molly muttering, "Och, lassie!" We succeed in tying in the reef, and the yacht is further eased. I lick salt off my lips. We are driving along under reefed foresail alone.

Suddenly the night turns to sound—an enormous blast of sound. For an instant I think wildly of a tidal wave, then I realise it to be a steam whistle. There is a scream and shouts. We see the lights and the towering bows of a ship bearing down down upon us, huge and menacing. I think we are dead. I think of Richard sinking to the bottom of the ocean, me faithfully with him.

A brilliant light illuminates our sail—the Captain has snatched up the Ready Torch. And the steamer is already swinging. The skipper has our helm alee. Even without the main and jib, we are shooting up into the wind. A blinding searchlight picks us out. The steamer rushes past. We glimpse men staring down, wondering what is down there; and then the ship is swallowed up in darkness. Our head falls off, and we run before the gale. At once everything is quieter.

I imagine the men on the steamer being struck rigid when they

looked down and saw in the glare of the searchlight all the scantily clad
girls running around below. I imagine a conversation with an off-watch
comrade: "You lot are crazy—couldn't be all dames!" "Listen, mate! I
saw 'em! Hundreds of 'em! Nothin' on, see!" And so a great saga of the
waterfront cafes would be born.

We have all made our way back to the cockpit where we are
collapsed. The skipper and Richard are talking and Peter is listening.
Peter looks at me in a worried way, and I grin at him. The skipper claps
Richard on the back.

The banging noise still sounds, nearer but not so violent. "Water tank
carried away under the after deck," says the Captain calmly. "Can't do
anything about it until it gets light. Second, suppose your watch drop
below and get on dry clothes—or *some* clothes—and have some tea or
chocolate and get ready to take the watch. Third—would you, er, like to
rest?"

"Oh, no!" I say. "I'm quite all right—thanks to Val."

"Good!" he says. "Val is a seaman and a brave one." I know I've
heard the skipper's highest commendation. He adds, "When I saw you
rolling over—I didn't know who it was of course—I thought nothing
could save you. I was just reaching for a life-jacket and flare when Val
leaped."

This naturally leads to a demand from everyone to know what
happened—most people were totally unaware of the incident. So the
whole story is told, and a wet Betsy gives me a hug. Peter looks as
though he'd like to do the same. I realise, as I know the skipper and
Richard do, too, that if I had gone over, the chances of my being picked
up again in the storm wouldn't have been great.

When we drop below to our cabin, Richard and I hug each other,
and I thank him for saving my life.

"At the time," he says, "I just acted. But I have been thinking ever
since, what if I'd lost you? Oh, Mary! I love you!"

"If you'd missed the shrouds," I say, "you'd have gone into the sea,
too. So we'd have died together. As it is . . . thank you for my life. I
love you."

"I suppose the sword is always hanging over our heads," he says.
"Come on, let's get back on deck."

"Val," I say. "If it had been the other way round, I couldn't have
saved you. That scares me. You know that thing we read about how
women should be in the combat forces—go to sea in warships? I thought
we should. Now—I don't. Not at all."

When we emerge on deck, the rain has stopped and the first signs of dawn are in the sky. Only the Captain and Roz and Beulah are still there. I look at Beulah in surprise.

"I'm taking Pam's place," she says. "She went below in hysterics during the, er, late emergency."

"Weak girl," says Richard with only a hint of scorn, but I know how deep the condemnation is.

We relieve the watch, but the skipper stays on deck, his wet shirt clinging to his great chest. The swells are very large and the wind strong from the west.

"Let me go and get you some tea," I say to him. "Or hot chocolate."

"Thank you, Mary," he says. "Very kind of you. Chocolate, please."

I bring up mugs of steaming chocolate for all of us, and we sit about sipping it as the light brightens in the eastern sky and the yacht drives on towards it with the boom of the foresail far out to starboard. The terrors of the night already seem far behind us. We all, I think, feel rather pleased with ourselves, coping so bravely with storms and near-collision. No Pams on our intrepid watch, and one hero, Val. The wind continues to moderate, so we go forward and shake out the reef in the foresail.

Turning over the helm to Richard, the Captain removes the cushions from the cockpit seat on the portside aft, lifts the seat itself, and tosses life-jackets out into the cockpit. Then he gets the torch and thrusts his head and arm down and peers aft. Withdrawing, he says that as he thought a water tank has come unbolted and the pipe unscrewed.

"Someone," he says, "will have to try crawling in there. I can't do it —too big. Val, too." He eyes Betsy and me appraisingly. "Third," he says. "Maybe you're the narrowest. Do you want to have a go?"

"Aye, aye," I say. "What do I do down there?"

"Well," he says. "You get yourself down there, first, and then—look, see that connection? That sleeve—that ring-like thing—will screw onto the tank. Then you have to crawl aft of the tank and swivel it around to that brace and put a washer and nut onto the bolt."

"But, then," I say, "I'll be behind the tank. Once it's in place, I can't possibly get past it and come out. What do I do then—live down there with people handing down cups of tea?"

"No, no," he says with a laugh. "You crawl that way and come up through the lazarette hatch." He takes the hatch cover off the hatch, which is in the middle of the after deck. "It's pretty small," he says. "Think you can get through it?" I nod, and he says, "Peter, will you and Betsy clear out the paint and gear from the lazarette so that Mary will be able to get over there?"

With an "Aye, aye," Peter lies face down on the deck, reaching down into the lazarette and handing paint cans and coils of line to Betsy.

Meanwhile I descend through the cockpit seat and worm my way to the tank while the skipper holds the light. I fasten the pipe connection. On his instructions I sound the tank, and it is empty.

"Three hundred gallons of water gone," he says. "In the bilges."

I crawl round the canted tank and shove it into place. The Captain shines the light down the lazarette hatch and passes down nuts and a spanner. I tighten the nut with all my strength. The tank is ship-shape again. As I work, I feel the big swells passing beneath the stern, lifting it, and I hear the water gurgling about the rudder.

Finally I crawl over to the lazarette—there is just enough headroom to crawl. The hatch opening, framing the skipper's face against a now-blue sky, is very small. I attempt to come straight out, but I can't get my shoulders through. I descend and turn over into a sitting position and reach one arm up to grab the hatch coaming; then I give a heave and my head again appears in the hatchway. I writhe and twist and get my shoulders through. "Made it!" I say, and Betsy says, "Hooray!"

With my hands on the coaming, I lift myself up and get my feet under me and stand up. Just as I stand fully up, my hips stick. "Ohhh," I say. "I'm sticking!"

"Try it catty-corner," says Betsy.

I sink down a little bit, thinking I resemble a jack-in-the-box, and twist and come up again on the diagonal. I cannot get through.

Richard laughs and says something to the skipper, who chuckles. I stick out my tongue at them. Richard grins and says, "Try dropping your jeans, and pull your shirt up."

I undo my belt buckle and, not without difficulty, unzip the jeans. Then I sink down a little and wriggle like a snake until the jeans drop down around my ankles. Then, pulling up the shirt, still on the diagonal, I come up again. The skipper puts his hands under my arms and lifts— and out I come, possibly with a case of compressed hips. He fishes out my jeans; and with an obligatory, "Don't look," I rapidly get them back on again.

"Ah," I say. "I was beginning to think that I was going to be a permanent fixture of the after deck, like a bust on a shelf. Or a hip."

"Lazarus from the lazarette," says Peter.

"Well done, Third!" says the Captain. "And thank you. —Now, for the bad news. No more showers. No more clothes washing."

"But we're all salty!" says Betsy. "We'll itch."

"I know," says the skipper. "I'm in the same, er, boat. But we've been blown off our course. Half our full water supply was lost; and,

90

unfortunately, we've been using the other tank, so *it's* half-empty. No showers! Minimum water for any purpose."

During the day, the wind and sea moderate still further. We get full sail on *Windrush* again, and the Captain gets some sun sights to fix our position. Richard and I sleep much of the day, arising in time for the first dog watch. But we are again asleep at twenty to midnight when Beulah comes to wake us for the midwatch.

"All right, we're awake," says Richard to her. We scramble reluctantly out of our nice warm bunk and put on clothes and jackets and pullovers. As we make our way to the galley for whatever has been made for us, we are joined by a very sleepy-looking Peter and a mop-headed Betsy.

"Yo ho," I say without enthusiasm. "Oh for the life on the ocean wave."

"I say!" mumbles Peter. "What an 'orrid time to turn out!"

As we emerge into the cockpit, the people on watch greet us with that hideous alert cheerfulness that marks those going off watch. The First gives us the course and says there's nothing in sight. Richard relieves her, and she stands up and stretches. "The skipper's in the saloon," she says. "Call him if there's anything. Good night." They go below.

The night air is soft. There is a steady fresh breeze just abaft the beam, and a golden half-moon in the western sky, which traces a yellow

moonpath shimmering across the dark heaving sea to us. We sip hot chocolate to the comfort of our 'midships region and cease to regret being ripped untimely from our bunks.

We talk a bit in quiet voices appropriate to the night. A light that Peter sees turns out to be a low star. Talk turns to England, places we like, Peter's Yorkshire and Dorsetshire and the Cotswolds. Betsy, who's seen so little of England, asks whether anyone has ever been to Tintern Abbey. No one has, though I say we've always meant to. Richard says perhaps we can all go together someday.

In response to a question from me, Betsy tells something of her doings since we were in hospital together three years ago. She had gone home, home being the Gloucester Neck of Virginia, where she had rested and read and painted. Then, as her strength returned, she had begun to ride again—it had been a fall at a jump that had put her in that hospital. Peter of course was interjecting all sorts of questions about the Bohun stables. The following year, Betsy went on, she had gone up to an art school in New York, where she had often wandered about the streets 'people-watching'. No harm ever came to her. I sometimes think she can make herself invisible when she wants to, though I've never actually seen her do it. But then of course one wouldn't see her.

She tells me about one of her paintings she thinks I'd like—a night-time dorm meeting when she was in college, done from memory. "What it was," she says, "was the scene as I came down the steps—all the girls in their housecoats, most of them sitting on the floor with their housecoats spread all around. I suddenly saw them as a garden full of bright flowers. In my painting you see it first as a garden, maybe . . ."

We all say that we should like to see it. Then Peter says he will go forward to be lookout, adding, "Come along, Betsy. I want to hear more about the horses." He looks at Richard, and they exchange grins. I give him a hopeful smile, too.

Richard is steering, and I am as close as I can get. We are silent for a time. Then I say, "Val, are you liking all this as much as I am? It's sort of hard sometimes."

"Oh, but I like it!" he says. "The rough with the smooth—a night like this or the storm last night. Not to mention hips in hatches. All good."

"I think everyone feels so," I say. "Except Pam of course. What I like is—well, here we are, miles and miles from land, sliding through the ocean like a fish, with all our friends in their bunks. And—and look at those sails against the stars . . . And I love you, even if you did slap me!"

"You punched me first," he murmurs unrepentant. "Hard, too." Then he leans over from the wheelbox and kisses me. It lasts until there is a small flap from the luff causing him to straighten up and tend to the ship. I look at his face in moonlight.

I hear four bells go—half our watch is over. We are silent again, and I think some more about our marriage as a ship, voyaging the sea with unknown dangers and harbours ahead. If one of us should die, that would be the ship breaking in two on a reef. Still, the final harbour is heaven, and our ship would sail again. I pray.

Richard, then, out of the depths of his thoughts, asks me if I need him, and I say of course.

"No, not of course," he says. "I was reading a book where the girl was always saying how she *needed* her lover and couldn't handle her life without him. Didn't seem right to me—a marriage founded on someone's neediness. Like having one person as a lifelong father or mother. How could there possibly be inloveness?"

"Oh, I see what you mean," I say. "And I agree. It's got to be two people who can cope alone but come together for joy and—and, well, completeness: that double vision you were talking about. I was coping with life, you know, even before wings—my books and all; and I think I could have coped and been sort of happy even if Daddy had been poor."

"You did indeed," says Richard. "Of course we have to remember that everybody needs a bit of mothering or fathering on occasion. Just not all the time. Each one has to have strength for the other, I think."

"That's us," I say cheerfully. "Especially since wings. My life is right, now."

"Yes, yes, yes!" he says. "As right as anything could be. The dancer unchained."

I stand up and sweep my gaze round the horizon and then lean over and kiss him, with passion and tenderness. It results in severe flaps from the luff and the vessel five degrees off course to windward. Fortunately the Captain does not hear the flap and come leaping up to put me in irons—the dancer chained again.

The remainder of the watch is without incident. Once I stretch out on the after deck and lie there watching the swing of the tall mainmast across the brilliant steady stars, listening to the splash and chuckle of the Atlantic sliding along the graceful, sea-kindly hull.

Mary writes about the famous rock
The next days are rather less eventful, which means partly that I didn't keep up this logbook very faithfully—and Richard only writes

under severe pressure from me. I've consulted the main ship's log, written up after each watch, but its entries—like "Wind NE by E, sea mod."—aren't very helpful in reconstructing the days. There was one dramatic event when Beulah tripped on a line and went over the side, and the skipper's "Man overboard!" went ringing through the ship. But the helm was already alee and a life ring sailing through the air. Then she was hauled dripping aboard, and the Captain gave us a stern lecture on the greatest danger at sea, next to fire. Especially on a night watch when someone might stumble into the sea and not be missed until too late. Nothing else broke the rhythm of the watches. We all longed for a bath, but not even Pam dared violate the Captain's order. The water got ever bluer. Once dolphins played about the bows all afternoon. Another time Molly caught a great fish, which we had for dinner. And once we saw a stove-in lifeboat drift by upside down.

Then one morning we awake to a cradle-like rolling, with a slatting back and forth of the booms. "We're becalmed," says Richard. "Let's go topside."

There, under a cloudless sky, our gaze falls instantly upon the great grey rock two or three miles off the starboard beam—Gibraltar! Fortress of England and gateway to the Mediterranean. Although we've expected to see it, we are thrilled.

"Let's get the sails off her," says the Captain. "It's going to be awhile before we get a breeze." He nods towards low clouds on the horizon. "Don't want to use the fuel for a run in under power."

After securing the sails, we breakfast. We weary of the rolling. Then the skipper says to the group of seven in the cockpit, "Who's for a fresh-water bath?"

There is a chorus of "Me!" "I am," and "How?" with a "Hooray!" from Beulah, the saltiest salt of all.

"See that long low cloud?" says the Captain. "Rain. No wind—see how it's creeping towards us. In about fifteen minutes, I reckon, we shall have a ten-minute shower." He then suggests that the men have a very rapid showerbath, leaving robes at the foot of the companionway, and hand over the rest of the rain to the women with their longer hair.

The men in fact take almost no time, and then we rush out of the saloon, shedding our robes at the ladder. Squeals at the chilliness of the steady downpour. We scatter out, soaping vigorously. Shelley cries to hurry and not be caught with soapy hair. The rain slackens. Betsy calls, "Wait, rain! One minute!" It obediently rains for one minute more. Stops. Sunlight falls upon us and we glisten. The sky is blue again.

Molly flaps her arms, drying. "Molly!" cries Beulah. "I'm going to catch you and then you'll be It!" There is a resounding slap on bare flesh, and Beulah skips away.

Molly looks wildly about and makes for me, crying, "Aha, lassie, you'll be the one the noo!" I dodge, laughing, and Molly runs on and slaps Roz's bottom.

Roz giggles and runs after Shelley. The wild game of tag goes on, punctuated with spanks and shrieks and giggles along with the thud of running bare feet, all probably very puzzling to the men below. I am tagged and scurry about amongst elusive ladies and finally give Pam a spirited slap. Then I scamper up the ratlines to the masthead. I see Betsy out on the tip of the long bowsprit, hanging onto the stay and trying to look, perhaps, like a figurehead. We exchange waves. I bethink me of a possible ship enjoying all this. But there is no ship, only the great grey rock in the distance. Zeus, very likely, is casting a glance from Olympus, having an eye for mortal maids.

The game dies away, and we go below, quite dry. As I come on deck again, dressed, I hear the Captain say, "Wind ho! All hands! Make sail!"

There is a line of glittering ripples moving across the water towards us. We spring to our stations at the halyards, and the sails go up with a rush. The breeze is upon us. The big schooner heels and comes alive and slides through the water. The familiar swish-swish of the bow wave returns. She is no longer a raft but a companion of the wind.

The skipper remarks, "We'll take her into Gibraltar and get supplies —and of course water. We should be there about five o'clock if the wind holds. Perhaps we'll have a night in."

It is, in fact, half-past four when *Windrush* stands into Gibraltar Harbour, all sails drawing. A great grey cruiser of the Royal Navy is lying at anchor with the white ensign fluttering from the stern. An officer on her main deck gives us a wave as we slide past to windward.

A launch swings alongside, learns we're out of London and in need of supplies, and directs us to a wharf. We approach it. The sails come down smartly at the skipper's command. The vessel glides on, still without the engine, though Shelley is standing by. The Captain puts the rudder hard over. The yacht swings, drifts neatly starboard-side-to into the wharf. Men throw us lines, and one says, "Very nicely done, Captain!"

The skipper makes arrangements for an immediate water hose and for fuel, and he gives a list of groceries and supplies to a ship chandler's clerk. The water hose comes aboard.

Down the wharf march three soldiers, very neat, wearing gloves. One of them carries a large bouquet of flowers. They halt with a stomp at our gangway. The leader snaps a low command, and they right-face as one man. The corporal says formally, "The yacht *Windrush* out of London, sir?"

"That's right," says the Captain with a puzzled look.

The corporal says woodenly, "We was instructed to deliver these flowers to the ladies of the *Windrush,* sir."

The Captain looks at Shelley, who steps up and takes the bouquet. The corporal salutes, says "Hup!" and they march away.

"What on earth?" says the skipper. "No one knew we were coming here, not even me."

Shelley suddenly shouts with laughter, and all eyes turn towards her. "There's a card," she says. "Listen, everybody. Here's what it says: 'To the Ladies who like to play tag! With deep appreciation!' And it's signed, 'From the ratings of H.M. Rangefinder Company.' So—the long and the short of it is that they were watching us this morning when we were larking about after the rain."

"Oh my God!" says Rozica. Roger laughs, and Richard chuckles. Suddenly everybody is laughing.

"But how *could* they see all that way?" says Pam.

"Lumme!" says the skipper. "I should have thought of that. We're not talking about ordinary little bird-watching telescopes. They have huge range-finders and fire-control telescopes. They read the name on the stern, you notice. They could probably have seen a mouse! And that rock was probably a solid wall of glass."

"I think I made a mistake climbing to the masthead," I say sadly.

"Think what you did for all those lonely chaps," says Richard with a grin.

The little fuel lorry arrives, interrupting the talk for the moment. When it departs, the Captain says, "I think that it might be as well to get underway as soon as we conveniently can. If this gets about—well, we shouldn't care for reporters and photographers, should we? So, as soon— Oh, good! Here they are now!"

A small electric lorry has arrived with the groceries, and we form a chain to take them aboard and below.

After it is gone, Shelley says, "As it is now—I mean, without further publicity—it's not so bad. Nobody's going to recognize us with our clothes on. But I agree, we should get underway." There is a general chorus of agreement mingled with laughter.

At that moment Rozica comes on deck in skirt and blouse, carrying her shoes and a case. "We're leaving the cruise, Captain," she says. "I'm sorry! Actually, I don't want to, but *she* insists." She nods towards the deckhouse. "And I feel sort of responsible for her until she is back in London." She glances at Richard.

There is a banging in the companionway as Pam struggles up with her case. The Captain and Roz talk apart, and then the Captain goes below and returns with an envelope, which he gives to Roz. People say polite goodbyes to Pam and friendlier ones to Roz. She looks at Richard with a wry little smile and offers her hand, which he takes. Then Rozica comes over to me and offers her hand, and I, too, take it. "Sorry!" she murmurs to me, with that little lilt of hers. "I'd like to know you better, Mary. Differently. Some day."

I say impulsively, "Come to see us in Oxford, Roz."

She gives me a quick smile and nods and turns away. She and Pam walk off down the wharf.

Less than an hour later *Windrush* is standing out to sea, and the famous rock, with H. M. Rangefinder Company and their memories, is fading away astern. Europa Point is abeam to port, and before long a gibbous moon will rise dead ahead.

Mary continues the journal with an account of France revisited

It is the forenoon watch several days and many sea miles later. The yacht is reaching on a northeasterly course, for we are bound for Marseilles in order to make a side excursion to Avignon. Richard has the watch and I am at the helm, although, since we are short-handed, Peter has been conscripted to the Captain's watch.

Beulah comes up on deck, wearing an apron and carrying a bucket of garbage which she empties over the lee side. A dorsal fin cuts through the blue water, and a huge shark surfaces in the wake. We catch a glimpse of rows of white triangular teeth. "Heavens!" says Beulah. "I'm glad it wasn't around when I fell overboard!"

I glance about for Richard, and he is not there. I instantly become certain that he has fallen overboard and been eaten by the shark. I consider leaping overboard and fighting the shark. Richard's head, smiling amiably, comes out of the companionway. I remember now that he had said he was going below for a moment. He hands me a cup of tea. All is well, and I spin the wheel a trifle.

Beulah says to us, "Lewis and I have come up with an idea. Pauline and Jean—on *Windrush!* Remember, they couldn't come originally because of guests? We think the guests may be gone by now."

"What a good idea!" I say. "Oh, I do hope they can come!"

"Sail ho!" cries Molly, who is lounging forward with a physics book. "Or steamship ho! Anyroad, a great ship is over yon."

The Captain comes on deck, and I point out the ship. "Steady as she goes!" he says. "Sail has the right of way over steam. See, they're altering course to clear. She's coming out of Marseilles. Mary—bring her to port a bit. See that spire? Steer for that. It's in line with the channel."

I bring her up a bit, and Richard sheets in a trifle. Richard tells the Captain about the possibility of adding the Verrières to the ship's company, and he is pleased. Fifteen minutes later I see a red buoy ahead and to starboard, and I say, "We're entering the channel, Captain."

"Steady as she goes," he says.

An hour and a quarter later we are tied up in Marseilles, and Lewis and I run down the pier to telephone Avignon. Pauline answers and Lewis hands the phone to me.

"Pauline!" I say. "This is Mary. Mary Vallance. We're in Marseilles."

"Oh, Mary!" she says. "I am so glad to hear you! And you are on the cruise, *n'est-ce-pas?*"

"Yes," I say. "And Pauline. We want to come to La Verrière Bleue tonight. Lewis and Beulah—Lewis is right here with me and says Hullo—they left their car in Marseilles when they flew to London. We can come in that and drive back in the night. Can you book tables for all of us? Ten of us?"

"Yes, yes!" she says. "But you must come here first, yes? And you must sleep here, if you wish. There is much room, our friends are gone —two days ago."

"Oh, good!" I say. "I was just going to ask about them. Because—well, two people have left the cruise—and we hoped that you and Jean could maybe drop everything and join us. The Greek isles, you know. Could you? Possibly?"

"Oh!" she says. There is a little pause, and then she says, "That might be, Mary. And you go to Greece! I should like that very much, but I shall have to talk with Jean. You come here, no? We shall talk, and then decide."

"Decide to come!" I say. "Please do! Well—we shall be there soon, I expect. Goodbye, Pauline. *Au revoir.*"

The Captain has arranged with the dock police for a watch to be kept on the schooner, for no one, naturally, wants to be left behind—and now he tells them that it may be all night.

Everybody is excited and pleased at the prospect of a break in the sea routine, and we bound about, breaking out dresses and shore clothes. I put on the Bluebell Frock—bought in Avignon in April—what a time ago!—and the pearls Richard gave me for my birthday. It seems extremely odd to be in skirts again—odd but nice. My legs feel freer.

And the others in their shore things look strange—strange but, again, nice.

Arriving at the street, we find Lewis waiting, for he had dressed swiftly and gone to the garage for the big convertible. Roomy as it is, ten of us require some wedging—four in front, including Lewis who is driving, then Beulah, then me, then the skipper, sitting more or less on a slant. And there are six behind, with Molly perched on Roger's knee. We drive out on the road to Avignon, some eighty miles away.

I remember that the Captain can be called Denis on shore, so I say, "Denis, you aren't the skipper in a tweed jacket and tie, are you?"

He smiles. "I'm jolly glad not to be for a bit," he says. "Anyhow, you aren't the model of a third mate, are you? Is this lovely lady in a pretty frock the same salty creature who was crawling about in the bilges with a spanner between her teeth?"

"Well, no!" I say, laughing. "Still, maybe it is good that we are getting to know the other side of each other."

"Yes," he says. "Fills in the image."

"All the same, Denis," I say, "there really *is* more of a difference with you than there is with me. Aboard, you are always the Captain— even asleep!"

"True," he says. "It's what's meant by the loneliness of command. Knowing that one is responsible, don't you know. No one to turn to. But inside, human—fallible."

There is a pause, and I hear the people in back talking about the silvery colour of the olive groves. Then the skipper—Denis—asks Beulah what she plans in marine painting. She says she's finished one—looking forward with the lee rail almost under. Lewis comments that he'd like to get out in the dinghy and photograph *Windrush* sweeping by. The skipper agrees to arrange it and expresses a hope to see Beulah's painting soon.

Avignon, with a swing past the Palais des Papes, and then the river house, with Pauline and Jean running to meet us. We all file up to the verandah where the luncheon party was, and Pauline offers us a choice of Dubonnet or sherry or pernod. I shudder at this last and speak for sherry. She tells me that we shall have our old room back.

Denis comes up, and I say, "Pauline, Denis is the Captain. Have you all decided?"

"We all hope you will," says the Captain with a warm smile, liking her.

"It is an attractive prospect," she says. "But have you thought that my Jean—he does not have much English? He might not understand the order to turn the star board." I giggle and Denis smiles. "Oh," she says, "Have I said it wrong? It was in a book."

Denis explains and then says, "Jean's English will be no problem, Pauline. Shelley, my wife and first mate—oh, she and Jean are talking now—she knows French well. Anyhow, Jean will soon pick it up—like Conrad, you know."

"Très bien!" says Pauline. "Then we come. Jean! Jean!"

Jean comes up smiling with Shelley, and Pauline speaks rapidly in French. He smiles more broadly and says triumphantly, "Eet is good! We are 'appy!"

Pauline laughs. "He works much on the English. With ten Anglo-Saxons, he will learn very fast. We go tomorrow? We thought much after Mary spoke, and we can do it."

"Jolly good!" says Denis. "Tomorrow it is, then."

"And tonight," Pauline says, "La Verrière Bleue. You will all be the guests."

Some hours later as two cars draw up on the Rue Jeanne d'Arc, I murmur to Richard to watch their faces when they see the ceiling. There is, in fact, a collective gasp from the six who have never been there, followed by a subdued "Och!" from Molly. Peter Shirley's blue eyes are wide with appreciation, and Denis first looks, marvelling, at the ceiling, then tenderly at Shelley's rapt face.

Then we are parted as the six couples go to their six small tables. Peter and Betsy are, of necessity, a couple. They do not object. They look up at the ceiling and down at the menu, talking animatedly the while. A gypsy-looking girl at the end of the room is playing the violin softly. The scene—the gypsy, the quiet couples at the small lamp-lit tables —is charming, but it is the luminous marvel of the ceiling that, like a full moon or a flaming sunset sky, compels a constant half-awareness.

Richard and I, after we have ordered, contrast this civilized scene with the night of the storm at sea, and then with the high slopes of Cader Idris in Wales far above the Barmouth Estuary. Not very originally, we compare our life to a tapestry.

"We're weaving ours with happy colours, aren't we?" says Richard.

"Yes—now," I say. "But . . . before wings . . . the Disaster, all sullen crimson and black. And then what? Grey? Grey for hopelessness— wanhope?"

"Well, but hope did come, didn't it?" he says softly. "Don't think about it."

"I have to, Val," I say. "It's part of the whole. I wish I could make you see it, too—what it was like with Mummy dead and growing up so twisted, knowing I'd never walk or play or even hold my head up right. Still, I was sort of happy: my books, you know, and sometimes Daddy's friends' children. But then Mercia dead, too, dead on the black rocks. Daddy did all he could, but I often wanted to be dead, also . . ."

"I know, darling," says Richard gently. "I do know, a little. Almost from the first time I saw you, when Uncle John came to see your father and brought me. You were only—what? fifteen? And I was so amazed at the books everywhere in your room—the *Odyssey* in Greek, I remember, and all the other poetry, Vaughan and Shelley and the *Faerie Queen.* And that strange book by Charles Williams that you lent me—which one was it, *The Place of the Lion?* And all the C. S. Lewis books. Even that day, you know, I could see what your life must be: all the books and you so twisted, but so—so bright-faced, too. I tell you, Mary, I couldn't get you out of my mind all year. —Ah, here's our dinner."

As dinner is served and we begin to eat in silence, my mind continues to dwell on that day of the advent of Richard into my small world. He had been on his way back to Holywell from Redrock, his home on the Eastern Shore. It was September, the beginning of his third year at the college. He was twenty then, much older than me. He had come to D.C. to spend a night with his Uncle John and Aunt Grace, who live in Falls Church, so he went up to his uncle's Washington office in order to ride home with him. And his uncle on the way home had stopped at our house in Georgetown to see my father. It was some legal matter that Daddy was handling for Uncle John's company. So, while they talked in the study, Richard had been brought in to me. That was the way we met. And of course what he felt was mainly pity, apart from amazement at all the books—over a thousand of them.

I didn't see him again until June—I was sixteen by then—when he came to Falls Church for a whole fortnight. He decided on his own to come to see me again. Actually, he came several times, especially towards the end of the fortnight. I think he had resolved, generously, to brighten my life—or maybe Daddy whispered to him that he was doing it— although Richard maintains that he was merely getting more and more interested in me as a person. Or half a person. I still think I was, mainly, a Good Work. Richard is generous. That was one of the things Daddy liked about him, for Daddy believes that the essential mark of a genuine gentleman is a sort of careless generosity, which Richard has, like Peter. Also, Daddy came to trust Richard's calm good sense. Once during that time Richard took me for a drive out into the country, lifting me into the car while Jolly fluttered around. Jolly is my old nanny and nurse, now Daddy's housekeeper. It was a lovely drive, and Richard and I talked a lot about everything.

And then he came back in September—Uncle John and Aunt Grace must have thought they were getting more charming—but this time he was definitely there because of me. There were more drives, and we got to be closer and closer in understanding. For me, of course, he—well, he was the main person in my life, except for Daddy.

That's the way things were when he went on back to Holywell for his last year. And almost immediately that short-lived passion for Rozica grabbed hold of him. Richard maintains that it was *because* he was already beginning to fall in love with *me,* which is hard for me to believe. But there is some connection, for even at the time he kept contrasting my dearness to him with this purely physical thing he was feeling for Rozica: and that was why, he says, that he kept on not doing anything about her. And then, when that desire for her faded as suddenly as it had begun, he wanted to see me. So he came down for a long lovely weekend in October, not to Falls Church but to our house, as Daddy had many times urged him to do. There were more drives amidst the beautiful autumnal colours; and it was on one of those drives, when we were going quite slowly along a country road, that something happened.

"Mary," he said, and paused an instant. "Mary, do you know that you are one of the dearest people in the world to me—perhaps *the* dearest? The one that means the most." I must have gasped or something, because he said, "You are!" as though I had denied it. "I'm not just saying it," he went on. "There's some sort of affinity between us that I've never felt with any of the girls I've gone out with up at Holywell. Or at home, either."

I didn't know what to say. I couldn't say that he was my dearest friend when I didn't have any others for him to be dearer than. Besides, I wasn't sure that I could trust my voice.

Finally I said in a slightly shaky voice, "I feel that, too. I think I would feel it even if I had a hundred other friends."

"Yes," he said. "I think we'd both have to feel it. I've thought a lot about the closeness I feel to you lately—whatever it is, affinity, friendship. It seems to me that when I was here in September a great flame of friendship flared between us. I don't know how else to describe it. The way we talked so eagerly about everything."

I think we were both saying, and honestly thinking, friendship— because anything else was so unthinkable with me being so crippled. And probably he was contrasting it with what he had felt for that Rozica, though I didn't know about her then.

"Mary," he went on, "you know how C. S. Lewis describes the three natural loves. And even affection, like love for your father, has a physical expression—hugs and kisses. Well, I think that—well, that friendship needs . . . well, a way of, er, expressing itself, like . . . well, you know, like holding hands, don't you?"

I think I gave another gasp, and, anyway, our hands found each other in an instant and squeezed, and then we just drove silently and blissfully on. I tried to think of him as the dear big brother I had never had. And our hands didn't let go, except for necessary moments, all that day. And other days, too. And it was now, during this long weekend—he cut about three days of classes—that we began to talk gaily, with joy and agony, of all the things we *would* do, if only I were somehow healed. This was the time when we invented the name "wings" for such a healing, however it came about. I say "however it came about" because, although there were no realistic grounds for hope at all—Daddy had taken me to all the doctors in the world in past years—Richard and I came to believe that somehow maybe God would act. Maybe Richard's love and prayers would be the key. God, perhaps, had just been waiting for him to come along and be my brother and friend, and for the flame of dearness and longing for wings that had sprung up between us. We did long for it so much. Of course I always had longed for healing, but it was so wonderful to have someone else longing with me. The longing seemed to me to double and redouble, soaring up like fire. Wings . . . just to be winged together . . . running along a beach together, sitting on a cliff together after climbing, and, above all, striding about beneath the dreaming spires of Oxford that Daddy had told such fascinating tales of. No vision of heaven could contain such bliss as our images of being winged together. Or, at least, it was utter bliss to me, and Richard says it was to him, too.

But the strangest thing was that, somehow, I, at least, continued to believe that the flame between Richard and me was—could only be—that of a magical brother-and-sister affection plus the affinity of friendship. I had read C. S. Lewis's *The Four Loves,* but I didn't think that what existed between Richard and me was inloveness—how could it be with me so crippled?—but all the other three loves.

Still, three loves are a lot, and it was almost inevitable that Richard should come down again in November. Daddy, of course, was just delighted by this whole thing of my new interest in life, and I expect he would have liked to give Richard half his kingdom. And I no longer felt like a Good Work. Most wonderful of all, it was agreed that Richard would come during part of the Christmas holidays. He would have to go

to Redrock for Christmas itself, but then he would come to our house—
and Holywell had a new thing where the students didn't have to be back
until midnight on the fifteenth of January. And who knew? perhaps God
would choose that time to use Richard as His instrument to heal me—to
make me winged.

So Richard arrived, beaming, at the very end of December, and we
and Daddy gaily lifted glasses of a delicious '57 Alsatian wine to drink in
the year 1961, destined to be the most momentous year of my whole
life. And Richard's.

The first days of the year went by like a happy dream. We were alone
together all day long, since Daddy was at his office, and sometimes in the
evening as well. We read poems together and ate delicious lunches that
Jolly made for us—she would have given Richard half her kingdom, too
—and we laughed and, above all, we talked, talked of our darling
subject, being winged together. It was such a hopeless dream, but so
much fun to dream it together. And, somehow, we would feel genuinely
hopeful while we spun the dream—maybe just because we longed so for
it together. Still, perhaps, as we constantly prayed, perhaps God *would*
work a miracle—carefully disguised of course.

The other thing we did was to go for drives in Daddy's car, which he
seldom used. The particular drive—the drive to Winebottle Mountain,
which is what we named it—came just two days before Richard was to
go back to college. We were having a 'January thaw' and the
temperature was in the seventies, as warm as a day in May, almost; and
Daddy was not going to be home until late. So we took a lunch and told
Jolly not to expect us till we came, because we shouldn't even start
homewards until dark and who knew where we should be by then. After
Richard had lifted me easily into the car and was stowing the lunch that
Jolly had handed him, she said to wait and went running into the house
and out again with a red rose, its stem carefully wrapped to keep it
moist, that had been amongst the flowers from the florist's that morning.
She leaned in and kissed my cheek, and we started gaily off.

It took us longer to get into the mountains than we had expected. We
had to drive far to the west to get near them and then find someone to
ask about the old back roads up into them. In the end an old farmer,
whose door Richard went up to, told him all he wanted to know. And
we didn't care about the delay: we were together and we were happy.
Our lunch, though, turned out to be more of an early dinner. Or tea.

We finally found just the place that the old farmer had told Richard
of. We went up the mountain on a dirt road and high up we came to a
little meadow, or clearing, with a trickling, splashing little spring coming

out of the rock face and running off down the mountain as a little stream. To the eastward, though, was the main beauty—two mountains sweeping up with a gap in between them that made one wish to go through it to see what lay beyond.

"See that gap?" said Richard. "That is the Gateway to Heaven. The old farmer said that everybody called it that when he was a boy, and it was called that in his grandfather's time, too. Nice name, isn't it? The Gateway to Heaven. Just right."

We did nothing but look at it for several minutes, sitting there in the car, which Richard had driven right into the little clearing, pointed at the Gateway. It was still warm enough to have the windows open, and, in fact, there was some quality in the mild breeze that made us think of April or May. But the trees all about were leafless, standing there in their bare grace, almost more beautiful than when they are leafy. Best of all, maybe, is very early spring with tiny leaves that don't hide the branches and twigs.

Richard got out the chicken sandwiches and the wine, and when he had poured our glasses full—it was another bottle of the Alsatian—he stuck the rose into the neck of the bottle. That's the way I remember that day always—the rose in the wine bottle. If our mountain had a name, the farmer hadn't mentioned it, so we named it Winebottle Mountain. Winebottle Mountain at the Gateway to Heaven.

As we ate our nice lunch and drank that lovely wine, a rabbit hopped slowly by, ignoring us or, perhaps, accepting us as large rabbits. After we had finished, Richard went over to the spring and fetched me a wineglassful of pure cold water.

And then I said, sort of lightly, trying to be funny, "Richard, what would you give for the wings?"

The sun shone in on the rose in the wine bottle, and Richard looked at me with his steady grey eyes, and time seemed to stop. Then I saw that there were tears in his eyes. And he whispered—he just whispered—"I'd give me!"

And then there were tears in my eyes, too, and rolling down my cheeks. We just sat there, then, not saying anything, looking through the Gateway to Heaven.

After awhile Richard got out and set the wine bottle and the rose on a small ledge above the spring, and got back into the car and backed it out onto the road. We drove on, upwards, between the trees, still not saying much, and it got dark. Richard said he thought we had better turn around, especially since we didn't know where the road went to. Then, after we were driving back, we began to see a light through the trees, realising in a moment that it was the full moon rising, enormous, incredible, in the eastern skies. We got just one glimpse of it through an opening in the trees.

"Oh, Richard!" I said—I always called him Richard then. "Let's go back to the Gateway to Heaven. And our rose."

"Yes, yes, yes!" he said. "I want to be there, too."

So we went back, parking just where we had been before. There was the rose in the wine bottle, a dark rose now but edged with silver light. In front of us was the Gateway to Heaven with the moon rising just there, in the Gateway. The magnificent sweeping lines of the two mountains that made the Gateway were also silver-edged and brilliant with light. The whole night was luminous and somehow hushed, except for the tiny trickle of the spring. We turned and looked into each other's eyes, shining in the moonlight—and suddenly, without thought or volition, never knowing how it happened, our arms were round each other and our mouths together in a kiss of unutterable love. For days now, maybe for weeks, a great wave had been rising above us, cresting over our heads, beautiful, urgent, unbearable in its power. Now it broke and thundered down upon us.

I don't know how long we stayed there at the Gateway to Heaven, kissing so wildly, loving each other with bursting hearts. I know we looked out once to see a great soft-winged owl drift by over our heads. And I know that the silver brilliant moon rose higher and higher over the Gateway to Heaven.

And once Richard whispered, "This is the peak of my whole life." Great tides of inloveness, of engulfing sweetness, swept between us, and we were content for ever in a kiss. It seemed impossible that any other two human beings could ever have loved each other as much as we did.

At last we forced ourselves to drive away, and we came down the mountain and home, totally in love.

"On the mountain," said Richard next morning, "you looked so girlish and sweet, I was almost overcome by it. I became almost convinced that you were winged and just didn't know it . . . and could run and dance." Sadly, it was not so; and yet the feeling that wings *must* come, now, after those life-giving kisses, was more intense than before. At the same time, I kept saying secretly to myself, "At least, I've had this —more than I ever dreamed of—and nothing can take it away." The truth was, in that dark midwinter, springtime caught me up; and soft as the owl's wings, like a drift of stars, came the kiss of urgent life.

There were more life-giving kisses, too. Most of those last two days before he went back, we kissed. Just kissed. Our lips were bruised with kissing. Not even talking much. And then he was gone.

That was the way it began. Of course that night wouldn't have been so overwhelming if the inloveness in us hadn't been all but impossible— unthinkable—to admit even to ourselves. So we talked of friendship and holding hands while the enormous wave crested and curled above us. Still, I often think what people who kiss and pet casually—or who spring casually in bed together—cut themselves out of: that overwhelming power of inloveness.

Anyway, Richard went back to Holywell, back to all those winged girls running around; and darkness crept in upon me again. I couldn't believe it. I don't mean I couldn't believe in our love. I did believe it, I clung to it. But not in our hope. It was too impossible—the twisted spine, the useless legs. Richard must know, too, how hopeless it all was; and, sooner or later, he would go away altogether and leave me to my books. And he *should* go away. I couldn't ask him to stay.

His first letter had been full of joy in "our magic love," and he said he was stunned by the beauty of that day at the Gateway to Heaven. But he was not able for a variety of reasons to come down either in later January or in all of February; and it seemed to me that his letters, full of his doings at the college, became somewhat impersonal. Once he said that we had been living "in a dream world of wings that January," but, he added, "we do have to live with things as they are." It was true, but it was chilling, too—the chill of the cold steel of truth. Then he wrote that he was having "a period of analysis and evaluation of everything." I knew then that he was going to go away. What else could he do? After that letter, for about a fortnight, there were no letters at all. I couldn't become absorbed in my books as I had used to do. The slow days crept past.

Then in early March Jolly brought me a tea tray and on it, also, was a letter from Richard. I had decided for some reason to be wheeled into the drawing-room that morning, and Jolly had lit the fire. Now she fussed about, mending the fire and pouring out my tea and adding milk, while the letter lay there, looking more fatal with every passing minute. I could scarcely stand it until Jolly was gone, and yet, in another way, I wanted her to delay. But she went away.

The first words of the letter, dated "March 4th, 1961, my 22nd birthday!" were: "Thank God, things are clear in my mind at last. I am able to see everything in perspective again." He went on to say that our parting in January and his return to the realities of college life and studies—including the remembrance of his brief passion for Rozica—had been unsettling to the point of making him uncertain of what was real and what wasn't. He said he had been thinking hard about what sort of a life we could have together unwinged; and he had faced the fact that such a life would mean for him "giving up such things as adventure and excitement and change." For four and a half pages, he showed me in detail, very realistically, what that life would be for him—"full of denials that make me weak with pain to think of." He was telling me all this, he said, so that I might know that he was "seeing things as they really are." By now I certainly did not doubt it. And he added that he was out of the dream world now and concerned only with reality.

Then in the middle of page five, after a space, he wrote:

> Mary, dearest, I cannot delay telling you any longer. I do *choose* our life together, wings or no wings. I have no illusions about it. It won't be easy. But the things we can have—love and friendship (I value our real friendship as deeply as our love), beauty, shared joy and pain—this is what I want. I love you and I am in love with you. To spend my days doing things to make you a little winged through my love—this, darling, is my dream and my *intention.* I have faced what it means. The battle is already won, my love. I hear the mighty triumph of our Brahms—our triumph! Love does conquer all. You are so dear to me, Mary. More dear than I can tell you. I am more deeply committed to our love than I've ever been to anything. And so, my darling, my Mary, we will go on together, hand in hand.
>
> With *all* my love, Richard.

P.S. I'll post this now so I'll know you have my word.

Only when there was the tiny, sharp splat of a tear falling on the paper did I know that I was crying—crying with a singing heart. I looked up at the picture of Mummy above the mantelpiece, and it seemed to me that her little smile was for me. Maybe she gave me a wink; I couldn't be sure. I had a sip of stone-cold tea. A thought went through my mind: could I *let* Richard commit himself to a thing like me? Then, instantly, I knew it was an unworthy thought. He *had* committed himself. He had made his own choice before God, the decision of a strong, brave, independent man. Since there was no faintest doubt of my deep and total love for him, I could only accept and trust. And thank our Christ for His love in us.

Late in March Richard came down for his spring vacation. It was a time of such happiness, such depth of love and beauty, that no words can capture it. I told him, again, face to face, that I accepted his commitment, and that I, in turn, committed my life to him, and that I knew it would be for ever. We both knew that this was, almost, our wedding—the exchange of vows. Once Richard said, "Something in me is fulfilled. It's like being freed." It was a strange remark when he had just bound himself to me, a crippled girl, but I understood, I thought, just what he meant. Another time he said, "I gladly devote my life to this beautiful thing between us, winged or unwinged. Next to God, it is the most important thing for me." And at the very end of the vacation he said, "Mary, when I kissed you goodbye then, it seemed to me that I suddenly understood why marriage is one of the sacraments. I was awed." He reached down and touched my hair and was gone.

We both knew deeply in that vacation what marriage was: the depth of intention in vows, and then, later, the consummation. We meant our vows as deeply as was in us to mean them. And that's why, despite Richard's quixotic withdrawal after wings, there was never any chance, really, of my accepting Peter Shirley's proposal in the punt, dear as he was, and going off to Yorkshire to be the future Lady Shirley; for I was married to Richard for ever in my heart and soul.

On Wednesday, three days after Richard had gone back to Holywell, almost at the end of March, Daddy said abruptly at breakfast, "Mary, there's a doctor that I want you to see. Don't get your hopes up. He doesn't think there's anything that can be done, but he wants to see for himself. I want to take you over to him at the hospital this afternoon. Will you?"

I said, yes, of course; and I didn't get my hopes up, except maybe a little. There had been so many doctors. Daddy didn't mention that this one was quite the greatest spinal surgeon in the world. And so I went, and there was an afternoon of testing and probing and giving me a spinal injection for x-rays, and later the rather horrid sucking-out again of the injection. At last Daddy, patiently waiting, took me home. That night, writing to Richard, I didn't say a word about it.

A few days later Daddy said, even more abruptly. "He wants to operate, Mary, maybe several operations if the first one is promising. He says there is no more than one chance in ten—but there is that. Do you want to go through with it?"

Of course I said yes; but I had had other operations, too, though long ago. So I didn't hope much, except, again, maybe a little.

But now I had to tell Richard, for I should be going into hospital in three or four days, and I should be there all the rest of April, including my seventeenth birthday on the twenty-fourth, and on into May, unless the surgeon—as was very probable—threw up his hands after one look inside. So that night I telephoned Richard, and we talked for more than an hour. I told him exactly how little chance there was for a real healing, warning him not to allow himself to hope. I was warning myself, too. He said he wouldn't hope too much, but there was hope in his voice, though he tried to conceal it. Perhaps I sounded as though I had a little concealed hope to him. He said he would come down right away; but I said no. "Please, darling, don't come—not until they have done the first operation."

On the day I went in hospital a letter came from him. I read it there in hospital, knowing that the first—and maybe the last—operation would be in the morning. Richard said that he knew how little chance there was and that he was being terribly realistic. But he said that I was to read again his Pledge, as we had come to call his commitment letter, and I was to remember that he meant every word of it, whatever was to happen in the operation. So I stopped reading the new letter and read the Pledge, which I had of course brought with me, and I whispered his final words: "And so . . . we will go on together, hand in hand." Then I went back to the new letter, which ended: "Winged or not, dearest, you are my joy, my delight, my world. To hold you in my arms is all I wish."

My heart was ready for the morrow.

Sitting here, winged, in La Verrière Bleue, under this blue heaven of the ceiling with Richard sitting across the table from me and friends all about, and the great schooner waiting, I allow these memories to slip through my mind, like sand between my fingers, each memory totally apprehended in the instant of its slipping by. Richard, too, is looking thoughtful. I glance about the small tables where the *Windrush* adventurers are, like us, finishing their dinners.

"Pray, why so silent, pretty maid, oh why?" says Richard.

"No silenter than you, my lord," I remark justly. "I have been remembering the days of our lives. Before wings . . . when we went to the Gateway to Heaven."

"Have you?" he says. "So have I. Thinking what your life must have been. I may have got inside it more than you know. After all, 'Wind Song' tells it all, doesn't it?"

"Yes," I say. "I wrote it not long after you came with Uncle John. You made the longing sort of peak. Even when you came back, and it was so wonderful, it hurt, too. You would stride across the room, looking like—like Apollo, and it would hurt so much because I couldn't . . . couldn't be an ordinary girl walking across a room. And then, when we began to talk about wings, I'd sort of believe, when we were together—believe that somehow maybe you could call to me, call to my girlhood . . . that's the way I always thought of it, because, you see, I wasn't really a *girl* because girls could walk across rooms and, er, jump. But when you weren't there, I thought I would never run through the grass to you; I would just have to stay a lump, and you would get tired of not having anyone to run with and just drift away . . ."

"But I didn't," he says, putting his hand on mine. "Did I, sweetheart?"

"No," I say sombrely. "But maybe you would have if I hadn't got well."

"Mary!" he says, astonished. "Don't you remember my letter—before we ever heard of that surgeon—my *pledge*, wings or no wings? Didn't you believe me?"

"Oh, Val!" I cry. "Of *course* I did! I don't know why I said that. I believed it completely! You were truth itself to me. Remember when I called you Richard of the Stars that time—my true knight! Even before the letter I believed—do you know when?"

He shakes his head. "When we kissed in the moonrise at the Gateway to Heaven?"

"Before that!" I say. "That afternoon. When the rose was in the winebottle and you said in that funny whisper, 'I'd give me!' I knew it was for ever. Daddy said once, 'Richard is a gentleman; you can trust him.' He didn't mean just truthfulness but that generosity—like saying you'd give you. Oh, Val! I don't know why I said that. It was an evil, untrue thing to say. Like a serpent. I'm *so* sorry!"

Richard looks at me tenderly, his hand squeezing mine. Then he looks slightly startled, for it appears to him—he tells me later—that my eyes are becoming larger and perhaps bluer. Then he realises that they are full of tears. One spills over.

"Remember, Mary," he says, "I loved you—and love gives us the power to know."

"Yes," I say. "You chained yourself with my chains, didn't you? Plighted your troth—your truth. I'm sorry I said that, Val. It's the worst thing I ever said."

"Here, dry your eyes!" he says smiling. "I know you didn't mean it. Listen. This is our life. Maybe there are parallel worlds, as you're so fond of supposing, where there never was a Disaster and you're a ballerina. Or one where Uncle John broke his leg that morning and we never met. But in this world we walk together. —And in this one . . . do you know what I think is about to happen?"

I shake my head, and he says solemnly, "I predict you are about to have—a period."

"Oh, heavens!" I say. "I am—I thought about it yesterday. No wonder I'm wallowing about in sorrows. But, Val, if I have a period in this world, wouldn't all the me's on all the parallel worlds be having their—my—our periods, too?"

"Not at all," he says with a grin. "You might be pregnant on some world."

"Lumme!" I say. "I'm glad I'm not on that world now—it would spoil the cruise. Except—well, I *am* on that world if it's another me! Good lord! who knows what I'm going through? Poor dear!"

"And I pacing nervously waiting," says Richard. "That is, if I'm your husband."

"Of course you're my husband!" I say. "Do you think I'm going to have a baby by a *stranger?* But maybe on that world you are cold-hearted and—"

"Certainly not!" says Richard. "I'm a good chap on all the worlds, if they exist, which I doubt. —Eat your sweet; it's good. —I want to ask you something. Haven't the wings and love made up for the Dark Ages? And aren't they *related?* I mean, without the pain for both of us, could we have had such joy? Not just happiness, joy? There has to be darkness to have the glory of dawn."

"And spring after winter," I say. "Maybe waking after death—maybe death is the gateway to heaven. It must be. Tropical places may be lovely, but no spring—that glory! You're right, Val. You brought spring —you're a—a crocus! —Val, there's something I want to, er, tell you . . ." I pause.

"What?" he says.

"Well," I say. "It is . . . that I love you. Extremely."

"Nut!" he says fondly. "I find some traces in me of love for you, too."

We look at each other for a long moment, and we love each other in a bubble of silence under the luminous blue infinity. Then you say lightly, as though the gay words concealed the awful loveliness of love, "Come and dance . . . in my arms."

We dance, as others are doing. I have small impulses to sing loudly about the glory of all the loves, or, better, head thrown back, to utter a joyful howl that will say it all. I do not give way to it. Only wolves perhaps understand that sort of thing. It might be good to be a joyful wolf.

The two cars drive back to the river house under a large misshapen moon just rising, and then we are in our familiar room, only the flowers on the table are white ones now.

We do not even turn on the light. After trips to the bathroom, we complete our undressing in the flooding moonlight. There is without words a sort of shared gladness and joy between us. "Mary!" says Richard, his voice low in the hushed room. "Mary, you were born to be loved." In his beauty he is like a figure on a Greek vase. I marvel as he walks to me across moonlight and eternity. All the emotions—joy and love and pain—that I have felt tonight seem to explode in me. I am bursting into a million stars, contained as Mary only by Richard's fierce embrace.

Mary continues the log of the voyage to Hellas

I wake happy. Slipping out of the encircling arms, I have a bath, then wake my Richard with kisses.

"Oh, Mary!" he says when he can. "Last night . . . " We kiss again, and he leaps up.

After breakfast, two cars roll towards Marseilles. A friend will drive Jean's back.

A few hours later *Windrush* stands out to sea, heeling in a fresh-to-strong breeze, Peter and I giving a small but spirited rendition of "Rule, Britannia" in the bows.

The skipper establishes new watches with Peter and Betsy on his, and Roger and Molly onto ours, which we now proclaim to be the Oxford Watch.

The breeze moderates in the evening. Shortly after dark, long before moonrise, cries from the watch bring everybody topside to see a strange and beautiful sight. Across the black waves *Windrush* is tracing a lane of luminous white—phosphorescence. Then Shelley cries, "Oh, look, everybody!" There beside the yacht are two torpedo shapes bathed in fire that circle and play. They are dolphins, friends of sailors, and they frisk about us for an hour, perfectly matching their speed to ours, perhaps somehow aware of the delighted eyes looking down.

Days pass, turn into weeks. We lose track of days, for it is the rhythm of the watches and ship's bells that shapes our lives. Once again, after spending several off-watch hours writing about France, mainly the night in Avignon, I neglected this logbook. And Richard, the lunk, whatever a lunk is, neglects it even more. He'll be glad someday that I wrote all these pages. But, actually, there hasn't been very much to write about during the long beat southward towards the toe of Italy, though we did stop one night in Naples for supplies. Then we pushed on, passing one afternoon those legendary monsters, Scylla and Charybdis. Since they are female monsters, I, who was at the helm at the moment, gave them a sisterly wave in hopes that they would entertain friendly feelings towards us. Of course all too often it doesn't work that way and sisterhood leads to bared stilettos.

One night Jean played his violin for those of us who were in the saloon, which was in a few minutes everybody who was off watch, with the watch themselves bending an ear from the cockpit. Others, then, were inspired to do something entertaining. Roger, for instance, had us howling with his inspired imitations of the famous, including a certain forgetful Oxford don and a magnificent growly Churchill. Then Molly did a Highland ballad for us, a typical line of which sounded like: "O ca' the daunton keckle blude, the pawkie mickle gawks." I may not, of course, have it just right. And Shelley sang for us in a remarkably pure soprano. I myself was inspired to write a play that was described by knowledgeable members of our company as quite possibly the greatest play for its length ever written. I put it on with Richard and Roger, and it had a run of two performances, the second performance being for those on watch on the first night. The props and scenery consisted of one large red bathrobe button, which was placed on the saloon floor just ahead of the three closely grouped actors who sat on the floor. The playgoers were informed that we were the Captain, Lieutenant, and Navigator of a rocket approaching the moon. This, then, is the drama, exactly as performed to great applause.

CAPT VAL [looking fixedly at watch]:   All right, Lieutenant, stand by . . . to fire the retro-rockets! Stand by! FIRE!

LIEUT DENBY [finger moving towards red button]:   Aye, aye!
NAV MARY [frantically]:   Not that button, you fool!
ALL [as finger hits red button]:   B-O-O-O-M-M-M!
                     [curtain]

A little later I wrote a verse, though whether it should be preserved
(if at all) in medical or literary annals is not certain. It came to be
written because, on three separate occasions, the nipples of one or more
of my breasts—up to two, that is—had itched: and each time, within an
hour, the schooner had run into a squall or a shower. I began to see
myself as a living barometer and so wrote this meteorological poem,
which I read to the company.

TITCH

> When nipples itch
> And judging from whitch
> It's rain she preditch,
> Then either the witch
> Is just a bitch
> And a hypocritch;
> Or if rain and sitch
> On the decks do pitch,
> Why, then, she's ritch
> With the benefitch
> Of her bitchy itch—
> Witch
>   Titch
> Whitch
>   Preditch!

I shall not speak of its reception, though it is possible that Jean's giant
strides in English were momentarily checked. And Pauline looked at me
as though "Titch" were not quite what she expected from the writer of
"Wind Song."

There were other events of course, and perhaps I should pass on to
them. Once Roger developed violent internal pains and collapsed; and
Molly, who had had a little spat with him that morning, was convinced
that he was going to die, and wept abandonedly in the saloon. But
Shelley, who had had some medical training, doctored him out of the
ship's medical chest; and Roger was restored to his wild Highland lassie.
Another time, while Richard was sleeping and I was comfortably reading
a science-fiction book out of my secret hoard, Beulah came into the

saloon and announced that we were not getting enough exercise. So to be companionable I joined her on the floor of the saloon where we kicked and bent. For a short while a craze for exercise swept the ship. Once when we passed a Sicilian fishing boat as we were emerging from the Strait of Messina, half the crew of *Windrush* were doing exercises on deck—mostly the feminine half. The five fishermen stood along their rail in shocked amazement as the big schooner swept by.

There came at last the moment, after we had sailed northeastward across the Ionian Sea, when—like the wandering heroes of the *Odyssey*— we made a landfall on Ithaca. Hellas was at hand, the Gulf of Corinth before us.

But, still, I did not maintain the journal. Nothing about the grandeur of the shores of the Gulf, and nothing about the trip to haunted Delphi, where Apollo, Lord of Light, still dwells high on mighty Parnassus. Then there was the Corinthian ship canal. And at last the Piraeus and Athens, violet-crowned.

There were long hours on the Acropolis and in the Agora. One reason that I did not write of it in detail is that any guide book, not to mention the accounts of master writers, will bring it all back. Also, Beulah has done two superb paintings besides the one of *Windrush*, practically lee rail under, as seen from the cockpit. One of them is the schooner at anchor, done from the dinghy, showing the coast of the Gulf and Parnassus in the background, and the other is just the sea and clouds. Betsy, too, has painted—a small, dark painting that is scarcely more than a suggestion of Delphi at night, but a haunting picture all the same. Not much has happened in the way of personal adventures, though I actually did find an Athenian coin with a little owl on it where they were doing some excavating: I spotted it and knelt quickly to tie my shoe and walked on with Athens under my toes. Richard thought I ought to turn it in, but I wouldn't: the museums are choked with such coins. Once Betsy and I went into Athens alone and just wandered slowly about, repelling the attentions of Athenian hoplites from time to time. Eventually we decided to go into a taverna near the Agora. There, after a preliminary struggle to establish the point that we were going to sit by ourselves and buy our own drinks, we were allowed to do so. But one of the aspiring hoplites muttered in English, "Aha! You like Athens but you do not like Athenians, no?" Quite unable to decide whether the answer to this query should be yes or no, I merely said politely, "It depends. Go away." Thereupon he retired, and we were left alone to drink our wine and observe the Athenians at play.

Another time Richard and I were on the Acropolis at nightfall, sitting on the stylobate of the Parthenon, looking towards the Aegean, a half-moon riding in the sky. We were talking peacefully of the ancient Hellenes. I quoted some lines of Sappho's in connection with their feeling for nature: the lines about the murmur of cool streams being heard amongst apple branches while deep sleep comes down. Richard put his arm around me. Suddenly there was a blinding flash of light. "The Bomb!" I cried, picturing Richard holding out his arms to me as our bones melted. We didn't melt, though. It was merely the floodlights coming on. But we decided that it was time to arise and go.

And this is all I shall write of the weeks since we left Marseilles. The yacht is still moored in the Piraeus, but she is ready for sea. Tomorrow we sail for the Isles.

Both Richard and Mary write of the Battle of the Cyclades. Mary begins

Two days later in the early afternoon, *Windrush* is ghosting over mirror-calm waters in a little cove with wooded hills all around and a waterfall within a few yards of the beach. The island is one of the Cyclades. Its town is on the other side of the island, and here there is no sign of habitation. The schooner eases slowly up into the breath of wind, and the anchor splashes down. Sails are dropped and secured, and both the dinghy and the raft that live between the deckhouses are put over the side. We shall spend the night at this tranquil anchorage, and we are planning a beach party.

The dinghy goes to and fro, towing the raft, carrying people and supplies ashore. From the after deck I call to you in the dinghy to ask where your bathing shorts are. My voice crying "Val-l-l! V-a-l-l-l!" rebounds in echoes from the surrounding hills, and I think that perhaps some god hears—perhaps Artemis with her bow. I find it very easy to believe that the gods are all about. I almost expected yesterday to see Poseidon with his trident emerge dripping from his sea, the Aegean; and now I think not only of the terrible huntress but of great Zeus, stern and majestic. I recall reading somewhere that the peasants of the islands are supposed to be deeply superstitious, and I wonder whether any memory of the old gods remains. Is the Christian God blended in their imagination with black-bearded Zeus? Do they have any recollection of Athene with her calm eyes beneath her helmet? Does Pan, god of the wild, the great god Pan, still play his pipes among these hills?

I shake off these speculations for the moment, seeing the dinghy returning. I find the bathing trunks and my own suit, and I put on a long-sleeved pink shirt in case it is chilly round the fire after nightfall. Then I go ashore.

Everybody swims in the cove, except Roger who has a headache and thinks he may be catching cold. Then we wash off the salt water under the tiny waterfall, and there are shrieks at its coldness from the less manly half of the company. I think that if there are any gods in the silent hills they must know by now that mortals have invaded the land.

When we are dressed again, Richard says, "Who's for a walk and a climb?" I say I am, but most of the others are for sunning and napping and say, not them.

Molly says, "Roger?"

"No," he says. "I'm not up to it. You go, Molly."

"Vurry weel," she says. "I'll gae alang, then. We'll no' be lang."

The three of us climb up through the trees, following the stream. After awhile we rest, no longer able to hear the sounds of the beach party. Of course they may be all asleep. Richard and Molly sit on a log while I first flop down on the ground and then get up and wander about. I am still thinking of the gods and all the nature spirits of the haunted groves.

"Mary," says Richard, looking around. "Where are you?"

I peep out from behind a tree and announce in a solemn voice: "It is true my name is Mary. But I have been changed into a dryad by Zeus and must live from now on in a beech tree, if I can find one. So farewell, O mortals, farewell. You will never see me more."

"Never, O Dryad?" says Richard.

"Well, hardly ever," I say. "A glimpse now and then as I slip from tree to tree. If your hearts are pure, of course." I smile merrily and disappear behind my tree.

Richard and Molly get up and move on towards the tree, but, sure enough, I am not there. I am watching them, though, and as they look about, I put my head out of a bush and give a high birdlike cry. As soon as they have looked and seen me, I smile as I think a dryad might and withdraw my head and creep rapidly out the other side of the bush.

"Mary!" shouts Richard. "Stop running about or you'll fall into a hole. Come back, O Dryad!"

The dryad does not reply. She is looking about for another place to appear to mortal gaze.

"Silly girl!" says Richard, smiling. I, of course, do not hear this untrue remark, but, later, Richard and Molly contribute their comments.

Molly grins and says, "She'll soon weary, nae doot, o' her wee frolic."

Once again they hear a high cry, and a hundred yards ahead they see the tousled head and blue eyes in the fork of a tree.

"She really does look like a dryad or nymph of some sort," says Richard. "All we need are the pipes of Pan." He waves at the flushed merry face and it disappears.

I run swiftly ahead, feeling more dryadish every minute. I spot a hollow tree that I can get into on top of a low bluff. Perfect. I run fast off to the left where the slope is easier. I want plenty of time to get settled-in when I reach my dryad-tree. I am nearly there and nearly out of breath when, whirling around a tree, I run straight into a big, roughly dressed man. I have a quick impression of his hugeness and a black beard, and then his arms go round me like a vise.

I utter a short high scream and struggle wildly, flailing about with the one arm that is free. I claw his face and almost break away. I am too frantic and breathless to cry out again. He grabs my blouse, which tears but holds me, and then he hits me and I sag.

Richard writes

When Molly and I hear Mary's short breathless cry, Molly laughs. "She sounds wilder every time," she says. "Yon was an eldritch screech."

"No, Molly! No!" I say urgently. "There's something wrong! She was frightened! Come on! Quick!"

We run in the direction of the scream, I shouting, "Mary! Mary! Don't play! Where are you? Mary!" We stop for an instant to listen. There is no sound. We run on.

Molly cries, "It was about here, I think."

We stop again, looking everywhere. Again I shout, "Mary!" and we freeze and listen. Then I spy the hollow tree and say, "She'd have made for that, Molly. Come on! Round this way!"

Suddenly Molly cries, "Wait! Wait!" She pounces on something, and then holds out a pink cloth-covered button with a tiny streamer of cloth attached.

"It's hers, all right!" I say.

"Anither one!" says Molly, snatching another pink button from the ground.

"Molly!" I say. "They've just been ripped off. God help her!"

"Val! Look!" cries Molly. She points. I see the print of a large hobnailed boot. "Oh, the puir lassie!" she says under her breath.

"A man's got—" I begin, when, suddenly, a high terrified scream peals out farther up the mountain and is abruptly cut off.

Mary writes

Recovering from the man's blow, I find myself slung over his shoulder, my legs dangling behind and a hand over my mouth. I try to think what to do. I realize that one deck sneaker is off my heel, and I wiggle my foot till it falls off altogether. I hope Richard will find it and catch the man and hit him.

The man is walking rapidly along a path. I think hard. Then I seize his middle finger between my teeth and bite viciously. The hand is wrenched violently away as I expected. I scream as I've never screamed in my whole life. The hand comes back in a smashing blow on my mouth. I taste blood from torn lips, or maybe from his bitten finger. He shifts his grip. Both hands press my face into his shirt. I try to bite through, but I cannot. I feel myself suffocating. I remember no more for awhile.

Richard writes

"That's Mary!" I cry when we hear the scream. "Come on! This way! We can run faster than a guy carrying a girl. Quick!"

We race up the mountain. We come to a path, angling up the slope.

"Follow it!" I say, running along it. I spot something red and snatch it up. "Her sneaker!" I gasp. "Good girl! This is the way! Come on!"

"Let us go softly and warily, though," says Molly.

"Right!" I say. We run on.

Suddenly there is a man's shout ahead, answered by another man's voice. Molly and I dive off the path and creep forward through the underbrush until we come to the edge of a clearing. From the shelter of the bushes we see a rough stone-and-mud hut. In front of it are the men, peasant types, roughly dressed, one of them carrying an axe. The other is a huge man with a short, very black beard and small piglike eyes, who carries, slung over his shoulder, an apparently unconscious girl. There is blood on her face, her blouse is in tatters, and one foot is bare.

I growl and tense and am about to spring forward, when Molly puts her strong hand on my shoulder and breathes, "Val, wait! Wait!"

A third man with a rifle is entering the clearing, and the man with the axe shouts, "Ho! Basil!" The man carrying Mary is grinning and talking, gesticulating with his free hand, which has blood on it. The man with the axe gestures down the mountain and asks some question. The bull-like one laughs and shakes his head. The other also laughs and brandishes his axe. The newcomer, Basil, who has joined them, grins and half-raises his rifle. Then they all laugh uproariously and go into the hut.

"Molly!" I whisper. "That big man with Mary—he must know there are only two of us, unarmed, and one a girl, so he thinks they're safe. I'll stay here. You go! Bring the men! Bring everyone! And guns! Don't get lost, for God's sake! Run like hell!"

"Like the Marathon runner!" whispers Molly. "Be canny and still! Wait for us! I'm off!" She unfolds her long legs and goes, running like a Highland doe.

I wonder whether I dare leap in there, punching. But if I do and fail, I may bring about Mary's death as well as my own. Dusk is coming on, and, while I crouch there, a lamp is lit inside. I decide I must know what's going on in there and run silently up to one of the windows, round the corner from the door. I peer in and notice at once that a heavy wooden bar has locked the door. Mary is lying on the bed. Her eyes are open, but her hands are tied to her side and across her mouth is some sort of tape. There is a smear of blood on her cheek. Her eyes seem enormous, and I think she is crying.

Meanwhile, the men. Each of them has a bottle of ouzo in his hand, and they are sitting at a rough table. They drink and cough. I feel desperate. I'm afraid of the ship's party getting lost in the darkness that is coming on. I want to spring through the small window, but I know that I'd be bashed on the head before I could even get in—if I *could* get through that window. I decide I must wait as long as I can before trying anything.

Mary writes

I am not crying, actually; but I am afraid and full of outrage. I think I've never known the meaning of hate and anger until now. I would shoot the men dead if I could. I want to stick long knives into them. The depth of my anger frightens me. I twist my arms in vain. I intend to bite anything that comes near enough, if I can get the tape off. But I am nearly hopeless. Even if you find me, what can you and Molly do against three men? Rifles stand in the corner, and there are axes. They must be wood-cutters who come up here periodically to cut wood, I think, and then I wonder how I can think of anything so irrelevant.

Then the big bull-like one that brought me here stands up. So do the others. One of them goes to the door and opens it and stands there, listening, for a moment. Then he slams it shut with a laugh and shoves the wooden bolt. They all three come over to me and stand looking down. They look enormous and brutal, especially the bull. His short curly beard glistens in the lamplight, very black. He makes an expansive gesture, pointing first to himself and then to the others, waving towards me with an open-handed movement, meanwhile running his tongue over his lips. The meaning is only too clear: they shall have their turns when he himself is done. I make a snarling sound behind my gag; it sounds like a wasp's nest, full of maddened wasps. They ignore it.

I think, this—this incredible thing—is really going to happen. I am actually going to be raped. Women are supposed to fantasize about such things. Here is the actuality that one must never, never admit can happen. Not the fantasy: the thing behind the fantasy. Fleetingly I think of the millions of girls this has happened to down the centuries. I despise these men—at the moment, all men!—with a loathing so intense that I wonder it doesn't stop their hearts in their coarse bodies.

Only a moment has passed since they came over. The man with a drooping moustache asks a question: he sounds worried. The bull answers, pointing down the mountain and laughing. Then he makes a throat-cutting gesture, closing his little red eyes, following it by a jerk of his head towards the mountain above. Again the meaning is all too clear: nothing to fear, at least for the moment, from below; then the dead body buried untraceably up on the mountain.

I wonder where you are. This is the end of all the happiness we have known. I think of you alone, wandering sadly about the streets of Oxford, without me to love you. Now tears for you and me do come into my eyes.

The bull bends over me and unbuckles my belt and yanks the blue jeans down. He moves to my feet and hauls them off. I lash out suddenly with the foot that has a sneaker on it and kick him savagely in the side. He says "Oof!" and staggers; then he slaps me viciously and my head swims.

Richard writes

All that Mary has described, I am seeing through the window with an anger and hate and horror that grab me and shake me like some giant hand. I want to kill—a terrible craving. I listen for the schooner's party, knowing it to be too soon—if, indeed, they ever find the place in the darkness. I think of firing the hut, but it is of stone. I know, now, that I cannot get through the tiny windows. I decide I shall smash the window with the rock I've picked up, distracting the bull at the last possible minute. Then they'll leave Mary and come out to chase me, and perhaps I can brain one with the rock or run in and grab a rifle when they open the door.

I see Mary's kick and mutter "Good girl! Well done!" Then when he slaps her, I suddenly remember the merry, loving dryad looking out from the tree. Something in me seems to be tearing—perhaps the last layer of civilised restraint.

The men have gone back and picked up their bottles again and are roaring out a song. Then the great bull comes over to Mary, taking care not to get within range of her foot. He tears the tape off her mouth and forces the bottle in. She gasps and chokes.

Then the bull sets his bottle down with a crash and turns and yanks his trousers off. Mary's eyes are huge in a face of horror.

At that point I go mad. I forget about the rock and the window. All that I am forces itself out between my lips in a cry that is half-roar, half-scream. There is insanity in it—and desolation—and a savagery of anger. Far down the path the schooner's party hear it and their blood runs cold.

The men freeze, and one drops his bottle. The bull, bending over Mary, is suddenly motionless. Then with infinite slowness, shrinking into himself, he straightens up. His face is drained of blood, death-white, his eyes wild and terrified.

I run to another window, and the terrible cry tears through the night again. My mind functions. I know I've hit upon something—the awful cry of Pan, god of the wild, could not have been more savage and lonely. The men huddle together, not even reaching for guns. Superstitious horror, Pan-ic terror, freezes their blood. I see from this window that the wooden bar has not gone far enough to bolt the door.

The schooner's party rush into the clearing in time to see me run back to the first window and give vent, once again, to the desolation of that frightful cry. I see the others, armed with two rifles and a pistol and cudgels. I motion imperatively and run to the door just ahead of them and leap in, uttering the cry for the last time.

The men don't move for a fatal instant, and I leap straight upon the bull, swinging the mightiest punch of my life into his belly. He half doubles forward, and I bring my knee up into his face feeling the nose break. He goes over backwards with a crash. One of the other men leaps for a gun. Beulah springs onto his back like a red-haired Fury, and Peter hits him savagely behind the ear with a pistol. The third man has got to an axe. A rifle cracks and at the same moment the Captain swings mightily with what looks like a cricket bat, and the man goes down with a bullet-smashed kneecap and a broken head. Lewis calmly lowers the smoking rifle. Then I see that the bull, sitting legs apart on the floor, has his hand on a rifle. I take a step and kick him savagely between the legs with my cleated climbing shoe, and at the same moment a heavier gun booms and the hand on the gun is a smashed red wound. The bull writhes like a broken snake on the floor as Roger keeps the gun aimed at him. The Battle of the Cyclades is over.

While the men are bound, I run to Mary. I try with trembling hands to untie her, murmuring, "Mary! It's all right now!" at intervals. Betsy finds a knife and comes over and cuts Mary's bonds.

Mary seems to be only dimly aware of what is happening. The bull's hard-handed and vicious slap added to earlier blows, she says later, had almost knocked her out, though she had been aware of the rape's imminence. She had known the terrible cries to be mine, but she had also believed that the earth itself was screaming.

She moans and shudders convulsively. She whispers, "Val . . . Val . . ." Then she whispers, "The bull . . . all dying . . . she . . ." The little whisper ceases. I look at her dear, battered face, and I bury my face in her stomach with tears burning in my eyes. Little shudders are going through her.

"Val!" says Shelley gently, taking my shoulders. "Let me look at her."

I stand up and see the great bull lying on the floor and am tempted to kill him, wounded and helpless though he is. I stare at him, and he stares malignantly back. But his face is bloody from the broken nose, his hand is ruined from the rifle bullet, and his crotch is torn and bleeding. The skipper sees my glance.

"That kick," he says with satisfaction. "I expect it has just about finished him as a rapist. The punishment fits the crime. —Val, did he rape her?"

"No!" I say. "Not quite. He was just going to when I, er, yelled."

"God!" says the Captain. "That yell—cry—whatever it was! It almost stopped my heart! I'm jolly glad you kicked the swine!"

"So am I, Val!" says Peter. "He quite deserved it—and if he had got that rifle . . ."

I go back to Mary. She evidently had seen the kick, for she is now muttering, "Kick him! Kill the bull! Hooray!" in what is little more than a bloodthirsty whisper. I stroke her brow, and she whispers, "Val! Val!"

Shelley says that Mary must be carried to the ship, and a stretcher is improvised from some of the furniture and blankets. There is some discussion of what is to be done with the men. It is decided that we shall be better off without publicity, let alone the struggle to get three wounded men down the mountain. The one with the shattered kneecap that the skipper hit with the cricket bat is still unconscious and breathing loudly. He is, according to Shelley, slightly concussed. The one hit by Peter with the pistol is conscious again and is the least mangled. The bull will not die, unfortunately; but he will probably not be the same man again. Still, one or two of them will be able to limp about in a few hours. The Captain and Roger take axes and thoroughly smash their guns and knives and the other axes, as well as the many bottles of ouzo. The lamps are extinguished. A broken knife is left in the centre of the room. One of the men will eventually be able to wriggle over to it and free himself.

Then the procession makes its way slowly down the Mountain of the Bull, as we shall later call it, four people carrying Mary. Fortunately there is moonlight. I am myself feeling exhausted, and I think that my exhaustion must stem from the cry. Aboard *Windrush* Shelley makes Mary drink a strong hot toddy and also gives her a shot. She is put to bed. We all have rather the feeling of warriors coming home from the wars, and most of us have a drink. We don't say much, except a few murmurs of "Good shot, man!" or "Nice hit you got in!" Everyone is drained, I especially. The Battle of the Cyclades will be discussed, but not tonight. During the night an armed anchor watch keeps the deck, but nothing breaks the silence.

Mary describes the aftermath of the great battle

Morning light streams through the port. I wake. I am not in Richard's arms, and I feel this to be strange. Then I see him, wrapped in a blanket and asleep in one of the saloon chairs beside my bunk. His face is dirty and has a long scratch on it. Instantly I remember with a gasp. The bull on the mountain. Everything after the slap is confused, though I remember his taking down his trousers, and shots, and Richard's boot smashing into him. And I have dim memories of being carried down the mountain. And I remember terrible cries. It is the sequence that is confused. I am sore and bruised.

I see the bull's face, black-bearded and full of lust. I see the trousers jerked down. Then it comes to me: I have been raped. "Oh my God!" I whisper. "Please, God, heavenly Father, do not let it be so." But I know it is so. It all becomes clear. He raped me, and Richard punished him for it with the awful kick. I feel a flicker of vengeful gladness about the kick. But I—raped! I feel dirty. My flesh has little crawly sensations all over. I shall never be clean again. Nothing will ever be the same again. I am changed for ever, different, dirtied. People will see it in my eyes, see that I have been raped and am dirty. I think I can't stand it. Then I think, "Oh, dear God! Maybe I have the bull's baby in me!" I shut my eyes for an instant. "I'll kill it!" I breathe. "I'll kill it!"

Then I think: "Stop! Don't be a fool! Be reasonable about this! If I'm pregnant, it can be taken care of. And the rape—it's over now! I'll live. It's just a—a happening. It doesn't mean anything. It's over! Nothing is changed inside where I live. Where my love for Val lives. I will not *let* this make a difference. I . . . will . . . not . . . *let* it!'' My resolution hardens, becomes steel.

Then I think: "We shall go up that mountain again today and find those men. And then I—nobody else, it is for me!—I will kill the bull. I shall shoot him where it will kill him. Van can kill him, too. Nobody else. Val and I. Yes, we'll do it."

Richard groans and mutters something and wakes up. He sees me looking at him.

"Mary, dear!" he says. "Are—are you all right?"

"Hello," I say. "Dear Val!" I am surprised: my voice is shaky. "Yes, I'm all right. Are you? Are you all right?"

"Tired," he says. "Exhausted. Emotionally exhausted, I expect. But I'm okay." He stretches. Then he says, "Your face is rather a mess. Your lip is cut and swollen, and you've got a huge green and yellow bruise on your cheek."

"Richard," I say. "We have to go up that mountain again—today."

"What!" he says. "I shouldn't think you'd ever want to see it again."

"I have to kill the man that's like a bull—the giant," I say. "You can kill him, too."

"But, Mary!" you say in amazement. "He's practically a ruin as it is."

"No," I say. "He has to be dead. Then I can be clean again."

"Mary!" you say. "I've never heard you talk like this before."

"I've never been raped before!" I say. "I have to do it."

"Mary! Mary!" you say. "You haven't been raped! Good God!"

"Not raped?" I say in an astonished squeak. "You're just saying that!"

"No, no!" you say, half smiling. "No rape, I swear to you. So let the bastard live. Listen!" You tell me what you saw through the window and what followed.

"Good! Good!" I say as he describes the Battle of the Cyclades, including the destruction of the bull. I am so relieved at not having been raped that—despite my harrowing experience—I feel quite cheerful, though shaken.

"All the same, Val," I say. "I know now about rape—all there is to know. Not only my thoughts lying there, seeing it coming . . . but this morning, before you woke up. I was a raped woman. I went through it all—all the horror and repulsion. How can men *do* things like that to another human being! I hate men—except you of course. Hate them!"

Richard looks at me. "Your father is a man," he says. "So is Peter. Don't fall into that error, darling. There are mad-dog men—and good men. Vicious women, too."

I think of Daddy, kind and gentle. And dear sweet Peter. And kind Roger. "You're right of course," I say. "I don't hate men. But, Val—why don't the good ones, like you and Daddy and Peter, kill the bad ones?"

"Well," he says with a grin. "We half-killed them."

"You should have killed them completely!" I say.

"I'm not convinced that it's Christ urging you to urge that," says Richard seriously. "Are you?"

"Well . . . no," I say. "Not convinced, I mean. I'll have to think about it. It didn't seem a time for turning the other cheek. Still . . . —I want a bath!"

I get up, creaking, and disappear into the shower. Other people are up and stirring. I meet Betsy in the passage as I return, and she reaches out a hand, which I take. She looks sad and worried, so I kiss her and murmur, "I'm all right—really!"

I put on clean clothes, and Richard and I go into the saloon. Everybody is there, even the anchor watch being secured now that daylight has come—except that the skipper and others glance out of the ports now and then, and the rifles are ready. Lewis and Beulah have made a large and delicious breakfast, the more welcome in the absence of dinner last night. Everybody is glad that I am not more destroyed by the experience, and they all glance at my bruised face—which looks worse than it is—and look at me lovingly. Pauline gives my hand a squeeze. I reassure them by eating a lot.

Then, after eating, we drink tea or coffee and talk, going over the whole adventure, fitting all the stories together. Just so, beyond a doubt, are epics created. And, in the epic tradition, we establish names. It is, we agree, the Mountain of the Bull, he of the black beard being the Bull. Or now, perhaps, the Steer. And it will be for ever The Battle of the Cyclades, which, we feel, has a fine epic ring.

We decide that the Bull and friends, knowing that there was but one man with me, had felt safe. Before the effete yachtsmen could summon help, the Bull and his companions would be safe in their village, with me untraceably buried.

"A nice little drama in three acts—three men, you see," I say; "and the curtains for me."

Molly tells the tale of her run down the mountain; and others tell of her arrival with electrifying wild shouts. Then she was so incoherent, stammering in her anger, that only Roger could understand her.

All the tales are told, including that of the sheer horror that everyone felt at Richard's cry.

"It was the terror of Pan!" I say. "That's what panic is, you know—Pan-ic terror."

"And now, thanks to Val," says Peter with a grin at Richard, "we all —not just those men—know quite precisely what it is."

The battle itself requires the most sorting out, but it is plain that everybody was brave, even me because I bit the Bull. But Richard of the Pan-cry and Molly of the winged feet are the great heroes of the saga.

Then Betsy says, "I know we had to do it to save Mary, but—well, can we justify so much violence? Like shooting them? I mean, could we have captured them without hurting them so much? I feel sort of smug about all of it, including Val's kick. But were we right to do it?"

"I have wondered about that, also," says Pauline.

"I wanted to kill them all," I say, remembering Richard's remark about Christ.

"Damn it!" says Richard. "I'm jolly glad I kicked him—he was reaching for a rifle. If I hadn't acted—of course, I didn't know that old Roger was about to shoot, and *he* didn't know that I was about to kick—"

"Like a rugger back," say Roger with a grin. "Well kicked, I say!"

"Well shot, Roger!" says Richard with a return grin.

"We had to act," says the Captain firmly. "Every single action was justified. Those men had to be stopped. If we had even hesitated—a civilised hesitation to shoot or hit instantly—one of those men might have got to a rifle or an axe. And then we might have had one or two shrouded bodies in a stateroom. Also, Betsy, remember: our guns were used to stop, not to kill. Peter used his pistol to club the one called Basil. Lew shot at the kneecap—and Roger at the hand that the Bull had seized a rifle with. Evil must be stopped. We stopped it."

"All we did was justified, I think," says Lewis, "including Val's kick. It wasn't 'nice'—but then we weren't having a nice, clean sporting contest, were we? Those men were going to rape and kill our Mary; and they'd have killed us all—or tried to—if they had got to their guns. And if the Bull is ruined sexually by Val's kick, as Shelley thinks . . . well, he's a rapist, isn't he? If Val has seen to it that he'll never rape some other poor girl, that alone justifies the kick."

"It ees so!" says Jean, to everyone's astonishment. "Val spike hees gun."

Everybody laughs, and the skipper says, "Spike is right—those cleats!"

"There's something else," I say. "Betsy spoke of our using violence. What *is* violence? Aren't 'violence' and 'violation' the same basic word?"

"Latin *violare*," murmurs Peter.

"Well, then," I say. "Those men were violating me—using violence. Right? I wasn't hurting them, only being a dryad. So how can defending ourselves *against* violence *be* violence? We weren't violating them."

There is a pause. Then Shelley says, "Sounds right. I'm going to have to think about the whole thing of violence and violation. But—thank God we acted!"

"Crew," says the Captain, "I think we had best turn our minds to decision. Do we rest up here a day or do we get underway?"

In the end we run across to a nearby island under power and find an anchorage there. The rest of the day we loaf and swim and talk endlessly about the fray. Two or three people go ashore but stay near the beach. In the evening, when everybody is relaxing on deck—Betsy and I are lying on our stomachs on the after deck—Shelley and Beulah come solemnly up from below. Each carries what I think at first is a plant and then see is a wreath of wired-together leafy twigs. They turn to Richard and Molly, who are fortunately sitting together in the cockpit, and they solemnly recite in chorus, each holding forth her wreath:

"In the name of all high Olympus, O Pan-Val and O Hermes-Molly, we crown you with laurel for Saving Mary from the Bull of the Mountain." Then they step forward and place a wreath on the head of each hero amidst clapping.

Mary continues with the story of a cave

The next morning *Windrush* is underway at dawn, and the regular sea watches are set. We visit several islands, including the Sacred Isle of Delos—sacred because Apollo and his twin sister, Artemis, were supposed to have been born there. We also experience one of the sudden fierce squalls that the Aegean is famous for. But the schooner is handled magnificently by a crew that have become seamen. Moreover, it seems to me that we all, even I, bear ourselves with the intrepid air of people who are not to be trifled with. Although I didn't keep up this journal, we have some splendid sailing in these days. And many of the island ports, with their old houses and crooked streets, dominated by their ancient churches, are very colourful indeed. Usually we anchored at night, and so had some grand conversations after dinner at night. That is all I shall say about these days before the next adventure.

It is a fine sparkling day. Second's watch in the forenoon. Richard is at the helm, and I have just climbed the ratlines of the foremast. All around me stretches the wrinkled blue surface of the Aegean—the wine-dark sea. Ahead and to port is a large island in the northeastern part of the Aegean. We are about to enter a cove the skipper heard about when we visited the principal harbour last night, a cove remote from any of the island villages.

Windrush on a westerly course is moving steadily towards the entrance with a moderate breeze on the beam. The channel is narrow, and I am aloft to read the water and con her in. The blue of deep water pales to green ahead.

"Come left—port!" I cry to Richard, who steers with the Captain standing beside him. "Steer for that rock!" The schooner swings to port.

"Now!" I shout. "Starboard! Come right! —That's well! Well that! Rudder amidships—steady as she goes! . . . Captain! We're in! We're over the bar!"

"All right," says the skipper. "Stand by the anchor! . . . A bit more that way, Val. . . . Now! Helm alee! . . . All right, Shelley, let it go! Down sails!"

Windrush glides on, is checked, swings to her anchor. The sails come down.

"Val!" I cry from the foremast. "Look at that cave!"

"I see it!" he shouts. "I'm with you!"

The small cove where the schooner lies is almost perfectly round. On the right, as one sees it when entering, there is a beach and beyond it a gentle slope leading up to a grassy bluff. On the left is a rocky incline, steepening to a cliff, and about two-thirds of the way up is the mouth of the cave. I see a fault slanting across the cliff face that I think we can work our way along.

Richard swarms up the ratlines to join me. Clinging to the shrouds, we study the cliff. "See that fault?" I say.

"Mmmm," he says. "If we land by that bush, I think we can work our way up to there—that greenish stone, see? And then traverse to the fault. And it goes almost to the cave—past that big rock anyway. There'll be some way to do the last bit, I expect. I can almost see the footholds from here. Let's go!"

We descend to the deck but find no more climbers.

"You're both quite mad," says Shelley. "Who wants to hang by their toes?"

"You'll be sorry!" I say. "We'll probably find Greek coins or something."

After changing our clothes, we paddle the life-raft over to the bush. The dinghy is in use on the beach run, making trips to and fro with people and supplies in order to resume the beach party that was interrupted by the call to battle on the island of the Bull, down south in the Cyclades. Here, we are pleased to see, there are no wooded fastnesses where enemy armies might lurk. Peter shouts from the beach that there is a fresh-water pool on top of the grassy bluff. Two heads are proceeding beachward in the water. The cove rings with merry cries. The water sparkles in the clear sunlight.

Richard and I find the ascent even easier than expected and gain the cave in no more than twenty minutes and disappear within. It is disappointingly bare of Greek coins and vases. There is only an empty packet of Players, which I set a match to and burn as we sit in the cave entrance waving to the people on the beach across the cove. I bury a shilling for someone else to discover some day. We are about half again as high as *Windrush*'s tall mainmast, and the schooner as seen from above looks trim and graceful.

"Well," says Richard. "Nowhere to go but down. Shall we try a dive?"

"Zeus, no!" I say with a shudder. "Keep your million pounds! What a thought!"

Richard grins and slips over the edge and moves carefully along towards the fault. I start to follow, then see him flatten himself against the cliff as a shower of small stones comes down from above. I look up and see the smiling face of Beulah peering over the edge; she and Lewis, exploring, have wandered around from the beach bluff.

"Get back! Get back!" I cry. "That's dangerous!"

Even as I shout and the head is jerked back, I see a section of the top of the cliff start to slip downward—straight towards Richard.

"Val!" I shout urgently. "Landslide! This way! Quick!"

He gives one hasty glance upward at the sliding mass, then leaps towards me. He is rather lower than the cave, but I manage to catch his hand. I am almost jerked over the edge. Then, frantically, I know that I cannot hold him—he is slipping! He will fall, die! I can't hold him! Suddenly, desperately, frantically, I am hauling him up, while his feet scrabble for footholds.

Simultaneously, the landslide, gaining in speed and mass—not just stones and earth but rock of the actual cliff face—goes by with a grinding roar, right over the spot where Richard was, and hits the water with a great splash.

But Richard is beside me.

"Good lord!" he says in a shaken voice. "Thanks, Mary! I thought—I thought I'd had it!" He swallows and runs his fingers through his hair. "Gods above, Mary!" he says in a stronger voice. "How did you do it? You just . . . aren't that strong!"

My heart is pounding. I feel very shaken. "Val," I mutter. "I don't know, I don't know! You were slipping, I couldn't *hold* you!—Val, Val! you were going to *die!* Then—suddenly I got twice as strong!"

"By George!" he says. "I know what it was." He is himself again, absorbed in an idea. "I read about it somewhere. It's called hysterical strength. Woman frenzied because her child is under a wrecked car—and she lifts it! Normally couldn't lift a bag of potatoes. That's what it was. You saved my life, Mary." He waves to Peter on the beach.

"It was the thought of you dead," I say, feeling exhausted. "I'm always imagining it, but—but this—this was the thing itself—you *dead!* I thought: God. I didn't ask anything: I just thought: God. Then I was pulling you up till you got hold. —That stupid Beulah!" She and Lewis, half way round the cove, are looking anxiously at us. Richard waves, and they wave wildly back.

"She didn't mean to," says Richard forgivingly. Then he says, "Mary! I just thought of something. My Pan-cry—could that have been analogous? Not a breakthrough into super-strength, exactly, but produced out of the same agonized intensity. I couldn't yell like that now —I don't know how I did it. I wonder . . . well, if there's some sort of reserve power in us that can be tapped through emotional intensity . . . maybe we could learn to control it. I've got to think about this."

"It certainly leaves you feeling exhausted afterwards," I say. "I'm feeling better now, but I could barely lift my hand after you were back up here."

"Yes," he says. "I could see you were done in. It's what you'd expect though, isn't it? Like running the mile all out. —Look, Mary! What's that? Behind the bulge, see?" He points.

About four feet above the fault that Richard had almost reached before the landslide, half-concealed by a protruding part of the cliff, there is a deep depression.

"Oh," I say. "That hole's where the big rock was, remember? I do, because I was thinking when we came along that I shouldn't care to have it fall on me. And now it has fallen. Look! you can see it sticking out of the water."

"I expect you're right," he says. "Are you recovered enough to start down again?"

I nod, and then grin as I see him give a wary glance upward. I climb over the edge and work my way towards the beginning of the fault, Richard close behind. When I get my feet on the fault, kicking away loose earth and rubble from the landslide, I find that it is much wider, almost a ledge, so much of the cliff above having slid down. I approach the bulge and stoop under it. Then I straighten up, Richard beside me, to peer into the hole where the great rock was.

A woman's large, dark-blue eyes are looking into mine, and it seems her rosy lips are about to smile. For a stunned instant I think she is alive. Then I realise, even as Richard murmurs, "Good lord!" that it is just a head, life-size, poised in a small depression on the floor of another cave opening up where the great rock was.

The head is of bronze but painted in the colours of life—and the paint, unlike any other Greek statue I've ever heard of, seems perfectly fresh, preserved in this airless space. The lips are copper. The eyes, dark as lapis lazuli, are glass. The face is noble and sensitive—and flawlessly lovely. It is apparent that the bronze, below the neck, has been cut through, somewhat irregularly.

"Oh, heavens!" I say. "What a lovely thing! What a find! It has to be a goddess—an Aphrodite. Aphrodite—Queen of love and beauty!"

"How in the world did it come here?" says Richard. "Looks like a part of a life-sized statue. Let's see if there is anything else in the cave."

We search carefully, but there is nothing else at all. The floor is rock —nothing could be concealed beneath it. The head itself is simply there alone. There is just enough of the swelling out of the neck into the body to form a sort of base. Even so the head rocks easily, as I determine by putting my hand on it.

"Listen, Mary," says Richard. "What do we do about this? Let's sit down and think about it while we are still the only two people in the world who know what's here."

We sit down in the cave mouth facing each other, on either side of the beautiful head, which we see in profile. We light cigarettes.

"Now," he says. "You're the classicist. How do you suppose she came here?"

"I've been thinking about that, Val," I say. "I don't believe there's the slightest doubt of her being an Aphrodite *and* ancient work. The worship of Aphrodite was strong in these islands off the coast of Asia Minor—certainly it was in Lesbos. Sappho in her poems—the few we have—is always referring to Aphrodite, almost never to the other gods. Of course Aphrodite was more than the goddess of love and beauty. She was the goddess of spring, and wherever she trod wildflowers sprang up. That's nice, isn't it? *And* she was the goddess of windy skies and calm seas, too."

"Strange!" says Richard. "The two don't seem to go together."

"No," I agree. "Not at all. Still, that's the way I remember it. Anyhow, I have the impression that shrines or little white temples of the goddess were apt to be on bluffs or headlands near the sea—and near the sky, too, you see. If so, that might account for this general area."

"True," says Richard. "But not for the cave. And not for the head torn off."

"Your guess is as good as mine about that," I say. "But here's mine. Someone who loved her—some worshipper—hid her here, to protect her."

"Against what?" says Richard.

"Well," I say. "Invasion, maybe. It looks to me as though she is, maybe, fifth century B.C. Or fourth. I mean, the sculptor obviously had full command of his technique, and yet she has the look, to me anyway, of having been done by somebody to whom the gods were real—the strict classical period. Or maybe the late sixth century. My history of the islands is pretty sketchy. I don't know whether the Persians occupied the island in the early fifth century—they must have done—or whether they would have been regarded as a threat to the statue. If so, that might account for her being here. Or much, much later, when paganism was dying and Christianity triumphing. The Christians would certainly have been a threat to the classical gods. She might have been hidden here by some last devout pagan."

"He did a good job of it," says Richard. "Now—what are we going to do with the lady?"

"How about the mantelpiece at Attica?" I say with a grin.

"Be serious!" he says. "What we're supposed to do is report it to the Greek authorities. In fact, anything else is probably illegal. Maybe immoral, too."

"Illegal, yes," I say. "Illegal because the government *says* it's illegal. But immoral? Governments can't make things immoral. Granted, Greece has some rights—Greeks do, I mean. I don't believe in 'the state'. But the Greek past is scattered all over the museums of Europe and America anyway. If we'd found it across the straits in Turkey, they'd say it was theirs."

"True," says Richard. "And ancient Greece is the ancestor of European or Western civilisation—not just modern Greece."

"Discoverers have rights, too," I say. "They always had in the past. In freer ages, when men made their own decisions. I don't think that, just because governments pass a lot of laws about what's theirs, it alters the fact that we have some moral rights as discoverers. That's why I kept that coin. Don't you agree?"

"What a sea lawyer!" says Richard with a smile. "Yes, I agree, discoverers do have some moral rights. So what's in your mind?"

"Oxford!" I say. "What could be more the heir of the Academy and all classical Hellas than Oxford? We can get Lewis to photograph the head in *situ*—not that that's very important in a case like this. No strata. No nothing. And then we'll take her to Oxford."

"I like that," he says. "It'll be there for the world. They won't have to say just where it comes from. Or if their conscience bothers them about the Greek law, they can hand it back. But I bet they don't."

"Listen!" I say. "We ought to visit a Turkish port. We've already been to Marseilles and Naples, both Greek places once. That's three different governments, four counting Greece, all with claims to Greek finds, only nobody will know which one. Except Oxford, and they won't tell, I hope."

"Right you are!" says Richard, entering into the spirit of the plan. "After a once-Greek place in Turkey, we could even go on to Alexandria and make it five governments. We can go out into the country and act a bit mysterious—I say! Don't we have good criminal minds?"

"That's why we love each other," I say. "But don't say criminal—say *individual* minds. Free spirits. Anyhow, it's agreed. —Now, let's get Lewis up here to take a lot of photographs, including one of the whole cliff face."

"Come to think of it," says Richard, "he was snapping away like anything when we were sailing in. With any luck, there'll be one of the cliff before the landslide."

We climb down—almost walk down, it's become so easy since the slide—and paddle the raft across to the beach, shouting, "All hands! All hands!" People leap up, stare at us—but see that we are smiling. So it's not another Bull.

Everybody is galvanized with excitement as we tell our story. There is a little hesitation—one or two disagree—about our plan to take the head to Oxford instead of reporting it, but we win them over. The skipper, glad that *Windrush* is the discovery ship, agrees to confuse the trail by putting into other ports.

Lewis is sure that his earlier photographs will show the cliff face, and he begins to take many more, some from the dinghy and even one from the mainmast top, showing the cliff from every angle, including the scar of the landslide, the new cave, and the rubble in the water's edge. Then he comes up to the cave and, after awed looks at the lovely face, takes dozens of flashbulb photographs. Everybody, in fact, braves the heights to see the lady as we first saw her. Peter Shirley, my fellow classicist, is especially full of wonder and admiration.

Then comes the problem of getting her down without risk of damage.

The head is heavy, and even though the climb is easy, it requires both hands. We consider the possibility of making a backpack for Richard, but he is reluctant. Peter points out strongly that the ancient paint must have an absolute minimum of handling or rubbing.

In the end the Captain takes charge. The gaff of the main is unshipped and carried ashore along with its tackle, and, after a struggle, is got up to the ledge where the throat or base is secured to heavy spikes driven into a crevice so that the gaff will swivel. Another line from the peak is run over the top of the cliff to a block on a heavy stake. We have, then, a cargo boom.

A tight metal box is hoisted up and swung round to the cave. There the precious head is carefully lifted up and laid in the box upon masses of shredded-up paper topped with quantities of cotton wool, much of it obtained from all the sanitary napkins that the female half of the company can spare—causing the irrepressible Beulah to remark that women are prepared for anything. The box is filled with more cotton wool and shredded paper until there is no possibility of the head moving, even the littlest bit, even during a storm. Then the box is shut and made watertight with melted wax and tape as well.

The box is then delicately lowered by the peak halyards into the waiting dinghy, which ferries it to the schooner. There it is lashed immovably in place in the portside stowage locker. The cave is checked a last time with torches—the cave that no one has entered, in all probability, for two thousand or even twenty-five hundred years, since it was closed with the rock. It must have been possible then, we surmise, to have rolled the rock into place. Finally we disassemble the rig, and all signs of our operation are done away with.

"Wow!" I say. "I don't think my heart beat once while the goddess was coming down the cliff. Certainly I didn't breathe."

"It was a seamanlike job," says the skipper. "All the same, I'm jolly glad it's done."

"If it weren't for me," says Beulah, who has been forgiven, "there wouldn't *be* any goddess. If we're going to log this as Aphrodite Cove, I think we should have Landslide Beulah, too."

It has been an exceedingly hot and busy afternoon for everyone, especially for Richard and me, cliff-climbers-in-chief as well as those at hazard. We change back into shorts and go ashore to a fire and the propect of food.

By the time dinner is ready, it is twilight, and just in the mouth of the cove a giant red-gold full moon is rising over Asia. I am staring raptly at it when Richard takes my hand and murmurs, "The Gateway to

Heaven . . ." and I remember that same moon rising in the far mountains of Virginia.

During dinner we talk, of course, about the great discovery. Richard remarks that Rozica will shoot herself for having left the cruise, and I say she'll more likely shoot Pam. Someone proposes that we should name this island, since we are to keep the real name secret. Treasure Island is suggested, but in the end we agree that Discovery Island will be better. Windrush Cove on Discovery Island, where Landslide Beulah occurred. Then we talk about the adventures of the whole voyage—the great storm when Richard's leap saved my life, showers and flowers at Gibraltar, Avignon and god-haunted Delphi, and of course the Battle of the Cyclades. It has been an adventurous voyage.

"Almost too adventurous for me at moments," I say. "Still, what ends well . . . Remember when I said that we should have adventures if we really wanted them? I was right, wasn't I? Or Daddy was."

We wonder what further adventures there may be on the long voyage home, but there is a feeling among us that the discovery of the goddess, the lady of love and beauty, marks the high point of the whole journey. So, despite new harbours, perhaps we shall be steering for the fair ports of home from this night on.

The talk dies away and a companionable silence falls upon us. We stare into the fire, lifting our eyes now and then to the rising moon, now silver and tracing a glinting moonpath across the cove.

Mary continues with the Moonpool

The dinghy crunches on the sand. Roger, who has been out to the ship to switch on the riding lamp—and has, I notice, left on the saloon lights—comes up the beach to the fire. "I just had a thought," he says. "It's a mild night—what about a moonlight bathe in that pool up there?" He gestures towards the bluff.

"My suit's aboard," says Betsy.

"Oh, let's not bother with suits," says the skipper. "After all, it's night."

Betsy glances at me, and so does Richard. I realise they are concerned about my reaction—so soon after the Bull. I do, in fact, feel hesitant, uneasy. But then I think rapidly: "I *must* not let it haunt me. After a fall, one gets up and rides. Now!" I smile at them.

"Besides, this is Greece!" I say. "Ancient Greece since we found the goddess. Think of Aphrodite. *She* wouldn't wear a bathing suit! Come on! This is the night of the goddess."

There are chuckles and murmurs of agreement, and we wend our way up the slope. There is the pool, round and dark. We pause, and someone starts to take off his shirt, so we all undress, leaving our clothes in a row of little heaps on the bluff.

In the brilliant light of the full moon we walk lightly towards and around the pool. Suddenly it becomes a pool of silver light as it comes between us and the moon. The Moonpool, I name it in my mind—the Moonpool of Aphrodite. One of the girls puts a toe into the water, sending silvery ripples across it. Open to the sunshine all day long, the water is warm, warmer even than the soft air. It is like a caress on our nude bodies.

A great hush lies over the island, and somehow no one talks above a murmur. There is a sort of pause as if to savour the moment. And then we are seized, all of us, by a joyous exhilaration—a lovely silent gaiety. Perhaps it is the spell of the goddess.

As the Moonpool receives twelve bodies, the silver mirror breaks into chunks and slivers of silver, ever changing geometric patterns of black and silver with the white forms of clean-limbed bodies appearing and disappearing. And almost the only sound is the splashing of water and little breathless laughs.

Richard looks at me with joy in his face and disappears suddenly beneath the water to rise across the pool. Shelley's face and her long dark hair emerge from the water. She smiles and whispers, "Oh, Mary!" and is gone. I swim rapidly across the pool, once touching some other girl's body with mine. Pauline and I are momentarily face to face, and we look at each other with deep love and understanding. I go out of the water and see Richard standing on the other side, and I run around the pool. When I get there, he has gone back into the water, so I run clear around.

In a little grassy space Pauline and Betsy are moving forward and back in a kind of dance. Pauline reaches out her slender hand and I catch it and, dancing, too, swing into the line. Peter and Jean stand watching. I am full of ecstasy, and I know we all are: we are all caught up in the same enchantment.

The three of us dance forward and into the water and swim away. I frolic like a dolphin. I go out of the water on the other side and stand looking, impressing everything into my mind for ever. The grassy plain of the Moonpool is dotted with shrubs bearing large white flowers. There are distant hills and groves. The schooner rides at her anchor below with her lights twinkling and the saloon ports glowing. The shimmering moonpath comes across the sea of Hellas. But in the centre of the world is the Moonpool, and we twelve, like the twelve great gods and goddesses of Olympus, frolic in and around it. At the same time, the girls in the pool are nymphs, not goddesses but frisking naiads.

Across the pool two more girls and now two men are dancing in the grass, hands linked. The skipper stands near the water, looking up at the moon and the drifting wisps of cloud, white against the dark sky. His mighty form is, in truth, like one of the great gods—Poseidon, brother of Zeus, he must be.

Richard comes out of the water, scattering silver drops, and strides towards me. He, too, is a god, I think—Apollo he shall be, the lord of light: the light of my darkness. As he come up to me, hands outstretched to take mine, smiling, I murmur, "O Apollo! Have you come down from Parnassus?" We stand there together on the little rise of ground. He is, I think, as beautiful as a god.

He says in a hushed voice, "Mary, you are lovely!"

"I was thinking that of you," I say. "Beautiful as the morning star!"

We embrace and kiss each other with warm lips and cool bodies, kiss lightly as though fearful of shattering so fragile an enchantment. Then, arm in arm, we stand looking.

He murmurs, "I have never seen a sight so lovely."

"It is the Moonpool," I say. "And the night of the goddess."

"It will be part of us now," he says. "For always."

We say no more, standing there, looking. I am conscious of the faintest breath of the night wind, and it is exquisite pleasure on my bare skin. Someone is chasing a girl around the pool. There are five dancers now on the other side, silent and graceful. A girl emerges from the water, her hips and hair streaming silver, and embraces one of the dancers. One couple, arm in arm like us, wander along the edge of the bluff, the female figure carrying one of the white flowers. Jean and Pauline stand together across the pool, looking at us, and we give them a little wave. Then we walk towards the pool and into it, where we stand hip deep.

We are the only two in the water now, and as we stand there without moving the wavelets die, and the Moonpool is again a disc of silver and black. I bend forward a little and look down and so does Richard. We see ourselves looking up at us. My body looks very slender beside Richard's broad shoulders, and my small breasts look fuller as I bend. This body, too, and Richard's are part of this night. Suddenly I am overwhelmed and shaken by a tide of joy at being this girl, alive, uncrippled—winged—with this man whom I love and who loves me and both of us part of this loveliness. It is, I think, bending with him over the silver mirror of the Moonpool, the utmost glory of my whole life. This—this moment!

Perhaps you sense what I am thinking, for your face is joyful. You move. The two in the water are shaken by a wave as they turn and kiss. You whisper, "Come away, my love."

We leave the pool and, nude under the moon, wander along the bluff where the great white flowers grow. The night is full of fragrance. You move your arm from mine in order to put it round me as we wander along. Our hips brush, and your hand moves lightly up and down my back. Little thrills course through me, and I feel my nipples tighten. You laugh a ghost of a laugh. In the place where we have come the flowering bushes grow in a semi-circle open towards the sea, and we stand hidden from all others in soft grass, looking down at the graceful yacht with her precious cargo, her lights twinkling in the water.

We draw a little apart and look at each other in the moonlight. The great hush still lies along the world. The night is vast, and luminous, and gentle. I feel a sense of harmony with it and with the purposes of our adored God who created this beauty and us, male and female, to be joyful. We look at each other and our eyes, too, are luminous, and gentle with our love and our giving.

"Mary, my love," you whisper with delight. "My winged Mary. You are my wings."

"Val," I whisper with answering delight. "For me, you and wings are one."

We move together, touch, embrace. I think fleetingly of the great blue eyes of Aphrodite in the cave. Every small particle of me seems to yearn towards Richard.

We sink down, never parting, into the soft, cool grass, and I lie on my back beneath the moon. A wisp of white cloud drifts among the stars. Richard leans over me with one arm under my head, and I see his shadowed face framed in stars. Val of the stars.

He makes a little sound between a laugh and a sob, and there is the ghost of answering mirth from me. Our lips smile and, smiling, join. We are flooded with passion, passion meeting passion. I cannot help it, I cry out, a wordless cry; and it is swallowed up in the vast luminous silence of the night of the goddess.

MOON MAGIC

Slip away in a dress of moonlight,
  Be lovely as a willow.
Run away and hide in midnight
  With grasses for a pillow.

The Study, Holywell, April, 1968—Richard

This reading of the journal with our lives at the crossroads is a strange experience. One moment I am lifted up into hope, another plunged into despair— wanhope. Despair of course is where I began when the letter came on All Fools' Day, saying so shortly that you were in love with an unnamed woman. A woman! You said you knew it would be a shock—incredible understatement!—but you couldn't lessen it and you had to have time, time to think—a month, you said —and I was not to make it more difficult—"Oh, please!"—by rushing down there or telephoning.

I did as you asked, Mary, despite my pain and, I must confess, anger. I wanted to hit somebody, whether you or that other woman or God I didn't quite know. Can one be cuckolded by a woman? I had impulses to wring her neck like a chicken's. Not, of course, very gentlemanly. Nor is it precisely ladylike to seduce someone's wife. But something, perhaps a curious trust in you, soon persuaded me that anger didn't meet the situation. And now, as I've studied the journals in hopes of understanding the impossible, over a week of that month has passed. Only a million years remaining.

Death or sickness one is a little prepared for in imagination. I was once prepared for your falling in love with Peter Shirley. But a woman! That I never dreamt of. I'd have said it was flatly impossible. The journal shows on every page how firmly based our marriage is. We are in love—or must I now say, were in love? We were, for sure—one can't be mistaken about response. So, can a woman who has loved a man—really loved with all of her—actually love a woman that way? That's the question of course. I am not indulging in—what shall I call it?—phallic arrogance. But a woman's loving a woman is an essentially different mode of loving: it is the coming together of identicals, or, as Simone de Beauvoir says, of mirror images. As opposed to reciprocals, like a nut and bolt, made for each other but different: the male splendour meeting the female splendour to make a whole. It's not that I can't understand your loving a woman, Mary—after all, I'm in love with a woman, myself. But you and she, two women, are like a yacht with two clipper bows and no rudder. When I think of feminine sweetness and softness, the image draws me because I am not that. But when I think of feminine sweetness and softness in the arms of feminine sweetness and softness, it seems—what does it seem? Wrong? Well, yes, but let's leave that out. It seems—sticky. Still, how can I judge?

I said the journey to sea, when our days were hard and beautiful, had lifted me like a wave to hope and dropped me down to wanhope. When I was reading about what you called your 'masthead resolution', I felt hope. And again as you described the days before wings and the Gateway to Heaven. The hope came from my conviction that you would be remembering, too. Can you have forgotten?

But then I came to the Bull of the Mountain. And I thought: have I found the clue I've been searching for? The clue to your 'impossible' involvement with that woman? You weren't raped, but you not only knew all the horror and helplessness of approaching rape, but you believed the next morning that you had *been raped. As you said then, you experienced the whole thing. I have always supposed that most women respond to rape with despair and weakness; but not you—your response was murderous. And your cry that morning rings in my ears: "I hate men—except you, of course. Hate them!" Although I've seen no signs of it in these four years, I am wondering whether your experience could have preyed on your mind, causing you to turn against all men? Could you, once loving a woman appeared to you as a real alternative, have turned to it with a sort of relief and sense of* rightness, *causing you to reject all men, including me? To reject me as a man, not as Richard? Against this theory, I put your justness and balance. Then, too, it would be a sort of cowardice; and you, my little lioness, haven't a cowardly bone in your body. Still, what has happened must have some explanation, and this theory must remain as a dismaying possibility. But I have another major journey yet to study.*

Journey to Hawaii

A seabird, soaring on strong wings through a blue dome of air, across which drift long ranks of snowy trade-wind clouds, looks down upon a deep-blue glittering ocean where a ship traces a long white wake and a faint disappearing wisp of smoke. Nowhere within the vast sphere of blue air and bluer water is there anything else at all. Only the bird and the trade-clouds and the westering sun and the ship, also west-bound.

Upon the ship, the SS *Molokai*, two people clad in wet bathing suits are just strolling away from the ship's swimming pool towards their main-deck cabin. The larger of these is none other than the hero, Richard, who has perhaps some affinity with the great god Pan—though fortunately, I feel, without goat legs. The other one—a female at that final, rather delightful stage of girlhood, the early twenties, where girlhood dwells with womanhood—is me, Mary, the writer of this logbook of our journey to Hawaii.

In our cabin we draw the curtains across our ports and strip off our suits and towel ourselves. Then I fumble in a drawer and find a notebook which I toss on the bed.

Richard, with the towel round his waist, seats himself determinedly at the desk; he has letters to write. I sneak over and lightly draw my fingernails down his bent back, causing him to drop his pen and straighten up. He turns his head and I kiss him.

"Love you," I say. I kiss the back of his neck, one of my favourite parts of him.

"I love you, too," he says, smiling at me. He picks up his pen again and remarks, "You made me make a squiggle in my letter to Mother."

"Think what a world of speculation it will open up to her," I say, propping myself up with pillows on the bed. "How came this here? she will think. Did a wasp sting my dear son? Did a hussy leap into his lap? Or was it a Hiccup caused by Drink?"

"Shhh," he says, writing. I hush and turn my attention to my notebook, in which I have now written the foregoing, having decided this morning that I shall, after all, keep a log, as I have done—with a little help from my hero—for our other two journeys in the past year.

One thing is certain: this new journey can't possibly end up with any such remarkable discovery as that in the Greek Isles at peril of Richard's life—the lovely head of Aphrodite. It has caused no end of learned excitement, especially in the efforts to date it. Some scholars firmly believe that it's sixth century B.C. and suggest that there must have been in Asia Minor some advanced sculptors, hitherto unknown. There are of course other opinions. At all events many savants are making pilgrimages to Oxford, where the goddess is on display in an air-tight case.

When we came back to Oxford, we found to our delight that Richard's election to a fellowship in modern history at Worcester College —there had been a hint of it before—was now an accomplished fact; and we laid on a great dinner at the Mitre to celebrate. Roger and Molly of course were there, and Richard had rung up Peter, who said he and Betsy, who was visiting the Shirleys, would come. In the end we had Denis and Shelley as well, since *Windrush* was in Plymouth. It was a grand evening with a perfect wine from the Mitre's vast cellars; and we found we had something else to celebrate that gave us more real joy than the fellowship—the announcement by Peter, just before our first sip of wine, that he and Betsy were to be wed. So we emptied our glasses in a toast to them, promising to come to the North Riding for the wedding— which we did.

So a good year at Oxford began, with Richard now a lordly don. Since I am reading Greats, which includes classics, my being one of the discoverers of the goddess did me no harm. At least, my tutor congratulated me warmly before asking me a severe question that I could not answer.

I said a good year at Oxford, but I should have said good Michaelmas and Hilary Terms, since we left on this journey a few days before the end of Hilary and must be back for Trinity near the end of April. How do I dare, it might be asked—even by me, someday, looking sadly back—how do I dare turn a whole vac into a holiday? I don't dare, in fact. But Richard, a don with no worries, argued that he would love me just as much if I were "Failed B.A. (Oxon)" and would forthwith stop loving me if I didn't come; and besides I was brilliant and would cope somehow; and, after all, couldn't I take a lot of books along? Overwhelmed by this donnish logic, I agreed; and I am here on this ship with Plato and Marcus Aurelius and others, and I've actually worked a lot. I ought to add, despite the nonsense above, that we did both want to see our families very much, and since we have long planned a journey to Hawaii —for reasons more important to me than to Richard—there was a degree of reasonableness to the idea of continuing west.

We flew from Heathrow on a grey day in early March to Dulles Airport at Washington, and my father met us there. An hour or so later we were back in the familiar Georgetown house where Jolly was making ready a delicious dinner. She was overjoyed to see us both—she was my nanny and nurse in the old days and came from my mother's village in Gloucestershire—and when I kissed her, she had tears running down her wrinkled cheeks. She is Daddy's housekeeper now. After greeting her, the first thing I did was to go into the drawing-room and gaze at the painting of Mother, dead these many years since the Disaster, smiling a little half-smile and with a twinkle in her eyes, which the artist perfectly caught. As I looked at the picture above the mantelpiece, Daddy sat in his chair by the fire looking at me. Then he said, "I had just said to her, you know, that I hoped we should have a daughter who would look like her—that was the response the painter caught. And you do, Mary. You have her eyes, those dark-blue eyes. And your expression, especially when you are amused and your face lights up, is hers."

"I'm glad, Daddy," I said, going over and putting my arms around him from behind and putting my cheek against his. "I remember her a little, you know—remember her as lovely. Oh, it's good to be home again. When are you coming back to Oxford, Daddy? That solicitor—what's his name?—who was up with you at Trinity College stopped me on the High last month to ask when you might be coming along."

"Oh, Haydon," said Daddy. "John Haydon. A rowing blue in our day. I might get over there in the autumn, not much before. So it's good that you could come home for a bit now. It's a happiness to see you here again."

So began a very pleasant visit of nearly a week. Daddy thinks the world of Richard, because he believes that Richard, in some mysterious way, had more to do with my being able to walk and run than the surgeon did—and indeed it may be true, somehow. I feel it, too. Anyhow, Daddy was delighted when Richard and I were married, although, he said when he flew over, he was in no way surprised. He smiled, then—it was just before the wedding in St Mary Magdalen—and said, "My dear, your eyes spoke to me of this long before you came to Oxford—long before wings, in fact. And you know, my dear, that if this is your joy, if this is your house of love, it has my blessing on its rooftree. Be joyful, as I was with that other Mary, your mother." He meant it, too. I am blessed, not only in Richard but in having my wise and humorous father.

We told him during the visit—taking turns to tell—of all our adventures at Oxford since we last saw him and of the voyage to Hellas, and I read bits of our logbook and then gave him the rest to read. Because he never criticizes or condemns, only makes shrewd comments that we think about later, we needn't keep anything from him.

The morning after we arrived, a Sunday, the *Washington Post* announced that the President had sent three thousand marines to Vietnam, and this worried Daddy a good deal. He predicted that, inevitably, there would be more troops sent. His view is that it's a genuine civil war in Vietnam, and that the people there should settle it for themselves. Richard and I hadn't thought much about it before, but we were impressed both by his concern and by his argument.

Daddy also asked Richard very specifically about his draft status, which gave me a small chill. Richard said that he had had the usual deferment when he went to Holywell and that the deferment was extended for his advanced study at Oxford. Daddy wanted to know whether his draft board knew about his marriage to me, and Richard said, "As a matter of fact, they do. My father shoots ducks with the head of the draft board and happened to mention it. And the man said he was glad to know it and would enter it in my file."

"Good!" said Daddy. "I don't think they'll touch you then. They want boys, anyhow. I'm glad you're out of it. I was a naval officer in the war against Hitler, as you know, and proud to be involved. But, somehow—well, this Vietnam thing is different. I don't like the looks of it at all."

Also while we were there, Martin Luther King tried to lead a march on Selma that was stopped by Alabama troopers. This civil-rights or freedom struggle is something that Richard and I have in fact thought about, with a great deal of sympathy for the black people. So when an acquaintance told us that there was going to be a demonstration at the White House about the Alabama action, we decided to go. I found some old paints and painted a picture of a Confederate Battle Flag—a valiant flag for which we have love and respect, for the South, too, fought for freedom. But underneath the flag on the big card, I lettered in the same red: CIVIL RIGHTS IN THE C.S.A.!

So, carrying our placard tacked onto a stick, we went to the demonstration, along with maybe a couple of thousand others, both black and white. People shouted, "Freedom! Freedom!" and we sang. Some of them looked at my card with a scowl until they took it all in, and then they smiled. One big black man said, "Right on, sister!" The great moment for Richard and me was when we all joined hands and sang "We Shall Overcome." I had chills going up and down my back, as Richard said later he did, and, at the end, I had tears in my eyes.

Then on Friday we borrowed Daddy's car and drove across the Bay Bridge to Richard's house, Redrock, on the Eastern Shore. I had never been there, though I had met his parents at his Uncle John's house in Falls Church and also in England when they came over to see us. The house is an old rambling frame house with long double galleries on the river side. It is set on a small rise of ground at a bend in one of the wide tidal rivers, surrounded by many acres of land, with no other house near. The name Redrock comes from a large reddish-hued boulder near the house that is unlike anything in that part of the country. There has been great speculation about how it came there, some maintaining that it is a meteorite and others saying Nonsense.

We were warmly received at Redrock, not only by Richard's parents but by his brother, Roger, who is my age, and his little sister, Cindy, who is a darling. During our stay we did a lot of riding, sometimes with Roger, to some of Richard's special places, and on Sunday we rode across the fields to the little Episcopal church, St Peter's, while the rest of the family came by car. We also spent some rather chilly hours on the river in Richard's old sloop. Not far up river from Redrock is a house called Tally-Ho where Richard's closest boyhood friend, Jim Cosby lived. Unfortunately, Jim was away in the Navy, so I could not meet him, but Richard entertained me while we sailed with tales of mischief and adventure he and Jim had got into. Once they had landed on an uninhabited island off the mouth of the river and had failed somehow to tie the painter securely. When they came back from exploring in the woods, the boat was gone, and they had had to spend a cold and hungry night on the island. Naturally, their families were frantic and were not cheered when somebody found the sloop and brought it to Redrock. It was not, in fact, until mid-morning that Richard and Jim, who had built a fire to make smoke, were found by a searching fisherman.

The Selma troubles were still going on while we were at Redrock, with federal troops alerted and most anything possible. Richard's parents, while believing that the position of the Negroes must be bettered, do not think that the Reverend Mr King should be going about it the way he is doing. Richard and I tended to be rather circumspect about our sympathies, although he once at dinner remarked that there might be worse ways than Mr King's.

All in all, it was a happy visit, and the Vallance table was always groaning with food. I felt that I knew Richard better after seeing where he first fell off his pony at the age of five and where he was caught in a squall with Jim on the river and overturned. I even met the girl he had his first date with—she was at church and is now married to someone else. She wouldn't have been right for Richard anyway. There was a good deal of talk about our Oxford accents, which are actually not so pronounced but are still a bit different to the Eastern Shore speech. All the while we were there the moon was waxing towards the full, and the last night we were at Redrock we saddled the horses and had a somewhat eerie ride along the river in moonlight.

The next day we drove, not to D.C.—Daddy was in New York anyhow—but to my grandmother's house near Culpeper, Virginia, for a night. Her house, too—where Daddy grew up—is white and rambling, though without the double galleries of Redrock. Since she lives so near to Georgetown, she would have been hurt if we had not come. Besides, we love her and wanted to see her—and we wanted just to be there where Richard and I have some happy memories. So, once again, a huge dinner—we shall have to diet when we get away from loving families and ocean liners. Dinner was followed by a pleasant evening telling her about Oxford life and our adventures. Of course she knows a great deal about Oxford already, from the days when Daddy was up at Trinity.

The next morning early we said loving goodbyes to her and, with a lunch she had made for us, we set off for the mountains. This was our day for revisiting the Gateway to Heaven, the old name for the gap between two great mountains. But we include in the name the little meadow, our special place, from which we see the Gateway. As we went out the drive of Grandmother's house we wished we could stop and pluck a red rose, but of course it was only March.

But then—in 1961, almost four years ago—it was Maytime, and the red rambler roses at her gates, and all over Virginia, were burning like flames. At the hospital the machines and the doctors had finished with me. That very morning, with the doctors and nurses smiling, with Betsy come back for the occasion, with Daddy looking as though he had inherited a kingdom, and with Richard shooting me looks of smiling encouragement—that morning I had taken two little steps and one longish one into Daddy's arms. And the doctor, looking pretty happy himself, said wisely: "Take her home now."

I was taken down to the car, with my head erect. Then Daddy, with Richard in the back seat, drove straight to Grandmother's, no one talking very much—all full of thoughts, I expect—but with everybody's face aching with smiling. My thoughts were spinning: the whole world was reborn. One thing I thought over and over was: now I know that Richard and I are going on together. He had pledged we would anyway, and I believed him. But that was belief; this was knowing. Like actually seeing Christ the King after faithful believing.

Grandmother was waiting on the steps. Our smiles told all, and she leaned into the car to kiss me. Then Daddy got out and told us to take the car and enjoy the Maytime. So Richard came round and we drove away, stopping at the gates for the perfect, clear-red rose, and then driving on through the shining Virginian countryside, lovely with new green and red roses and tiny bright-blue indigo buntings flitting across the road like bits of sky. And ahead of us rose the Blue Mountains.

Soon we were climbing the road into the mountains, heading for our meadow where the spring trickles down. The day was fresh and shining, we were in love, and—I was winged! I would run and dance. Not today, but soon. My heart was bursting.

There was the meadow, unchanged. There we looked at the pure lines of the two mountains sweeping up to make the Gateway to Heaven. I told Richard to take my shoes and stockings off. And then he helped me out of the car, since my legs were still terribly weak. He had already put the rose in a winebottle on the ledge above the spring. And I stood there in the grass on trembling legs. I stood! Stood straight as a pine tree, with the Virginian sky arching overhead. Then I walked, as I was determined to do in this place, walked through the sweet young grass—I who had not walked a step since I was five. This was Wingsday. A few steps in the grass. And then, still standing, though Richard was holding me up, we kissed, there beside the spring and the rose at the Gateway to Heaven.

Sitting in that grass, later in that same exultant winged summer, I wrote how it all was, a poem about the coming of wings.

Once you whispered: I'd give me!
And the day grew still with the holy gift
Of generous love. The winebottle rose
Blazed in that silence, and your eyes
Were grave and glorious with that troth.
My grace was to accept your pledge,
Go hand in hand. And in that clasp
There was the glory of our wings.

Miracle in the altered air.
Girlhood charged with the wonder of spring.
Loving past all reality,
Astonished by bliss, all-over bliss,
Like free-fall bathing in sun-soft air,
All crazy sweetness, hand in hand
Among red roses: blithe in Maytime
And morning and a thousand hours.

There was a moment of seriousness that day, the day of wings, that foreshadowed the poem. I told Richard of the conviction that had grown in me during those long weeks in hospital that, if I did stand and walk, it would be because our merciful and loving Christ had accepted Richard's pledge, knowing in eternity that it was for ever, to go hand in hand with me even without wings—and *I* had accepted and believed. "Somehow, love, you made me winged," I said, smiling a little.

Tears came into your eyes, and you reached over and took my hand, but you didn't say anything for a minute or two. Just held my hand. Then you murmured, "May will always come in for me with a flutter of wings."

All that glorious summer after Richard had been graduated at Holywell—all that summer of a thousand hours we stayed there at Grandmother's, exploring the green countryside and driving often to our mountain meadow, always with a rose. I call it a meadow, but really it's a glade. Or a meadow for deer. Anyway, it was our place, part of the Gateway to Heaven. And we dwelt at the gateway to heaven in every sense that winged summer: we lived with joy, thanking the Most High. Every day I would walk a little farther. Then I began, a little, to run and climb tiny slopes. The sound of that gurgling little spring, trickling away unnoticed as we read or ate or talked, was part of our lives. One night— it was Midsummer's Night—we stayed up there in our mountain meadow until morning, always about to go but never quite doing it because we were so happy under the moon and stars. At last the stars paled, and the light grew, and we saw what we shall never forget—dawn in the Gateway to Heaven, the mountains edged with flame.

Always that summer we brought books and lunches up there with us —always chicken sandwiches and my grandmother's apple pie, the best apple pie that ever was. So hundreds of hours in our meadow. Hundreds of pieces of pie, also.

And now—four years later, on our way to Hawaii—on this bright, mild March day we had chicken sandwiches in the old way and four wedges of that apple pie, though we had to supply a red rose in our imagination. When we came to the meadow I ran round it twice, while Richard watched smiling lazily, and then I made an enormous leap right into the spot where we had always sat by the spring. We had our chicken sandwiches there today, too, and the first two pieces of pie. The spring trickled with the same sound, and the mountains of the Gateway were just as pure of line. After lunch we had a drink of the cold, clean water. Then, standing where we had stood on Wingsday, we stood, remembering, and kissed with all our love. The years shrank away to nothing. We could hardly believe that what was then but a dream, going off to Oxford, had come true.

Then we drove away, holding hands. As the day drew on towards evening, we wended our way downwards, eating our reserve pieces of apple pie. It was twilight when we drove through the farm country and a great full moon rose ahead of us, making a perfect ending for our day, although we wished that we might hear one whippoorwill calling to his distant lady love.

When we got to Georgetown, Daddy had been home for about an hour, so we all three had a late supper in the study. Daddy had been somewhat uneasy, as had Jolly, about me going back to Hawaii, because of what happened there before. But now, knowing that I was comfortable about it—and knowing that Richard would be there— Daddy, at least, had come to feel that it was a very good thing. So it was an altogether cheerful little midnight supper. Afterwards I went into the drawing-room to have one more look at the picture of my light-hearted mother.

Next morning early Daddy took us to the airport and with his usual generosity pressed a cheque upon me; and then we went aboard the aircraft. A few hours later we were in Frisco, whence we sailed the same evening under grey skies out through the Golden Gate. We stood shivering on the upper deck while the liner's hoarse whistle blew and the land receded into night.

The voyage has been very pleasant. There is more of boredom in six hours on an aircraft than in six days on a ship. And in the timeless days on shipboard, suspended as it were between the place one has left behind and the place ahead, it is possible to see one's life with a detachment from place that is unique. If the great ships yield to aircraft, our lives will be impoverished.

The ocean has been, day by day, getting bluer and bluer as we move south, and in the last day or two flying fish have appeared and with them the long trade-wind clouds. I feel the mood of the Islands creeping over me again. We have met some pleasant people, particularly Mr and Mrs Sawyer, who are both archeologists connected to the Metropolitan. They and we are at the Captain's table—we because of some rumour about our Aphrodite find, perhaps. I myself am feeling rather cold towards the genial Captain, for, having heard a man in the saloon talking about being on the bridge, we asked the Purser to arrange our going up there; and he told us this morning that, while Richard would be welcome, the Captain thinks it's bad luck to have a female on his bridge. Can such a silly superstition still exist in the world? Bad luck, indeed! *Windrush* didn't sink, I noticed. Anyhow, I have a plan against the Captain.

I see that Richard must have finished his letters, for he is reading a science-fiction book that I am just waiting to get my eyes into. There is nothing else about this voyage so far that I need say. No dramatic events —perhaps because I wasn't on the bridge. Hiss!

This is the last night before Honolulu. Consequently there is to be a grand dinner and then a gala dance with free champagne, courtesy of the steamship line. We have decided not to go to the dance, even though I have an evening gown, old but dear because everybody proposed to me in it. We don't feel in the mood for a dance and consider champagne the most overrated of wines anyhow. But we decide to dress for dinner.

So, as the second gong for dinner sounds, Richard is impeccable in a white mess jacket and black evening trousers and I am in my pale-yellow gown. As we descend the broad carpeted stairs from the main saloon to the dining saloon, I holding firmly to Richard's strong arm so as not to trip and dive spectacularly into someone's soup, I notice that one of two young Stanford men we know has his fork stopped halfway to his mouth and his gaze on me. I am pleased—my gown is still working. I smile at him.

At our table the Captain and Mr Sawyer and Mr Phillips all rise, and when we are seated I am told how lovely I look: in rather a fatherly way by Mr Sawyer, whose wife is beside him; more emphatically by Mr Phillips, whose wife is on their sugar plantation in Kauai; and very bluffly and bravely indeed by the Captain, who has no wife. I consider forgiving him but do not. The waiter gives us champagne and brings soup.

Mr Sawyer, across from me, begins a tale of an archeological dig in Syria. He and Mrs Sawyer highly approve of us, Richard for being a recognised scholar, even in so recent a period as mediaeval and renaissance England, and me for being a fledgling Grecian. They know of course about the head of Aphrodite and the speculation about the locus of the find—one school urging Egypt and a late date, the other Asia Minor—and Mr Sawyer has hinted that really Asia Minor is much more likely, isn't it?

The Captain is bored with archeological talk, but, quite apart from my genuine affection for the Sawyers, I have no sympathy for the Captain. When Mr Sawyer ends his tale and sits back beaming, I ask a question about ancient superstitions. Mrs Sawyer, who is expert in this area, answers my question and speaks amusingly of a number of odd beliefs.

There is a slight pause, and then, just as the Captain is about to launch some hearty witticism, I say in a clear voice, "What astonishes me, Mrs Sawyer, is the *persistence* of superstition into the modern age. Among half-educated persons, of course. You are no doubt aware of the barbaric superstitions concerning women—for instance, the belief that if a woman stepped over a spear lying on the ground, the spear would be mysteriously weakened and would have to be destroyed. Now, would you believe me if I told you that I personally know of a ship captain who actually believes that a woman on his bridge would bring bad luck?"

I can tell that Richard is repressing a smile; and the Captain is getting very red. Mrs Sawyer glances at me and then at him, and she smiles.

"Surely not!" she says. "Unbelievable! Surely it must be in some very backward region. But I am most interested. I'm writing a book, you know, about ancient superstition; and this primitive survival might make an interesting paragraph. Where did you come across this captain?"

Richard here interjects, "Captain, have you ever encountered this sort of childish superstition? I realise, of course, that none of the skippers on *this* line would hold such backward beliefs. Would they? I'm afraid that most people wouldn't want to travel on a ship with a superstitious Captain, if it got about."

"Very bad publicity!" says Mr Phillips.

"Ahem! Garumph!" says the Captain, very red-faced, indeed. "No, no! Not on this line! But all this reminds me that I've been meaning to invite you ladies to visit the bridge—no superstition on this ship, ha, ha! How about you, Mrs Vallance? Mrs Sawyer? The men, too, of course."

"Why, thank you, Captain!" I say. "How very nice of you. Perhaps in the morning. Mrs Sawyer—I've just remembered that that reference—the superstitious captain, you know—has to do with a Japanese sampan captain. That wouldn't help you, would it?"

She looks at me with a twinkle in her eye. "No," she says. "In that case it really wouldn't help."

"That reminds me," says Mr Sawyer, who has missed all this. "The Syrians had a curious belief about snakes. It seems that they had the souls of women . . ."

On second thought, *did* he miss what was going on?

As we go up the steps, Richard murmurs, "Well rowed, Lady Margaret Hall!"

In the saloon, men are putting up Hawaiian decorations—grass skirts and shields—in preparation for the dance. Having decided to have coffee, we thread our way among these objects, stepping over them, to reach chairs. As we seat ourselves, I see one of the men pick up a spear, which bends and then breaks in the middle. Did I step over it?

Richard, who hasn't noticed—fortunately perhaps—says for me to order while he whips back to our room for his book. After I've ordered, one of the Stanford boys, George, pauses to tell me how beautiful I look. He is shocked when I mention that we aren't going to the dance. He urges me to change my mind, believing perhaps that his urging will be decisive, despite my having a husband. Not many girls, I expect, have said no to him. I say no, and Richard returns. George goes off. I tell Richard.

He laughs. "George is getting into practice for American suburban life—affairs, you know. Maybe you are missing out on a good thing. If you divorced me and married him, you could live in a suburb with lonely ranchhouses eaves-to-eaves to each other and wall-to-wall carpeting, and have affairs and divorces in the usual way."

"Oh, you mean the 'good life'," I say with a shudder. "It ain't for me, pal."

"I hardly thought so," he says. "Thank God! —Hush up now! I've got to find out if the space liner lost in the time-warp will ever get home. Only twenty pages."

I hush and occupy myself with various thoughts. I wonder whether I have the power to make spears break. Might be useful some day.

Finally Richard says, "Ah!" and closes the book. "You can have it now," he says. "Why don't we go out on deck?"

It's a moonless night with a million stars overhead and glinting in the dark waves. The bow wave, white and faintly luminous, swishes continually away from the ship.

We stand at the rail for a few minutes and then go to our cabin. I want to find out about the space liner, but I feel guilty about leaving the beauty of the night. Was it Emerson who said that, if the stars were visible only one night in a thousand years, the whole world would lie out on its back that whole night. But some people never look.

In the room we take off our evening things and read, very tranquil and comfortable. We can hear music from the ship's band in the distance. Once we get into a big discussion of space travel, which fascinates us both, and we create a little fantasy about our having a small, really advanced space yacht. Anti-grav of course and faster-than-light drive. We name it *Starrush*. After our first tour of the solar system, before we left for the stars, we would bring *Starrush* to London and land, light as a feather, by the Round Pond in Kensington Gardens, where we would give interviews to the *Telegraph* and *The Times* and perhaps the Queen would come to tea. And a little plate on the hull would say: "This vessel was constructed by the West Dorsetshire Bicycle and Rocket Shop."

We laugh, and then decide to go out on deck again to see if we can see the loom of Honolulu. In the corridors the music is louder, and we pause to listen to part of a Beatles song. On deck George is throwing up champagne at the rail, and we don't stay out long.

Mary writes upon the landfall and making port

I am awakened by the sound of voices on the deck outside our port. I bounce up, nude since we slept that way last night, and part the curtain a crack and peer out. I see a coast and tangled green foliage in the distance.

I fall upon Richard, crying, "Val! Val! Wake up! Land ho! We're here!"

He smiles radiantly, leaps up and applies his eye to the crack. "Dear, dear, dear!" he says. "Long way off." He collapses again. His eyes close.

I reach for the water glass and pour some water into his naval. He suffers this. The small lake in his navel quivers and rises and falls with his breathing. I take a pen from the bedside table and dip it. The small lake is now a small blue ocean. I contemplate it. Then I tear two minute snips of paper and launch them upon the blue sea.

"What are you doing, crazy girl?" says Richard with his eyes shut.

"I'm having a navel battle," I say. "Look! Don't move! HMS *Victory* is about to open fire!"

He opens his eyes and lifts his head and looks.

"Ahhh!" I say. "*Victory* has rammed the Frenchman! It's all over!"

"A mad wife!" he says. "You *are* mad, you know. Quite mad!" He sits up. The ocean spills over. "See?" he says. "A blue navel. —Good morning, love!"

"Just remember," I say. *"Your* navel has just had what may be the first navel battle in the history of the world. And you owe it all to me! Where in the annals—"

"Oh, do shut up!" he says with a grin. "Nut! Crazy girl!"

At breakfast the Purser comes with the Captain's compliments and an invitation to me to come up on the bridge. "Er, what did you do to him?" the Purser adds.

"White female magic," I say with a grin. When the Purser goes, we decide to spare the Captain. "After all," I say, "he might get so nervous that he'd run the ship onto the rocks, and that would prove it."

We finish packing and go out on deck. The ship is steaming slowly westward along the south coast of Oahu towards Honolulu harbour. Shoreward we see the surf, deep blue and foaming white. Beyond the shore with its graceful coconut palms, the land slopes up towards shadowy mysterious mountains with their heads lost in massed trade-wind clouds, where perhaps the ancient Polynesian gods still live. My skirt billows as a breeze catches it. I feel a stab of joy—joy to be returning to the Islands winged.

Mr Phillips, the planter, comes by and points out Koko Head that we're just coming up to, with Diamond Head soon to be in sight. When Richard comments on the pronunciation, of Makapuu—Ma-ka-POO-oo—Mr Phillips says to remember that it's always the next-to-last syllable that is stressed. And, he adds, *a* always like the one of *father, e* like the one in *obey, i* as in *pique,* and *u* like *rule* or an *oo* sound. "A simple rule of thumb, isn't it?" he adds. "I'm always running through it for mainland friends."

We thank him and he says, "I must go below to pack, so I'll say my aloha now—aloha to the Islands—welcome." He goes off.

"Saves me telling you," I say. "Look! Diamond Head is showing." I see the Captain looking down from the bridge, and give him a friendly Smile #3.

The ship docks in Honolulu harbour with the band playing "Aloha Oe," and there is a flower *lei* for every passenger. We go ashore to a waiting car that we'd laid on in advance, and tip the steward who brings our cases to the car for us.

Richard gets behind the wheel and says, "You navigate. Where away?"

"Well," I say. "We can try to find Moani ridge and the house and get settled in. That's a long way off towards Pearl Harbor. Or, since it is still morning, we can go to Waikiki Beach, the other way, back towards Diamond Head. Why don't we? That's why we wore our bathing suits under. We've got all day."

"Okay, Waikiki," he says. "Which way?"

"I ain't quite sure," I say. "It's been a long time. Anyhow, turn right."

"Right it is," he says, starting the car, while I breathe the fragrance of my lei.

Honolulu—everything familiar yet strange. I see streets I remember—Nuuanu, King—and the shops with the marquees built out over the sidewalks against the swift tropical showers brought by the trade winds. On the streets the same colourful mixture—Oriental, Caucasian, Polynesian in endless combinations and permutations, with dashes of Melanesian and Micronesian—and lots of white-clad sailors and khaki-clad soldiers. Some of these give me the eye, and I hear a long-drawn-out whistle.

"Imagine me!" I say. "A whistled-at girl in Honolulu! Think of that!"

Mary remembers Mercia

Waikiki—great hotels and palms on the right, fronting the famous beach and the sea; shops and residential side streets on the left, against the background of the mysterious mountains. And Diamond Head looming over all, on ahead.

Suddenly, unexpectedly, I am overwhelmed with the memory, the living presence almost, of Mercia. Tears spring to my eyes and roll down my cheeks. Mercia, so loving and so dear. I glance down at myself, and half expect to see—something different, something twisted and frail. Oh, Mercia, Mercia.

Richard glances at my tear-streaked face and swings off to the left onto a quieter street.

"It's Mercia!" I say in a trembling voice. "She—she's here! As though it were—were yesterday!" I cry harder.

Richard swings the car around and parks some distance from the boulevard but facing back towards it. There is a glimpse of the deep blue of the sea past a hotel. A palm shades us.

He sits there quietly, a comforting hand on my leg. My tears slacken.

"Tell me about it," he says in a peaceful voice. "I know a bit, of course. Partly from your father."

"Well," I say unsteadily. "I always knew we'd come to the Islands, some day. And I thought I'd tell you here, when we did. I—I didn't think it would be like this—it was all so long ago. But Waikiki—we were here first in a hotel. And it's not long ago at all! It's only yesterday! I almost expect to see her walking along this street, smiling . . ."

My heart stops. A slender figure comes round the corner, and for an instant . . . But it is someone else. I sit there, remembering.

Trade clouds sail overhead. There are island flowers upon my breast.

"It was when I was eleven," I say. "And Daddy was sort of frantic about my situation. It wasn't that I wasn't being taken care of, of course —he and Jolly did all they could. And a really good tutor, you know. But no friends my own age. How could there be? There wasn't any fun or play in my life at all—I hardly knew what they were. Just the books, you know. And then Daddy got this great idea of taking me on a trip to Hawaii and taking my cousin Mercia, too, to help take care of me."

"How old was she?" asks Richard.

"She had just finished her second year at Bryn Mawr," I say. "About as old as I am now. But I was only eleven—pale, bookish, not laughing much . . . and—well, she was just everything I was starved for. Light-hearted, funny, impulsive. And so warm-hearted and generous. She was pretty, too: big brown eyes and dark hair and slender. She seemed beautiful to me. But what I remember was her funniness. She made me laugh. I laughed and smiled all the time with her.

"Well, so we came, and we stayed here in Waikiki, at the Moana Hotel just down the street—I want us to go there later. And the two weeks Daddy had planned on were such a success—Mercia was always making me laugh—that Daddy was just delighted. So he got another great idea. He had to go back to Washington, but Mercia and I should stay on. Mercia agreed right away—she didn't mind staying out of college a year, she said. Daddy would pay for everything, of course. I've wondered since why Mercia agreed so easily. I have an idea from some little things she said that maybe there was a situation at college that she wanted to be away from; and then, too, there was me. I mean, she knew she was doing something pretty enormous for me. Well, there were about a million telephone calls—to Uncle Rob and Aunt Kate, to my doctor, to Bryn Mawr—and it was all arranged. Daddy is nothing if not persuasive. So then he found this little house for us, Umoani, the one we're going to tonight. He left us there and flew back to D.C., but he would come to see us about every six weeks."

"And you were happy?" murmurs Richard.

"It was the happiest time, those months, of my whole life, up to you and wings," I say. "It's funny, talking about being happy, considering the way I was, but—yes! I was incredibly happy! We lived in this queer little house on the Moani Ridge—*moani* means the scent of flowers, fragrance, drifting down the wind. And Umoani, the name we made up for the house—well, *u*, someone told us, was hill—so it would be fragrance drifting on the wind over a hill. So we lived there in Umoani, which was only three rooms and a big lanai or porch, and it was partly built on stilts over a pool. One went over a little bridge to the front door. And there were frog things, called bufos, in the pool and they croaked at night. And flowers. And yellow shower trees, leaning over the house and pool, dropping blossoms. We were always on the lanai, and it was like being outdoors."

"It sounds idyllic," says Richard.

"You'll see tonight," I say. "Oh, Val, I was so happy. We read poetry aloud, and laughed. It was all so gay! And I wrote a poem, my first poem. Do you want to hear my first poem, age eleven? I've saved it for telling you about Mercia and all."

"A poem I've never heard?" says Richard. "Yes, of course!"

I fumble in my bag, saying, "Mercia may have helped me with a word or two, but I really did write it. —Ah, here it is. Listen."

"Wait a minute," says Richard. He puts his arm around me and draws me to him and kisses me on both cheeks and both eyes. "Now read it," he says, smiling.

I smile back. "Here it is," I say.

YEARNINGS

Yearned to be a princess in a tower
  When a prince came gaily singing,
When I laughed and blushed and tossed a flower
  And golden castle bells were ringing . . .

Yearned to run out naked in the showers,
  The kiss of rain upon my breast,
Brushing cool damp petals of the flowers,
  Seeking out some tree-root nest . . .

"Not bad!" says Richard. "Especially the second, er, yearning. First one is bookish—you wouldn't have known what to do with a prince if he *did* come."

"No," I say. "I just thought I ought to want that. Still, when you did come riding . . . Anyway, the other . . . to run out in the rain, the quick bright rains of the Islands . . . or just to run . . . Well—I was telling you how it was—how happy I was! Mercia was so sweet. And for me—well, she was like life itself! I adored her! I suppose I had a crush on her, but what does that mean except that you love someone with all your heart?

And she loved me, too. She used to call me 'little owl'—because I was so solemn, you know. She would read to me and tell me stories. She was full of love, just by nature, I think; but it seems to me that I got to be sort of special to her. . . ."

"Here," says Richard, handing me a lighted cigarette. "Was there anything in particular to make you think so?"

"Well," I say. "Mostly it was just something I sensed. But one evening she was reading Keats to me—the 'Nightingale'—and, well, you remember the line about Ruth? How the nightingale's song is heard by her with her sad heart, 'when, sick for home, / She stood in tears amid the alien corn . . .' And when Mercia finished reading the poem and looked at me with a little smile, I said something like, 'I'm Ruth, and being sick for home is like longing to walk and run with you.' And Mercia got tears in her eyes and came running over and kissed me on the mouth. . . ."

"How did you feel about that?" asks Richard.

"Oh, Val!" I say. "It was pure heaven. I wanted her to kiss me again like that, but she never did. It was just that once. Well, anyhow . . . we had a car that Daddy had got us, and she would sort of hoist me into it, and we would drive around the island. And sometimes we would go to lonesome beaches, and she would get me down to the beach itself in the little folding wheelchair, and we'd sit there watching the big waves come in and making up stories . . . and she'd run into the water and have a swim—she was a good swimmer—and come back happy and wet. Sometimes we'd have a fire on the beach with the sound of the waves and the millions of stars . . . It was so lovely!"

There is a little silence, and I hear the palm tree rustle above us and smell the wild white ginger.

"And then?" murmurs Richard.

"And then it all came to an end," I say. "One of those afternoons on the beach. She was telling me some story about Tahiti she'd read—I don't remember what it was about, except that she was pronouncing *aloha* the way they would do, maybe, in Tahiti, with the 'l' changed to 'r'—*aroha*. And I would giggle every time she did it, because it sounded so funny. I had learned to giggle, somehow; and she would laugh, too. She had a very gay little laugh. So then she went for her swim, and when she started down to the beach, she said, '*Aroha,* owl dear! Till we meet again.' The song, you know—'Till we meet again.' So she said, '*Aroha,* owl dear! Till we meet again. O *aroha!*' And we both were laughing. And she walked down to the waves, and I was calling, '*Aroha,* O *aroha!*' after her, and laughing . . ."

I suddenly sob and pick up my lei and bury my face in it and cry. Richard strokes my hand lightly.

After a moment I go on in a choked voice: "She went down to the waves, walking so lightly. A big wave was just curling over and she dived through it and came up on the other side and waved. So she just swam about, waving every now and then and smiling. But she got farther and farther out. I know now that it was a current—we'd never been at that beach before, and of course there wasn't another soul anywhere in sight. And then she seemed to realise what was happening, because she started to swim hard towards the beach. She swam like that for a long time, but she didn't get a bit closer. And then she just seemed to give up . . . I thought she called out once. I thought she called out, 'Aroha, little owl!' And I was trying to crawl down the beach and crying . . ."

Richard makes a small sympathetic sound.

"That's all, really," I say. "I don't remember. I know it got to be night and stars. I suppose I was exhausted with crying and screaming. I remember some man carrying me. And then Daddy came and took me away. I don't even know where I was before Daddy came. I never saw our little house again. I remember hearing a man in another room saying that her body had been washed up on the black lava rocks somewhere."

Richard squeezes my hand a little, and then strokes it again.

"It was a long time ago," I say. "But it all came back. As though I'd seen her only yesterday, full of gaiety and—and life. And, also—well, the Islands! I love them! It was here that I was so happy, and, just because I was happy, I almost broke my heart with longing to be well, to be like Mercia . . . to run lightly down a beach, as she did. I—I could hardly *stand* it to be such a—a lump! Oh, I wanted to be winged and lovely . . . maybe so Mercia would love me. —And when she died—a second Disaster, really—it was like all the darkness closing in again, only worse than before. I was ill and almost out of my mind for a long time. And it was like the Islands had been drowned in the sea as well as Mercia. I wish you'd known her . . ."

"I wish so, too," he says gently. "At least, you've made me know her a little. I'm glad you've told me now—not before, I mean, and also not later. Now, at the beginning of the Islands. Are you glad, too? How are you feeling?"

"Happy," I say. "Happy and, well, peaceful. But, oh! I wish I could see her just once—now. And that she could know about wings and all. But, Val—everything's all right. And maybe she does know . . ."

We sit there peacefully for a little while longer. I listen to the palms rustling and look at the bit of blue sea past the hotel. Richard seems lost in his thoughts, fitting the story of Mercia, I expect, into all he knows about my childhood.

Mary continues her account of the first day

After a time we leave the car where it is and walk down to Waikiki Boulevard and along it. We stop in a shop and buy some beach towels as well as *tapa*-pattern shirts. Then we are on the famous beach at Waikiki, having stripped down to bathing suits. Diamond Head looms majestically to our left, and far out to sea the big waves begin to crest—this is the king surf—and rush foaming, cresting, towards the beach. A brawny Hawaiian beach boy goes by carrying a surfboard.

I give Richard a light spank and say, "Val can't catch Mary-the-flash!" I run rapidly down the beach with Richard in hot pursuit, to the accompaniment of a subdued cheer from four young men under a beach umbrella. When I feel that Mary-the-flash is about to be overtaken, I whirl towards the ocean and dive beneath a wave and swim out to sea. Then I feel myself seized round the hips. I turn just in time to see Richard take a deep breath, so I gulp one down too, just before he pulls me under. There, below the surface, our lips meet in a real if salty kiss. Is nice.

"Aha!" he says as we surface. "My woman does not escape me so easily!"

"Girl!" I say. "Or both."

We swim on out and attempt to ride the waves by swimming very fast towards shore until overtaken and lifted by a wave. But they always slide out from under us.

"Val! Val! Hullo!" cries a pleasant baritone voice. Two men with surfboards.

"Jim!" cries Richard in amazement. "Jim Cosby! What a place to meet! —Mary, this is my old friend, Jim Cosby. From Tally-Ho, just above Redrock. Jim, Mary, my wife."

Jim tosses black hair out of his eyes and smiles. "I've long wanted to know you, Mary. Val, we came out just to see if it really was you." He introduces his companion as we all tread water and the waves lift and lower us. The friend, an amiable blue eyed young man, is Bill Wingfield, who immediately suggests that we share their surfboards, pushing his towards me.

He steadies it while I crawl on, face down, as far forward as I can; then he crawls on, partly on top of me. Richard and Jim on the other one are paddling shoreward.

"Paddle, Mary!" says Bill. "As hard as you can."

We paddle. A wave passes beneath us, but it boosts our speed. The next one catches us, and we ride away on top of it very fast for about thirty yards, then slew round and turn over. We try it several times, and then I say I'm tired.

"Me, too," he says amiably. "And thirsty! How about a drink?"

"Love it!" I say, swimming shoreward, seeing the others sitting on the sand.

The four of us move up the beach to the terrace of the Outrigger Club where we have planters punches, and then sandwiches. Jim Cosby and Richard are full of reminiscences of the old days—hunting and sailing and, later, dating together. Some of the stories I've heard from Richard. They've not met since the Christmas of their last year of college —Jim being at Annapolis. Now he's a lieutenant (j.g.) in a destroyer, USS *Randolph*—better known as *"Rakish Randy"*—at Pearl Harbor; and Bill, a year or two behind him at the Academy, is an ensign. They say we must come and dine aboard.

We talk, too, about the Islands, and Bill, an enthusiastic skin diver, talks fascinatingly about the underwater beauties along the reefs. Finally, having changed out of our suits in the rest rooms, we say we must go.

They stroll back to our car with us, Richard and Jim in the lead, still filling each other in on the last few years, and I follow with Bill. He is not so tall as Jim but very strong and muscular, and, I learn, a Californian. He remarks that he had meant to take me to dinner if I were not attached to my pursuer on the beach.

"I suppose the Navy trains men to make quick decisions," I say. "Even if wrong."

"Mostly a matter of shape," he says with a grin. "One look at the lines of a vessel, and you know whether to chase her or sheer off."

"Of course," I say. "But a fine little merchant ship might have a cruiser escort lurking in the mist. Then you'd get sunk, wouldn't you?"

He gives me a quizzical look, and then we are all at the car. We give them our telephone number and make vague plans for meeting again soon.

As we drive off, Richard says, "Jim's a civilised sort of chap, isn't he? Bill's a good sort, too—though perhaps a bit sorry that you aren't unattached. —Mary, are we on the right road? We didn't come this way."

"That's all right," I say. "Right direction—the mountains on our right. It's all coming back. Here one always says *makai*—towards the sea, and *mauka*—mountainwards."

We drive on, talking of the Islands. Suddenly I cry, "Oh, stop! Stop!

Go into that parking place—that *puka*. A *puka* is any kind of a hole. Anyway, see that little street over there? It should be—yes, it is!—Mynah Bird Lane. I have no idea how I remembered it, I was only there five or six times. Well, in there lives, or used to, a big fat lovely Hawaiian lady named Momi. I told you about her once, remember? Supposed to be descended from King Kamehameha, not to mention an English Duke in some irregular way. Still, a very high-born lady."

"Is she the one with the little girl?" says Richard. "The one who used to tell you about the little people in the mountains?"

"The Menehune," I say. "No, Momi's daughters were grown up. The one with the little girl was Iolani—the one who was a hula dancer. About twenty-eight. Married a soldier at the end of the war with Japan and went to New Jersey with him. Then she ran away—she hated it or him!—and came home. And Momi's other daughter that we knew was Makaleha—sort of a Polynesian Beulah, lively and merry. Anyhow, the whole family, especially Momi, sort of adopted Mercia, and me, too. We'd come here and eat poi and fish, and Iolani would dance while everybody clapped to keep time."

"Did you ever write?" says Richard. "After—well, after you went home?"

"No," I say. "I didn't even know their last name. Also, when Daddy took me home and Mercia was dead, it was all like some beautiful dream that . . . was over. But now I'm longing to see them. If they're still here. And still alive. Momi is probably in her sixties now. Let's go in, shall we?"

"All right," he says. "I'd like to." He starts the car and turns into Mynah Bird Lane.

"It's at the end, I think," I say. We pass a couple of ramshackle houses. "Yes," I say. "That's it." The lane ends and a path goes up to the wide lanai of a big frame house, much in need of paint where it can be seen through the scarlet bougainvillea and hibiscus. Also scattered about are two yellow shower trees and a big poinciana. A tiny naked brown girl pursues a little boy clad only in a t-shirt. As Richard turns the car off, we can hear the chattering of mynah birds in the trees.

"The real Hawaii!" I say. "Or, at least, realer than Waikiki. Put on one of your leis again and come on."

We go up the path to the wide-open door and knock, and a slender girl with a creamy complexion and long dark hair down her back appears.

"Iolani!" I exclaim.

The girl looks astonished. "Oh, no!" she says. "I am Leilani. My mother was Iolani, but she is dead. Did you know her, in New Jersey?''

"No—here!" I say. "Leilani, do you remember Mercia? And the little girl who couldn't walk? That was me. Remember—you told me about the Menehune?''

"Oh, I remember!" she cries. "The poor little one with the head that leaned over—and you are well! And Mercia, so beautiful, drowned in the sea. Oh, come in! Come in! Momi is here, and Makaleha, my aunt, comes behind you."

We whirl around to see a huge brown woman coming along the path smiling, treading lightly despite her bulk.

"Makaleha!" cries Leilani. "It is the little twisted girl who was with Mercia!"

"Oh," says Makaleha. "The little Mary! Malia! And you stand on your legs! And hold your head up! Oh, we are glad to see you!" She throws her arms around me and kisses me. "Come in, come in to Momi!"

"This is Richard Vallance," I say. "Or Val. My husband."

They extend warmth and welcome to him, and we all go into the big airy house to Momi, who does not look much different to what I remember, except for the greying of the once-black hair. She is even bigger than Makaleha. There are more explanations and introductions, and I am hugged to Momi's bosom, too. They lament Mercia's death, and tell us that Iolani went back to her husband in New Jersey, leaving Leilani, and she died there in less than a year. It is plain that all of them are about to regard us as family—long-lost, but still family.

"We must have a luau for Mary and Val," says Momi. "A luau because the little Mary has come back to Hawaii nei. And the Mamos will come." The Mamos, it is explained, are three Hawaiian women, all huge, all named Mamo, who live together and delight in the planning and arrangements of the outdoor feasts called luaus.

Momi presses us to stay with them, but we explain that we have rented the little house on the Moani Ridge where I had lived with Mercia, so we are told warmly that we must come many times to see them. Momi is sad that Iolani is not here to know that I am well.

"I wish she were here to dance the *hula*," I say. "All these years I have remembered the beautiful dances of Iolani. I used to cry because I could not ever dance like her."

"Leilani dance the hula, too," says Makaleha. "Just as good. She has been to the secret school—the hula school—and now she teaches the hula there. Leilani! You dance, no?"

Leilani stands, lovely as a willow, and her hips sway. Her hands make incredibly graceful movements. She murmurs, "The trade wind over the ocean . . . and now the rains come . . . and the palm trees sway and bend . . . and now the clearing and the rainbow . . ." All these things the lovely hula hands delineate, while the slender body sways and the graceful hips circle. Meanwhile, Makaleha and Momi sway on their chairs and their hands clap lightly. Soon I, too, sway and clap.

Leilani stops and smiles. "You like, yes?" she says.

"I never dreamed the hula was so beautiful and said so much," says Richard, considerably moved. "Thank you very much, Leilani."

"Oh, Leilani!" I cry. "My thanks, too. I can't tell you how much I wish I could do that. All this—it's like coming home. Like something in my blood . . ."

"You Island girl!" says Momi firmly. "You kama'aina!"

I explain to Richard that *kama'aina* really means native-born but is sometimes used for the old Hawaii hand, one who belongs to the Islands.

We say now that we must go, promising to return soon, and with many alohas and waves we drive away. I am utterly delighted to find them all again.

Heading westward—*ewa* of Nuuanu—we pass through colourful, flimsy Chinatown and eventually get onto the highway that goes between the canefields, parallel to the south coast, to Pearl Harbor, passing by the gates of the big Air Force base, Hickam Field. At the Pearl Harbor Navy Yard, the sentry allows us to enter when I say that we are just going to the Sub Base and out again. At one point the road passes near the harbour itself, and we see a great many vessels scattered across its placid waters, including the huge bulk of an aircraft carrier.

At the Sub Base gate we are waved through, and the sentry on his little island snaps to poker stiffness and salutes with a click of his heels. Shouldn't we respond somehow? Hoist the flag? Then I perceive that he is in fact saluting the car behind us, which flies the three stars of a vice-admiral. Nevertheless I give him a snappy salute back, and he looks as shocked as a poker can.

Richard is laughing. "Next thing," he says, "you'll be joining the Navy to get saluted. I suppose you thought that salute was for you—admiral!"

"Of course it was!" I say in a gravelly voice. "Attention! Man the guns! Shoot!—I mean, Fire! Full speed ahead!" I salute again and say, "Clear for action, Mr Vallance!"

Three sailors walking towards the gate whistle. I give them a stern admiralish look, and one of them yells, "Hey, baby!"

"Get sunk!" I cry and zoom past.

We turn off on a narrow road towards the mountains and come to a fork with a sign that points to Aiea one way and Moani the other. Then we come to the small village of Moani, where we stop and buy milk and groceries, and follow the road winding up the mountain. After a false turn, I find the lane that leads into Umoani, to which we already have the key. We park the car, and there is the little house, just as it always was. Shower trees bend over it, and its big screened lanai and the footbridge are reflected in the pool.

A cat sits at the edge of water. "Ah," I say. "A *popoki*. Here, *popoki!* Puss, puss! Poki, poki!" But it moves off. We have disturbed its fishing, and it is disgusted.

We go over the little bridge. Inside everything is spotless. There is a big bed on the lanai and screens that can be placed around it. We unload our groceries and cases. From the lanai we can look down the mountain and across the Ewa Plain northwest to the Waianae Range and the flat top of Mount Kaala, the highest on this island. I am astonished at the way names, unthought of for years, come flooding back. The other mountains above Honolulu—the mountains that we are in—are the Koolau Range.

I sit down on the bed on the lanai. Richard, thoughtful as always, murmurs that he'll stroll about a bit, and goes out. For an instant it seems to me that no time has elapsed since I last sat here. When Mercia and I left that afternoon, never to return—until today—the yellow blossoms were drifting down into the pool, just as they are doing now. Almost I expect to hear the gay little laugh from the other room and the sweet voice saying, "Ready in a moment, little owl!" And surely that was a rustle, a light step, in there? My eyes blur, and I whisper, "Mercia?"

Then there is a heavier step on the bridge, and Richard returns. My own dear Richard! He glances at me and comes over and sits beside me, putting an arm about my waist. I bury my face in your shoulder for a moment, and then we kiss. I am back in the reality of now.

"I love you," I say, and we sit there peacefully.

After awhile I stir and say, "Okay. I'm in business again. The question is, do we dine here on bread and milk and beans, or out?"

"I think I'd like to go out," says Richard. "By the way, where are we going to sleep—here or the bedroom?"

"Oh, here!" I say. "Much nicer! And let's go to the Royal Hawaiian Hotel—very grand, or at least it used to be—for dinner. Just the two of us. And listen: didn't Lewis Hughes send you the name of some club? The Hula Club, where they do the real old-time hula—not the haole hula. We might go there, too?"

"I've got it in my pocket," he says. "What's *haole?*"

"Paleface," I say with a grin. "White race. That's us. And you are a *malihini*— newcomer—whereas I, at least according to Momi, am *kama'aina.* All clear, *kane?*"

"All clear so far," he says. "Except that Makaleha called you Malia?"

"Oh," I say. "Mary in Hawaiian speech. Richard would be Likeke—I asked Momi when you were talking to Leilani. And *aloha*—that magic word!—means both hullo and goodbye, both in a loving way. Don't ever say *aloa,* by the way; it's *a-lo-ha. Aloha oe* is farewell to thee, and *aloha nui* is much aloha—lots of love—and *aloha nui nui* is still more."

Richard hops into the shower, and then I do. An hour and a half later two well-dressed *haoles* are dining sedately on the terrace of the Royal Hawaiian. Over my left shoulder Richard can see the dark silhouette of Diamond Head. There is no moon, but the sky is ablaze with stars, seemingly hung lower than in northern latitudes, and there is a shimmer of starlight on the restless sea. We sit beside a low parapet, over which is the beach, not far from where we were this afternoon. On the other side of us is the line of big open doors leading into the enclosed dining room, where we can see huge murals of native Hawaiian scenes. At one end of the room Hawaiian girls in grass skirts are dancing the hula. A man sings and at intervals the girls cry plaintively, "E-a, e-a . . . e-a." The night air is soft.

In the Island intonation, I say, "You like? Yes?"

"I like—yes," he says.

"You good-kind *haole,"* I say. "Soon Hawaii nei will be yours as well as mine."

"And not long," he says. "After Leilani's dance and the welcome from them all."

"I can't get over finding them like that," I say. "And so unchanged, after ten years—except for Iolani being dead. And as you say, the welcome."

Richard picks up his glass of wine and takes a mouthful. "Shouldn't this be coconut milk or something?"

"Probably," I say. "Actually there is, or used to be, some sort of a native drink made from the *ti* root—t-i not t-e-a—called *okolehao.* The name means 'iron bottom' or something, so I expect it was pretty rough."

As the waiter serves our dessert of fresh pineapple and papaya,

Richard says, "I'm already beginning to sense—and like—the Hawaiian mood. Astonishing, isn't it, that it can be so different to the Mediterranean mood? The same ingredients, I mean: sun and blue sea and balmy air."

"Yes," I say. "And both different to, say, South Florida—or honky-tonk Southern California. Traditions and history make the difference—think of Greece with its memory of Aphrodite and Pan and the old high civilisation. Hawaii has old gods, too."

"Has to be a strong tradition though," he says. "What's left of Spain in California?"

"Oh, it's *all* going," I say sadly. "Commercialising—out to ruin all that is old and fragile. Coco-colonisation. They'll make this a Miami Beach, damn them."

"No one can say no," says Richard. "But let's not think about it tonight."

I agree that tonight isn't the time for meditation on the ruin of everything. I look seawards, aware of flower fragrance drifting on the wind, and even in starlight seeing the combers far out racing in. I see an exceptionally bright star, low in the southern sky, that actually traces a slender star path over the heaving waters.

"That star path," I say, pointing. "It's like our life, shimmering, dancing . . ."

"Hand in hand," says Richard. "Always."

We return to the car and find Beretania Street. Since the name is the Hawaiian version of Britannia, dating from their effort to give themselves to Queen Victoria, it causes me to essay a brief burst of "Beretania rules the waves!" This in turn causes Richard to say fondly, "Ass!"

We find a lighted door between two dark shops with "Hula Club" on the frosted glass.

"Look!" says Richard, parking. "That girl coming out. Ask her if we can go in."

The girl walks by. I do not speak.

"Oh, Mary! You little coward!" says Richard. "Why didn't you ask her?"

"I didn't want to scare her," I say with a grin.

"Liar!" he says, also smiling. "Brave Mary! Ha!—Well, let's go in."

There is a narrow stair and from above we hear a babble of voices. At the top, we are about to be denied admission when, to our delight, Leilani waves from a table and calls that she will sponsor us. She is with a dark-haired, powerful man, bronzed by sun and Polynesian blood, whom she introduces as Kahana, and who is also Kenneth Lawrence, professor of literature at the university—and, she adds, her fiancé.

We join them as urged and drinks are ordered, and we all begin to get properly acquainted. Leilani, herself, is at the university in her last year. Her great love—apart from Kahana—is the hula, which she dances professionally under the name Leilani Moana, because, she says, she does not wish to use her father's name. "He was the G.I. who was unkind to my mother. I think that is why she die when she went back to him in New Jersey. She thought she ought to go; but she would not take me, to that. She made me stay with Momi."

A Chinese girl comes up and murmurs something. Leilani says, "Please excuse me for a few minutes. I promise to dance."

"Moana?" says Richard. "Not the same as Moani Ridge, where we live?"

"No, no," says Kahana. *"Moana* is the ocean, and *moani* is the fragrance drifting down the breeze. Very different. —Oh, you knew that, Mary?"

"Yes," I say. "Mercia and I—you know about Mercia? Yes, well, we sort of made up a name for our house—Umoani. Like the flower fragrance drifting over the hilltop."

Kahana chuckles. "Hill is *puu,"* he says. "And *u* is breast. So Umoani is more the meaning of the scent drifting across a breast. Still, that is not so bad."

"Not at all!" says Richard laughing. He grins at me. "Even better," he adds.

A door beside the bar opens and Leilani in grass skirt and a twist of tapa over her breast comes out. She is barefoot with her hair down her back, and she wears a lei.

She dances, and a man strums the ukulele. Many of the people sway with the music and beat their palms together softly. Sometimes someone sings a line or two. Then the dancing ends with a rain-in-palmtrees patter of applause.

"Oh, Leilani," I say. "That was lovely! I wanted to jump up and do it, too, just as I did when I was eleven."

"Then why don't you learn?" she says. "Are you serious? Do you want to do it enough to dance a little every day at the school?"

"But, Leilani!" I say. "Isn't that the secret school—just for Hawaiians? How could I? I'm a *malihini.* And *haole."*

"No, no!" she says. "You are not *malihini*—you were here long ago. Not even *haole,* in a way. Momi made Mercia, and you, too, part of our family—daughters—and that is a thing with meaning, for Momi has the blood of kings. That means nothing—and everything." She puts her slender hand on my arm. "Today, at our house, you said being there and the dancing were like something in your blood—and Momi, Momi who knows, said, 'You are Island girl come home.' Is it so?"

"Yes, yes," I say. "It was almost the only bright time in my childhood. You know how I was. Yes, it *is* coming home. Somehow."

"Yes," says Leilani. "Momi say so. So—we are family . . . sisters . . ." She smiles.

Impulsively I lean over and kiss her. "Yes, sisters," I say.

"So, you see," she says, "no *pilikia* about the school. You go there one, two hours each morning and you learn one, two hulas."

"Mary, do it!" says Richard. "I know you want to—and I've got that writing to do. Do what your family tell you to do. Besides, I want you to dance the hula for me in Oxford."

Everybody laughs, and Leilani says, "You are family, too, Val. You will do it, then, Mary? I tell Madam Pele tonight."

"Madam Pele!" I exclaim. "But she is—I thought she was the volcano goddess."

Kahana and Leilani laugh. "So she is," says Leilani. "But this one is the *kumu*—the teacher. The head of the school. We do not call her that to her face—but she erupts sometimes. Then you will understand."

We plan our meeting in the morning and also plan a drive round the island after the dancing. Leilani dances again, and then we take our leave.

As we drive homeward, Richard says, "What a splendid pair! It's pretty fantastic to come half round the world and find a family. More evidence for my theory of compensation, do you think?"

"Maybe," I say. "Only, I hope we've already paid for our good luck and don't have to pay for it later by getting squashed by a bulldozer knocking down the last tree."

"I think you've paid," he says. "Not only the Disaster but Mercia. Wonder you didn't go right round the bend and get hauled off to shrinks."

"What could they do?" I say. "They couldn't bring Mercia back. Or persuade me I wasn't sad. They can't change anything that's real—death or sorrow or guilt."

At Umoani we bathe and then we are nakedly in the big bed on the screened lanai.

There is a sonorous croak beneath us, and you say, "Gods above! What's that?"

I giggle and say, "That's the bufo I told you about. A frog or toad or something from India. It'll sing us to sleep." I am on the screenward side of the bed, and I pull myself to a sitting position and lean over and look down. "We have a pool full of stars," I remark.

You raise up and flop face downward across my lap and peer into the pool. There is a faint splash. "Something jumped in," you say. "All the stars danced."

You twist about on your side and lie there looking up at me with your head in my lap. Your face is dim in starlight.

"If the *u* of Umoani is breast," you say, "what is breasts?"

"Oo-oo!" I say. "Maybe."

"Your oo-oo's are two hills in starlight," you observe. "Each with a tower upon it." You reach up and touch a tower. "Ah," you say, "one of the towers has added another story." You touch the other one. "It, too," you add. You squirm about, possibly looking for a third one. But I gather you in my arms and we kiss with passion.

The bufo gives a loud croak, and we jump and chuckle. "It's jealous," you say. "I bet that bufo has no bufess, and he wants some fun. Sex is fun."

"Wholesome," I whisper.

"Let's see which it is more of—more wholesome or more fun," says Richard.

Then we cease to talk about it.

Mary tells of the hula school and round the island

We wake very early, bathed in sunlight. It is well that we wake early, for we did not remember to arrange the bamboo screens. Anyone standing across the pool would have seen two humans as nude as ponies sleeping there. But no one is about, and the petals of the yellow shower trees drift down upon the water.

We depart early so that I may show Richard the Nuuanu Pali, which is a dramatic cliff as well as a pass through the mountains. The trade winds are funneled through it in a half-gale. I throw over a box I've brought: it falls for a hundred feet, and then is seized in the hand of the wind and hurled back far above us. But the cliff goes down hundreds of feet to the windward side of the island, and only a few miles from the foot is the blue of the Pacific.

At Mynah Bird Lane Leilani comes running out. "You have bathing suits, yes?" she asks. "Good. We come back to dinner here after round the island. Will that be all right? —Yes? Well, I tell Momi, and then we go."

"Now," she says when she has returned. "Go this way—the school is in Kalihi Valley." Bright drops suddenly patter down. "Oh," she says. "The rain comes. Go fast."

There is sunlight all around us, and, as the rain descends, the drops sparkle. It stops as quickly as it began. Arching across the sky is a brilliant rainbow. This, I remember, is the land of rainbows—trade-wind showers and rainbows almost every day, sometimes several in one day.

Leilani says that she saw Madam Pele last night, and I shall be accepted in the school as part of Momi's family.

"Oh, Leilani!" I say. "I'm afraid I can't learn it right!"

"Do not worry," she says. "I am good *kumu*."

We turn into a driveway that is little more than a track leading back to a small parking area. Here we say aloha to Richard, who is to be back with Kahana in about two and a half hours. He looks as though he would like to come along and see the dancing, but it is forbidden. He drives off with a wave.

Leilani and I continue down the lane, she explaining that her one class at the university this afternoon is not meeting. We arrive at the rather unkempt precincts of a frame house with a long verandah. On it stands a woman, just verging on plumpness, wearing a long, flowered wraparound called a *holoku*. Leilani murmurs that it is Madam Pele.

"Aloha!" she says as we come up. "Aloha nui! Come in! You are welcome!" She looks energetic, and her black eyes are sharp and lively. "Mary," she says, "come with me."

We enter a room where seven small nude girls about eight or nine dance as lightly as seven small feathers to the hula music of a record player. Leilani remains with them, while I follow Madam Pele into the room beyond. The sound of girls' laughter comes down from upstairs. Every window in the house appears to be open, and the fragrance of flowers is on the breeze that blows in.

"Now," says Madam Pele. "You want to learn the true hula, yes? Not the haole hula. And you will work hard? You are not just playing?"

"No, no!" I say. "I want to do it right. The true hula!"

"That is good!" she says. "Now. Take off all clothes."

I do so with slight self-consciousness. Then, at her instructions, I bend from side to side, and walk about, and sway my hips.

"You move well," she concedes. "Leilani say you do. Now. You put on the grass skirt. It is what you wear at the school. The school uniform, like England, no?"

I think of English schoolgirls in grey-flannel skirts and blazers and me, bare-breasted and bare-foot in grass skirt, but I agree gravely that it is very like.

For the next hour or more, under her guidance, I work on the swaying of the hips and the little steps of the feet. Finally she says that I have got the basic pattern and it is enough for today, but I must practice it much. I must do it in my dreams at night.

"Now," she says. "We go to Leilani for the hands." She leads the way upstairs where there is a very big room in which there are eight other girls about my age. Madam Pele says I am ready to begin the hands and departs.

Leilani introduces me to the others and has me watch for awhile. A small record player in the corner plays the same hula over and over again. The girls roll their hips and take little steps—the little steps that I have been practicing—and move their hands in the intricate imagery of the dance. The hands are certainly the centre of meaning, and beauty too. Then, after I have watched for two or three run-throughs, during which Leilani has corrected this girl or that on some movement, she has me take my place in the line. As the music plays and we move our hips and feet, she shows us how to hold our arms and how to interpret the words with both arms and hands: this is the way the rains come . . . and this is the angry sea . . . and this, the bending of the palm trees. Gradually I learn the Hawaiian words and their meaning. There is one moment when I am doing the rain that I and the music, the swaying of my hips and the sinuous movement of my arms and hands and fingers, become all one. It is only for a moment, but Leilani smiles at me, and I begin to love what we are doing.

Then it is all over for the day. I am told where to hang my grass skirt —my own peg on the wall—and after dressing I run back upstairs and hang my skirt there.

She and I go out the lane again, and there are Richard and Kahana, smoking and deep in talk. They ask me how it went, and I tell them about my morning. Meanwhile, Richard gets the car underway and is directed to head for Diamond Head. He and I are in front, Kahana and Leilani in back.

We pass Diamond Head, looking up at the great black bulk above us and down at the sea pounding at the foot. Then we drive more or less eastward along the coast road. We are, in fact, returning along the coast we observed from the liner.

The top of course is down. Most of the time the deep blue of the ocean is visible on the right. The air is mild with that caressing quality that comes when it is neither too hot nor too cold. The sky is very blue with the long trade-wind clouds moving across it. There is another rainbow towards the mountains. We are all feeling very gay and Kahana remarks, as I turn round to say something to him, that my eyes are the same blue as the sea. He says it with a kind of approval in his voice. It occurs to me that sea-blue eyes, in the days before the *haoles* came, might have enabled me to set up as a goddess of the sea. Or, again, they might have qualified me as a sacrifice.

We pass Koko Head and our road comes round to trend more or less north-westward. Before we have gone far in this direction, we turn right on a sandy road leading to a little cove or bay below the headland of Makapuu Lighthouse. We change into swimming things behind some bushes and go down to the beach. Here there is neither reef nor king surf with the waves cresting far out. Here the big swells come close to the beach before they curl over and crash down upon the sands. I remember vividly a happy little picnic on this beach with Mercia long ago. Only, I—and I look down at my lithe, hula-dancing body—am not helpless in that little wheelchair. I glance up to meet Richard's eye, reading my thoughts.

"It's quite true, Mary," he says with a tender smile. "You can run down the beach at Makapuu-by-the-lighthouse. Or even dive into the waves—if you're man enough!" He looks dubiously at the great waves falling upon the beach with their prolonged soft roar.

"Thanks for understanding, darling," I say. "As for the waves, pooh! The eyes of my foremothers are upon me! Not to mention Leilani's and Kahana's. Can I hang back?"

"*My* foremother wouldn't go into a fishpond," says Richard.

Leilani runs down the beach, her long dark hair flying, and dives neatly under the curling crest of a great comber. A moment later she bobs up like a mermaid beyond the surf.

"It is easier when waves are big," says Kahana. "Timing is the secret." He, too, runs seaward, slowing so as to dive just as a great wave begins to curl.

"Yay, Mary! Go!" I cry and gallop down the beach, see a swell uprearing, and dive through. "Yay!" I repeat as I surface and look about for friends. I see Kahana about a mile overhead, he being on top of a swell; and a moment later I am on high, just as Richard surfaces. We sport about awhile and go in—the trick here being to get one's feet on land between waves. I don't quite do it, but claw my way up the beach anyhow.

The warmth of the sun falls tingling and delightful upon our skin as we lie in the sand. We talk a little and Richard makes some remark about the Bull of the Mountain.

"A real bull?" says Leihani. "A bull with horns?"

"A horny bull, at least!" I say, and Richard chuckles. This leads, naturally, to our telling the tale, with Leilani interjecting *"Auwe! Auwe!"* the Hawaiian word of lamentation, as we tell about Mary in peril.

"What a story!" says Kahana at the end. "Wish I'd been there to biff him one. Or two!" It occurs to me that one of Kahana's biffs might well be enough.

"Should we move on?" says Leilani. She yawns and stretches sinuously and suddenly kisses Kahana.

We drive on in a northerly direction, pausing in a village to buy some little apple bananas. To our left the Koolau Range is a green, buttressed barrier wall—green with moss, not trees—and to our right the deep blue of the Pacific.

"Kahana," says Leilani. "Do you think Sacred Falls? Would you two like to climb a little?"

"Let's do," I say. "Perhaps we'll see a Menehune—if they really exist."

We turn off on a rough road towards the Koolau, and at the end leave the car and proceed on foot. We come to a rushing stream, dotted with boulders we can cross on.

"A god called the Pig-child lives up here," says Leilani gravely. "He will let us go up if we do this each time we cross water." She picks a green leaf and places it upon a rock with a smaller rock on top of it. "A-stone-on-a-leaf-on-a-stone," she says. "If not, the Pig-child roll great stones down upon us!"

"No doubt," says Richard, waving towards the hundreds of giant boulders all about. "Plainly there is a rash *malihini* under each of those."

"That is right," says Kahana, plucking a leaf for the next crossing.

We follow a dim trail upwards, crossing and recrossing the stream, not forgetting the proper propitiation. The towering mountain walls close in on either side of us. The air grows cooler. Finally we see ahead the snowy plume of Sacred Falls. We come into the shade of the mountains, though we can see the sunlight on the high walls above. And then we arrive at the place where Sacred Falls plunges down from far above into a dark pool. The gorge is filled with the sound of the falling waters. It seems a fitting place for the Menehune or for the old gods.

We sit on the rocks for a few minutes, just looking. Then Leilani asks whether we want to have a quick dip, since we still have bathing suits on. We take off shirts and shoes, and wade in.

"This is madness!" I cry. "It's twenty degrees colder than ice!"

Once we are in, with final shrieks and howls, it seems not quite so cold—or we become unable to feel. We swim towards the falls thundering down into the pool, but beyond a certain point, no matter how powerfully we swim, we cannot go. Nor can we hear each other, over the roar of the water.

No one cares to stay in more than two or three minutes; in fact, two or three seconds might be thought to be excessive. We scramble out, wrap shirts around us, and make off down the path towards sunlight and warm beaches.

On the way down we spy a patch of wild white ginger growing in a wet little glade, and we go over to look at it and smell it, damp and fragrant and lovely. A trade-wind shower patters down briefly; no one much minds, for we shelter under a broad-leafed tree and stand there looking at the white flowers in the rain.

A half hour later, having recovered the car, we are again stretched on the sands of a lovely white crescent of beach, deserted but for us. Here we have our lunch, glancing out now and then at the deep glittering blue of the ocean. It surges and and gleams and seems alive; the air is filled with the tang of it as well as the sound. After eating we drowse awhile in the sun, and then we wander down the beach. There are few shells, but Richard finds a blue-green glass ball, which Kahana says is from Japanese fishing nets. It has floated thousands of miles, perhaps over years, taking on its colour from sea and sun, to be at last washed up and found by Richard. After swimming again, we play catch with the fishing ball. Richard, running to catch it, utters a yelp and sits down suddenly and examines his foot. He has stepped on a sharp stone. The skin is not broken, and he makes light of it, but I notice that he limps slightly.

We drive on towards the northern part of the island, the coast unrolling before us in panoramas of sea and headland and mountain, each seeming to us more magnificent than the one before. Eventually, far to the north, after a last swim in the sea, we turn inland to come down through the middle of the island into the Ewa Plain. Now there are mountain ranges on either side of us, although more distant, and we are driving through plantations of spiky pineapples. The sun is touching the saw-toothed peaks of the Waianae Range. Then it slips behind, and the mountains become inky black against a flaming sky.

"Val," I say. "This is Hawaii. It's like this most of the time—not too hot, not too cold, sky and sea. How can we ever go back to lands with icy winters and fogs and hideous summers? Let's just stay here and be beachcombers, shall we?"

"And renounce the dreaming spires of Oxford?" he says. "No more the bells of St Mary the Virgin ringing the changes and Great Tom booming through the mist? No more grand dinners at the Mitre? No more of England when the roses blow on a perfect day in June and swans and punts are on the Cherwell and the skylark is singing in the sky?"

"Oh, Val!" I exclaim. "You're a poet! That's a strong magic, too."

"I wish to see England very much," says Leilani. "But I could not stay. I could not stay in San Francisco when I went there. The Islands—they are something in the blood—they call and call to come back."

"Yes," says Val. "I know they will—and I have only just got here."

"I think I would die in the cold grey cities of the north," says Kahana. "Two years in New Haven nearly finished me—I kept remembering the windward beaches and the flowers and the soft Hawaiian nights. As Leilani says, the Islands call . . ."

"They called to me—always," I say softly. "But I was afraid, too. Now, thank God, that fear is gone, and the Islands—they really are part of me. When we go to England, I'll tell my lei to go home! —Val, when you leave the Islands, you always throw your lei overboard. If it drifts ashore, you will return. If it drifts out to sea, you never do. But of course you don't know which it did."

"We will swim out and get yours," says Leilani. "You come back!"

I look up at a brilliant star riding in the dusky blue of the twilight sky. Then I begin to sing in a low voice the Hawaiian words, never forgotten, of Queen Liliuokalani's haunting "Aloha Oe." When the refrain comes, Leilani and Kahana join in, and Richard comes in on the two lines originally written in English—"one fond embrace" and "until we meet again."

When the last line is done, Leilani says, "Oh, you will come back, Mary. If you have remembered that all these years, you are truly an Island girl, as Momi says."

We approach the turnoff to the Moani Ridge, and I say, "Leilani, when will Momi be expecting us? Have we time enough to run up to Umoani and shower? Besides, I'd like you all to see it—it's where I lived with Mercia."

"Oh, yes," she says. "Plenty time. I wish to see it. Momi, who was there with Iolani, my mother, told me of it."

She and Kahana are enchanted with the little house and the bridge and the pool, and we make plans for them to come for an evening next week. Richard leaps rapidly into the shower to wash away the salt, while I do the hula for a few minutes with improving suggestions from Leilani and croaks from the bufo. Then Leilani showers, followed by Kahana.

The telephone rings, and Richard, limping slightly, answers it. He turns to me and says: "It's Jim Cosby. They want us to come to dinner on *Randy* tomorrow. Any reason not to?" I shake my head, and he tells Jim we shall come. I hear him telling Kahana and Leilani about meeting his old friend from the Eastern Shore in the middle of the Pacific. Then I hop into the shower.

When I come forth again, Leilani says, "We want to ask you something. The luau. Momi said we should ask you. Would you like to go to a real, old-time luau? The way it was before the haoles came? It's a big secret, you see, and you have to swear not to tell anyone about it—not even that there is such a thing. And especially not when or where—the secret beach. Never tell where it is, even afterwards. And you must promise to do all we tell you. We dress in the old way and do the old things. Yes?"

"I promise," I say. "I swear. Everything. I don't get sacrificed on an altar, do I?"

"No, no!" say Kahana and Leilani together, laughing. "But we tell you no more!"

"I promise," says Richard. "Grass skirts for wahines is the old way?"

"No," says Kahana. "They came later, from Samoa. It is *tapa* cloth—the word is *kapa,* really. You'll see. Not for awhile, though, not until the moon is full."

At Mynah Bird Lane there are cheerful greetings when we arrive. Makaleha's children run happily about. We meet her husband, Eho, a dark amiable man of about thirty-five. They are all so welcoming that we really do feel part of the family—more than warmth, a belonging. The big airy room with its *lauhala* mats is just the same as it was when Leilani and I were little girls. Leilani tells Momi of my remembering "Aloha Oe" in the Hawaiian all these years, and she beams. "Island girl come home," she says. "I knew."

We gather round the table, and Richard has his first experience with the Hawaiian 'bread'—*poi,* a thick grey paste, slightly fermented, slightly sour, made from the pounded-up root of the taro. The first taste evokes vivid memories of Mercia laughing at me when I first tasted it long ago.

"You eat it with your fingers, Val," says Makaleha. "Like this." She dips two fingers into the bowl; and then with a curious twist of her wrist gets it to her mouth.

Richard gives it a suspicious look, and people chuckle. "Looks like wallpaper paste," he mutters. He puts a finger in and licks it unenthusiastically.

"Val," says Kahana. "Do it this way." He illustrates the scoop, and Richard does it. He keeps on trying it throughout the meal—the main dish is a fine baked fish—and it begins to grow on him. I tell him to think of the faint sourness of good rye bread.

After dessert of fruit we all sit on the dark, flower-scented lanai, Richard and I sunk into an old punee, or couch. I am conscious of the soft breeze touching our cheeks. There is talk of the Islands, especially Momi's recollections of long ago: she had been born only a decade after the American planters and businessmen had seized the kingdom and overthrown the Queen—a conquest motivated by greed. Richard and I writhe a bit, there in the dark, at our link with the despoilers; and in my resentment I strengthen in my mind my links to my Hawaiian family— Leilani, my sister, and Momi, who lifted me in her strong arms long ago. Sitting there in the dark on the rickety lanai, touched by the flower-scented breeze, I am a Hawaiian girl glaring defiantly at the bulldozers.

A little boy comes out of the night and whispers to Leilani and runs off.

"Oh, Mary, Val!" she says. "You must see! It is the night-blooming cereus!"

"Is this the night?" I say. "Mercia was going to take me, but—but she couldn't."

"The aloha of the Islands!" says Momi. "You go."

"I say," says Richard. "Will somebody please explain? A flower? 'The night'?"

"Forgive us," says Kahana. "Only one or two nights a year it blooms. And so, when the night is near, there are watchers. So tonight is like a welcome to you."

The four of us troop out to the car again. "We go first to the wall of Punahou School," says Leilani. "Turn left here." We arrive and park, as other cars are doing.

All along the old grey wall stretches a row of spiky plants, and each one lifts—tonight—an enormous white cup-shaped blossom towards the night sky. Unearthly.

"In the morning," says Kahana, "they will all be gone. Or most of them."

"The old gods," I say. "They come down from the Koolau in the night and drink from the flower cups. Then they throw the cups away."

From Punahou we drive up to the little volcanic crater called

Punchbowl to see more of the flowers, then drop Kahana and Leilani at their places and continue homewards to Umoani.

Mary's account of Navy Day

In the morning—it is Saturday, the day we dine aboard the destroyer—there is no hula school, though I practice for an hour. Later we go into Honolulu to shop and explore before going on to Waikiki to swim and sun. I notice that Richard is limping.

"It's that stone bruise I got yesterday," he says in response to my alarmed look. "Nothing really, but sore as the devil."

We go home after lunch to nap. We are to meet Jim and Bill at the Pearl Harbor Officers Club for a drink before going on board the ship. It is a guest night, so there may be other women. I wear a pale-blue frock and Richard a white linen jacket, and thus arrayed we roll down the hill to the Sub Base Gate, where I tell the sentry that we are going to the Officers Club. He says, "Yes, Ma'am!" and salutes. Controlling an impulse to salute him back, as Richard grins, I merely give him a Smile #3 and drive on. A lady.

Lieutenant Jim and Ensign Bill have evidently been keeping watch, for they meet us at the Officers Club door and lead the way to a table on the big lanai facing the harbour. We can see a giant aircraft carrier and two haughty cruisers. By turning our heads a bit, we can see the shadowed mysterious mountains. As we had expected, the Navy men are immaculate in gleaming white uniforms, cut on sort of princess—or perhaps prince—lines, with gold buttons and high neck and black-and-gold shoulder-boards.

As the planters punches they have ordered arrive, Jim, with his charming smile, says, "We have just found out—just in the last ten minutes—that *Franklin Pierce,* the big carrier over there, is having a dance tonight. We thought perhaps you all would like to go. Bill and I may go, though the lady I usually take to such affairs is on the mainland. Still, there are wives and daughters . . . The dance won't begin any before nine. Do come if you find the thought appealing."

"Yes, do!" says Bill.

Richard and I exchange a look. In his grey eyes a small Richard shrugs and gestures, palms out, to indicate it's up to me. A tiny Mary in my eyes smiles and tilts her head a bit and opens her eyes wide to indicate that she has never been to a dance on an aircraft carrier. The tiny Richard smiles and bows. The tiny winged Mary gives a small hop and then nods sedately.

The full-sized Richard turns to Jim and says, "Sounds like fun. We'd be glad to."

"You will be perfectly all right as you are," says Jim. "But I remember you saying, Mary, that you had brought an evening gown because of that reception in Washington. If you'd like to change—a good many of the women will be wearing long dresses—there'll be plenty of time after dinner."

Richard glances at me and sees that the tiny Mary in my eyes is frisking about in a long dress. I, in fact, say, "Yes, I'd like to change. More fun. Besides—"

"Besides—it's up there waiting," says Richard with a grin. "Mary, why don't you tell them your news?"

I wonder briefly what my news could be, then remember the hula school. I say, "Oh, yes, I shall. What it is—well, I have been admitted to an ancient institution of learning, rather more select than Oxford. Or Annapolis. Also, different."

"Good heavens!" says Jim. "I can't imagine what it could be. You're not, er, taking the veil, are you?"

Richard and I laugh. "Hardly that!" I say.

"Tell us!" says Bill.

"I am most intrigued!" says Jim smoothly. "You could hardly have joined the Buddhists, I suppose. You do mean here in the Islands, I gath— Good God, Mary! You don't mean the secret hula school, do you?"

"Ah," says Richard. "You know about it, do you? That's it."

"How could you be in it?" says Jim. "You have no Hawaiian blood. I know girls—Navy Juniors—who have tried and tried to get into that school. Or even find it. How can you be in it?"

"She is, though," says Richard. "She was here when she was a little girl. And she and her cousin were sort of adopted into a Hawaiian family —blood of King Kam-something."

"Kamehameha," I say. "So, you see, I'm an Island girl, a native, er, maiden. Unlike all you *haoles.* You like, no?"

"Well," says Bill with a grin. "I like. When can we see you do the hula?"

"Not for awhile," I say. "It's more complicated than it looks. Especially the hands."

Bill grins again, and says, "I wasn't thinking of the hands."

"This is really fascinating," says Jim. "I'm really interested in Hawaii —the whole culture. And there's nothing with deeper roots than the hula."

"Mary," says Bill, "when I see you do the hula, I shall be inspired to write an immortal sonnet. Ah, it's taking shape in my mind already. It will begin, 'My heart leaps up when I behold a grass skirt on our Mary—so was it from the front view—so is it from the back . . .'—something like that.''

I laugh and say, "Bill, I seem to catch the faintest echo of one of your masters. It would be interesting to know just where you'd go from there.''

A waiter comes up and says to Jim, "The officers' motor boat from *Randolph*, sir.''

"Very well,'' says Jim, reaching for the check and signing it. "Everyone ready?''

At the club landing a boat about thirty feet long waits with its coxswain at attention. I am handed into the boat. Bells ring. The boat shoots away. We ride in a tiny cabin decorated with elaborate mats of knotted and woven rope. Through a port I see the flaring bows of a cruiser, and through the open companionway of our boat I see the coxswain standing in the stern holding the tiller. He suddenly snaps to attention and salutes, and a moment later an admiral's barge with a two-star flag goes by. After awhile there is a shout and an answering shout from our coxswain, who then rings his bell a lot. The boat slows, creeps forward, bumps. We have arrived, and we ascend the gangway to be welcomed by a pleasant young man who is Officer of the Deck. Jim and Bill give us a short tour of the ship, and I am eyed with interest by sailors scattered about the decks. Finally we are led up to the bridge.

A boatswain's mate, whose open neck discloses a pelt that would do credit to a bear, comes up and says, "Mr Cosby, sir. Could I speak to you and Mr Wingfield?''

They say they'll be right back and go off with him. Richard goes over to the big wheel and stands there, turning it a trifle.

"All right, Vallance!'' I grate. "Helm alee! Full speed ahead! Prepare to ram!''

He laughs. "Hush up or they'll hear you. Be a lady even if you are a pirate.''

"All right,'' I say sadly. "The last round is fired. Strike the flag.''

Jim and Bill return and escort us to the wardroom or saloon—a comfortable room stretching the width of the ship with a long table in the middle. Several officers who are reading or talking rise when we come in, and Jim performs the introductions. The officer with two-and-a-half stripes on his shoulders is the famous 'Brassjaw'—as he is called behind his back—the executive officer. He smiles cordially enough, apologizing for the Captain's absence. I am tempted to respond to the introduction with a "Hullo, Mr Brassjaw!" but am deterred by the thought of Jim and Bill led out to be shot.

As we are seated, I at Brassjaw's right and Bill beside me, Richard to the exec's left with Jim, one of the other officers says, "Tim's not coming down, sir. Says he's not feeling well." I remember that Tim was the Officer of the Deck we met as we came aboard.

Only once during the dinner does the conversation touch upon anything serious. Bill makes some comment on the Navy's strike of forty carrier bombers against North Vietnam that was in the papers this morning, and I think of Daddy's prediction of a bigger war. Someone remarks, indiscreetly, that he supposes that that is where *Franklin Pierce* will go when she sails on Monday. A lieutenant says that it looks as though the U.S. isn't playing any more, and he bets that North Vietnam is having second thoughts about supporting the Vietcong. I can't contain myself any longer.

"I think," I say, "they're not going to stop no matter how much we bomb them."

"You're right, Bob," says Brassjaw to the lieutenant. "They'll back down now. Nothing can stand up to our fire-power if we decide to use it. It'll soon be over."

I seethe. It is exactly as though I hadn't spoken. Perhaps only men are allowed to have opinions about wars. True, my opinion came from Daddy—*he'd* be listened to—but I'm a woman. In my mind, Brassjaw is made to walk the plank on *Windrush,* me standing by with a cutlass: there is a big splash and he is gone.

Richard says coolly, "Did anyone notice what else was in the paper this morning concerning Vietnam?"

There is a momentary silence as everyone checks the memory banks. Jim Cosby says, "Something important, Val?"

"*I* think so," says Richard. "At Columbia University. What the paper called a marathon teach-in—not just students but faculty, against what we are doing. It's going to spread!"

Jim looks thoughtful; but Brassjaw laughs and says, "I hardly think a few hot-headed students are going to change the United States government. I think President Johnson has decided to win this war and get out. That's the way it will be."

"Sir," I say sweetly. "Do you remember the American general who said, 'Let's win this war and get out!'—General Custer at the Little Big Horn it was!"

There is a burst of laughter, and Brassjaw reddens slightly and glances about. The laughter is checked, but I am smiling and figuratively wiping my dripping cutlass on my napkin.

Brassjaw says, "The situations are hardly comparable, Mrs Vallance."

I merely smile, and the conversation returns to a lighter tone.

After dinner Jim says that if we are going to change for the dance we had best be starting. A boat takes us to the Pearl City Landing at the northern part of the harbour, and we all climb into Bill's old Plymouth, I in front to show him the way.

As the car heads towards the mountains, Bill says seriously, "You know, Val, I think you may be right about the protests spreading. My brother at Berkeley says that anger about Vietnam is kind of in the air." Then he laughs and says to me, "That was a mean blow you gave old Brassjaw about Custer. I thought I was going to explode."

"Take the right-hand fork, Bill," I say. "He deserved it."

At Umoani Jim and Bill admire the bridge and the pool, then say they'll come back for us about eight-thirty. We suppose they are going to the Club for a drink, since Richard had mentioned that we hadn't laid in any liquor.

As I take off my dress, I compliment Richard on remembering the teach-in. Then, pawing in a drawer, I say, "Listen. —Where's my yellow slip? Oh, here it is! —What I was going to say is, you're limping like anything! How can you go to a dance?"

"Oh, I can shuffle a step or two," he says, tying his bow tie. "And you can dance with all the admirals, can't you?"

I stick my head into the long evening slip and begin that writhing journey that every woman must make alone. From the depths I say, "Brave Val! Brilliant Val!"

"Not for me to deny the judgement of my peers," he says modestly. "Or my peeress. Still, why these laurels?"

"The teach-in," I say. "I wanted to crush Brassjaw, for ignoring me, you know; and suddenly you charged like the cavalry. Why didn't *I* remember the teach-in?"

"I never said I loved you for your brains, did I?" he says kindly. "Not that you didn't blast him with that Custer thing. Jolly good!"

"What an interesting subject this has become!" I say. "You love me for my sea-blue eyes?"

"Can't be that," he says, "since I love you when your rather improbable eyes are shut."

"That's nice," I say. "Why then? Carnal reasons, I bet. Woooo!"

"God knows!" he says. "I often wonder." He comes over to me, looking very handsome in his white mess jacket, and puts his arms round me. "I do, though," he mutters.

Then he says, "Can you possibly clothe that beautiful form before the Navy walk in? It's eight-thirty!"

"Good lord!" I say, and leap for my pale yellow gown and slither into it like a snake. "Aha!" I say. "Saved!" I dab a trace of Essence de Floozie behind my ear.

The two white-uniformed figures come up the walk and over the bridge, the outside light striking gleams of gold from their shoulder-boards and buttons. They say I look beautiful, and we go out to the car. We park right next to our own car at the Officers Club and go in to have a drink there, since there will be no bar on the carrier.

Then Jim says, "Perhaps we should dance now? There's a boat halfway to the landing. Shall we go?" He rises, tall and debonair, and we all troop down to the landing and stand, with three other couples, looking across the placid water, shimmering with reflected lights, at the vast bulk of the carrier and the approaching boat.

A short time later we enter the side of *Franklin Pierce* and move through a maze of metallic caverns, where perhaps trolls live, and arrive at what Bill says is one of the aircraft hangars, now gaily decorated as a ballroom with a band at one end and a colourful throng, almost all the men in white and gold.

I dance first with Richard, but I can tell his foot is hurting him. "Val, dear," I say. "We shouldn't have come! Don't try to dance! Just sit and watch, and we'll go home soon."

"All right," he says. "I think I shall. Just watch, I mean. But no hurry about leaving. I'll be fine." As the dance ends, he sits down, and we explain to the others.

The next dance I dance with Bill, a very good dancer, although he holds me rather tightly. Then I dance with Jim Cosby of Tally-Ho, who is graceful and gracious. There is an interval, and Bill brings both Richard and me cups of punch. I discover that, whether the Navy is dry or not, the punch is far from a soft drink.

Brassjaw comes up and claims me for a dance, and I feel the hardness of his muscles beneath his uniform. I mention that I should like to go to sea on *Randy*.

He shudders slightly and says, "A warship is no place for a lady. Still, there is no doubt that you would brighten up the decks."

No retort occurs to me, since I am too truthful to deny that I'd brighten the decks.

The dance ends, and Bill comes up to reclaim me. When we are out of earshot, he says, "Rank hath its privileges, but once is enough for him. More punch?"

"Yes, please," I say. "Only not so strong, Bill, please." I sit down with Richard.

Jim comes up. "Where's Bill?" he says. "Oh, here he comes." As I take the cup of punch from Bill, Jim says, "Well, children! The situation changed is! Tim is sick—remember, he didn't come down to dinner? Anyhow, *Randy*'s just signalled: they're sending him over to the hospital. Brassjaw says I'm to go back and take the deck. I'm sorry to break up the party, at least as far as I'm concerned."

We all make sounds of sympathy. Then Jim says, glancing at Richard, "An idea just occurred to me that—just maybe—you'd like to come along, Val, since you can't dance. We could sit around and talk, and Mary could stay here with Bill and dance?"

"I'd like that!" says Richard. "Why don't you, Mary? You're the dancer unchained."

"Do say yes!" says Bill. "See, Jim and Val can drive around in Val's car, and *Randy* will send a boat. Then Jim can put Val ashore when he's ready to go home—and I can run you home in my car. Perfect!"

It is apparent that the majority have made up their minds. I look at Richard, torn between a desire to go whither he goes and the realisation that he and Jim will really enjoy a chance for a good long talk. Richard winks at me.

"All right," I say. Richard says he'll probably leave *Randolph* about midnight or half-past and that, since the dance ends at one, he supposes I'll be along about one-thirty. He smiles at me and limps off with Jim. I look sadly after him. Who knows what dangers he may run into without me there?

Bill and I dance several times, and then he proposes that we go up and stroll on the flight deck. It is enormous—acres of it. The stars seem to hang low, and the trade-clouds, white and tumbled even in starlight, drift across the sky. Bill puts a brotherly arm about my waist as we stand looking.

Then I realise that the arm is not brotherly, it is drawing me closer. "Bill!" I say, warningly.

"One kiss?" he says. "Mary, you're enough to drive a man crazy!"

I hear this with interest. Perhaps I am a danger to men. Deadly. Not a bad thing, I think.

"I'm so sorry, Bill," I say sweetly. "I'm getting cold. Let's go in, Bill, please."

We dance again, and he holds me even more tightly than before.

Possibly I shall have a row of little American eagles engraved down the front of me.

During the next hour or so I dance with Bill and again with Brassjaw and with the lieutenant, Bob. At some point, an older man with the broad stripe of an admiral comes up to me and says, "Tonya, m'dear!"

I remark that I am, in fact, not Tonya; and Bill introduces us. Then the admiral asks me courteously to dance, and as I move into his arms he says, "Thank you, Tonya, m'dear!" So I decide that, okay, I will be Tonya for him, enshrined, perhaps for ever, in his heart as Tonya. So I look at him as Tonya might and say goodbye, when the dance is over, in a Tonya way. He says, "Thank you, Tonya, m'dear."

I remain Tonya for the next three minutes with Bill. I am recalled from being Tonya by the sudden awareness that Bill's voice is becoming a little blurry—he is drinking too much—and I don't know how Tonya would cope with that. On the other hand, I don't know how to cope with it myself, now that I am Mary again.

Finally, almost midnight, fearful that Bill may drink too much to drive, I ask him to take me home. Somewhat to my surprise, he agrees without protest.

At the Officers Club, though, he insists on having one more drink, and I assent reluctantly. I like him better unblurry.

"You're a pal!" he says. "You're a good little girl, Mary baby! There's only one thing wrong with you."

The waiter brings the drinks, and Bill scrawls a signature.

"There's only one li'l thing wrong with you," he repeats. "Do you want to know what that one li'l thing ish? Do you?"

"I suppose so," I say. "I expect you're going to tell me anyhow. I'm not pretty enough. That's it!"

"Oh, no!" he says solemnly. "You're beautiful! Your eyes are beautiful. Your shape ish beautiful!" He pauses, but my diversionary tactic has ultimately failed, for he resumes, "There's just one li'l thing wrong with you. Do you know what that one li'l thing ish?"

"No," I say. "Bill! Shouldn't we go now?"

"It ish that you have a hard, hard heart!" he says. He looks at me solemnly, and I suppress a desire to laugh.

"That's right," I say. "Very hard! It's been that way since I was a little girl. Nothing will change it. —Come on, Bill! We've had our drink. Let's go!"

I am relieved when he agrees and more relieved when he maneuvers his car successfully and even skillfully out of the Navy Yard. Perhaps he is not as drunk as he sounds. In due course, he makes the turning to the village of Moani without being reminded. I begin to relax. I do not notice that beyond the village he takes the fork that leads to Kahili Ridge, where there is a small, closed-down Army post. It is very dark between the trees since there is no moon.

Suddenly, I see the entrance to the Army post go by.

"Bill!" I cry. "You're on the wrong road! Bill! Turn around!"

" 'Sall right, baby!" he says. "Don' worry! Relax! Jus' wanna show you the view. Almos' there." He swings the Plymouth off on a small side road to the left and says, "See, baby! Trusht Bill Wingfield!"

"Bill!" I say. "I want to go home! Now!"

He turns left again and the trees thin and he stops. Far below are the twinkling lights of Pearl Harbor and the Ewa Plain.

"Pretty!" he says. "There'sh *Randy*. Besht damn' destroyer in the Fleet!" He puts his arm around me.

"Bill!" I say sharply. "Take me home! Now!"

"No, no!" he says. "Nish here! Pretty girl! View!"

Suddenly, powerfully, he pulls me to him with a grip like steel. I remember that he played football for Navy. I struggle, but my arms are pinned to my sides. How can I hit him if I can't get my arm free?

"No, Bill! No!" I cry. "Let me go! Val—"

His mouth finds mine, and he kisses me hard. I do not kiss him back. He fumbles at my dress, holding me firmly. I try to twist away, but I cannot. I become furiously angry. He is unzipping my gown down the back.

"Bill!" I cry. "Stop it! You're drunk!"

He breathes heavily and says, "Aw, c'mon, baby!" He pulls at my slip, then yanks, and I feel the shoulder straps break. He fumbles with the fastenings of the strapless bra, still holding me firmly. He hauls the bra out and flips it into the back seat. My gown is half off my shoulders.

"Officer and gentleman!" I say freezingly.

He kisses me again, and I feel his hand on my breast. I growl during the kiss. It ends.

My mouth is close to his ear. I screech at the top of my voice. He jumps and relaxes his grip. I yank out an arm and slap him hard.

He draws back a little and says reproachfully, "Aw, c'mon, Mary! Don't be like that!"

I find the door handle with my right hand and open it, giving him the hardest punch I can manage with my left. I leap out and, holding my dress from falling off, run into the woods.

It is pitch dark in there, my dress is falling off, and I have on very high heels. I feel far from the compleat woodsgirl.

Suddenly I stumble and fall. My torn slip has worked its way over my hips, meaning that it is torn through the waist, and tripped me.

I hear Bill stumbling about, and I crawl behind some bushes.

"Mary! Mary!" he calls. "Come back! Don't be a damn' fool! Mary!"

I do not reply. I reach around and zip up my gown, wish for blue jeans. Stuffing the ruined slip into a bush, I hear the car start, and guess he means to turn it so that its headlights will shine into the woods. I take off my shoes and, holding them and the skirts of my evening gown, circle around towards the road, keeping clear of the light.

I see Bill's white figure stumbling into the woods. I run to the open door of the car with the thought of leaping in and driving triumphantly away but see that it would take so much backing and turning that he could easily run back. So I take the car keys and then, seeing him turn back, I also vindictively snatch his uniform cap off the seat and run back into the woods on the dark side.

Still shouting, "Mary! Come back!" at intervals, Bill gets into the car, probably intending to point it in a new direction. Then I see him scrabbling about on the floor with matches flaring at intervals.

I know it will be several minutes before he thinks of it being me that took the keys, so—still carrying my shoes as well as his cap and keys—I slip back to the little road well below the car and run swiftly down it. I pause at a bend and look back. My last sight of Bill is in the flare of a match on the ground outside the car: he is crawling about on hands and knees. I hurl his key ring far off into the woods and run on.

"Ha, ha, ha!" I mutter, slowing down to a walk. "Where now the mighty Wingfield? The Navy's sunk! No girl, no keys, no hat! Yay!"

I turn onto the road that leads down the mountain, and I become aware that my feet are hurting. I brush off the gravel from the torn stockings, and then, realising that the feet are no more than rags, take off the panty-hose altogether and throw them away. The bra is gone, the tiny flat compact that was in it is gone, the slip is gone—and now the panty-hose. What will be next?

"Clear for action!" I say sternly but softly to a bush.

I listen for overtaking footsteps. I put on my shoes and limp down the road, not very fast because of the heels, pausing every now and then to listen.

The night is very still. There is no breeze, which makes it seem as though a great hush lies over the world. Somewhere a remote dog barks in a lonesome way. There is no moon, but a million stars wheel overhead. The only sound, apart from the lonesome dog, is the click of my heels and the rustle of my long dress. Pretty soon I take the shoes off and go barefooted again, padding on with only the rustle.

I become aware that I've still got the visored uniform cap. I look at it in the starlight, seeing glitters from the eagle and anchors on the front. I consider throwing it away, but decide it is my trophy. So I put it on my head to avoid carrying it, and I push it back to a rakish angle.

I can't read my watch in the starlight, but I know Richard will be frantic before I get home. He isn't very far away as the mynah bird flies, since the ridges are parallel, but the only way for me to go is down to the fork, almost to the village and then up again on the Moani Ridge Road. I wish, suddenly, that Richard were here, too, also padding along in bare feet.

"Solitude is sweet," I murmur, "but solitude is sweeter if you have someone to whisper 'Solitude is sweet' to." Did Daddy say that? I cannot remember.

There are no houses or lights anywhere. I come to the Army post, but it is dark and padlocked.

"It is no easy thing," I say to myself, "to be a good girl in this world. Next time, if there is a next time, I shall carry an emergency kit with sneakers in it."

I think of the hula school. It is as well, I think, that the girls do not have to be chaste maidens, never kissed. I picture Madam Pele pointing a stern finger at me, saying, "You are defiled. Go!" And Leilani weeps as I slink sadly away into the ocean to drown. I enjoy this scene for awhile. Then I think that, even in such a school, my struggle ought to redeem me. Now Leilani and the others are clapping while Madam Pele puts the uniform cap into a glass trophy case with a small card, neatly lettered, saying, "In defense of virtue."

It occurs to me that *Randolph* is sailing in the early morning and that Bill will be hanged at the yardarm if he's not on board. "Ah," I mutter unforgivingly. "Keelhauling is too good for him! And it's a long, long walk to Pearl City!"

I think about Bill, whom I once liked. What is it in so many men— otherwise intelligent and affable—what corruption makes it possible for them to violate the integrity of another human being? I know that Richard would not do that, nor of course would Daddy, nor Peter Shirley. Nor Jim Cosby, I'm certain. But Bill—just like the Bull of the Mountain, except for manners. A *little* Bull. Then I giggle slightly: instead of the Bull of the Mountain I have Bill of the Mountain. Or Bill of the Hill.

I wonder what he is doing. I picture him crawling about in the woods, his white trousers stained—still looking for the keys with matches, if he has any left by now—possibly still mournfully calling, "Mary! Come back!" I giggle at the image.

I pad along a bit faster. I wish I had a cigarette. I sing the "Aloha Oe" in a soft voice. Then I do some poems, not loudly but with, I think, moving power. Shakespeare blends with the soft Hawaiian night.

I decide I'm rather enjoying myself but would enjoy myself more if I had sneakers on and a shorter skirt. And a cigarette. And perhaps a sandwich, country ham.

My feet are hurting in the bruised way, so I put on my pumps again until they start hurting in the going-downhill-in-heels way.

Suddenly a man's shape looms ahead, and my heart beats hard. But the shape says "Aloha" in a calm deep voice and goes by on bare feet. I murmur "Aloha," and, after a minute, I look back and see him turning off the road into the trees. I decide he has a hut in there. Why didn't I ask him if he had a cigarette? I further decide that I can't be far now from the fork.

I take off my shoes again and pad onward. I hear a crackling sound behind me and freeze, ready to dive into the bushes. I listen intently but there is no pound of heels, no further sound. I decide it was a fruit falling off a tree, not Bill. I wonder whether he has gone to sleep in the car up there, and I wonder, too, whether his being drunk is any excuse for what he did. Not much, I decide, although he is a man who oughtn't to drink. Still poised, listening, I look up at the infinity of stars in the sky. A faint breeze brings me some flower fragrance. I hope my darling yellow gown is not ruined. I wonder what Richard is doing. I pad on.

Richard is, in fact, dozing at Umoani. His evening has been quiet and serene.

He and Jim Cosby had driven swiftly round to Pearl City where, in accordance with the signal from *Franklin Pierce,* a boat from *Randolph* waited. With occasional turns on deck by Jim, the two of them had sat in the wardroom over coffee and talked long.

The log-keeper has only an imperfect account of what they talked about, possibly some things not suitable for her ears. But they talked of the days on the Eastern Shore when Jim was at Tally-Ho and Richard at Redrock. They also talked about Jim's dedicated love for the Fleet. He said that when he married, it would have to be to a woman who could accept that the Fleet came first for him. Richard asked him if he would be prepared to have his wife put something else, perhaps a career in physics or law, first. Jim smiled and said, "Certainly not!" His wife, he said, might, and probably would, put the children first; but she would have to accept the rôle of an officer's wife and hostess. Many a career had been made or marred by the sort of wife a naval officer chose. Richard told him something of our idea of putting love first; and Jim said courteously that it was splendid, but not for a dedicated naval officer.

At this point the quartermaster of the watch came to the wardroom door and said, "Sir. Officers hailing *Randolph* from the landing, sir."

"Call away the motor boat!" said Jim, and added to Richard, "Would you like to come topside, Val? Or wait for me here?"

"I'll come up," said Richard. "Actually, it's after midnight. I think I shall start for home."

When the boat returned, it proved to contain Brassjaw and the lieutenant named Bob. After they had come aboard and salutes were exchanged, Jim said, "Sir. Did you notice whether Bill and Mary were still at the dance when you left?"

"Last I saw of Mary," said Brassjaw gruffly, "she was dancing with an admiral."

"They left, I think, before we did," said Bob. He added in a lower tone, "Bill had had quite a lot to drink."

"Take the deck for about fifteen minutes, Bob, will you?" said Jim. "I'll go ashore with Val for a moment and come straight back."

"Sure," says Bob. "Sir, I relieve you."

Richard and Jim went down into the waiting boat. After telling the coxswain to make the landing, Jim said, "Don't worry about Bill. He can hold his liquor. He'll get her home all right." Later, as they walked towards the car, he urged Richard to come down in the morning to the Pearl Harbor channel where it went alongside of Hickam Field if he would like to see *Randolph* underway. Richard said he and Mary would probably come.

They exchanged goodnights with a handshake, both of them delighted by the good fortune that led to their paths crossing in mid-Pacific.

At Umoani there is no Mary, not that you expected there to be. You get out of your clothes and go to bed to read and wait. The bufo croaks contentedly. A mango falls with a thump somewhere near. Holding the book, you wonder what I am doing. You open your eyes and realise that you've been asleep for two seconds, dreaming of Oxford and . . . and something. You can't quite remember. Pity. You read for five minutes. The book slides down. You sleep.

The bufo thinks, "Ah. My voice lulled him to sleep. What a lovely croak! I bet he would like to be a bufo, if he were awake of course.

Where is the blue-eyed girl? I wish she would come. I'd better save my voice for her. Where can she be?"

But the girl does not come. The stars wheel above the quiet earth.

You wake with a start. You smile. Then suddenly you look at your watch and leap up. It is two-thirty.

"Dear God!" you mutter. "Where is she?"

You wish you could call the *Randolph* and talk with Jim. Maybe he could send out search parties. You think about a wreck and you shudder, yet what else could it be? An awful conviction comes to you with overwhelming force that there *has* been a wreck and I am dead or dying.

You pull yourself together with a decisive effort and force yourself to think. You spring to the phone and call the police to ask whether there has been a wreck involving a naval officer and a girl in a Plymouth. They say no. But, you think, a wreck would be between the Navy Yard and here. Perhaps Bill has driven into a tree or over a cliff. You yank on shirt and trousers and shoes. You prowl back and forth, peering out towards the driveway, listening. You wonder if you dare leave the phone to go and search. But where would you search?

Suddenly you feel that you can't stand it without at least driving down to Moani village. You run out to the car. You roll down the mountain without starting the engine, feeling that you might hear a cry in the night. You look sharply on both sides with the headlights on high beam for wrecks or signs of a car going off the road. You have gone about two miles. Then you coast round a curve and brake hard.

There in the glare of the headlights is a girl in a long yellow dress, hobbling along. On the back of her head is an officer's cap, and, in the instant of the beams falling upon her, her mouth is open in song and her arm is flung dramatically out. Her other hand holds up her long skirt. Her words reach your ear: "On top of old Smo-o-o-o-ky, all covered with dew . . ."

You coast rapidly up to her, saying, "Mary! Mary!" and opening the door.

"Hullo-o-o!" says the apparition. "I thought you'd be along. Cigarette—quick!" She clambers wearily in. . . .

Mary relates the aftermath of Navy Day

A little before nine o'clock on a Sunday morning a couple sits in the sunshine on a bench placed among carefully tended flower beds. The man wears a grim expression on his face. The girl wears a naval officer's cap perched rakishly and incongruously on the back of her head. Almost at their feet is the water of the Pearl Harbor channel. In the middle of the channel a long, lean, grey destroyer moves sedately towards the sea.

On the forward deck, immaculate as always, is Lieutenant James Pickering Cosby, USN., standing poised and alert. He sees the two and waves. There are crewmen at the rails, and two or three of them are snapping photographs of the girl with the officer's cap and her grim-faced escort. Several officers stand on the bridge, among them Ensign Wingfield, who does not wave, and a man with gold braid on his cap visor, who must be the Captain.

The girl with the officer's cap on her head stands up, and then she steps down to the channel's edge. The Captain looks at her. Other officers and men look at her, also.

She takes the cap off. She holds it up at arm's length, dangling from her hand as a scalp might dangle from the hand of a Red Indian maiden. Then, just as the slow-moving destroyer is abreast, she casually, even contemptuously, sails the cap out into the channel. It soars high, with a glitter of gold. Cameras eye it. It falls into the water. Lieutenant Cosby smiles broadly. The Captain's lip seems to twitch. Ensign Wingfield does not smile. The girl stands there as the ship steams on to sea. . . .

Much earlier this same morning a worried Jim telephoned us. I spoke to him after Richard in order to assure him that I was all right. I also told him exactly what had happened. He said that Bill, dirty and footsore, had arrived, capless, on the landing during morning quarters. The car was still on the ridge. This much the whole ship knew, along with the fact that Bill had left the *Pierce* with me. Now Jim said, with his meticulous Southern courtesy, that he would let the rest of the story—me pinching the car keys and running off—be known to protect my good name. He then spoke to Richard again—Richard who was in the mood to tear Bill into very small pieces indeed—to explain that Richard needn't bother: Bill was going to suffer agonies of embarrassment.

Thus, by the time *Randolph* steamed out the channel, the story must have run round the ship—and half the crew watched with fascinated interest when the girl sailed the cap into the water. Standing there, looking after the departing vessel, I decide that the story, perhaps with photographs, will become famous in the Fleet and haunt Bill for years to come.

"Bill, baby!" I murmur to the stern of the ship. "You have just been sunk!"

I turn around and Richard is grinning. He appreciates, better than me perhaps, what a ribbing Bill will have to endure—remarks about great lovers in the wardroom, innocent questions from the men about mountain climbing, and isn't that a new cap, sir? Richard and I ceremonially shake hands and depart for a long nap and a lazy day.

Next morning at the hula school, after I have got into my grass skirt and bared my rather bruised feet, I tell Leilani what happened. "*Auwe, auwe!*" she exclaims as I tell her of the struggle, then she grins as I go on. She says that Madam Pele must hear—and so I learn why she is named for the volcano goddess. We witness an eruption. We are awed. She grumbles. Molten lava bubbles to the top and spills over. The flow obliterates the wicked Wingfield. It broadens. It overwhelms the entire U. S. Navy. Ships sink. Then the Army. Then all males. But she presses me to her heaving bosom. Finally she insists on looking at my scratched, bruised feet and rubbing them both with coconut oil. Then we turn to our dancing. . . .

Mary writes of Dancing Days

Up to this moment, the eruption of Madam Pele on the morning of our fifth day in the Islands, I have written in detail about everything. And that evening we went off to Mynah Bird Lane for dinner and still another retelling.

Now I am again writing at Umoani in the afternoon—but some days later.

If there has been any theme, any motif, in this journey to Hawaii, it has been dancing. These have been dancing days. Not only the dancing on the carrier, but Leilani's lovely hulas and my own daily dancing at the school, as well as dancing at Umoani to show Richard what I've learned. I do, in fact, almost hula in my sleep, and my fascination with it—one of the most graceful and expressive kinds of dancing in the world—grows. I love the sound of "dancing days"—it is a wingèd thing and wingèd word. And there have been all the light-footed dancing girls at the school, and dancing seas, dancing sunlight reflected by rippling water, dancing flowers in the trade wind. And the dancing gaiety in Richard's grey eyes. Life itself, it seems to us both, may be seen as a dance, sometimes gay and frisking, other times solemn and mournful. A dance with a partner: is not love itself a figured dance?

And then heaven itself, not only the Great Dance that lies beyond but heaven as it includes some of this life—all that is most truly loving of course and all that is most lovely, too.

These days since I last wrote have been no less dancing days. I have continued to dance two or three different hulas, including the one called "Moku Kia Kahi," which means a one-masted vessel, like a little dancing sloop. We have in these days been much with Kahana and Leilani, here and at Mynah Bird Lane and at the Hula Club. We have also gone to the windward beaches, sometimes sitting round a driftwood fire, hearing the sound of the waves, until quite late. The moon has been waxing, and we have swum at night with moonlight on the heaving ocean. And there have been dancing showers and rainbows without number.

Once the four of us wound our way up a long zig-zag path that climbed the windward barrier wall of the Koolau Range until we reached the very top. We did not see any of the little folk, the Menehune, though of course they may have seen us; but we did see a wild boar, who fortunately went his way, and we saw some shy lovely flowers. We ate a late lunch just below the actual knife-sharp crest of the Koolau. Where we were was sheltered and windless, but we could hear the wind and had only to raise a hand for it to be in the trade wind. All the green, windy, sunny island lay below us, encircled by the dark blue of the vast Pacific Ocean.

One evening we had Jim Cosby to Umoani to dine, and he gave me a small bundle that contained not only my long-lost bra but, more welcome, the tiny flat silver compact that had been in it—a gift from my Gloucestershire grandmother. Jim said he thought Bill was genuinely ashamed, and perhaps I'd get a letter from him some day.

So we have walked or danced through the bright days of sun and shower. I have worn hibiscus in my hair and Richard has worn hibiscus on his shirt. Sometimes we wander up the road, Richard and I, to where the road ends above Umoani at the edge of a wood. Once we wandered into the wood among the white-trunked koa trees and discovered a small, grassy ledge, very secluded, whence we could see almost the whole sweep of southern Oahu, from Diamond Head in the east to Barbers Point Light in the west.

Here we had a long afternoon's talk about our life, where we were headed and whether that were the right heading. We strongly believe in such periodical examinations—otherwise it would be just drift. What we talked about mostly—Richard lying on his side with head on hand and elbow and I sitting with my knees drawn up to my chin—was love, not just love for each other, but love as the centre of all. God's love poured abundantly into us with the imperative command that we pour it into others: and we were asking: were we doing it? Love must be given to individual persons, if it be truly love, not to faceless groups. We talked all afternoon until it was almost too dark to find our way out of the wood. And that night we found a name for our little secret place—Kulahola, meaning golden hours.

Sometimes during these days I have tried to read Marcus Aurelius, but my mind would wander from the page. And one afternoon, aware of the flower scents drifting down the breeze, I wrote a small poem instead of working. After all, what has a Stoic emperor of Rome, writing in crabbed Greek, got to say to an Island girl, dancing with naked breasts and a red hibiscus in her hair where the yellow shower trees drift their blossoms by the sea?

We sat beneath our own yellow shower tree at Umoani on the grass by the pool, and I read my little poem to a dreamy-eyed Richard.

> Diamond Head lowers
> A brooding sphinx
> Pondering her riddles
> Of drifting flowers:
>
> Whether your lei
> Shall drift to her
> Calling you back
> To Hawaii nei.

Mary's account of the Great Luau

At Mynah Bird Lane where we have spent the night, we awaken to a sense of excitement and anticipation. This is the day of the great luau. We spring up, dressing in old clothes, and have a bite of breakfast. Other people, including Kahana, have spent the night here and others are arriving by the carful every minute, for the expedition to the secret Moana Beach will leave from here. The lanai and yard are full of laughing groups of Hawaiians and part-Hawaiians with innumerable children running about and screaming. In the lane are parked two large, high-sided, ex-Army trucks with their tailboards down. Everybody will go in them.

I go out after breakfast to see what's happening. I am dressed in a battered blue-denim skirt and khaki blouse; my legs are bare, except for sandals. Since Richard and I are so tanned by now, we are as dark as most of the others, all of whom have at least some Polynesian blood. I espy Leilani talking to Kahana, Eho, and another tall man by the tailboard of one of the trucks, and I go up to them.

"Good morning, Mary," says Kahana. "What confusion! Mary, this is Haokea."

"Good morning," I say, smiling at Haokea. "Perhaps I am Malia today. Do you all go in this truck? Can I come, too?"

"No!" says Haokea explosively. "This is *kane* truck! Men's truck! You *wahine!*"

"She doesn't know, Haokea," says Leilani, and to me, "We'll go in the other one. We go soon now."

Eventually the confusion is sorted out, and, after a fond and disapproving farewell to Richard, I climb into the crowded wahine truck along with Momi and Makaleha and Leilani. We sit on the floor with the sides towering above us. Once the tailgate is shut, we can see only the sky from our seated position. As the truck starts with a jerk and rumbles out into the street, I think that if there should be a wreck I should certainly land on some enormous bosom and be safe.

The trucks, with the kane truck in the lead, head out the Pearl Harbor road (as I can tell by the position of the sun) and then, after skirting the harbour, travel in a more or less northwesterly direction across the Ewa Plain. Our truck is a babble of feminine chatter and laughter, with children crawling about all over the place. After a long time I become aware that the truck is on a smaller, bumpier road with almost no traffic on it, but I couldn't tell where we turned off if I wanted to. Then, after more time has elapsed, it stops. I extricate myself from a little girl and stand up to see what there is to be seen.

We are on a more or less straight road with undergrowth and trees on either side. Ahead there is a small hill, and one of the men from the kane truck is standing on it. He shouts and waves—an all clear, I later decide—and suddenly two small trees on the left side of the road move away like Birnam Wood on its way to Dunsinane. As soon as the trees are gone, the kane truck shoots into the hole and disappears. We follow. I look back. The trees are being moved back into place; their roots seem to be bagged. The men who moved them and the lookout come running in, past us, to where the kane truck waits. Then the trucks snort and bump along a track through the trees that is almost invisible to my eyes. I sit down again and jounce along, watching tree branches go past overhead. This goes on for a long time. Finally the truck stops and the engine is switched off. The men who have driven our truck come back and lower the tailgate, grin at us, and run off towards the kane truck, parked some distance away. We are here, but where is here? There is still nothing to be seen but trees. We crawl out.

Leilani says, "We leave all our haole clothes and everything here, under the canvas. Leave everything."

Some of the women are already opening big bundles of bright-patterned lengths of cotton cloth, which is to be our substitute for the original *kapa* cloth. Leilani comes up to me and says, "For you, Malia —the white ginger you love on blue." We undress to a hum of laughter all around. Then, naked, I wrap the soft cloth about me under the arms as I see other women doing. Leilani and Sara, one of the girls from the school, both laugh, and Leilani says, "No, no, Mary—Malia! That is for the older, married *wahines.* Of course you and Val *are* married, but not with babies. We thought—Momi decided—that for today you should be, like me and the girls in the school, not married, yes?"

"All right," I say. "Whatever you say—whatever Momi says. So what do I do?"

"That is good," she says. "And Kahana is telling Val. We who are not married, we leave our breasts bare. See?—like this!" She wraps a length of white cloth round her waist, tucking it in to make a short skirt. Sara is doing the same, except that hers is purple with orange flowers on it.

"Lumme!" I mutter, but I follow their example.

Then we walk along the track, as most of the other women are doing. A group of men, neatly if not extensively dressed in loin cloths, come out from behind their truck and walk along with us. Despite a passionate outcry to Richard once against bras, I feel somewhat self-conscious at having uncovered breasts before men, especially walking since they bounce a bit. I meet Richard's eye and he gives me an amused look, and I manage to grin back. I encourage myself with thoughts of Eve's braless state, as well as with the observation that lots of breasts bounce much more than mine.

"How now, the ancient Minoans?" Richard murmurs.

"Never heard of 'em!" I murmur back. "Never heard of bras, either."

I notice, though, that the men do not stare. They are, indeed, so natural and easy in manner that I decide it's better to be half-undressed with Hawaiians than to be fully dressed with Frenchmen or Italians. Soon I cease to be self-conscious and feel as natural as I do at the hula school. After all, why not?

We come over a little rise, and there before us is Moana Beach. In the immediate foreground there is a parklike grove of trees, where a group of girls and women is sitting or half-reclining. Beyond the grove is the crescent of sand and sea. Inshore the water is calm and clear green. Farther out there is a reef and beyond it the intense deep blue of the ocean. Waves break against the reef in showers of bright spray. At either end of the curving beach, the cove is bounded by great black cliffs. One of the men who is walking beside me tells me that the cliffs stretch along all this part of the shore, except for this one place, where the unbroken reef and surf make it impossible for a boat to land.

We pass women who are tending a pot on a fire, and others who are pounding something with stones. Naked children and dogs are scampering about everywhere, and some of them are splashing in the lagoon. Out on the reef are three or four men with spears, and, even as I look, one of them darts his spear into the water and pulls forth a rainbow-hued fish.

Haokea, who is standing beside me waving to a small outrigger canoe on the beach, says, "We go out there now."

"It looks like fun!" says Richard.

"When? Now?" I say. "Can I come? Will you show me how to spear fish?"

"No!" says Haokea gruffly. "Kane work! You no go! You stay here! Do wahine work!" He sounds cross.

Leilani laughs. "She does not know the old ways yet, Haokea. She stay! Go on, kane!"

He grins a little and says, "Teach her to be wahine! Aloha!" He runs lightly off with Kahana and another. Kahana calls, "Come on, Val!"

Richard grins at me and says, "See you later, wahine!" He runs down the beach.

"Hisss!" I say. "What am I supposed to do? Have a baby this afternoon?"

"Today," says Sara solemnly, "we are wahines of old Hawaii." She smiles and adds, "It is true that if we were here for always, we might urge some changes in the old ways. But this is today."

"No," says Leilani seriously. "There wouldn't be many changes, because the old ways would be natural and right if civilisation broke down—women would do what they have always done. And the men— they do not fish for fun or sport. They hunt for food, and they do it best. And we have our functions. So on this day do not think twentieth century. It's never been heard of. Do you see it anywhere?"

I glance about, then look more intently. The trucks are invisible, over the hill behind the grove. There is nothing anywhere—not a watch or a radio, not a shoe or a book. I do not even see a pair of spectacles.

"You see?" says Leilani. "It is gone. If you went back up the hill, there would be no trucks. There never were. Honolulu is grass houses only. Perhaps we never find the way back to the twentieth century. You will see! We are wahines of old Hawaii, now, always."

I see Richard, tall and bronzed, spear in hand on the reef. He plunges the spear in and brings up a fish. Kahana claps him on the back. Maybe it's true; maybe we've slipped through a time-fault and are here for ever.

"Only fish," I say. "Only coconuts. Only poi."

"That's right," says Sara. "And the sea and the sky."

A fisherman on the reef pulls up a writhing octopus. I lose a measure of enthusiasm for reef fishing. He slaps it to his face, and the arms wrap about his head. I lose still more. Then, as the fisherman bites it, the arms go limp, and he throws it down. Let the kanes have it.

In Oxford, I think, the spire of Oseney Abbey splits the sky, and the Black Prince, perhaps, is waiting for a fair wind for France. And here: old Hawaii, sunny and bright, yet with savage wars of its own and human sacrifice. I look at the wahines round the fire and in the grove and the naked children playing. Close at hand are the shadowed mountains of the Waianae and the long snowy trade-wind clouds drift overhead. I look at Richard, brown and powerful there on the reef, with his spear in his hand, and I see only a Polynesian male, a warrior among other warriors. A seabird cries. A woman by the fire says, *"Auwe, auwe!"* A young wahine is giving her breast to her tiny baby. It is a scene by Gauguin. Then I think, no, no—there is no Gauguin. Captain Cook has not been born. I look down at my flowered skirt and bare breasts. How else could it be? Suddenly it is perfectly natural: it is all true. I see a tall kane coming towards us, and I don't feel shy. The sun is warm on my skin and hair, and I am wahine and this is the way things are and always have been. Immemorially. Now, today, in this space we call the present, there is no machine civilisation anywhere. That was a dream in the night, perhaps a nightmare, already fading. The sand, the trees, the wahines, the kanes on the reef, the sun falling on my breast, and the encircling sea —this is the real.

The powerful kane who was walking towards us comes up and says, "Aloha!" in a deep voice.

"This is Noke Tom," says Leilani. "Aloha, Noke Tom. This is Malia."

He gives us a wide grin and says cheerfully, "Momi say to me, 'Blow the horn for the Breaking of the Lagoon,' and she say, 'Tell Leilani.' How long?"

"Now!" she says. "The girls are chosen—seven. And all know except Mary. Blow, Noke Tom!"

"Hokay!" he says; and he lifts a curving shell to his lips and blows a long mournful blast that echoes off the cliffs. He goes down the beach blowing further blasts. I see the canoe, full of men, coming in from the reef.

"We play now," says Leilani. "Ceremonial capture. We who are maidens are captured and carried off into the lagoon by the men. What happens is this: we three—you and I and Sara—and four other girls, those who are old enough—" She glances delicately at our figures and goes on, "We all stand at the beginning of the beach in a line. And the unmarried men, ten of them, are back in the grove. Then when the horn is blown again, they run to the wahine they choose, pick her up, and carry her into the lagoon. Perhaps originally he was supposed to be taking her off to his own island. Anyway, the first kane to reach the water is the King of the Luau and the ones who get no girl are laughed at as boys."

"And is the first girl carried into the water the Queen?" I say.

"Oh, no!" says Sara. "Momi is always Queen. There is no honour for us. We wait on the man who captures us when the time for eating comes."

"Unfair, unfair!" I say, lapsing slightly towards the twentieth century. "I shall run into the sea by myself and swim away."

"No!" says Leilani. "That you must not do! They would catch you. Anyway, we are supposed to *want* to be captured. Our honour is being chosen. Of course, with ten men, we all will be. Come on! The men are landing! We leave our clothes by this palm tree, yes?"

"WHAT!" I say explosively. "We are naked?"

"You wouldn't want to get your skirt wet, would you?" says Leilani, grinning. "And bathing suits haven't been invented. Remember—this is before missionaries. Or Queen Victoria. And you promised to do all the old way, no?" She drops her white skirt. "The kanes will be naked, too," she adds.

"Help, help!" I mutter to myself. I look around, possibly for a policeman. I see a naked man striding towards the grove. Then I drop my skirt with Leilani's, and murmur to Sara, "I hope this ceremonial capture isn't supposed to be followed by an actual rape. If so, I spend my day in a palm tree, coconut-bombing kanes!"

Leilani marshals the seven of us in a long line with two-yard intervals at the top of the beach. "You face the grove and the men," she says to all of us. "It will be a little while yet—the kanes must choose the one they will try to get. And listen—listen, Mary!—when the horn blows and you see them running, do *not* be so afraid you run away! That is the big disgrace! And you get caught just the same."

She takes her place beside me in the line. There is a silence over the beach. I hear the crash of a wave on the barrier reef. I hear, or at least feel, the beating of my own heart. The older people, with the children beside them, sit in the grove and look at us. The naked men at the back of the grove—a clear way has been left for them—are also looking at us.

One of them is making a joke to another. I see Richard and he grins at me, but I do not grin back. He is one of them.

I am nervous. I have never felt so naked in my whole life, or quite so vulnerable and—female. My knees tremble slightly, and I can't make them stop.

"I know now," I mutter to myself, "what the bait in a trap thinks about." I glance down at my sunlit body—that particularly intimate, for me alone, view of myself; and I think that in this moment I am not primarily the human but primarily the female. Still, I think, I am thinking this, which is human.

"Blawww!" The long blast of the horn rings in my ears. Thinking ceases. I feel. A great roar goes up from the men. I hear a sound like a sob from some girl.

The men come bounding through the grove. My heart starts to thud. I am for a moment dizzy, blind. My sight clears. The men are much closer. They are gigantic! Naked! I forget that this is a game. I breathe in short gasps. I am terrified and excited all at once. Everything in me wants to run away.

I see a tall, black-haired giant running towards me, arms outstretched and low. Again my eyes blur. My heart will choke me! I can't breathe! I want to be seized! I must run!

I half-turn. Suddenly I am swept up. Taken! An arm round my shoulders! Under my knees! I hear him grunt, say "Ha!" I feel the jarring of his pounding feet. I glimpse my knees against the sky. Somewhere a scream. We are falling through space!

Shock! Shock of cold water! Water closing over me! I gasp and struggle. I am being held, raised.

It is over. I look at him. *Richard!* Richard captured me! And I never knew it to this instant. "Val!" I say weakly.

He is grinning. "My wahine now!" he says. "Won you fair and square! Thought Noke Tom was going to get you, but I made it. He swerved off and grabbed Sara. Anyway, Kahana with Leilani was first. He is King. Let's go in."

I nod, feeling exhausted, even though Richard has done all the work. I paddle in, seeing Sara and Leilani sitting on the beach.

"See you later, love!" says Richard. "You're doubly my wahine now. See that you remember it! And as they say, see that I get plenty pig, plenty poi." He goes off towards a group of laughing men, discussing, as men have always done, the hunt.

I sit down with Leilani and Sara. I still feel shaken. We are silent.

"Well," I murmur finally. "I'm certainly glad I didn't get my skirt wet."

The others giggle, rather weakly, and Leilani says, "We know how you feel. After all . . . Anyway, it will be a colourful memory. A kind of initiation, maybe. We did not tell you before, because we didn't want you to—to be nervous."

"Just as well!" I mutter. "We don't, er . . . do quite that sort of thing at Oxford."

"No," says Leilani. "It's not the way I think of Oxford. And no woman in her right mind . . . no woman *with* a mind would want to be so, so—"

"So female!" I say.

"Yes," she says. "So female. No woman with a mind would want to feel so female all of the time. Still, it may be good to be reminded now and then . . . about what lies beneath. The, er, differences, no?"

"I ain't likely to forget for many moons," I say with a small grin. "If ever! But I agree, Leilani. I do. No wholeness without the truth."

"We talk more later," says Leilani, lapsing back into the half-pidgin Island rhythm. "We go now. Do wahine work."

We arise and walk back into the lagoon and swim about for two or three minutes and then walk up the beach together. Some of the men are standing near the palm where we left our skirts, but as we walk towards them I do not feel the least bit shy. Perhaps it is, as Leilani said, that I have had an initiation. Anyhow, I feel proud, proud to be a woman, and I walk lightly towards them.

The men look at us, and we look back. To me, there seems to be admiration and grave approval in their glance, which also seems to me to be open and sunny. We walk to our skirts, there beside the men, and bend and pick them up and wrap them round us as naturally as a woman in England might pick up and put on a cardigan. I feel that this is good; and then I think that the way men stare and snigger in the supposedly civilised countries is not good. Evil perhaps.

Leilani remarks as we walk away, "Do you know, in the Hawaiian language you cannot curse or be obscene. One must learn the English words to do it."

We join the other wahines and are put to work. Momi is the high command, but the three Mamos are her lieutenants. There is poi to be stirred and dried octopus to be pounded and fruit to be cut or arranged in wooden bowls. Some kanes are digging a hole nearby, and Makaleha tell us that in that spot the pig has been steaming since last night—a number of people spent the night on the beach. First, she says, the pit was dug. Then many stones, long-heated in the fire, were put in. Then a bed of wet seaweed with the pig—*puaa*—on top. Then more seaweed, more hot stones, and then earth.

Now the pig, tender and juicy, is brought out of the ground. The luau begins.

The kanes gather in the grove, sitting cross-legged in the grass. Each of us wahines has a man she must serve. The older wahines serve their husbands. We serve the men who captured us. Once the jovial, shouting men are seated, we start for our particular men. I give Richard, who is seated with Noke Tom, Haokea, and King Kahana, a drinking nut—one of the young coconuts full of milk that the men climbed for earlier. Then I bring him a koa-wood bowl full of poi. Finally I take him a broad stiff leaf of considerable size, which is laden with baked pig, raw fish and cooked fish, edible seaweed, and several other foods. Richard grins at me and murmurs, "Plenty pig, plenty poi!" and Haokea guffaws. After the kanes with women have been served, the men who have no women queue up, leaf in hand, with the children for their food.

A Mamo calls some of us girls over to her and gives us bowls and platters to pass round to all the men. I have a wooden bowl of kukui-nut meats and Leilani a shallow wooden bowl of cut-up fruit. I am struck by her beauty and grace as she stands poised, waiting, her long hair partly caught on one shoulder and partly down her back, the dark bowl of red fruit held in both hands just below her breasts, contrasting with her creamy brown skin. One of the other girls reaches out and steals some kukui nut from my bowl and then reaches for more.

"No, Watee!" says Mamo. "It is laxative. Take after eating, maybe."

We proceed on our mission. As I offer the nutmeats to Noke Tom, who takes a pinch and puts it on the side of his leaf, he says, "You good wahine! Plenty pig, plenty poi! I catch you next time." He grins at Richard, who grins back and says, "Maybe, Noke Tom." I smile impartially at them both and move on.

I pause at one point, between two groups of men, and look about. Through the trees are the slopes of the mountains, bright in the afternoon sun. Amongst the dark heads and muscular bodies of the men move the slender girls in their gaily coloured skirts, moving with light steps, while drifts of petals come down from the pink and yellow shower trees.

The men are at last finished, stuffed indeed—plenty pig, plenty poi!— and most of them sleep where they are.

And we at last serve ourselves and gather some distance away, all the women, and eat. I am wildly hungry, and the baked pig is wonderfully succulent and delicious. We eat and eat. Between bites and swallows of coconut milk, Momi and the other older women, including Madam Pele, tell stories of other luaus. I ask if any girl has ever run away from the charge of the men, and there is laughter from the women who hear the question.

"You wanted to run fast, Malia, yes?" says Momi. "It is good you stayed. But girls have run away. We all want to and yet not. When they run, though, they are caught. Except Noela, when I was a girl. She ran and the kane could not catch her. That year there was only him with no girl—no one to help him—and he was slow with short legs. He had to keep running after her. All through the luau she ran away. She was afraid at first, but also she did not like him. And then she laughed. All the kanes shouted jokes at him, and all the wahines began to cry out to her not to be caught. When he stopped to rest, she stop. She never caught."

One of the Mamos tells of the time the littlest man could not lift the fattest girl. "He tried and tried, and she said he was no real kane. And then he got mad and took her foot and dragged her to the lagoon, screaming. Later, though, she marry him."

The talk and laughter die away, and one by one the wahines curl up to sleep. I go over to the stream to wash the grease from my fingers. Then I go a little apart and lie down under a yellow shower tree. The grass is soft, almost covered by the pale yellow petals. My eyes close. They open when a shadow falls across my face. It is Richard bending over me. He lies down beside me in the petals. We kiss with drowsy pleasure, sleep.

I wake and find that in our sleep we have come to be in each other's arms. I look up through the yellow blossoms and dark branches to blue sky and rose-coloured cloud. It is near sunset. I stir and Richard wakes. A little naked girl about five years old looks at us solemnly. We both smile warmly at her, and a delighted smile breaks out on her face. She runs away. We kiss and sit up. Some people still sleep but most are awake and stirring.

"Oh," I say. "I feel so good!" I yawn and stretch. "I think I was made to be a Polynesian girl. I seem to take to this life."

"Even the capture?" he says with a grin.

"Even that—now and then," I say, also grinning. "Although at the time . . ."

"Look!" he says, pointing. Sara and Leilani and Haokea are strolling unclothed towards the lagoon. Noke Tom follows. "Come on! Let's go, too."

"I'll leave my skirt here," I say. "Seems to be the proper thing. And I've got over every single squeam!" We both walk nude towards the water. "Why not?" I add. "Skin is very nice-looking stuff. I may even go bare-breasted on some summer evening strolling down Piccadilly. Naturally, I'll wear heels since it's Town."

Richard laughs. "And then, I suppose, you'll go up to a bobby and say that a man is following you. Three years later when you get out of Holloway Prison—"

"With a blouse supplied by the Crown," I say. "Val! Stop a minute." He pauses, and I say, "What were you thinking about just then?"

"Why, London and all that," he says. "And—how good the sun feels. Why?"

"Oh, it's so unbelievable!" I say. "We walk along joking about bobbies, and now we're standing here talking with people all about. And we're stark naked!"

"It is sort of incredible," he says. "But good. Here comes Kahana."

"Yes," I say. "Sort of—well, before the Fall, you know."

Kahana comes up to us. "Aloha," he says in his deep voice. "Good-kind luau, yes?"

"Aloha, King!" I say. "Plenty good!"

He grins and then says in his civilised vein, "You two are pretty adaptable. Both Leilani and I—and Momi—thought you would be. Anyhow, you seem to have gone native, as they say, rather easily."

"We were just talking about that," says Richard. "We think it's good."

"It *is* good," says Kahana. "There is some truth in the Noble Savage idea, after all." He grins cheerfully at us and wanders towards the lagoon.

"I don't know what Rousseau would think about some Noble Savages like us talking about being Noble Savages," I say. "Come on. Let's swim."

We walk into the calm waters of the lagoon and swim about.

The sky is spectacular with sunset. The flaming colours of the sky, including a wine-like red, are reflected in the still lagoon. We come out of the water and walk along the edge of it to the cliffs on the end of the beach, where we sit on a rock and look back at the sunset. Although we're nude, we are perfectly comfortable in the balmy air. The sky over a great dark mountain is a glory of streaming colours and the lagoon has become crimson. The colour falls upon us, too: Richard and I are

208

rose-red, and the sand is reddish gold. The far end of the beach is already in the shadow of the other cliffs, and the mountain is a bold black silhouette. The night creeps down the beach. The lagoon darkens. The fire that has been lighted halfway down the beach seems to burn more brightly. The last of the rose colour fades from our skin.

"Another jewelled day," I murmur. "To hang on our necklace of days and hours."

"So many of them, here in the Islands, have been," you say. "How good living can be!"

"Mmmm," I say. "When there's beauty—and love. I've been loving you a lot all day, unbeknownst to you."

"Silly girl!" you say in a tender voice. *"Not* unbeknownst to me! Every time you turned those blue eyes towards me, I knew." You put your arm round my waist. "Mary," you say. "You nearly broke my heart at the Breaking of the Lagoon. You looked so frightened, as if you wanted help. All I could do was be the one for you . . ."

"I'm glad you were the one," I say.

We fall silent as the dusk gathers round us. From the fire down the beach we hear the sound of an ukulele and a girl singing.

"Val," I say. "Did you know that Rupert Brooke came to the Islands? Listen."

> Warm perfumes like a breath from vine and tree
> Drift down the darkness. Plangent, hidden from eyes,
> Somewhere an *eukaleli* thrills and cries
> And stabs with pain the night's brown savagery;
> And dark scents whisper; and dim waves creep to me,
> Gleam like a woman's hair, stretch out, and rise;
> And new stars burn into the ancient skies,
> Over the murmurous soft Hawaiian sea . . .

My voice trails away. And then I murmur, "Mercia and I used to read all his Island poems."

"Just perfect," you murmur. "Perfect for this moment. And beautiful." You bend closer and kiss me, your hand behind my head. Then you straighten up and say, "Come on, love. We'd best go back to—oh, look!"

Two women are dancing with supple grace in the firelight. We wander, hand in hand, down the beach, detouring to find my skirt and his loin cloth. Torches are moving along the reef where some of the men have gone back to fishing. We move into the outskirts of the throng around the fire and sit down.

We do not sit quietly for long, or at least I don't. Madam Pele comes round the fire and beckons me to follow her into darkness. There I find Leilani and others from the school.

"We do the 'Moku Kia Kahi,' " says Leilani. "Tuck skirt in well!" There are six of us from the school, supplemented by Leilani. We wait while four very fat women, including two of the three Mamos, wearing loose flowing holokus, which they have to hold off the ground, dance— dance lightly despite their bulk—and sing. They sit down laughing, and the ukuleles begin the rhythms of our hula. With little steps, hips swaying, we dance into the firelight. Some of the women in the audience sing, and they and the men beat time with their hands. For some reason I think of Peter Shirley in far-away Yorkshire, perhaps with the Hunt, Peter splendid in his pinks, and I wonder what he would think if he could see me now. But it seems to me right and natural that I should dance thus by the sea, for that is what young wahines do. The hula ends and we return into the darkness. "All pau!" says Madam Pele. "You hula girls now." I wander back to the fire.

Some of us sit in a little group, while other people dance or sing. Leilani and Richard are talking about Island customs, when they can hear each other. I look into the fire in a dreaming way, watching the sparks ascend into darkness. Noke Tom is sitting a yard or so away, half-facing me. I look at the firelight shining on the brown skin of his great shoulders, highlighting the muscles of his arm, but I am scarcely aware that I am doing so. Then I change my position slightly, and as I do see my legs, rosy in the firelight. For an instant I am faintly shocked—not at their nudity but at my not being the twisted creature of past years. It haunts me still. I shudder and feel restless. I murmur to Richard that I'll be back soon and slip out into the darkness.

As soon as I am away from the fire, I see the moon, large and golden, sailing up above the cliffs at one end of the beach. I wander along the edge of the lagoon to the other end of the beach and sit on a fallen palm tree, looking at the distant fire and the torches of the tireless reef fishermen and the rising moon. I can hear singing from the fireside, distant and sweet; and I can also hear the boom and sigh of breakers on the barrier reef. The trade wind stirs the coconut palms, a rustling sound, and the breeze touches me lightly. I think dreamily about the wonder of wings, a wonder that thrills me yet. I hope I shall never take it for granted. Or take any beauty—poems or stars or the splendour of the sea —for granted. But wings! Wings after such hopeless pain: maybe I appreciate the particular wonder of being a light-footed, dancing, running girl with all life open to her more than any other girl in the world.

Maybe I'm more aware, and appreciation rests on awareness. In heaven, I think, perhaps everyone will be eternally what they most completely were in life. Socrates, the elderly truth-seeker. St Joan in shining armour still. Shelley or Catullus, the intense young poet. Churchill, the lion's growl of England. This man will be the soldier, that the businessman. One woman, the dowager; another a singing voice; and many, mothers. And I, then, will be the girl—the dancer unchained. The girl in love with life.

I abandon this theory before it can crumble, and think about the Islands—how they are dearer even than I knew, and how it has been a coming home to a part of myself as well as to Hawaii nei.

A feminine voice says, "Oh, there you are!" Not Leilani. Not Sara. Yet familiar, known. Who, then? I see a slight figure walking lightly down the beach towards me. That light tread—oh, known! But—but . . .

"Hullo, Mary—little one!" says the voice. "Aloha, little owl!"

I know. Oh dear God, I know! Little thrills chase up my back.

"Mercia! Mercia!" I cry. "Oh, Mercia!" I hold out my arms. My breath catches.

"Oh, no, owl dear! I can't hug you, honey," she says with a little laugh. She stands there, smiling, looking lovingly at me as she used to do. Her hair, never long and very fine, moves in the breeze.

"You came back," she says. "Back to the Islands, where we were so happy. Back to our little house. Our Hawaii. It was right to come."

"Mercia!" I say in a shaky voice. "Is it really you? —Oh, it is, it is! Oh, Mercia! It was so awful when you—when you went away. Awful darkness! And I cried and cried, longing for you—and the Islands. You were the only . . . only bright thing there ever was . . ."

"Little Mary, I know," she says gently. "I know. Believe me, I would have come to you, in the darkness, if it were allowed. I loved you, little owl—did you know how much?"

"I loved you, Mercia," I say. "Oh, you were all the sweetness, all the laughter in the world. I still love you. Oh, so much! Oh, Mercia—dear, dear Mercia! And I wanted you to know about me—walking. I'm—I'm different!"

"I see that!" she says with a happy little laugh, looking at me in the moonlight with her large eyes shining. I follow her gaze, looking down in the light of the moon at my body, again with the faint shock of delight.

"Yes, honey," she says. "Different. Winged in beauty. You're not Ruth now, 'sick for home . . . in tears amid the alien corn.' You've come home. And you've wanted me to know. I do know, Mary. I came to tell you that I know."

"I wanted wings to be with you, Mercia," I say. "I wanted to run along beaches with you."

"Oh little owl!" she says. "I knew that, even then."

"Mercia," I say, "I think I was in love with you—if a little girl of eleven can be—that year by the sea."

"Yes," she says in a low voice. "I felt it . . . and, Mary, it was good and right, then. And then Val came riding, finding you in the darkness— a very great good!"

"Oh!" I say. "You know about Val!"

"Of course I do, little owl!" she says, laughing. "You needn't tell me anything! I have heard the bells of Oxford. Mary dear, I can't explain, you know, but loves go on. Here in the Islands, I was watching over you. I wanted to. And now—well, we have choices still—I want to go on . . . watching over you, in a way . . ."

"Oh, Mercia!" I say. "I'll be so happy knowing that. I'll never forget!"

"Mary, little one," she says. "You and Val, loving each other and loving your love—that is true and holy. Offer that love to God, blessed be He. Never forget what you know: that your love for Val and his for you is part of that Great Dance you were writing about the other day. And in the figure of the Dance I, too, have a part that is full of joy. Your part is loving Val with reckless love."

"Mercia, Mercia!" I cry. "I do, I do! And I love you so much!"

She steps closer to me, steps so lightly, as she always did, and her lovely eyes shine in the flood of moonlight. She looks at me with her eyes full of love, and then she smiles her gay, impulsive little smile.

"Reckless love!" she says softly. "Shut your eyes, Mary. And do not move."

I shut them and sit very still. I feel her hands brushing lightly, gently, over my strong legs, then my arms, and then my face and hair. Something touches my lips, light as a feather. I kiss it.

"Darling," Mercia whispers. "Darling little owl. Walk in love all your days. *Aroha,* little owl . . . until we meet again . . . *aroha* . . ."

"*Aroha,*" I whisper. Then after a moment I murmur, "Mercia?" There is no reply. My eyes still shut, I whisper again, "Mercia? . . . "

I open my eyes. The wavelets in the lagoon glitter, flashing silver under the moon. There is no one near. Far down the beach, with his long, easy stride, is Richard coming towards me.

He comes up to me and says, "Oh, there you are!" and I hear the echo of another voice saying those words. "Mary, darling!" you say. "What are you doing, sitting alone in the night?"

"But I haven't been alone!" I say. Then, suddenly, I cry out, wildly, *"Aroha!* Oh, *aroha!"* I burst into tears.

"Mary, dear," you say, sitting down beside me on the log and putting your arms around me. I bury my face in your familiar shoulder and sob. You stroke my hair. After a moment or two, you say gently, "Mary, what is it?"

"Mercia!" I say between sobs. "She—she came and talked to me. She said sh-she loves me, and she is with me, t-t-too! And she said that you and I should love each other with r-reckless love. Reckless! And offer our love to God! And she said—oh! she said *'Aroha!'* You remember, I told you . . . how we—we said that?"

"I remember," you say, while I sob harder.

Then, suddenly, the tears are gone. I tell you about it all, from Mercia's first words until you came with the same words. "And she called me 'little owl' just as she always did," I say. "And then, when I closed my eyes, her fingers touched me lightly all over and there was a little light kiss, and she said, *'Aroha,* little owl . . . until we meet again . . . *aroha.'* And when I opened my eyes, she was gone."

"Strange and beautiful," you say. There is a short silence. Then you say, "Mary, how was she dressed?"

"Why, I don't know," I say. "I didn't notice. I kept looking at her eyes."

"Well," you say. "Was she like you, with breasts bare? Or some kind of blouse?"

"I just don't know," I say. "I don't think her breast was bare, but I don't have the impression of a blouse, either. But I saw her smile, and her eyes were shining in the moonlight, like the lagoon . . . and she touched me lightly, like the wind . . ."

"Was it the wind?" you say. "Could you have drifted off to sleep and dreamed it?"

"Oh, no, no!" I say. And then, "Oh, Val—I don't know! It seemed as real as this. Terribly real. She laughed. Her hair moved in the wind."

"Well, we don't have to know," you say. "Perhaps it's best to leave some things open. Maybe we're meant to. But what she said is true and right. It makes her seem even realer to me. —Also, there is this. When I was looking for you—when I first spotted you, way down here at the end, I had the impression that there was somebody with you. When I got closer and saw you were alone, I was slightly startled. —Well, shall we go back?"

"Look!" I say. "Oh, look! The one thing I wanted you to see—the lunar rainbow! Look!" I point. Over the sea on the horizon arches the rainbow—in moonlight. The moon is still low above the eastern mountains; the lunar rainbow on the western horizon. Faint but clear the colours shine against the night sky. It fades.

"Oh, I'm so glad you've seen it!" I say. "I saw it once before with Mercia. It's rare. —Val! I saw it with Mercia, and now with you right after Mercia! Right after she told us to love each other with reckless love! Oh, Val!"

"Good lord!" says Richard. "Even I have got a goosebump or two. The thing itself—that ghostly beauty! And then—at this moment!"

"Yes," I say. "Let's go away now . . ."

We walk slowly, hand in hand, along the curving beach, gleaming white in the moonlight and holding in its arms the moving, shimmering lagoon.

As we near the fire I say, "I want to swim under the moon. You?"

"Yes, yes!" he says.

We hang his loin cloth and my skirt on the branch of a small tree up the beach, and stroll towards the lagoon.

"There's some poem," I say, "about how you can never know Hawaii till you've hung your every garment in a tree and swum in a bathing suit of moonlight and a breeze."

"Best kind," he says. "Very fetching, too."

We pause at the water's edge, and I look at him, tall and splendid in the white pour of moonlight. I think how clean and strong his face is with its fine brow, deep-set eyes, and patrician nose. Then I look down at myself, seeing my body as objectively, almost, as a sculpture.

"Val," I say, seriously, "I am beautiful and you are beautiful. We shan't be always. People are young and beautiful, and then they lose it— and long to have it back. And some never have it, as I almost didn't— and they break their hearts with longing. I know! Val, we mustn't take what we are for granted, ever! Oh, love, we are beautiful as running deer in our own way. I know we love each other's body, but let us be joyful about our own, too. Do you know what I mean? Do you? A gift of our God? Look! I am beautiful!" I run my hands over my hips and strong thighs.

Richard looks at me with an indescribably happy expression.

"Oh, Val!" I say, ecstatic. "We are a beautiful part of this beautiful night—we are one with it! The curve of my hips is the curve of this beach. Your shoulders are the mountains that hold the sky suspended. Be joyful! Be wonder-*full!*"

"My love, thank you!" he says. "I am joyful—more than I can say. Mary—keep us aware. Always!"

We step lightly into the lagoon, and the water embraces us. There is no one on the reef now, but occasionally white spray leaps up from the smash of seaward waves.

"Look," says Richard. "Some of the others are coming."

Leilani and Sara and another girl join us in the water, and girls' laughter rings out. Once I swim up beneath Richard and give him a wet and salty kiss. Other people come into the water all along the beach. There are splashing sounds and cheerful cries. I float on my back and look up at the moon. Then I close my eyes and just delight in the silken feel of the water.

Suddenly I find myself lifted right out of the water in the powerful arms of a man. My eyes snap open, and I look up into the smiling face of Noke Tom. He is standing in water up to his waist.

"Oha!" he says. "Look what I catch in the lagoon. A wahine!"

"Plenty pig, plenty poi!" I say in a surprised squeak.

"That good! Good-kind wahine!" he says. "But pig and poi not all for kane!"

"Tom!" I say, realising that Noke Tom means Persistent Tom. *"Val's* wahine!"

"Auwe, auwe!" he says. "Too bad! Well, I fish some more! Aloha, wahine-of-the-lagoon!"

He lowers me back into the water with a grin, and I swim away with an "Aloha, Tom. *Auwe.*" As I swim I mutter to myself, "My 'auwe' means that I half-wish you had kissed me, Noke Tom. I need to— where's Val?" I find him eventually, sitting chest deep in the water, and I sit beside him.

My breasts float and move with the water, and I giggle. Richard looks and chuckles and says, "Ah, my two little responsive dolphins!"

"Eat out of your hands!" I say. "Val, these tropic nights are dangerous. The kanes get ideas!" I tell him about Noke Tom.

"That dog!" he says with a laugh. "I get ideas, too!" Your hand moves under water.

I jump, "Ohhh!" I breathe. I collapse and disappear beneath the wavelets.

Richard hauls me up, chuckling. Then he gives a sudden start. I, too, have hands.

He leaps up and hauls me up. "Come on, wahine!" he says. "Quick!"

We splash out of the water and run down the beach, swerving into the glade.

Suddenly we fling our arms about each other. I am pressed against Richard's warm body, lifted for a moment off the ground by his strong arms. We kiss hungrily, fiercely. I am shuddering with passion. We sink down, mouth to mouth, into the grass. Richard caresses me, and I can feel a shaking in his body. "Mary, Mary!" he whispers. I moan. My fingers move over his back. "Oh, Val!" I whisper. "Val, now!" We press ourselves together. I think fleetingly, "One flesh . . ."

The trade wind rustles the trees above us.

Somewhat later we walk back to the lagoon. Richard says, smiling, "What was that about the tropic night being dangerous?"

"A lovely danger!" I say, also smiling.

We pause by the dark lagoon with its silver gleams, watching four girls playing like mermaids in the water.

"Listen, Val," I say. "Here is another poem, or part of one, by Rupert Brooke . . . 'Tiare Tahiti' it's called."

> Crown the hair, and come away!
> Hear the calling of the moon,
> And hear the whispering scents that stray
> About the idle warm lagoon.
> Hasten, hand in human hand,
> Down the dark, the flowered way,
> Along the whiteness of the sand,
> And in the water's soft caress . . .
> Spend the glittering moonlight there
> Pursuing down the soundless deep
> Limbs that gleam and shadowy hair . . .

"This night!" says Richard. "That poem's this very night, isn't it? We have been right inside those lines."

Hand in human hand, we walk into the warm lagoon, feeling, indeed, the water's soft caress. Two Island people joining four others in the blue Hawaiian night . . . playing . . . smiling . . . pursuing down the soundless deep limbs that gleam and shadowy hair . . .

Late in the night the wahine truck, laden with dozing women and girls and dogs, follows the kane truck back down the centuries under the silver moon. At Mynah Bird Lane, Richard and I sleep together on a narrow punee.

Mary on Aloha

We wake to a *kona* storm slashing across Honolulu with sheets of

216

rain. I am still in my luau skirt and Richard in his loin cloth, though our haole clothes are across a chair. Sara, also in luau skirt, appears in the doorway and smiles at us.

"You come to breakfast, yes?" she says. "Come like that."

We smooth our hair a little and splash some cold water in our faces and go to the table. In addition to the family, there are various others there, people too sleepy last night to go further.

Momi gives us a beaming smile and says, "You really Island people now. Not many haoles ever go to that luau."

"I know, Momi!" I say. "We are so grateful!" I jump up and run around and kiss Momi's cheek, and she looks pleased. "That's from Mercia, too, I think," I add.

While we eat our papaya, we see the storm rumbling away into the distance, and sunlight strikes down through the trees. Mynah birds set up a racket in the big spreading poinciana.

After breakfast Richard and I go out on the lanai. "Mary," he says. "We'd best go to the travel agency and book a flight in about a week— Summer Term begins a week from Monday. Ten days!"

"Auwe, auwe!" I moan. "I suppose so—as late as possible. The dolphins will be sad, though."

"What *are* you talking about, missy?" says Richard. "What is this talk of dolphins?"

"My breasts!" I say. "No more freedom. You said they were your dolphins."

"Dolphins don't bounce," he says in a donnish way. "They, er, glide. Come on!"

"You go. You do it," I say. "I'm not going down there with bouncing dolphins, that's flat! Or, no, not flat—that's the problem, isn't it? Anyhow, you do it. I'll stay here. —Oh, ask them if they'll drop our leis out."

"Okay," he says. "I'm glad you don't have seals instead of dolphins, crazy girl. At least, dolphins don't bark!" He dresses and drives off.

While he is gone, I tell Momi and Leilani about Mercia. I add that, whether it was a dream or something more, its happening was a sort of double sealing to the Islands. We are still talking about it when Richard drives in.

He comes up onto the lanai and flops down. "Mary—we go tomorrow!" he announces. "Nothing all next week—even these are cancellations."

"Oh, no!" I cry: "Oh, I don't want to go. I'm not—not prepared."

"Must!" he says. "One good thing. It'll give us about a week to get ourselves together before Term begins. So, now—we've got to go to Umoani and pack and arrange about the car. —Oh. They muttered about it, but they'll drop the leis."

Momi and Leilani are listening sadly to this. We promise to come back, and Momi says that we shall not be able to stay away now. I know it. Leilani says that she and Kahana will come to the airport in the morning, but we urge Momi not to. And they will have to say all our alohas to others of our Hawaiian friends for us. They urge us to come in tonight, but we think we shall spend our last evening alone.

Then with kisses and alohas and a few tears on my part, we drive away.

Richard says we have plenty of time to pack and suggests our driving around a bit before we leave Honolulu. First we drive up to the Pali to look our last upon windward Oahu. Coming down again, we just drive at random round the city including streets we've never been on. One of them takes us up a narrow valley towards the mountains. The houses become fewer and the green valley walls draw in. The air is cool and fresh. Then, almost at the end of the road, we see a parklike little glade with a stream tumbling through it. Sunlight pours down through the trees at the edge of the stream, and splashes of light fleck pools of shade. We decide to go over and sit on a rock for a while.

After a long silence, during which we are adjusting our minds to leaving the Islands, you say, "Last year about now—a year ago next week —we were sitting in the *Broom* at Dover, on our way to Provence. All our adventures there and in *Windrush* and in Hawaii, all lay ahead. Not to mention my *viva* and fellowship."

"What a year!" I say. "Adventure and beauty and loving friends. And, above all, our own love—our glad love, as you once called it."

"We have known what few ever do," you say, "—something perfect."

"Mercia knew—if it *was* Mercia," I say. "Reckless love. Love that doesn't weigh things up. When you loved me before wings, that was reckless love. Not recking . . ."

"Before I found you, Mary," you say, "I thought I could never love completely—always something reserved. But I love you completely—with all of me."

"So with me," I say. "All. It means waking up glad in the morning."

"Mary," you say. "That night when you didn't come home—you were walking down the mountain—I thought it *had* to be a wreck. It—it was almost more than I could take . . ." You pause and swallow. Then you say intensely, "Mary, I stagger myself when I think of all you are to me. You are my love, my world, my everything!"

I turn and hold you very tight, and we kiss, gently, with a timeless bliss.

Then, smiling a little, we get up and walk, hand in hand, to the car.

At Umoani we pack, see the neighbouring landlady, arrange about the car, and give the *popoki* a final pat. Then we have a small dinner and wash up as darkness falls. I read a bit, but Richard is restless and roams about. After awhile he goes across the bridge and stands there, looking across the Ewa Plain.

He comes back in and says, "The moon is above the Koolau Range. It's too lovely to read. I'd like to walk up to our special place, Kulahola —if we can find it!"

"Oh, let's do!" I say. "We can find it. I think."

And we do. The white-trunked koa trees are faintly eerie in the moonlight filtered through their leaves and branches, and we have to do a bit of searching about, but eventually we emerge onto our little grassy ledge.

I immediately slip out of my clothes and am nude. "Ah!" I say, pleased. "I am myself again." I sit down in the grass. After a surprised look, you do the same.

Below us is the sweep of the moon-blanched land. We can see the jewelled cluster of lights that is Honolulu in the distance, and farther still the vast darkness of the Pacific. Over us arches the luminous dark blue of the night sky. It is utterly silent save for a tiny breeze that makes a faint stir in the koa wood.

After a silence, I say, "This morning in that valley, everything was spilled gold and velvet shadow. Sunlit loving. And now all is moonlit— black and white. Not black so much as darkness. Your hair is darkness. Darkness in the wood, except for the white trunks. But this is the same world as that earlier one."

"Yes," you say. "And you, moon-white, breasts tipped with darkness —you are the same girl who was rose-red in the sunset by the lagoon last night. A rose-red girl, breasts tipped with roses."

"Heavens!" I say. "That's beautiful!" I pause and then say, "And Oxford? Hurrying home through the midwinter dusk and cold to the fire and tea, and the bells sort of muffled in the dusk—that's the same world as that of the shimmering lagoon, isn't it? Two visions of everything. Like poetry—the doubled vision."

"The doubled vision is the true vision, surely," you say. "To hold both together. And, of course, the most important of the dualities is the feminine vision and the masculine taken-in to the oneness—'one flesh'—that man and woman together can be. The deep truth of what Jesus said on marriage is clearer to me every day."

"Oh, yes!" I say. "Wholeness. The one complete wholeness—whole vision. Like seeing those dualities. Like seeing truth and beauty as one . . ." I pause, looking into the vastness of the night. Then I say, "I sometimes think that I show us the truth of beauty, and you show us the beauty of truth."

Again there is silence but for the faint stir of the koa wood. Then you put your hand on my thigh, and I bring my knees together, enclosing it.

"Mmmm," you say. "So warm and soft . . ."

"But somehow," I say, "your hand is warm on my leg."

"Inner fires," you murmur. "A moonlight princess of snow, cool and white, melting into darkness laced with flame."

You draw me close to you. Our bodies, cool and warm, come together, and the darkness is laced with flame.

A seabird sweeping through the dome of morning towards a great black rock rising out of the waves espies another larger bird on ahead drop something white and rush onward. Aha, thinks the seabird, it has dropped its fish; I shall catch it. The seabird swoops magnificently down, seizes, and soars high above the rock before he discovers his prize to be inedible. Falling from the indignant beak, flashing through the morning air, the linked *pikake* leis drop down to Diamond Head.

The Study, Holywell, April, 1968—Richard

The journey to Hawaii raises a new question in my mind, but it disposes of an old one. On balance, I feel a greater hopefulness. One thing that contributes to hope, Mary, is simply your poem, "Troth"—especially with your saying, "Somehow, love, you made me winged." Both came out of the deepest places in you, Mary—and your troth is your truth. You will remember.

The dreadful question I raised after the journey to sea, whether man-hating might be the explanation of your turning to a woman, is the question that is now disposed of, thank God. Mary, if your experience with the Bull—the near-rape—had been preying on your mind, you would have reacted to Bill Wingfield's stupid conduct with far greater upset and rage than you did. Instead you dismissed it yourself, with amused scorn, as a coming from the Bull of the Mountain to Bill of the Hill. A lesser thing. It's not significant and that's what's significant. Like the famous dog that didn't bark in the night. Your account of your walk down from the ridge was not only amusing but amused. You were less angry at Bill than I was myself next morning. So I simply scratch the possibility of some sort of man-hating or rejection of men. With relief.

On the other hand, there is a new question—the question of Mercia. When you told me that story with tears, there in Waikiki, I was deeply moved. And I was moved again, reading it in the present. But, reading it, I was struck by your saying you'd had a crush on Mercia. And by your response to her kissing you on the mouth, and your wishing she would do it again. I hate this business of looking with suspicion—of contaminating, as it were—the innocent past, like the once-funny episode with Jacqueline or even the gentle talk with Pauline. And yet —I can't avoid it—Mercia does seem significant. That kiss, Mary: what would be the effect of it upon a starved, impressionable little girl? Especially in view of Mercia's death and the terrible darkness that followed for you? Schoolgirl crushes, I gather, flame up and then fade, and the girl wonders what she saw in her Latin mistress. But Mercia tragically dead, dying before your eyes: that might enshrine her for ever. And Mercia coming, or seeming to come, to you on the beach at the luau would renew the whole experience. Mary, I do wonder whether I may not have discovered the essential clue?

I shall now defer all further comment until I have written of the past year at Holywell. But, first, the little, happy one-day journey to Tintern Abbey.

Journey to Tintern Abbey

The long June evening is luminous and serene. Mary has gone to the other side of the village to consult the Vicar, old Mr Osbaldistone, on some matter concerning the care of roses, so, for the moment, I am alone here in the garden of Greyfell save for Fluky, our black border collie, curled up at my feet. Our Yorkshire guests, Peter and Betsy Shirley, have gone for a walk. The roses on the garden wall that I can see from my bench beneath the great beech seem in no need of care—they are a glory against the stone.

I have been thinking about the close friendship among the four of us over the last few years, and about how unimaginably different everything would be if Mary had said yes to Peter that morning in the punt so long ago. Not really so long ago: that was 1963 and now it's 1966, but it seems long because so much has happened since. At all events, the four of us are very close indeed, and I think there is for all of us a sense of rightness in the way things have worked out.

Mary is perhaps leaving the Vicarage garden, with a last wave to the Vicar, about now. Then she will walk briskly down Oriel Street, crossing the High Street and continuing along Oriel to Greyfell, which is athwart the street and ends it. It is, in fact, the oriel window above our door that gives the street its name, though one would think they would have named it Greyfell Street. When she gets to our door, she will perhaps turn right and come along to the garden gate. I glance up. She is there. She has come soundlessly across the grass and is standing by the seventeenth-century sundial, looking at me.

She is smiling a little and one of her hands is just brushing back a wisp of hair—perhaps it was that that caught my eye. Her hip is touching the sundial, and behind her the mullioned windows of the oldest part of Greyfell are glittering in the last beams from the west. I see the beloved face, the large sea-blue eyes, the generous mouth with lips made for smiling, the short fair hair, and the slender woman's body that has walked beside me so long—beside me, indeed, before there was any walking. I look at her with a little sense of awe at the mystery of the one flesh of husband and wife.

Mary's thoughts, she tells me later, had also flashed over the past, from the rose in the winebottle at the Gateway to Heaven way back in '61 to our journeys of recent years to Provence and the Greek Isles and Hawaii nei: images superimposed upon this quiet Oxfordshire garden with me sitting so quietly under the spreading beech tree with, she said, a half-smile on my face. "Love," says T. S. Eliot, "is most nearly itself when here and now cease to matter." And for both of us in those moments, seeing our life in its wholeness, touching lightly upon the remembered past without losing the awareness of the tranquil here and now that the past has led to, our love was most nearly itself.

Looking at her there by the sundial, I say out of my thoughts, "Mary dear, you create my world anew by being here."

"And you mine," she says out of her thoughts. "Our love is born today as well as yesterday. And tomorrow."

I smile and she runs three steps into my arms, held out for her. Then she sits beside me on the bench. Fluky gets up and stretches fore and aft and licks both my hand and Mary's ankle. Deciding that they are much the same, possibly with thoughts of his own about one flesh, he plops down across our feet. Poki, the calico cat, stalks across the garden intent on some mysterious errand, her white-tipped tail raised high like a banner.

Greyfell, long owned by Mary's family, became available to us less than a year previously, but already it is home. It is, we think, perfect for us: the quiet village, the splendid garden, the mellow Cotswold stone of the house, and withal an easy drive from Oxford. We hope to live here all our days.

Mary tells me of her call on the Vicar and says there is a plan afoot to put on a one-act play in the church. Mary has agreed to play the village girl, and I'm to play the king.

"Oh lord!" I say. "I can't act."

"How do you know unless you have a go?" she says. "Besides, I'm not sure you'd have to do much acting—just be yourself at your most majestical."

I say that we'll see. Then she says, "Listen, Val. Didn't you say at dinner that you don't have to go into college tomorrow?"

I nod. "Yes," I say. "And I was thinking that we ought to plan something. A picnic, maybe. A visit to Minster Lovell. Too bad Roger and Molly are in Scotland."

"Minster Lovell's too close," says Mary. "Oh, I know! We're always talking about going to Tintern Abbey. Let's do it, and find a picnic spot round there?"

"Ah, good thinking!" I say. "And here are the long walkers come home. We'll see what they think."

Peter and Betsy are in instant agreement, and Mary and Betsy start planning the picnic. Betsy says, "Do you know we planned this day two years ago in *Windrush?* Remember? It was a night watch with the four of us, and we were talking about places to go in England."

Next morning I wake early, but the bed is empty of Mary, so I spring up. I go to the window to see sunlight pouring down and the leaves glistening—a shining day. I bathe and descend to find Mary and Betsy busy in the kitchen, not only getting breakfast but packing a hamper with the picnic.

"Val," says Mary. "Rouse the sleeping baronet, will you? Breakfast will soon be ready."

I climb the stairs, thinking with regret of the death of Peter's father, whom I had barely known but liked immensely. I knock at Peter's door. No reply. I go in.

"Pete!" I say. "Arise! The bird is on the wing! The bacon's on the fire! Wake up!" He waves a hand. "Wake up!" I say. "Sit up. Show a leg!" Peter swings himself up, sitting on the edge of the bed, hair tousled.

He grins. "G'mornin'!" he says. "I'll be down in no time."

In no time plus twenty minutes we are all seated at a table on the garden terrace looking cheerfully at a large platter of eggs and bacon and sausage, not to mention a Maybowl of strawberries in hock.

We eat hungrily, along with the food absorbing fresh air and warm sunshine—altogether a splendid mixture. A thrush in the old apple tree sings a morning song, not only twice-over but lots-of-times-over. I get up and pluck a red rose for Mary and a white one for Betsy and have another glass of hock as a reward.

A short time later *Kleio,* our rather ancient dark-green Bentley, top down, moves with quiet stateliness down the High and out into the countryside. Her name, we consider, is a nicely blended nod to both history and the classics. I am driving with Mary on my left and Fluky sits, full of intense interest in this promising day, between Peter and Betsy in back.

Since our village is in western Oxfordshire, we are very soon in Gloucestershire, where Mary was born and where, indeed, up near Stroud, her grandmother and many other members of her family still live. The countryside is beautiful and fresh as if, apart from the ancient Cotswolds villages, it had been created this very morning. We follow back roads, being in no hurry, heading for the Severn.

Mary is half turned round, discussing people-watching with Betsy, who is an inveterate people-watcher.

"It's quite astonishing," says Betsy. "Astonishing how much you can know them, if you really *look* at their faces."

"And love them," says Mary. "Once, just after I'd read Brother Lawrence, I'd try, when I was walking along the street in Oxford or London, to love people—actually love them—who were total strangers. What was so amazing was how many of them, old women, all sorts, would seem to feel it and turn round and smile."

"It's not the same, though," says Betsy. "Understanding and loving, I mean."

"Not the same," I say. "But good companions."

"Can't say I've ever thought about loving strangers," says Peter. "But the folk I know a little. My solicitor, for instance. Or my tailor—Mr Carter at Hall's in Oxford. You still go to him, too, don't you, Val? Or the farmers round my village. They're the ones I feel affectionate towards." He pauses, and I nod.

"The ones God gives us to love," says Mary. "I read that somewhere and never forgot it. The ones in our path, so to speak. There's something strange about love, you know. The more love you give away, the more you *have*. And the less you give away—the less you love—the less you have."

Peter chuckles. "It's thrifty, then, to be a spendthrift." We all laugh.

"Oh, look!" says Betsy. We are driving along a narrow country road, scarcely wider than the car, and the hedgerow on the left has given way to a velvet lawn dotted with ancient oaks and beeches and, beyond, a great towered house, built of the golden-grey stone of the Cotswolds.

"How lovely!" says Mary. "Oh, how I hope it is still somebody's home. It would be so awful if some government thing were in there. That house should be lived in and loved."

Having briefly owned and loved the great house ourselves, we drive on. I notice after awhile in the rear-view mirror that Peter and Betsy appear to be napping in the back. Fluky, too. I look at Mary, and her sea-blue eyes are turned towards me.

"I was just thinking of Holywell," I murmur.

"Snow," says Mary. "Snow in the birch woods. Snow everywhere. Ice skates on the pond, and Mary in peril. Er, why are you thinking of it?"

"Lumme!" I say. "I seem to have punched the stream-of-consciousness button in you. But it fits in. I was thinking of my senior year. When I sort of committed myself to you, even though it looked, you know, as though you'd be crippled always. If only I—we—could have looked ahead and seen . . . all this. Oxford, Greyfell, everything. It all seems so—so inevitable, somehow. But of course it wasn't."

"No," she says in a low voice. "We might have parted. Then the wings wouldn't have come—I believe it. My love, you did make me winged—somehow."

"Well," I say, moved. "I, er, loved you, you know."

Somewhat later, as we are driving through Chepstow on the far side of the Severn, Mary cries, "Val! Here's where we turn!"

"Mistress Mary!" I say. "That sign's as big as a—a mains'l."

"You'll be sorry some day," she says. "You'll take a wrong turning and drive into the ocean, but I'll never speak. Just calmly swim away."

The road winds about. Suddenly the ruined abbey rises before us. We park and go in. Green wooded hills surround it. Although the great abbey is roofless, the walls, unlike Glastonbury, rise substantially intact. The Cistercians built soundly as well as beautifully. The floor of nave and chancel is thick green grass. A Jersey cow is eating it. The glass of the windows is of course long since gone, but the stone tracery still remains in the great west window. Although we are in green Wales, the large east window, above what was once the high altar, frames the green of England over the river Wye. A skylark, invisible in the pure blue of heaven, pours down song.

"A perfect anthem for this church," says Mary.

We explore. There is a flight of steps in the north transept leading up to a a gothic arched doorway, beyond which is a small locked wooden door.

"I say!" says Peter. "That'll lead to a spiral staircase in the walls, up to the clerestory and perhaps to the top of the walls. I wonder if they'd let us go up?"

The custodian displays an initial hesitation, but Mary, knowing that Peter had written a monograph on Fountains Abbey, saves the day.

"This gentleman," she says grandly, "is Sir Peter Shirley, a distinguished historian of architecture. This abbey is, er—architecture. Sir Peter is writing a book."

The man weakens and gives us they key, telling us to lock the door behind us to prevent others from going up. The door opens easily and we see stone steps, very narrow and hollowed in the centre, spiraling up into the gloom. We start up in single file, Peter in the lead. Betsy locks the door and gives me the key, since I have pockets.

"If you lose it," she says, "we'll have to stay here till we die, and then we'll be the ghosts of Tintern, moaning in the walls."

"Oooooo!" Mary moans in a wavering voice.

"Rather feminine ghost you are," I remark as we climb.

"What's wrong with being a feminine ghost?" says Mary. "We're the best kind."

"To apply the logic that awes my students," I say kindly, "this was a monastery for monks."

"Who knows what went on?" says Mary darkly. "Ooooooo!" Her quavering moan is, in fact, eerie, there in the pitch darkness as we trudge upwards, round and round.

"Light ahead!" says Peter. In a moment we have come to a narrow doorway, through which the sun shines blindingly. It opens onto the clerestory gallery. "Did you notice," Peter says, "only the north transept has a clerestory."

Since the steps continue upwards, we do too, and eventually emerge through a trapdoor onto the thick ruined walls. We peer gingerly over the edge and see the cow, looking very tiny, in the quire. We sit and are silent.

Looking at the beautiful ruined abbey church, I reflect, as perhaps the others are doing, on mutability: the monks who built this church for the glory of God, toiling in the sun and in the rain through the long slow decades, watching the mighty walls rise, feeling, surely, pride and joy. And then the long, long centuries when it was a living church: the processions, the masses, the chanted plainsong—they must have felt that the great church was for ever. The steps we came up, with their centres worn down by inches: yet how few of the monks would have had occasion to use them. But even once a day for thousands upon thousands of days . . . it must have seemed for ever. And then the fierce-eyed reformers, the destroyers of the dream. The flung stone shattering the Queen of Heaven in the blue stained glass.

"It's full of ghosts, isn't it?" says Peter.

"Yes," I say. "I've always wondered how the reformers could bring themselves to do it, even with their beliefs."

"It's curious," says Peter. "Men build, patiently ar. ' beautifully. And men destroy. They always have done. Always the barbarian at the gates."

"Not only buildings," says Mary. "The barbarians burn the books, too. Not so successfully perhaps. And barbarize the language. Like Americans using 'home' when they mean 'house'. And I read somewhere that homosexuals are calling themselves or being called 'gay'—What an awful thing! One of the loveliest words in the language—and no synonym. For lovers of the iron of English, it's a very sad thing. Anyway, I will never use it for that. Never!"

"No," says Betsy. "Never. But they do need a non-insulting word, I think."

"Oh, yes," says Mary. "But I wonder what's happened to our ability to form new short words out of unused syllables or abbreviations. 'Homosexual' could be abbreviated to 'homex'—or a new sound, like, er, 'lon' or 'zay'. It would sound odd at first, but it would soon mean whatever it was meant to mean."

"Let us be preservers, then," I say. "Speaking of which, I'm beginning to think that some lunch would preserve me. Shall we go down?"

Less than an hour later we are seated round our picnic in a meadow that runs down to the Wye. Besides soft green grass and a Jersey cow that looks like the sister of the one in the abbey, there is a knoll with a cherry tree on top.

"Oh, glory!" I say, after sandwiches and tarts innumerable. "Was anything ever more comfortable than a full belly and birdsong and soft grass by the river?"

"Only heaven," says Mary. "And it must be like this, only without that fallen ant that just bit me. If heaven doesn't have tasting in it—claret and Stilton—and smelling sun-warmed grass, it's a lesser place. And that can't be."

Betsy says drowsily, "Maybe all the little monks from the abbey are having a collation in a meadow in heaven. And I think heaven must have naps . . ."

We are silent. I dream something about monks sitting sadly on ruined walls.

I wake. A rabbit five yards away looks at me and twitches its nose. Then it hops off in an unhurried manner as if at that very moment it had remembered an errand. Later, in its burrow, it will tell the tale of its heroic approach to the sleeping giants. Fluky, who would be truly interested in the rabbit, sleeps in the grass, as does everyone. I

228

soundlessly arise and wander off towards the little hill and gaze at the river.

Mary wakes and sees that I am gone. She immediately pictures me— she later tells me—carried off in a lorry by scowling men. Then she sees me.

I look round and she is coming towards me, barefooted in the grass. I hold out my arms to her, and she begins to run, her hair blowing in the wind. She rushes into my arms.

"Oh, darling!" she gasps. "Running in the wind, like 'Wind Song'— 'Barefoot, wind-blown, and free!' "

"I love you, Mary-maid!" I say. I kiss both cheeks, then her mouth. The soft blue sky arches overhead. A robin chirps in the cherry tree. The moment is an unexpected glory.

" 'The wind's winged girl,' " I murmur. "Mary, can you say that last stanza of 'Wind Song'—the chanting one?"

"I think so," she says. We sit down in the grass.

> I would go as the wind goes—a girl
> Blown by the wind, as light as a drift
> Of cloud, as gay as a flurry of joy,
> The wind's winged girl, beloved of
> The wind, blown lightly along and away . . .

Her voice trails away. "There's more," she murmurs. "It has all come true, hasn't it?"

"Yes, thank God," I say. "Mary, our love is the most perfect thing I've known. And never more perfect than in this moment—here on this English hill beneath the cherry tree."

"Yes," she says. "Richard, write this day in our neglected journal, will you?"

There is a rapid patter of flying paws. Fluky, who has just discovered where we are, rushes up like a small joyous whirlwind. We congratulate him warmly. Then we return to the others, who are beginning to awaken.

"Friends," says Peter, "looking at the sun with a countryman's eyes, not to mention a quite unnecessary glance at my watch, I perceive that it's time we were starting back. You will remember that Betsy and I are dining and spending the night with the President of Magdalen."

As we drive towards Oxfordshire, we talk a little about the modern novel.

"If I ever write a novel," I say, "it's going to be a happy one—even if happiness ain't art. Anguish is the thing in the modern novel. Driven types who can't have erections or who hate everything. Cheerful types who love life ain't allowed."

"I don't agree with that view of life," says Peter. "Driven types, I mean. Maybe that's why I like John Buchan and Rider Haggard. I don't need to be reminded of how grim and sordid life can be."

"Actually," I say, "it's a view of life—people who are puppets of dark sexual gods, living without hope or meaning—that is impossible for Christians. And happy people who are trying to be good are just as much a part of reality as those others. But literary standards today aren't set by Christians, are they? Imagine a novel where two people are in love with each other at the beginning and still are at the end. No, it's not art— they say—unless the iron claws come down and get you after the first chapter."

"Of course," says Betsy, "the iron claws do sometimes come down.'"

"True," I say. "But even then—people aren't always in pain. Life is episodic. Happy one minute, sad the next, then happy again. Gaiety, tears, irrelevance. Sometimes romantic—which life dares to be— sometimes not."

An hour or two later Mary and I deposit Peter and Betsy, bathed and resplendent, on the High in front of Magdalen, promising to pick them up in the morning. Then Mary and I decide to wander about Oxford in the luminous evening. We do so, walking down Queen's Lane, hearing the sound of change-ringing bells floating through the air. We go into St Mary Magdalen and kneel together for a few moments in gratitude for this day. Apart from two women wandering about, the church is empty. Then we stroll back to the car. The ancient golden stone of the colleges is mellowed still further by the long slanting light. Two dons pass us, their gowns floating about them. One is saying, "Not at all, my dear fellow. You have misread Pliny, if you . . ."

In the car again, we drive out the Woodstock Road. At Greyfell we have a bite to eat and feed the animals, and then go out into the garden.

"Twenty-four hours ago," I say, "you were at the Vicar's, and we hadn't even thought of going to Tintern. And then you came home and we created today. Now it's done, and here we are again."

"Dramatic unity," says Mary. "Of time, at least. And we did jolly well creating it, don't you think? A happy story, like those you were talking about."

"Splendid!" I say. "Especially your run up the hill. I couldn't think of a thing to improve the day, could you?"

"No," she says. "Still, there must be something that could have made it better. Let me think. Ah, I know. We move the clock back, okay? We are coming down that staircase in the walls again, and—who was behind me?"

"Before we got to the clerestory or after?" I say.

"Don't make things complicated," she says. "Before."

"I was," I say. "Afterwards, Betsy was."

"Okay," she says. "We are coming down in the dark, and suddenly you stumble—"

"Not likely!" I say. "I never stumble."

"Damn and blast!" she says. "Will you shut up? —All right! Afterwards, then! Betsy is behind me, and, suddenly, *she* stumbles! And she falls into me, and I throw out my hand to save myself from falling into Peter. The domino theory, you see. And I grab a projecting stone that my hand encounters in the dark. Well, that saves me; but I say in a very tense voice, 'Wait!'—because, you see, I felt that stone move. So I wiggle it, and everybody says what's happening, and the stone comes out—"

"And falls on your foot!" I say. "And you scream—"

"No, no, no!" she says. "I do *not* drop it on my foot, and I wouldn't scream if I did. I would be too brave! What happens is, I lay the stone carefully down. And then I light a match—'the quick sharp scratch and blue spurt of a lighted match'—and there in the hole is—guess what?"

"A black-widow spider!" I say. "The pistol that done in the Major."

"Those wouldn't have made the day nicer," says Mary. "Certainly not! No, what was in the hole was a leather bag. Or the decaying remnants of a bag. And spilling out of it are golden sovereigns, glittering in the light of the match. Did they have sovereigns at the time of the Reformation? Guineas? Anyhow, gold! Lots of gold! So, then—"

"So, then," I say, "we all start fighting in the dark, mad with greed! And at last the sole survivor staggers out with the boodle and turns the key on the carnage within. And the dreadful question as that bleeding figure staggers towards the Bentley—the awful question is: who is it?"

"And," she says, "will Scotland Yard find, written in blood by a dying hand on the abbey stones, the single sprawling letter M or R or P or B? Anyhow, you ruined my story. I was going to tell how we used the money to found a new abbey. Now I'll never tell!"

"Well," I say, smiling. "Maybe we'd better leave our day as it really was. Perhaps in some other reality you found the gold or the black-widow spider. Perhaps in this reality that gold is really there and won't be found till the Cistercians return."

She smiles and gives my hand a little squeeze. "That would be nice," she says, and quotes: " 'What might have been and what has been point to one end which is always present.' "

"That's T. S. Eliot, isn't it?" I say. "Yes. Reality is certainly more complex than people like to think. Sometimes it seems to me that I just glimpse, at moments, realities beyond what we think of as reality. God and spiritual reality—well, I'm certain that that reality *is* real, but it's beyond comprehension."

"My mind is collapsing under all these realities," says Mary. "Why don't we go in and pursue reality in bed?"

"It is well that I know you," I say. "Otherwise I might wonder what you meant. Anyhow, I'll be off to the shower."

I am in bed when Mary comes dewily forth from the bathroom and gives her hair about three strokes with her brush. She comes over to the bed and looks at me. She suddenly bends down and kisses me. "Oh, Richard," she whispers. "I had forgot that we must die."

"Yes," I murmur, aware of mortality. "We must remember. But we live now and it is good. And, past that dark door, we shall live again, and that will be good."

She comes into the bed, after kneeling a moment by it, and I reach up and switch out the lamp. The casement is already wide, and the white curtains are moving a little in the gentle breeze. St Margaret's is striking the hour, but I do not count the strokes.

We lie there wrapped in each other's arms, as we have always gone to sleep. We are very sleepy and loving. We give each other a small, additional goodnight kiss, and Mary seems almost to drift off to sleep in the middle of it. I murmur drowsily, "Sleepy little girl . . ."

But we don't quite go to sleep. It is too delightful to be clean and affectionate on the very brink of slumber, and we don't want to leave our sleepy delight. Several times I drift off but come back, once to a tiny kiss on my ear. I kiss the top of her head.

Far away in the night a solitary bell note sounds from the church tower. The white curtains blow at the window. A distant owl hoots. The last thing I hear is a rather girlish little sigh, a peaceful sound.

Journey to Holywell

The Study, Holywell, April, 1968—Richard

So the journal ends, almost two years ago in the garden of Greyfell. Shall we ever go home to Greyfell? I wonder. The journal, though, the journal written by Mary, ends almost exactly three years ago at Kulahola, ends with a re-affirmation by Mary of the complementary wholeness of Richard and Mary. Now, as I begin to write of this present year, the image of deep love between a man and a woman in those far islands lingers in my mind like the flower fragrance borne on the trade wind. As does the image of Greyfell. —In your mind, too, Mary?

Studying the journal as I have done through the greater part of April, pondering every word, has been a strange and rewarding experience. That double vision of man and woman we spoke of at Kulahola is something I've been deeply experiencing in her parts of the journal, combining what she writes about with my own memories of the same thing. But it has not been a double vision only: it has been a *triple* vision. The third vision has been that of an intelligent stranger who knows nothing about us save what is written. What, I've asked myself, would this objective stranger see in this passage? What would he think of that one? Would he consider it sincere? Would he think it an expression of genuine love? It is he who has given me the clues and insights that I have remarked on in my end-of-journey notes, and he who tells me our love has been deep and genuine.

But I shall not attempt a final summing up of my judgment of the past just yet, for the past is not yet complete. What of the three years since Hawaii? Since we didn't keep the journal, except for that one day of Tintern Abbey, I can't say much, especially of the early part of the three years. One strange thing about the picture presented by the journal, dealing as it does with our adventurous journeys, the picture isn't balanced with the more work-a-day and humdrum side of our lives, a side that was of course there. Like other people we had boring tasks and colds and involvements in church and university. About those years I shall only say that it was in the summer of '65 that we moved into Greyfell, a house long owned by Mary's family and suddenly vacant; and we moved in just in time to welcome Mary's father there when he came to Oxford in the autumn. In thinking about that half-year, and 1966, and early '67, I see nothing that throws any light upon our present crisis. But the latter half of '67 and the early part of this present year—our journey to Holywell—appears to me to be a time I should write about, if only because it was the period immediately preceding Mary's involvement with the mysterious Miss X.

This Holywell period has been the time, especially, of our being caught up in something rather different to anything else we ever experienced: the anti-war movement and all that goes with it—protest, rock music, drugs. We were of course somewhat prepared for it. Mary's father had long ago predicted an expanded war, and we ourselves had done a bit of predicting when we dined in the wardroom of the USS *Randolph.* Oxford itself had become aware of the war, and there was considerable feeling against it. And in the summer before Holywell there had been a demonstration in London that we had played a small part in —the Angry Arts protest. Still, nothing had quite prepared us for the major upheaval that was happening in the States.

We arrived there in late August of 1967, I on leave from Worcester College, Oxford, to teach a year at Holywell. It seemed good to us both to be there again. The professor whose place I was taking for the year had rented us his fine old house on the edge of campus—high-ceilinged rooms and a beautiful New England doorway and fanlight.

And almost at once we became aware of the intense feelings on campus and, indeed, in the whole country about the undeclared war in Vietnam. The opposition to the U.S. involvement seemed to be based mainly on the idea that we should not be interfering in another country's civil war. Then, too, the U.S. had pledged to hold free elections in South Vietnam and then refused to allow them, supposedly because of a secret CIA report that Vietnam's George Washington, Ho Chi Minh, would win hands down. If this was true, the U.S. position was fatally corrupted. Fair is fair; and if the South Vietnamese would choose Ho at the ballot box, then we had no right to prevent it. We listened and, increasingly, felt that America was fighting an unjust war. We sided with the protesters and then, little by little, were moved to active protest.

Once in my sophomore year at Holywell, way back in 1959, Jim Cosby, who was then a midshipman at Annapolis, came up to visit me. I was at that time rather anti-scholarship—that is, people who wrote footnotes instead of poems or novels. On a trip to New Haven to visit a common friend I held forth, to Jim's amusement, on scholars; and when we got back to Holywell I wrote a poem on footnotes, which, in view of all the footnotes on poems, is a rather man-bites-dog sort of thing. I have digressed into this anecdote because I now—in 1967—took out that old poem and altered and polished it into my first poem about the sixties.

FOOTNOTE [1]

[1]Spectacled little scholar
Scribbling away in the stacks
Walled off from life in the library
Turning out lifeless books
Books about books that live
Forming the learned footnotes
Concepts to classify
Label but never believe
Sonnets and songs to dissect
Muting both music and meaning
Adoring nothing at all
Not life or the Christ or the poem
Branches and trunk without leaves
Lost in a lifeless limbo
Of ambiguities
While kids cry freedom and cops
Strike blood at the barricades
And about the buttressed towers
Is the roar of the rising wind

Mary approved of this. The thrust of the poem had now become, not against scholars—after all, I was one myself—but against the timid and, above all, against the sort of scholar who never connects up ideas and life —who talks about freedom without believing in it, who deals learnedly with the New Testament accounts of Jesus but thinks his objectivity would be impaired by belief. Strangely enough, he never supposes that disbelief mars objectivity.

The faculty at Holywell were divided, as I suppose faculties everywhere were. The older men, the majority in fact, were shocked at the disloyalty of the protests, the decline of patriotism as it seemed to them, and the questioning of authority. Not to mention the long hair. Many of the younger faculty as well as a few of the older ones were beginning to believe that America was fighting a war of aggression that was inherently unjust. Moreover, they—I should say we—believed that there was a higher ideal of patriotism than acquiescence to injustice.

We were sounded out, by students and faculty alike, from the moment we got settled in at Holywell. We could not have avoided the question had we wished to, for everyone was talking about the war one way or another, even if they seemed to be talking about long hair or the Beatles. Actually, the anti-war people asked us point-blank where we stood. The other party didn't ask in so many words, or even state a position; they simply grumbled about the long-haired types or the decline of patriotism, meanwhile peering at us to see whether we would grumble back. The old idea that America was always righteous—always the 'good guys'—was one that men who had fought against the genuine evil of Hitler found it hard even to question. It was, I suppose, one of America's most deeply rooted fundamental assumptions.

Anyhow, we answered roundly that we thought the war wrong. Then, when "Footnote[1]" was printed in the *Holywell Holler,* our position was made quite clear; and we were at once drawn into the anti-war group. There was a chapter of SDS on campus, and I spoke to them one night about the Angry Arts thing in London and the vigorous anti-war feelings in Oxford.

It was a strange thing all the same for Mary and me to come from Oxford, which somehow always remains serene and civilised despite Roundheads or Reformers, into this American storm. We were, in a way, prepared. We had been sympathetic to the black Freedom Movement— or black and white, I should say—and had even been involved in that small demonstration in Washington at the time of Selma. And of course our friends in the States, not to mention the newspapers, had kept us in touch with what was happening. But in Oxford the bells rang as always and people went to tutorials and what was happening in America seemed very remote. Not so in Holywell. Peaceful New England town, yes, and nothing like Yale or Wisconsin or Berkeley, but compared to Oxford it was the eye of the storm.

All the threads of protest came to our ears: the whole case against the war—and against the government. Speakers came to Holywell, including SDS leaders and black leaders. Mary and I talked a great deal about it. If anything, she was more angry, more eager to take some sort of action than I was, possibly because she was closer to the students. But there was no disagreement between us. The thing was, it—the war, the whole 'sixties thing'—took so much of our time. Somehow, we read poetry less, listened to music less, took fewer walks. And that may be significant.

The bombing of those hapless people in Vietnam especially filled us with anger. And the anti-war protests, however spirited, did not seem to be accomplishing anything at all. Out of my anger—our anger, I should say—I wrote a darker, angrier, bitterer poem.

FAITH

"In God we trust" our coins proclaim.
Only, what God? what holy name?
The great Apollo, lord of light?
Wisdom, thou of the triple helm?
Jesus, loving his enemies?—
The Christ who healed the cop's slashed ear?
Is there, I wonder, a lord of bombers
That don't turn into butterflies
In shaken skies above Vietnam?
A god whose heaven is falling flame?
Old Mars would do, or some beast-name—
Moloch perhaps or the Lord of the Flies.
"In God we trust"—and in his name
Devote our billions to his claim.
Credo: we believe in, not
—Not the owl and not the light,
And not in Him whose "Father, forgive"
Haunts still the blood-stained centuries.
Ours is a different, darker spell,
The pattern of a pentagon:
Conjuring the power but not the glory.
Is there a god of murder to proclaim?
—In his name.

That poem was widely reprinted in the so-called 'underground' press, and I was right pleased one time, on the occasion of calling at the office of a theologian in another college, to see it, framed, on his wall. He must have been a Christian. More important, perhaps, for this account of our journey to Holywell, the poem does suggest how we felt—where, as they say, we 'were at'—when it was written. I remember vividly Mary's fierce approval when I first read it to her. I may speak of it further later, but it is important to note that, although we weren't going to church much, we both thought of the world—and the Vietnam war—in a context of solid Christian faith.

It was in connection with this poem, I think, that Mary remarked shrewdly on a difference between her poetry and mine: her poetry—"Wind Song," for instance—was almost always personal 'inner' poetry, while mine tended to be impersonal and 'outer'.

We realised increasingly as time went on, as I suggested earlier, that the anti-war movement was not a thing in isolation but, rather, tied up with a number of seemingly unrelated things. Long hair for men, for example, is almost invariably a clear signal of an anti-war stance. But it is also a signal of defiance of constituted authority. All, then, are part of 'the Movement'. But the whole Movement is closely linked to folk music and the stirring rock music of the sixties. The long hair was almost certainly triggered by the Beatles in England, and their songs breathed a cheerful defiance of authority. The lovely, soaring voice of Joan Baez, whom we heard in concert soon after coming to the States, seems to express the highest ideals of the Movement, first as Freedom Movement and now as Anti-war Movement. Mary adored Baez and said she had a winged voice. But no less a part of the Movement are the great songs of Bob Dylan, whether hauntingly sung by Joan Baez or, with somewhat raucous impressiveness, by Dylan himself. Mary and I tend to see the music of the sixties as the key to the decade, so far at least. The reason that so many older people have seemed pathetically bewildered by what's going on is their refusal to avail themselves of that 'key'—the music. Finally, as a part of the sixties, tied up with all the rest, is what's called 'the drug scene'. It is important, as is the music, to the story of Mary and me; but I shall come to it later.

One other aspect of our emotional involvement was, and of course still is, the very real possibility, if the war continued to expand, of me being drafted. I had a deferment as well as a wife and had reached the ripe old age of twenty-eight—twenty-nine last month—but still there was the spectre. Mary was terrified of it, and I myself didn't much care for the idea of stumbling about the rice paddies shooting at folk I felt rather friendly to in behalf of a cause I didn't believe in. Thus we could join in with spirit to the shout, "Hell, no! We won't go!" as well as other, less printable chants.

We had scarcely got ourselves settled-in at Holywell and become known as anti-war people when the massive March on the Pentagon began to be planned and talked about—a great and peaceful march on the centre of the warmaking activity, the Pentagon, which had become a symbol of aggression. The idea was, of course, to show the American people how great the opposition to the war really was. A considerable contingent from Holywell planned to charter a bus or two and go, along with other contingents from Yale and Dartmouth and Smith and Mt Holyoke and everywhere else. And of course Mary and I planned to go, not only to express anti-war sentiments but to have fun.

Thus in late October, on a beautiful Indian summer day, we found ourselves near the Reflecting Pool in Washington, along with tens of thousands of others, waiting for the march to begin. The sky was a deep October blue and the pure beauty of the Doric columns looming above us on the Lincoln Memorial lent something of their austere majesty to the scene. There were banners and signs everywhere expressing anti-war sentiments, often with humour and always with vigour, and signs also identifying groups, such as Harvard Divinity School or Indiana University. The mood was lighthearted, not grim; and everybody was friendly to everybody else. It remains in my mind as a fine thing: to march, not to a war shouting Hurrah but against a war shouting Peace. Mary said she wondered if perhaps Jesus might be here, walking around in blue jeans with a merry smile on his face.

We sat about in clusters on the grass with the shining Doric columns above us, and sometimes we took little tours among the various groups. There was so much affection and comradeship that it was, I imagine, quite like one of the be-ins or love-ins they were having out on the west coast. Hand-rolled pot cigarettes—joints—were being smoked and passed about freely. We smoked our first pot there—everyone was doing it— and got high in a sunny sort of way and enjoyed it. It seemed to make the sky bluer and the columns purer in their splendour. We felt that it made us see more: the individual twigs and leaves of the tree, and the bird in the tree, too. There were lots of speeches, but we knew all the arguments and soon stopped listening. The march had by now begun, though our turn was a long time away. One of the things I remember most vividly was the long ranks, ten or more abreast, swinging out gaily with their banners and signs, laughing and shouting.

It looked as though Holywell might not march for hours—there must have been over a hundred thousand people there—so finally I rallied our group and we watched our chance and slipped into the march, forming two or three ranks. We had a golden banner with "Holywell for Holy Peace" stencilled on both sides of it, and it floated above us as we marched onto the bridge over the Potomac. We were all shouting, "Peace—*NOW!* Peace—*NOW!*" like a chant, and then we began to sing about how we all lived in a yellow submarine.

There was a delay of some kind up ahead on the Virginia side, and the long column, marching on the left side of the bridge, slowed and stopped. After awhile there were immense cheers from behind us, but we couldn't see what the cheering was about. Soon the cheering came nearer —and louder. And then up the right side of the bridge came the tread of marching men, real marchers keeping the step, and the sight of the nation's flag. We could see, first, a proud little man, stern-faced, carrying the colours, then a sign in the first rank of the briskly marching men: "Veterans of the Abraham Lincoln Brigade Against Vietnam!" They went by like heroes, eyes front, to immense cheers. Soon after, we began to move again.

At the Pentagon the scene became grimmer. There were troops everywhere, and U. S. Marshalls with armbands arresting everybody. We couldn't get anywhere near the the door and tried to circle round the crowd. But across the road was a line of troops with rifles at the port-arms position. We tried to persuade one unhappy looking soldier to let us through. He evidently wasn't allowed to answer, but he rolled his eyes in the direction of his sergeant. Mary talked to him a moment or two about how wrong the war was, and then she reached up and put a flower in the muzzle of his rifle. I heard later that a couple of soldiers— perhaps Mary's soldier was one of them—had flung down their rifles and leaped into the ranks of the demonstrators and disappeared as people gave them coats and shirts to hide their uniforms. Other soldiers were less sympathetic.

Later we got into a melee near the troops and marshalls on the terrace. A moment later from a little distance I saw a U.S. Marshall grab Mary and, worse, hit her quite needlessly across the shoulder with his club, probably a baton sinister. And then this unpleasant-looking fellow started to drag her off to jail, I struggling through massed people towards her. Suddenly, though, Mary twisted out of her loose denim jacket, all in one motion, and ran like a hare, the Marshall right behind her, towards me and a cluster of our people. We opened a way for her in, but the Marshall was just reaching to grab her again when I, rather unpeaceably, struck him a massive punch in the pit of the stomach. Not many of the small pleasures of life have ever been quite so satisfying. Our people closed round us while the Marshall croaked desperately for air and then staggered off. Mary wasn't much hurt, only a big purple bruise from his baton, but the incident made us much more aware of repressive authority. Later, in her inimitable way, Mary invented the pleasing fancy that the Marshall took her denim jacket home with him and put it, stuffed, in his trophy case, labelled "A wicked chick".— Sounds like you, Mary. My new slogan, you said, should be "Punch for Peace!"

After the great march was all over and we were back at Holywell, I kept thinking about the meaning of the day—people marching for peace. A month or two later I had occasion to be in Washington again, and I walked back to where the march had begun. All was quiet except for a few winter tourists, and I sat down on the steps of the Lincoln Memorial and wrote a poem trying to tell how it was and what it meant.

MARCH ON THE PENTAGON
Retrospect: Lincoln Memorial

That October was a sort
Of Indian Summer. We lay about
Here on the sun-warmed grass beneath
The radiant columns, smoking pot,
And still we hoped for America.
Then with the long ranks moving out
We raised our banners: home-made signs
For Peace held high into the blue
October air, and laughed, and stepped
Out lightly towards the Pentagon.
"Peace—*NOW!*" we shouted, and we sang.

Let these be famous: let men raise
In bronze these blue-jeaned brigadiers
Amidst the clubs: let history praise
Not only endless ranks of spears
But those who marched for peace with cheers.

There were to be other, smaller demonstrations later that fall and winter, and our anger grew deeper. But for our personal crisis, Mary and I would probably have planned to take part in the big march on Fifth Avenue in New York this month, with a look at the Columbia University sit-in. It's strange that Mary, who is so much the poet in "Wind Song" and who has been of us two the more enraged about the war, has not been moved to write any poems about it. She says she can't write angry poems—whereas anger pricked my muse into spirited activity. At all events it seems to me, looking back from this cruel April, that we were terribly dominated by the war from September to mid-March, almost as much as people fighting wars are. No, that's too extreme; but there's no doubt that it was the dominant thing in our lives. And the importance of that is that other aspects of our lives suffered. Our love, for example, we took for granted more than we had ever done. And, I fear, our religion: thoughts of our Lord Christ didn't come often into our conversation, or into, at least, my mind. I can't say about Mary—but perhaps I ought to be able to say.

Looking back from my present self-imposed isolation—on the plea of urgent work—it seems to me that in the months leading up to this April our living room was always full of people, both students and faculty, talking about the war and kindred subjects. Or listening to rock. Or of course both at once. And when our living room wasn't full, we were likely to be in somebody else's house, or at a meeting, or perhaps on our way to a vigil or demonstration. Certainly Mary and I spent less time alone together and, except in the early autumn, took fewer walks—yet we had always known that long walks together in the deep country were a refreshment to our souls and our love. Of course we never decided against those things; we simply drifted into a different pattern. When we came back to Holywell from the March on the Pentagon, for instance, we inspected Mary's shoulder with its huge bruise. Then, while I made some coffee, Mary put a Dylan record on. We sat there listening, feeling, I think, that he was speaking our language. He was, too, in a way, but only, I think, the language of one part of us. There were too many parts of us, including the joy in life and love and beauty that so filled the pages about Hawaii, that we seemed cut off from. —Do you agree, Mary?

Each of us made a close friend at Holywell, and those friends play some part in the story of the period.

My friend was (and is) Timothy Gannet, who is in the English Department—Chaucer and the Elizabethans are his loves. He has an exceptional intelligence and, although as deeply involved in the Movement as I am, keeps an admirable objectivity about everything that is going on. At the same time he is open to experience—he is the only other member of the faculty who marched on the Pentagon—and he is a gay and valiant comrade. Tim and I have spent innumerable hours discussing and analyzing the whole sixties phenomenon. He is rather frail physically but makes up for it in restless energy; and he has a vein of crazy humour that delights me. He is, in fact, the only friend I've told about what's happening—that is, Mary's love for the mystery woman. Of course there isn't much to tell, except the fact. Tim's idea is that Mary is simply experiencing a new thing and will come back once she's come to the end of it—whenever and whatever that may be. I wish I were as confident, but—"knowing how way leads on to way"—I doubt sometimes if she will ever find her way home.

Susie Wainwright, a student, is Mary's particular friend. After all, Mary, who is not yet twenty-four, is scarcely older than some of our students. Susie is very fair—a mop of yellow hair—amiable, slightly crazy in an endearing way, intelligent, and slender to the point of lankiness. She seems to drape herself over furniture. She and Mary share a passion for Joan Baez, especially "Farewell, Angelina"—which they have played about a thousand times. I have often come home from classes to find Mary and Susie talking briskly, with that song playing in the background. Or come home to find a note from Mary that she was going over to the girls' dorm to see Susie. Probably playing "Farewell, Angelina" over there, too.

One of the subjects of their talk—and this may be significant—was the put-down of girls in the Movement. On the local SDS planning committee, for instance, there are only men; and at the meetings the girls mostly sit silent. And it's pretty much the same everywhere. Certainly some of the male leaders seem to think that the girls are there simply to make brownies and to cheer and to swell the ranks. So Mary and Susie had a point. But they were going beyond that valid point, beyond the Movement, picturing women in offices taking orders from male bosses and women at home being bossed about by their husbands. Mary always generously exempted me, as she in fact had to do, so she could not speak from first-hand experience. I asked her mildly whether she thought Peter ordered Betsy about, or Jean, Pauline, or Roger, Molly. She giggled a bit at the idea of anyone ordering Molly about, and said we were all untypical.

Some of the time, it seemed to me, Mary and Susie were echoing some sort of feminist line they had heard somewhere but didn't understand all that well. Then I began to hear references to Agnes— Agnes says this or that. I asked Tim about an Agnes, though of course I could have asked Mary, and Tim grinned and said he knew her all too well, since she was in the English department. Temporarily, he added. Anyway, Agnes was a rather sour woman, unmarried, who taught Freshman English. Tim said she would not be retained because she simply wasn't doing the job of teaching students to write. And apparently Susie and Mary had been to Agnes's flat a couple of times and had learned there of the slavery of women. Agnes had given them a book on female oppression as well as feminist tracts, and Mary and Susie were always talking about them. I read them, too, and, after being somewhat impressed at first, I decided that they were one-sided, and many of them fanatical.

One afternoon Mary and Tim and Susie and I had a drive up into the Berkshires, and during the course of it we stopped at a roadside place for gasoline. The man who ran the station had a newly caught wildcat in a cage, where it was rightly feeling angry and unhappy. We tried to persuade the man to let it go. Later Mary and Susie decided, without evidence, that it had been a female and was a symbol of all caged females.

When I heard that, I said, "That's rubbish, Mary! Who's caged? Molly is a redheaded wildcat—but Roger ain't caging her. Is Betsy caged? Is Shelley, mate of the *Windrush?* You're not caged! Beulah's not! Agnes, regrettably, isn't! What woman is if she doesn't *want* to be? Don't cut down the trees looking for snakes that aren't there." Mary uttered a small wildcat growl but looked thoughtful.

That night I wrote a poem.

PUSSYCAT

Once I saw a wildcat, newly caged,
A-snarl with savage longing to be free,
Small but unappeasably enraged,
The needle teeth all bared at tyranny.

I thought: Could women once have been like that?

Before the building of the cages,
Before the bars made home a trap,
Before the breaking of the ages,
Before the bowl of milk and slap?

It took awhile to make a pussycat.

The haunted hills and open starry sky—
Do they really linger in your dreams?
Was there once a savage growl,
Before contented purring on a thigh,
Before the catnip mouse and bowl of cream,
The pitiful miaul?

But now perhaps the genes are pussycat.

These days, indeed, in talk you greatly dare,
And after all the law is kind,
And even for the fair what's fair is fair—
Still, questions linger in my mind.

The difference: whether God intended that?

The lion roars his splendour on the hills:
He *will* be free and if he must he kills.
Small pussy—you have fangs and claws in fact,
But dare you with pawsful of daggers *act?*

Renounce the deference due to ladyhood,
As in your wildcat talk you say you would—
Be *sure,* though, in your blood you hear the call,
Dream still a dream of freedom on the hills.
For it, pussy, will you hazard *all?*

Thus only claim the deference due to lords:
The ancient courtesy of swords.

I did not dedicate this poem to Agnes, though perhaps I should have. I did send her a copy by campus mail, having met her by then, and received from her a look of extreme hauteur, more duchessy than wildcattish, when we passed on the steps.

First, though, I read the poem to Mary and Tim and Susie one night, reading it a second time when they looked a little blank. Which side was I on? Then Tim chuckled and puffed clouds of smoke from his pipe. And Mary, again, looked thoughtful.

The poem, in fact, led to a considerable conversation, not about the admitted injustices suffered by some women but about the differences— or lack of differences—between men and women. The talk began on Saturday night, after Tim and Susie departed, continued late, and was resumed Sunday morning. I wish I had written it down while it was still fresh in mind. I do remember that the talk began with me remarking that by and large, with the exception of a few minor injustices, a girl's position in the early sixties—the time of wings, the time of our journeys —was close to ideal. A girl could be or do almost anything she chose— not handed her on a legal platter, but won—and yet could still claim "the deference due to ladyhood." Mary acknowledged that she had felt as free as a bird after wings—that wings and freedom were almost one. But she had been free as a girl is free, not as a man is free—and she hadn't had to think about earning a living. If she had had to think about it, lots of possibilities would not have been open to her, because she was a girl.

At first Mary was suggesting—and I was sure it came from the embattled Agnes—that, apart from physical differences, men and women were just the same. The apparent differences—men's aggressiveness and women's passivity or, better, unaggressiveness—were merely the results of conditioning: parental pressure, books, films, society. I laughed aloud at that, I remember, and said she might think otherwise about that if she had grown up at Redrock.

"What do you mean?" she said in an annoyed voice.

"Dogs," I said. "Horses—stallions and mares. Roosters, too. At Redrock we didn't tell our mares and bitches to be a lady—and they didn't read books, although one little bitch puppy ate three chapters of Melville. Seriously, Mary, there's a world of difference. I had a little collie bitch one time, and she was a born lady: gentle, sweet-tempered, and, well—just plain feminine. And the males: full of adventure. They were the ones who were always off to see the world. If they were penned up, they were the ones that leaped the fence or dug under—and went gaily off, ready to fight an elephant if one happened along. And, Mary! you remember my grey stallion, Caesar! Why, Mary, it's ten times as hard to break a stallion. *No one* except someone who grew up in a city could suppose for a minute that there isn't more to male and female than the anatomical. Our ancestors who never doubted down through the centuries that men and women were different—that common judgement of mankind—based their judgement firmly on the observed world of nature. We've got to start with that."

"Yes-s-s," said Mary. "There is a difference, though you must admit it's hard to put your finger on. But that doesn't mean that a woman couldn't be a good doctor or engineer."

"Of course not!" I said. "I've often thought that women, who for millions of years have had to be sensitive to what might be wrong with little inarticulate children—or with husbands!—might be *better* doctors. Better surgeons, too, with their deft little fingers—if they weren't having their periods."

"Well, then, you see?" she said. "The differences don't *affect* anything."

"Oh yes they do!" I said. "You missed my point. I wasn't saying that a woman would be a good doctor in spite of being a woman but *because of it.* Queen Elizabeth was a great *queen:* she used her womanhood, hinting at marriage to keep foreign kings from invading when they might win all by marriage. On the other hand, thinking of Caesar—my stallion —and the male dogs adventuring, I'd a lot rather have my country defended by men."

"Oh, me too!" said Mary. "I admit that. Now that I think about it, I expect there are some jobs that women will probably never be very good at, just because of what a woman's nature is. And some things a man won't be good at."

We talked on for many hours, agreeing more and more deeply that what humanity has always and everywhere believed, that there are deep and innate differences between men and women—however much civilised life tends to hide them—is true. And we agreed that fatherhood and motherhood, while both are good and necessary, are not the same things and not interchangeable.

"Male and female, created He them," I said at one point. "I think it's certain that God intended men and women to be complementary, not identical. I think that Jesus—God incarnate—did *not* come as a man because of Jewish prejudices, but because He could be no other."

"Oh, I think that, too," said Mary. "Agnes doesn't, but I've always disagreed about that. She doesn't know anything about Christianity—or marriage, either. In fact, she doesn't know very much about anything from experience. Anyway, she was saying that women ought to be priests! Or priestesses. And I was saying, how could they be when they are supposed to *be* Christ at moments? I was thinking about her and Daddy the other day: she's really a very uneducated woman."

"I expect so," I said. "What this discussion really comes down to is that men and women are, or should be, fully equal in *value* but not necessarily equal in *function*. A nut and bolt are equal in value. And if the likes of Agnes were to try to persuade all the nuts to function as bolts, how would we hold the sum of things together?"

"I've always felt joy at being a girl," said Mary. "A joy and pride based on the idea that I had something unique, *qualitatively*, to bring to our marriage, just as you did. You know how we used to say that wholeness in marriage was to have the binocular vision made up of both qualities? Well, I've just realised that Agnes has been trying to take that away. What's so strange is—well, she's been talking about what she calls the liberation of women—and *I'm* feeling liberated by being a girl again! I mean, liberated by the idea that I'm not just a smaller man but something different through and through. Different in quality. Yay!"

"This world has difficulty," I said, "in coping with qualitative differences." Thus this—this *unisexism*! A unisexist *has* to be ignorant!"

"It's perfectly simple," she said. "For a girl to wear pants on *Windrush* or climbing Cader—that's a kind of freedom. But then to wear a skirt—nothing binding around the crotch or knees—that's a different freedom. Qualitatively."

"Nut!" I said. "Whisper that to the women with quantitative behinds who wear trousers when they're *not* climbing mountains. *Tight* ones!"

There we left the discussion, but it seemed to me from small things she said that Mary did have a sort of reborn joy in being a woman. She must have talked to Susie, too, for there was much less talk of Agnes. In fact, I think that she and Susie may have begun an anti-Agnes faction. It seems to me that all this may have some bearing on our present crisis, but the trouble is I don't know what bearing. —Will you tell me some day, Mary? I wonder.

A final element of the sixties, as it impinged on our lives, must be touched on: the drug scene, as it is called. Soon after we got to Holywell, we became aware that 'grass' or pot (marijuana) was everywhere—as well as LSD and mescaline. The newspapers and magazines were viewing with great alarum, and so was the Holywell administration; but nothing could stop it, because it was a part as well as a symbol of the whole congeries of protest and defiance, long hair and rock. Mary and I, at first, looked askance at this aspect of the sixties scene, for we had been brought up, like everybody else, to believe that marijuana "reefers" and—even more—hashish were the way to crazed and murderous deeds, as well as hopeless addiction. The first thing we learned was that none of that was true. We were assured of its untruth on every hand, and we noticed ourselves that pot seemed to lead towards beatific smiles rather than students running amok. Increasingly, we became curious, wanting to find out for ourselves. And I've already mentioned our smoking pot at the great march in October. Thereafter we considered it virtually harmless.

Of course we smoked it again from time to time, though there is certainly no addiction. We would smoke it with Tim and certain other friends. And then one evening in November—before the conversation about male and female—Mary went with Susie to see *The Graduate* at the campus theatre. I had seen the film with Mary earlier, but couldn't go along to see it again owing to a lecture to prepare. So off they went.

After the film, Mary went along with Susie to some girl's room in the dorm—not apparently for the first time—to smoke some grass. There were about ten other girls there and one illegal guy, all smoking and listening to records. Mary and Susie stayed for about an hour, and then, fortunately, went away. Ten minutes after they left, the other ten girls and the luckless chap who was with them were 'busted' in a big campus crackdown. And all were expelled. In the course of the electric excitement caused by the bust—in fact, it was Susie who hared over to tell Mary about it—I learned, with relief, of their narrow escape. And of the fact that she had more than once smoked in the dorm. After Susie left, I threw out the proposition that maybe Mary, as the wife of a don, was not as free as an unmarried girl like Susie, who had only her own neck to risk, to take such chances. Mary bristled slightly, being very likely a wildcat, and muttered something about cages. Then she slammed off and into the shower. Then she came back, smiling. She was sorry. She just hadn't thought of possible danger to me—or to her, either.

That could scarcely be called a disagreement, or only the flick of one, but we had a deeper disagreement over whether to try LSD. Tim had said a couple of times that he would rather like to try it, and Mary had talked to some people who had had quite fantastic experiences with LSD or mescaline or the 'sacred mushroom'. One of my colleagues had tried it, under controlled conditions, and spoke of it in terms from Huxley— the opening of the doors of perception. On the other hand, there were the frightful stories of 'bad trips' and hospitalization and death, although death as a result of some error of judgement, such as endeavouring to fly out of a tenth storey window.

Mary wanted us to try it. It might, she said, be a great adventure.

We'd never know unless we tried it. I was curious myself, but it seemed to me that all the evidence wasn't in on possible long-range effects. Suppose it actually damaged the brain? Suppose one of us attempted to fly out of the window?

"Then he'd fall ten feet into the flower bed," said Mary. "And there's not one bit of evidence that it does damage the brain."

We argued about it, inconclusively, several times. Finally she said, all right, then. If I were going to be so unadventurous, she'd do it alone. Or with Susie.

"Mary!" I said. "We said once that we'd do things together—or not at all. What about that? How could you do it alone—especially if it *is* such a great adventure?"

"Well," she said. "You're right. I shouldn't have said that. We do have to go together. But you won't *go!* Look. Here's a situation where one of us wants us to *do* something, something positive. Or do I mean affirmative? Anyway, moving *towards* adventure and experience. Right? And the other one is hanging back, not for any solid reason but just— just caution. How should we decide a difference like that?"

"Just caution?" I said. "Mightn't it be just as true to call it sanity?"

"Okay, sanity," she said. "Same thing! Sanity *often* means caution, hanging back, doesn't it? Lots of people in Columbus's day were far too sane to cross the great ocean. Or too sane to want to fly in one of them new-fangled airyplanes. Maybe sanity is a sign of growing old."

"Ugh!" I say. "Torpedoed! You're making a jolly good argument, you know. And I suppose—on that question about the negative and the affirmative—I suppose, when it comes to venturing upon new experience, the affirmative *ought* to be stronger. Remember that, next time *I* want us to do something! Anyway, now—we'll do it. Bring on your acid! Let the portals of perception swing wide . . ."

And that's how we came to trip. I asked Tim if he wanted to do it, too, and he said he did. Moreover, he knew where to get some LSD—or 'acid'—that was genuinely pure, with no 'speed' in it. And one night during the Christmas holidays, with nothing on hand for the morrow, Tim arrived with three red-and-blue capsules.

"They're six-hit caps!" he said. "Each one is enough, supposedly, for six little trips. What shall we do? Each take about half of one?"

"Let's drop the lot!" I said, determined not to be outdone in venturousness by Mary. She looked slightly frightened, I was glad to see. "We don't want just a high," I added. "If this is a great experience, let's have the whole of it."

So it was bravely agreed, although I fancy we were all a bit scared.

And we bravely and ceremoniously swallowed the stuff. As I sat back, waiting for the room to dissolve or whatever it would do, I thought Mary looked a little wild-eyed.

An hour later—nothing at all had happened. We even went out and strolled about the wintry campus. Then we played some Beatles records. Still nothing. We began to suspect that we had been given sugar capsules.

"Mummy!" said Mary in a little girl's voice. "The Emperor doesn't have any clothes on."

As she spoke I was looking idly at the cream-painted mouldings of the archway into the dining-room. Just as she finished speaking, a broad band of brilliant crimson shot up the moulding and round it. "Wow!" I cried. "It's working!"

"I'm tripping!" cried Tim.

A moment later Mary cried, "So am I! So am I! Colours! Everything wiggling!"

"Remember!" I said, seeing streamers of yellow and blue and crimson. "Relax! Go with the flow! Don't fight it or panic!"

But, despite my words, I was feeling thrills of panic. Something was happening that couldn't be stopped. Where would it lead? Should we ever come back? I looked at a coffee mug on the table, and the lines of its pattern were writhing like worms. I shut my eyes, and the colours flashed across the inside of my eyelids. But then, rather suddenly, a sort of peace crept over me, and I began to go with the flow—no longer caring where it might lead. The panic was gone. I looked at Mary through the flashing colours—only the three primary colours for me— and she was smiling a secret smile to herself, so I knew that she was all right. Tim was rapt but peaceful.

The night was fantastic, most of it impossible to record, though I tried to fix some things in memory. I remember at one point putting on a record of Strauss's mighty *Thus Spake Zarathustra,* and was nearly overwhelmed. The immense music seemed to fit our inward voyaging. Another vivid small memory—or gigantic—came just after I had lighted a cigarette. I found myself poised in empty space between the stars. Peacefully I watched the great wheel of the galaxy slowly and majestically turn, seeing its spiral arms and all its billions of stars. Eons I hung there. Then I found myself in the room again. I looked at my cigarette after my eons in outer space: it hadn't yet greyed with its first ash.

Here is the poem I wrote the next day about the inner-space trip.

PORTAL

Doorway between the rooms
Mouldings a century rigid
Suddenly what was cream
  (Scream) is shot crimson
    Lines writhe and crawl
      Panic thrills along the nerves
        Mind going blowing
      Wind on the sea of nowhere
    No turning off
  Fare inward voyager
Now dark tidal peace floods
  Primary colours burn in the dim room
    Sail on Odysseus before the wind
      Time opens upon Eternity
    While first ash greys a cigarette
  Hanging in the winds of space
And the wheel of the galaxy is music
  Through skulls eggshell-thin
    Tendrils reach and intertwine loves
    Pale globes of light are cosmos
      And at the still point of All
        Utter presence without lineament
        The Love
        Pouring joyously into souls
      Familiar never-seen abstract shapes
    Yearning Loveward to be filled
    Then burning crimson blue or gold
  Now this dark cylinder of soul
O known
  Intense blue lights along that dark
    Burn like suns with loving
      O ecstasy in the knowing
      All manner of thing is well

This rather spectacular poem represents of course my trip only, and I shall never while I live forget the experience—or so it seemed—of being in the presence of God. I did not, even in imagination, look upon the face of God and live—nothing of shape or appearance. Only the sense of a Presence so utterly majestic, so utterly vast, and so utterly loving that I can't help but think—or, rather, *feel*—that it had some relation to truth—objective truth outside my head—which alone would give it any importance. What made it seem like a glimpse of truth was, in that Presence, to see, not it but friends I recognised despite pure abstractions of shape—cubes and cones—as being Betsy or Peter or Tim or Mary herself, and see them yearning towards the Presence that was Love and being filled by it—how could I have imagined that? I was aware enough, while it was happening, to say to myself: "Remember this! Oh dear God, let me remember!"

Tim and Mary both said that they, too, had seemed to experience something of the divine, but either the experiences were more nebulous or Tim and Mary hadn't made the effort to remember that I did. At all events, we were glad we had tripped, and we decided that it might be worth doing again at rare intervals.

I have been thinking about my God-experience, if it was that, since I got the terrible letter from Mary on April Fool's Day. What I keep thinking about was the joyousness of the Love's pouring itself into the souls—a joyous, laughing torrent of love. C. S. Lewis speaks of "majestic rivers of foamless charity" in one of his poems, but I shall always think now of sparkling, laughing torrents of joyous charity.

I was not far from despair at the beginning of this month, thinking about that letter. But, somehow, lately I've been thinking about that joyous love, the laughing torrent. It is, I'm convinced, the essential truth of the universe: that God's love is like that. And Mary knows it, too. —Mary, I pray, often, that you *are* knowing it . . . now.

One time years ago Jim Cosby and I sailed from Redrock down the river and out into the Chesapeake to Scudder's Island, the same island that we had been marooned on when we were little. Now, though, we were about sixteen or seventeen. We anchored and had a swim, and then we sat naked on a rock and talked. Jim was telling me about the longing he felt, and had always felt, for the great ocean. It was that longing of course that was taking him to the Naval Academy. But he described it as a kind of joy—the very thought of it. I understood that, for I had the same sort of longing for beauty: hills and trees and ocean, too. Later, though, my longing was for Mary winged. But whatever I longed for, it always seemed to me when I had got it that there was some other joy on beyond that was what I really longed for. And in this bleak April I decided, with the help of my image of the joyous, laughing torrent of God's love, that what all my longings—and everybody's—are for is, quite simply, God. And it seemed to me that I could turn over this business of Mary's love for that woman to that joyous God . . . and, somehow, all would be well.

Now I am almost done with this journey to Holywell and ready to ship all I've written off to Mary. After the LSD trip there wasn't much to break the routine of our winter days except a Christmas trip to Redrock, which was pleasant, as always. Lots of uncles and aunts about, but Mary and I did a good deal of riding, as well as some sailing during a warm spell. Since my father is quite anti-war, we told him of our activities, including the March on the Pentagon. Dad was hilarious at Mary's escape from the U.S. Marshall, though I suppressed my punching him. Even as it was, one of my uncles was a bit gruff about the march and muttered about the flag and ancestors who had fought and bled. Finally I said, "Look, Uncle Charles, not all wars are the same. Our own family fought against the United States in the days of the Confederacy. And if I had been alive when Mister Lincoln invaded the South, I'd have been galloping right behind General Lee on Caesar. At the Pentagon I was doing the same thing." Uncle Charles grinned a little and afterwards mellowed considerably. He even gave me approving looks from time to time, hearing perhaps rebel yells round the Pentagon.

Back, then, to the snows of Holywell. Early in the new term, with Holywell locked in snow and ice, there came a letter from Leilani, full of trade-winds and white ginger, urging us to "come home to the Islands." Even as Mary read the letter aloud, sleet was slatting against our windows; and we were instantly seized by a longing for Hawaii and spending the summer there.

But our plan had been to spend a month with Mary's father, since he had been tied up in Frisco during the whole of Christmastide. When the idea of the Islands was broached, Mary exclaimed, "Oh—poor Daddy! He'll be crying unfair, unfair! And I do want to see him so much."

So did I. He was the wisest and best of men. Of course he wouldn't in fact cry unfair, unfair. He wouldn't say a word. And that made it worse, since it *was* unfair.

So we devised a Vallance compromise. Mary would betake herself to Georgetown in the middle of March and spend three weeks or so with her father, and then in June we'd go down together for another week before going off to the Islands.

Thus on Monday, the eighteenth of March, Mary departed, promising to ring up often. I was not overly cheerful about our being separated, nor at the prospect of lonely meals out of tins. Still, I looked forward to some good talks with Tim.

Mary rang up that Monday night to say that she was there and had just had a great talk with her father. I heard from her again on the following Sunday. Then nothing more. When she didn't phone on the next Sunday, I planned to ring her on Monday—but the letter came.

Apparently she didn't trust herself to tell me on the telephone.

There has been, though, one chink in the shell of silence. Today—April twenty-fourth, her birthday—there came a brief note from her father, saying only: "Val—Hang on, old chap. Can't talk about it, but don't surrender the ship; don't strike your colours." I feel somewhat encouraged. Perhaps more than somewhat.

I should also record that last Sunday afternoon—about nine in the evening in England—I put through a call to Yorkshire. To Peter Shirley. I told him all about it, which of course took about a third of a minute. He took it calmly and was a great comfort, saying with warm certainty, "Val, she will come back!" Still, he was a bit shocked. Then he said, "Speak to Betsy." I could hear him shouting, "Betsy! I say, Betsy! Come and talk to Val!" Then her small voice came down the line: "Hullo, Val. What is happening? Is it something about Mary?" When I had told her, she was silent a moment. Then she said, "I'm not quite surprised. Her own love of being a winged girl—well, it made her feel that there was a sort of . . . magic or glory in all girls. She could imagine, you know, that something like this—another woman—might be . . . I don't know what to call it, a sort of fulfillment, maybe. But, Val—it *won't* be. Not for Mary. It might take her a little while to find out, but she will. I know it."

This seemed wisdom to me. Betsy is a sort of seeress anyway. And she, like Peter, was seeing with loving eyes, which may be the truest vision.

Perhaps I ought to say that, in addition to the journals, I've read right many books on sexuality, including homosexuality, but it's very clear that no one understands what causes it—masses of contradictory theories couched in ponderous and disagreeable language. I seriously doubt whether I'd trust a psychiatrist to guide me across the street. One theory that I thought about a little was that everyone is bisexual, able to go either way, leap in bed with anybody. I don't really believe it, since I cannot discover in myself any inclination towards other men. I even developed a counter-theory: that homosexuals and heterosexuals alike were concerned with the "other"—the person who attracted them—while the so-called bisexual is perhaps concerned with what gives him pleasure. Still, I suspect that they are 'really' one thing or the other.

My story is complete. This afternoon I'm going to pack the whole manuscript—from "Wind Song" to "Journey to Holywell"—and send it off special delivery to Mary. I think she needs it to make a just decision, And she is fair-minded enough to read it.

The question now is, what do I have to say in conclusion? What, if anything, is the fruit of my intense concentration upon the past?

First, then, I will lay it down that Mary's love for me is as genuine and deep as any woman's love for a man could be. Her own writings in the journals establish it.

Second, I am firm in my conclusion that, whatever I thought when I read about her reaction to the Bull of the Mountain, Mary was *not* thrown into a man-dreading and, hence, man-hating deformity. She is too sunny and valiant and balanced.

Third, I have decided—admittedly, I could be wrong—that Mary is not 'really' a lesbian, only now discovering her true sexual nature. I decided this on the basis of all our love over the years. Even in this perilous time, I affirm my belief that Mary is a woman who cannot be permanently happy with another woman—who will find her joy with a man. After all, I *know* the joy she has found, her response to my love-making.

Fourth, I believe that Mercia is the key: a schoolgirl crush, born and then truncated in circumstances of such heart-rending beauty and pathos that it was bound to be enshrined in Mary's heart. All the more so after Mercia's seeming appearance by the lagoon at the luau: Mercia torn on the black rocks but Mercia smiling by the lagoon. I think Mary is, as it were, *continuing* her crush, with Miss X as stand-in for Mercia. If I were to speculate about Miss X, I should guess she is a bit like Mercia, gentle and tender. Perhaps a little older than Mary.

Fifth, if I am right about the crush on Mercia being continued with Miss X, then it would be reasonable to suppose that, like other crushes, it will run its course quite swiftly. I hope so. If it does, then Mary will be free of it for ever.

Sixth, I think of God and that joyous torrent of His love. I think Our Lord the Spirit is at Mary's elbow—and that perhaps will be decisive.

Those are my conclusions, right or wrong. Somehow, the rats of fear that have been gnawing at my bowels have withdrawn. I hope that Mary herself at some not very distant day will point out where I have hit the mark and where I have missed.

And Mary—I love you. Happy birthday!

Now I shall box this up and take it to the post office.

Richard Vallance

Journey to Urania

The Study, Holywell, April, 1968, Richard

Two days after posting the journeys to Mary, special delivery, the postman knocked at my door with a big envelope, registered special delivery, from her. So the pattern works itself out.

Mary's letter

Richard—I've made a decision that has been full of pain. I know you are also in pain, but I must ask you, whom I've hurt so deeply, to try in your courtesy to understand. Please, then, Richard, do *not* look to the end of this first. Go with me in my little journey and understand why I *must* decide as I have done. . . .

As I begin to write about it all, I think of you, Richard, steadfast and valiant, and you are like a rock. And I think, too, of—Deirdre. I murmur that magic name, a small Celtic poem in itself: Dee-*err*-dray. And I see her, too, the soft eyes and sweet mouth, her face framed by her dark hair. Her face is quiet, a little sad. Deirdre of the Sorrows—I shall always think of her so. And thinking of that name, Deirdre of the Sorrows, I hear her lovely, slightly husky voice, hear it singing or reading a poem or pronouncing my name. But the sorrows were mine, too—such pain as I've never known since wings.

Although she was as English as an old apple tree in Hampshire, she was also as Celtic as her mother's blood and songs could make her. But it was in America, curiously, that I met her. Or not so curiously perhaps, since it was England, England seen from afar, that was immediately a bond between us, for I am my mother's daughter. A bond of primroses in an English wood and the Downs magnificent and bare against the sky.

I left Holywell still wrapped in snow and ice and went south to early spring in Georgetown, as Richard and I had agreed I should do. I was sad about leaving him for so long, but I was looking forward to being with Daddy. When I arrived, Jolly kissed me and hugged me and made a marvellous dinner. And Daddy was just quietly glad. And it was good to be home again. One of the first things I did, as always, was to go into the drawing-room and look for a long time at the painting of Mummy above the mantelpiece. I always come home to her as well as to Daddy.

We talked, Daddy and I, with honesty as we always have done and, in the end, perhaps more deeply than ever before. The first evening, after we had settled down in the old leather chairs in his study, we got caught up on our news of each other. He told me about the complex case that had kept him in Frisco so long and was now won by his firm—a very amusing story, as he told it. And I told him what we had been doing at Holywell, including the acid trip. If he was at all secretly alarmed by that, he didn't show it. Just smilingly listened with complete attention. Sort of an acid test, perhaps. I read him Richard's poem "Portal" about his trip and told him what I could remember of mine. That led to my going back to what at the time was completely believable, Mercia's coming to me there by the lagoon at the luau. Of course Daddy had heard about it before and had, in fact, read the journal. I would trust Daddy with anything. I said I didn't know whether to believe that it was really Mercia, what did he think?

"That's always the question, isn't it?" he said. "We cry out for proof that God *is,* but I often wonder what we would consider proof. If an angel radiant with light appeared in the Senate Chamber and was seen by everyone, I doubt that the unbelievers would become believers, don't you? They would mutter about a trick of the opposition or mass hallucination. The only thing one can say about your experience with Mercia is this: that God knew before the world was made—He saw it happening in His eternal Now—that you would believe, at least at the moment, that it was Mercia."

"But, Daddy," I said, "if God knew, then it was real even if it wasn't."

"It was a real *experience,* wasn't it?" he said. "And your joy was real, wasn't it? And you are still glad it happened—as, I may say, I am, also. Isn't the truth this—that we need a better definition of reality? If we believe God is, that believed fact compels a different definition of reality."

"I'll have to think about that," I said. "The meaning of reality. Val said something a bit like that, too. Anyway, as you say, I *am* glad it happened and glad she said what she did."

"Particularly what she said about reckless love," said Daddy with a smile. "Reckless love is perhaps the only real love."

"Speaking of which," I said, "perhaps I'd best ring up Val before he goes to bed."

After I'd talked to Val, Daddy told me to feel free to use his study to write in, if I wanted to, and also to use the car whenever I liked, since he rarely uses it.

In my bed that night I thought how glad I was to have come to be with him.

The second evening we had a big discussion on the war, and I told him more of our anti-war doings, including the big march here in Washington. He had been out of town then, too, so we hadn't seen him after we came back from the Pentagon. He laughed when I told him about escaping from the U. S. Marshall, having looked rather grim during the clubbing part of the story. When I told him of Richard's powerful punch, he laughed again and said, "Good work!" I finished the story by reading Richard's poem on the march, which Daddy liked and asked for a copy of.

He asked me, then, to read some of my own poems, particularly "Wind Song" which he loves the most. I read two or three, including that one. Then he said, "There's one you haven't read to me for a long time. One you wrote before wings—'Nocturne'. —Would you like to read me that one?"

"Good heavens, Daddy!" I said. "I don't have it—in fact, I don't know if it still exists." It was a poem I had written long ago when Daddy and I were staying in a borrowed cottage near the shore. One evening I had asked Daddy to carry me out in the twilight to sit on a stone wall and leave me there till I called.

"Ah," said Daddy with a grin. "I can remedy that. I still have the copy you gave me." He went over to his desk and then handed me the poem. "Read it."

So I smiled at him and read it.

NOCTURNE

Alone I sat on a low stone wall,
　　My skirt tucked under my knees:
Unheard in the night a tear can fall
　　—With wind in the trees.

The wind and the high stars overhead
　　And a girl alone in her dream:
Till something past dreaming came in its stead
　　—To be or to seem.

A warmth and a cry, a weight, a shift
　　(My heart-leap thrilled the alarms):
A little head for my hand to lift
　　—A babe in my arms.

One moment appearance was complete—
　　Was it faith that failed to go on?
One moment of bliss and the night was sweet
　　—And then it was gone.

I prayed in the night grown suddenly chill
　　Under the stars grown old:
I prayed to a god remote and still
　　—And my breast was cold.

"You know," said Daddy, after a little space of silence, "that seems to me to be an exceptionally fine little poem."

"I know," I said. "I got a little poetry-chill. As though it were somebody else's poem. Yet remembering, too."

"Mary," he said, and paused. "Do you think that perhaps you should write a poem about Mercia on the beach? Isn't there a link?"

"Do you mean—?" I began, and then, "Oh, heavens! I see! Both, er, *appearances.* But, Daddy, Mercia existed, so, maybe, she did come. But that baby—my baby—how could it be, er, real? I never *had* a baby . . ."

"I don't know," said Daddy. "Except that past, present, and future would seem, somehow, to be all one in eternity."

There was a little silence. Then I said slowly, "I'll have to think about that. And copy the poem for Val; I don't know that he's ever seen it. Daddy, you do think of upsetting things, don't you?"

But that was Daddy. Always something to think about later.

On the fourth day I met Deirdre.

If 'April' showers hadn't come early on this first day of spring, so that I decided to take Daddy's car for some morning errands, we might never have met, although she lived but five doors away in the direction of Wisconsin Avenue. It was raining slightly, and I was just backing the car out into the narrow Georgetown street, when she came along and paused because the way was blocked. I saw her through the right-hand window of the car, a little shorter than me, perhaps a few years older, striding along with a country walk, something curiously right in the graceful casualness of her clothes. I have since thought that it was, perhaps, the look of England that made her seem so right. Anyhow, she strode along and she paused. And at just that moment, the wind gusted and the rain came blindingly down.

And I, moved by some obscure impulse, leaned across and opened the far door and said, "Good heavens! Come in, won't you?"

And she came in and shut the door.

We sat there, laughing about it a little, while the rain beat down. And, somehow, almost at once we were talking of England—a rainstorm on the South Downs she had walked in. Her name was Deirdre Digby, and there, in that name, were the two sides of her. Like me, she was staying with her father, and he was a captain in the Royal Navy—Captain the Honourable John Spencer Wentworth Digby, RN, in fact—and Naval Attaché at the Embassy. She, herself, was on her way to the Embassy—she had meant to walk—to have lunch with him. Indeed, she was here from London to be with him, because her adored mother, the mother who had given her the name Deirdre as well as something wild and lovely in her voice, had recently died.

And when I spoke of Oxford, she said a little sadly that she had always meant to go up to Oxford and to Lady Margaret Hall, but various family complications had postponed her matriculation from year to year. And then had come her marriage, a marriage to a second cousin that had been an absolute disaster from the first, although more years had passed before she had finally extricated herself. Now she was firm in her resolve never to marry again. In recent years she had lived in London, working in the Home Office and sharing a flat with a woman friend.

I didn't find all this out during the rain, of course. We sat and laughed and talked of England, she in that husky voice. And when the rain slackened a bit, I drove her to the Embassy. The car radio, I remember, came on with the melody of a folk song with roots in Wales, and Deirdre hummed along with it for a moment and then, spontaneously and naturally, began to sing it in Welsh in a low, soft, somehow thrilling voice. I think I may have fallen slightly in love with her while she sang. At all events, I begged her to come along to Daddy's house when her luncheon was over, and she said she would. Then we arrived at the British Embassy, and I watched her slender figure go up the walk.

And she did come. We talked and laughed and played one or two records. And then we got to reading poetry to each other. It began with one poem I wanted her to hear, but then she urged me to read more, saying over and over how excitingly I read poetry, so I read several more, all dear to me. Then she hunted about for some of her loved poems, finally running over to her house for one special book. She read poems with the same thrilling quality in her lovely voice that was in her singing. When she finally left, just before Daddy was due to arrive, we were already planning tomorrow, and other tomorrows were being implied since we both had our days free while our fathers were at their offices. Somehow, when she left, it seemed very natural for me to kiss her on the cheek.

The next morning, as we'd planned, I went over to her house, where she had a fresh pot of smoky Earl Grey tea all brewed. While we drank it, she told me she had dreamt of me in the night, and I practically interrupted in excitement with "Good heavens! I dreamt of you, too. But I can't remember it, except it was by the sea."

"But, Mary—I do remember mine!" she said, smiling. "Oh, it was so strange! I dreamt I was walking in a royal forest—huge old oaks and beeches—and a doe came running through the forest. And, Mary, it had blue eyes and it was you! But that's not all, because, then, the doe changed into a collie, all red and gold—and the *collie* had blue eyes and was you, still running towards me. And then the collie turned into a blue-eyed girl—you, for sure—running still, running to me. And then I woke. Now, you tell me what it means, Mary Vallance!"

Well, I thought, we both thought, it ought to mean something important, but we couldn't decide what. A strange, haunting dream, even just hearing about it. All that day we talked and talked, discovering all sorts of things, from Devonshire clotted cream to the glorious new Coventry Cathedral that we both loved. And once she sang some folk songs, including "Willow, Willow," and I was very deeply moved.

She insisted that I come to lunch with her and her father at the Embassy that day, and I found him to be a very pleasant and witty gentleman. I knew without a doubt that he and Daddy would like each other, so Deirdre and I conspired and determined that Captain Digby—and of course his daughter—should come to dinner at my house on Sunday. This was done. Deirdre was impressed with Daddy, and the two men began that evening what I'm sure will be an enduring friendship. In fact, as Daddy found out very quickly, the Hon. John had been at school with my mother's brother—my Uncle Hal in England—whom he called Tadders for some obscure reason, and had actually once danced with my mother. So Daddy just made a little gesture towards the portrait over the mantelpiece, and Deirdre's father looked and said, "I remember." Also, of course, both fathers were naval types, and Daddy's ship had been in English waters.

I called Richard that night, after they had gone, and said that I had met some extremely nice people; but I didn't feel that I could tell him what Deirdre was like over the telephone, so I didn't try.

Deirdre and I saw each other every day. We spent long, happy hours with each other. Sometimes we drove about in Daddy's car, one time going down into Virginia to the Northern Neck to see Lee's old home, Stratford Hall. Sometimes Jolly would make a picnic basket for us, as she had used to do for Richard and me. And of course there were the mornings or afternoons—usually both—at one house or the other, laughing and endlessly talking. Deirdre had a wonderful sense of humour, and we had a lot of little special jokes. And always we would, sooner or later, turn to poetry, which was almost our secret world.

Although we laughed so much and joked, there was an underlying sadness in Deirdre, a hint of melancholy. I knew it sprang, in part at least, from her mother's death, but I thought it might come, too, from the wasted years of her marriage. I told her, of course, about Richard, but I didn't talk of him and our love much, for I thought it might make her sad because of her own awful marriage. She told me about that, and she spoke, too, of Irene, with whom, until recently, she had shared a flat in London.

Very swiftly, and very naturally, we became closer and closer friends, Deirdre and I. One day I told her what my childhood had really been like after the Disaster, the dark, imprisoned, hopeless years; and there were tears rolling down her cheeks when I finished. Then she came over and kissed me without a word. After that, somehow, we got to talking a lot about childhood, and we would spend time sort of dreaming awake about how much fun we might have had if we had been little girls together. We pictured ourselves as children in different settings, climbing an old apple tree in Hampshire or paddling in salt water pools and looking for shells at the seashore.

One day she was reading Keats, and she read his "Ode to a Nightingale." Hearing that poem in her lovely husky voice moved me very much, especially when she came to the lines about Ruth sick for home. Deirdre looked up to see my eyes full of tears. I told her then the story of Mercia and her death on the black rocks . . . and then of Mercia coming to me by the lagoon. She listened with absorbed attention, her chin on her hand; and when I was telling her of Mercia's death, Deirdre's brown eyes were full of tears, as mine had been earlier. Then she reached over from her chair and took my hand for a moment.

Deirdre of the Sorrows. Why do I always think of her so? For one thing, of course, the music of the name seems to fit her. But also, even more, because of the hint of melancholy in the sweet husky voice and in the big brown eyes. Maybe that is why they fascinated me—when we were apart I would find myself longing to hear her voice, and I would see her eyes looking at me. Even behind her gay laughter there seemed to be a ghost of sadness, and that laughter would echo in my ears when she was not there.

And then one morning, late, when I had been especially longing to see her and was thinking that I wasn't going to be able to stand it unless she came pretty soon, she was suddenly there. Jolly had let her in, and I hadn't heard her ring. So I was a little startled, though happily so—a wave of happiness went over me. Deirdre smiled, perhaps at my wide-eyed startled look; and she said, sorry to be late; and she came over to give me our little good-morning kiss. She bent down and put her arms around me, as we always did, and kissed my cheek. But I felt a sort of trembling in her arms. Or was the tremble in me?

I don't know which it was, but, suddenly, overwhelmingly, I had to kiss her on the mouth. Blindly I turned my face a little. Maybe she blindly turned her face a little. Our lips met. Something warm and lovely pouring through me. It seemed to me that our lips were clinging of their own volition. But a shock was building up in me, too. And then, without my awareness of the parting, the kiss was ended.

We both pretended that it hadn't happened or that it was nothing—a variation, merely, of casualness. We talked of ordinary things. What they were I don't remember, but I remember that my voice sounded unnatural in my ears. And something was trembling, somewhere inside of me. I wanted to kiss her again; I wanted our arms around each other. I thought I would die of wanting it. And it seemed that it would be so right, so good. The image felt like goodness and sweetness. But, also, somehow, not right. I was confused. Torn. I could not think. I said that her tea was cold; I would get her some fresh. I carried her cup into the kitchen to empty it. I came back and poured out more tea and added milk, not looking at her. I set the cup down beside her, still not looking at her.

Then I did look at her, and she looked at me, and her face was wet with tears. The soft brown eyes were full of tears. A century passed in that look. I felt my heart breaking.

"Dear God!" I whispered. "Deirdre! Oh, Deirdre!" Then I fell to my knees and buried my face in her lap. Without lifting my head, my voice muffled in her lap, I said, "Deirdre, Deirdre!"

"Oh, Mary!" she said, her voice choking as she said it. She stroked my hair.

I could hear Jolly singing upstairs, and somewhere in the distance— the window was open—a radio was playing "Sergeant Pepper." Otherwise everything was very still. We stayed like that, not moving. Once there was a small sound, like a tiny sob, from her. Time had ceased to exist.

After this had been for ever, she said, her voice shaking a little and huskier than usual, "Mary. I'm going now. Will you call me this afternoon?"

With my face still buried in her lap, I nodded and whispered, "Yes." I reached up my hand and felt her take it. She gave it a small loving squeeze. Then she let it go.

She stirred and I took my face away without looking at her and buried it in my hands. It was wet.

"Stay there," she said above me. "I'll let myself out. Bye, bye— Mary."

"Deirdre!" I cried. "Don't go!" Then I said, "No, never mind. I'll call you. Bye, bye."

The door closed.

I continued to crouch there on the floor for a few minutes.

Then I rushed out to the car and drove to Rock Creek Park. It was still morning and a Wednesday, so there were not many people about. It was a grey day anyhow. The one man that did attempt to speak to me got such a snarl that he practically reeled.

I sat there on a bench for a long time, not thinking at all. I watched a bird and looked at the budding leaves.

Then, like a leaf falling upon my hair, the thought fell into my mind: I am in love with Deirdre—her sweetness, her warmth, her gaiety and sadness, her brown eyes, her mouth, her lovely husky voice. So I added a word to the thought: I am in love with Deirdre—terribly! I wanted us to go on being happy together. But I wanted, now, to hold her and be held. I wanted warm, lovely kisses. I wanted us to hold each other, laughing a little, straining towards each other. I wanted that husky voice to murmur, "Mary, Mary, I love you!" into my ear.

Another leaf drifted down into my mind: Richard. Val! Just that. It stayed there beside the first thought. Then I added something to this one, too: Richard—oh my God! I wanted to think about Deirdre. I made myself think of Richard. I called forth his image, but he seemed pale, remote, his steady grey eyes looking at me. He didn't smile. I thought of Richard saying, when I was a lump, that I was his dearest friend—and shouldn't we hold hands? And Richard whispering, "I'd give me!" His kiss—and wings. He and I driving in the Berkshires and coming home exhausted with happiness. His merry grin and crinkled eyes. Richard—so quiet, so strong, and yet so vulnerable. And so totally trusting: oh agony in that thought! I knew I loved him enormously.

But Deirdre—beautiful of face and form, beautiful of soul looking out of gentle brown eyes, haunting me. The warm bond of living poetry. Longing for her like Ruth sick for home. The warm mouth that I ached for, as once I ached for Mercia to kiss me again.

But Richard—comrade in storms at sea and in quiet hours at Oxford, hearing the bells. Richard, so dear, so generous, so loyal. The night of the goddess by the Moonpool. Richard of the wings—the *wings!*

Deirdre.

Richard.

Oh my God!

A little girl ran happily along Rock Creek. I was just a lady sitting there, nothing to do with her world. Would she ever be torn like this? Could a person actually die of being torn apart? I held up my hand and looked at it; it shook a little. I breathed deeply.

Then I thought with wonder: It is possible, it *is,* to love two people at once. The thought shook me. I looked at the thought, and I knew that, not only was I in love with somebody besides Richard—oh my God!—but I was in love with him, too. I was really, truly, in love with both. What I felt for Deirdre—oh, Deirdre!—was no brief emotional infatuation, even less merely a physical desire. It was truly love; and, I knew, she felt it, too. But I loved Richard, a living love.

And yet I couldn't bring Richard's image as near to me as Deirdre's was. *She* was warm and alive; he seemed remote and a little cold. I didn't ache for him as I did for Deirdre. Was that significant?

Then I thought—a shattering thought—what am I doing? making a choice? Could I leave Richard? Never, never! He's my blood, my life, my breath. Then—leave Deirdre? Leave her when I'm all one ache for her? When I'm longing for the sound of her voice, the touch of her lips? I can't! I can't!

I moaned aloud, but there was no one to hear. I clenched my fist till it hurt. Nothing had ever been so impossible. Nothing had ever been such agony. I wanted help, but there was no help. Or was there? Perhaps I should pray? But how could Christ understand a thing like this? How could He take away the agony? I turned my mind away from the fleeting thought that He, having known agony, might understand very well. I didn't quite admit the thought that Christ would want me to do some awful, impossible thing like leaving Deirdre, but it was a thought below thought. No, I wouldn't pray now. How should I know what to pray for? I didn't want to think about Christ. I didn't think about Him.

I wanted to think about Deirdre. I thought about her.

Eventually the thought crept into my mind: if I do not see Deirdre, I'll never know what it all means. I can't go back to Richard not knowing. It wouldn't be fair to him. Why wouldn't it? Never mind, it wouldn't be fair to me. Anyway, I *can't* not see her. I must see her. Must. I won't think any more. Not now.

Then I went back to the car and drove home and dialled her number. My hand was shaking a little. Her voice came along the wire after one ring.

"Deirdre," I said. "This is Mary. I must see you."

"Yes," she said. "Come, then. I'm alone."

A few minutes later she opened the door for me and led the way into the little garden room they call the parlour. She turned. We stood there an instant, just looking at each other. Then she raised both arms just a little, her small hands hip-high, palms out. It was question and it was invitation, as I chose.

I stepped into her arms, all questions answered, at least for that moment in time. Our lips met, clung. Fleetingly I thought of Mercia's kiss. But I held the soft reality of Deirdre. A woman. I was a woman. Our breasts pressed together.

After a long moment, she pulled me down beside her on the sofa, murmuring, "Oh, Mary, Mary! I wanted this so much!"

"I love you, Deirdre," I whispered. "Oh, I love you!"

Our lips were together again, as if they could not live apart. Thrills chased each other over my body. We did not speak again, except for small murmurs, for a long time.

Finally, as if it were by common consent, we drew a little apart and looked at each other with speaking eyes. My lips felt bruised.

"Shall we have some sherry?" she said in an unsteady voice.

I nodded, and she rose to pour it out. After handing me my glass, she sat down in a chair facing me and raised her glass.

"Let us drink to the meaning of Mary and Deirdre," she said softly, huskily. "And to womanhood."

266

"To the meaning of Mary and Deirdre—and womanhood," I said, also softly.

We drank, looking at each other over our glasses.

"You said you love me," she said. "I love you. That is the meaning of us, isn't it? The love of women . . ."

"Yes," I said. "We are the same. I know you as I know myself. When we stood there kissing, I felt your breast pressing into me, and you, I knew, felt mine pressing into you. That's it, isn't it?"

"Yes," she said. "That *is* it. You are swift to know. But, Mary, what of Richard?"

"I don't know," I said. "I tried to think. But I am riding the tidal wave."

She laughed a little at that. She was caught up in the same tidal wave. She had sworn to herself that she would not make the first move, because of Richard. If I had not telephoned this afternoon, she would have gone away.

I told her about Rock Creek Park, a little. Then I said, "How can I think when I'm torn with longing for you, Deirdre? It would be easier, maybe, if you were another man. But loving a woman . . . it's not just a matter of degree. It's a different thing altogether. It's a difference in kind. Isn't it?"

"Yes," she said. "I think so. But, then, I don't think I ever loved a man. I tried to persuade myself that I loved my husband, at first. But I didn't really. I didn't know what love was. And then, when I fell in love with Irene—I did love her, you know—I said to myself, 'This is what I was made for, loving a woman. Someone who thinks the same way I do —*feels* the way I do.' You know, don't you? I put my hand on your breast a little while ago. What did you do, Mary? What did you think?"

"Mmmmm," I said. "I put my hand on yours, didn't I? And I thought: my hand is feeling the softness of her breast and *her* hand is feeling the softness of mine. And we're each aware of the other's hand. A terrible closeness. It made me dizzy. Like everything spinning round. I almost fainted. Or—that nice old word—swooned."

"That's it," said Deirdre. She smiled. "That's what is so lovely about women loving. That is, for those who *find* it lovely. You do, don't you? Yes, I know you do. That's one thing you know now, isn't it? That you are one of those who do?"

There was the sound of the front door opening. It was the Honourable John. He glanced in. "Hullo-ullo!" he said. "Nice to see you, Mary." He went on up the stairs.

"Stay for dinner," said Deirdre.

"No," I said. "I'm not up to being company. I'm off."

I rose, and so did she. We kissed quickly, warmly. "Till tomorrow," she said.

That night Daddy and I did not talk. I pleaded a headache and went to my room. I wrote a note to Richard, knowing it would be like a sword thrust. But I had to do it. I had to have time. I could not speak to him.

I did not sleep much that night. I did read a short novel about the love of two women Deirdre had given me as I left. And I thought about something that Agnes, a Holywell teacher, had said one night when Susie and I had been at her place—something some feminist had written: "The only totally liberated woman is one who loves other women and is independent of men." At the time I had thought it nonsense, for it seemed to me that men and women were meant to be mutually supportive. But now I was remembering it and wondering. Could it be true?

I dreamed about Oxford. Some woman, perhaps my former tutor—I couldn't remember—was saying to Peter Shirley: "Mary of course is a lesbian. Isn't that *interesting?*" And Peter was saying sadly, "So that was it." What "that" was, I was not to learn, for Jolly was just coming in with my early tea. As she set it down and drew the curtains, making cheerful remarks about the rather gloomy day, I realised that the dream had sprung from the lesbian book I had been reading last night, and I snatched it off the table and put it under the covers.

When Jolly had gone, I thought about the word 'lesbian'. I thought about Sappho and her roses—the beautiful poems about the beloved Atthis and Anactoria. I suddenly remembered that the Greeks had called lesbians Uranians, the name coming from Aphrodite Urania, goddess of love in its higher manifestations. Sappho was a Uranian on Lesbos, and in the end even the Hellenes had come to call women lovers Lesbians. Still thinking of Lesbos and Sappho and her girls, I remembered the Moonpool and wondered, with a faint sense of disloyalty, what the night of the goddess would have been if we had been only women. I imagined Deirdre, nude and beautiful, there at the Moonpool, coming up to me with her graceful walk and her tender mouth, her dark hair round her face and her eyes shining in the moonlight. But Richard . . . Apollo . . . —I jerked my thought away, back to Deirdre in Georgetown.

Deirdre, with a name like a poem. Deirdre with her soft brown eyes —oh, eyes like Mercia's! And longing to kiss her, as I had longed to kiss Mercia. Deirdre and I in the Islands, on a beach, dressed only in *pikake* leis. I could smell the fragrance, here in the Georgetown morning.

Lesbian. I am a lesbian, I thought. Am I? I must be, mustn't I? I know now what it means. I long for what it means, but am I a lesbian? Deirdre is, and am I not the same? Oh, Deirdre! I want your arms holding me.

I sprang up and bathed.

When Deirdre came, after Daddy had gone to his office, the day was like the day before, without the shock. We kissed as if we could not kiss enough.

In retrospect, it seems to me that, during all those days, we spent hours and hours mouth to mouth, wrapped in a kind of sweet ecstasy. One whole day, when we were quite alone in her house, we dispensed with clothes altogether, loving each other's nude female body.

But we talked, too, talked eagerly, telling each other about our past lives in detail, talked as though we could not get enough of talking, either. The words fairly tumbled out. Once when I was telling her about Pauline and Provence and the little dinner party in the house by the river, Deirdre said: "Imagine that little dinner with only women present —one of them being me, if you please, Mary dear. How different it would have been with no men to dominate the talk! Men talking and women murmuring, 'How wonderful!' " I agreed eagerly. It was only later that it occurred to me that the men hadn't dominated it a bit.

We talked a lot about the world of women, a phrase that she was fond of. An intimate world, where the women spoke freely of what they felt. And a gentle world, as femininty itself is gentle. Gentle voices, light steps, soft cheeks. Who ever heard of a woman raping another woman? The Bull of the Mountain, abetted by Bill Wingfield, became in our talk the symbolic opposite to the world of women. In a way I knew it was a false opposition, for Richard slipped into my mind, along with Peter and Jim Cosby, and of course Daddy, whether I would or no. Still, I banished them as swiftly as possible, for I wanted to be a true believer in Lesbia. I only glanced over the wall around the world of women surreptitiously. I was beguiled, enchanted by the idea of femininity and gentleness and sweetness as an enclosed garden, full of flowers. I was proud of my womanhood in a new way, almost as though it admitted me to a very lovely secret sorority—the world of Lesbia. Or Urania.

So the days slipped by, each as enchanted—and as passionate—as the one before. Deirdre spoke often of London—of the two of us in London and what we should do. And this, too, I found delightful. At the same time I knew, in a corner of my mind, that eventually I should have to think of Richard and make decisions. But not now. This was lotus land. Tomorrow would be time enough. Deirdre did not press me. Occasionally she gave me little questioning looks.

During all these days, now drawing into weeks, I had avoided any discussions of a serious nature with Daddy. He didn't, I was sure, have any idea of what was going on.

One morning—morning is when I think, if ever—I abruptly decided that I must talk about everything with Daddy. Maybe he would tell me what to do. I didn't tell Deirdre what I planned.

That night, after we had dined and gone into the study, as we usually did, we talked a little about a new development in one of his cases. Then, when he had finished an amusing anecdote about the opposing lawyer, there was a pause.

"Daddy," I said. "Daddy dear, there is something very per-found I want to ask you." Per-found, a childish mistake of mine, had come to be our joking way of saying that something was important.

"I am all attention," said Daddy, smiling at the old word.

"It's this, Daddy," I said. "You know that I've spent a lot of time with Deirdre Digby in these past weeks, and you know how sweet she is. Well, not to mince about the matter, I have, er, fallen in love with her, and she with me. Er, lesbians! And I don't know what to *do.*"

Daddy looked at me and the smile in his eyes was undiminished. It was a comforting look. "I had surmised as much," he said quietly.

"Oh, Daddy!" I said. "You see too much! But what *am* I to *do?*"

"You will do what you decide to do, won't you?" he said with a grin.

"But I *can't* decide," I said with sudden anguish.

"Not to decide *is* to decide," he said, still smiling. "That's the truth, Mary. Decision by default of decision. Or more simply decision by drifting. Or, you see, decision through careful weighing of the alternatives. Which line have you been following, Mary?"

"Er, drifting," I said, miserably. I suddenly felt cowardly. "I'm a coward," I added.

"Bravely said—at least," Daddy commented.

"All right, Daddy," I said, smiling a little myself. "I have decided this much, anyway. I will become brave and, er—think. But let me ask you this: Suppose I decide to leave Richard. Suppose I decide that I am —well, really a lesbian. What will you feel about it? Will you wish, in your heart of hearts, you know, that I weren't? What I mean is, will you *mind?*"

Daddy looked at me, his eyes still smiling, and he tapped out his pipe and began to refill it. He didn't say anything while he was doing it, but that didn't bother me, for Daddy never speaks until he knows what he wants to say.

"I know what you're asking me, Mary," he said finally. "And I'm rather glad that you asked: I think the answer needs the question. Let me answer you briefly first: I do not mind."

"I am very thankful, Daddy," I said.

"Mary, my daughter," he said. "After the long suffering of your childhood, you have come out into the sunlight, not twisted in body—or mind. You have become what I value, an independent human being. You have a mind and you use it. I'm not saying of course that you mightn't make a mistake. But you're honest enough, independent enough, and thoughtful enough to recognise it if you do. And recover. You are like your mother in that."

"Thank you, Daddy," I said. "If I am so, you had a lot to do with it."

"Who can ever measure?" he replied. "Now, my dear, have I answered your question? Yes, I think so. For I have told you, truly, what is most important to me—that you be fully human, which is to be independent of mind, making your choices with integrity. I shall be sorry for Val's pain, if you decide for Deirdre, for, as you know, I have great respect and love for Val; but that is a separate matter. It is not important at the moment. You are. *What* you are. Mary, the *integrity* of your decision is more important—to me—than *what* you decide." He paused and gave me a steady look. Then he said, quietly, "Mary, dear—I'm proud of you."

I jumped up and kissed him, and then I said that I thought I had the best father in the whole wide world, and added that I never thought of him without thanking him in my heart for all he had done for me since the Disaster.

"And, Daddy, for your own integrity," I added.

He knew I meant it. He got up and made us each a whisky and soda.

"Mary," he said, after he had resumed his chair. "I needn't tell you that the pain of your childhood was my pain, too. Pain for you, and pain for myself—the end of the happy companionship with my other Mary, your mother. I loved her deeply—and still do. Some people seem to love deeply only once. But she was gone, and you—well, I needn't enlarge upon that. And then, as I put it earlier, you came out into the sunlight. Partly, we must remember, through Val. I was always glad about you and Val, because there was kindness in your marriage. It seemed to me a gay and generous love. But of course you must not stay with Val because of gratitude alone: it must not be a chain. There may indeed be other reasons to stay, and reasons to go: only you can decide. But, Mary: it's not the style of house you live in that's important: it is whether it's built to withstand the storms."

He looked at me with his warm smile, and then got up and came over to me and just put his hand on my hair and looked down on me, still smiling.

"You'll do," he said.

He returned to his big leather chair and took a meditative sip of his whisky. Holding his glass, which caught glints from the fire, he said, "There's one thing more, Mary." He looked suddenly serious, though his eyes were kind. You asked me what I felt—whether I minded, to be precise—and I've answered you honestly. But, my dear, there is another question, isn't there? Not for me to answer, though."

"What do you mean, Daddy?" I said. "What other question?"

"Whether Christ minds," he said gently. "I expect it's a question you have asked and answered, isn't it?" He held up his hand as I started to speak. "Wait, Mary," he said. "You must not suppose that I know the answer or think I know. I don't myself even ask it. The answer for me must come from you—what you do. What you choose. If the God we believe in has a word for you, He will certainly not speak it to me. It is, you see, your question. What you are—what you decide—that will be my answer." He smiled and said again, "You'll do."

I smiled back, loving him enormously. Although he had left it all to me, giving me his trust, and although I felt that I had a huge stack of thoughts on my mental desk to work through, I suddenly felt that I might be able to do it.

All I said was, "I'll be mindful, Daddy. Thank you for your trust."

In the morning, as I drank my early tea in bed, I decided to tell Deirdre that I must take the afternoon to write some letters. Then I would think. Or try to.

But when she came, a little later, she said that she must leave early enough to change and lunch with her father and some people from England at the Embassy.

Then we kissed each other good morning and talked happily about all sorts of things. I put the thought of decisions out of my mind, except for the fleeting one that I could never leave her, never. I looked at her, the soft lovely contours of her face framed in her dark hair; and her big brown eyes looked into mine.

"Your eyes," she said softly. "Blue pools under the summer sky."

"Your eyes," I murmured, unable to think of anything for brown eyes to be like—"your eyes are the eyes of love, Deirdre." As always I loved to speak her name.

Then we were in each other's arms, there on my bed. Two women loving . . .

When we had come through passion, still holding one another tenderly, we lay there, smiling a little at each other. A bird chirped on the apple tree in the garden.

Deirdre sighed, a gentle little sigh. "Oh my Mary," she murmured. "I love you so much." I stroked her cheek. Then she murmured, "Our loving is so incredibly beautiful. Heavenly . . . it's as though we went together to the very gateway to heaven . . ."

A little shock went through me. I wonder if she could have felt it. In all our talking I had never mentioned that secret meadow at the Gateway to Heaven. Now she, lovely Deirdre . . . the love of women . . . the gateway to heaven . . .

Deirdre stirred and looked at the watch on the arm that was round her.

"Good lord!" she said. "I must rush! Call me this afternoon—after two-thirty."

When she had gone, I abruptly decided to go back to Rock Creek Park. It was just such a morning as the other time, a weekday, rather chilly with dampness in the air. A grey sky with patches of blue. I sat on the same bench as before. Had I ever been away? Yes, because the buds on the trees were little young leaves now.

All right, think, I told myself.

What was I going to decide? I thought about Deirdre and how I loved her. I thought about Richard, remembering. I remembered his steadfast love when I was a lump. I remembered love and passion and all our gay adventuring. I remembered our meadow at the Gateway to Heaven. How strange that Deirdre should have said that! Which was the gateway to heaven? The love of Richard or the love of Deirdre? Or both?

A thought grew in my mind. Could we, could we possibly . . . all three . . . ? People do. Surely Richard would love her, too. Mightn't a threesome be a richer love, more full of delight? Oh, it's possible, it is, it is! Oh, God, to kiss Deirdre without loss or guilt! But—but what would Richard be doing while I kissed Deirdre? How strange—only two can kiss. As though we were *designed* to be in pairs.

Designed. I suddenly felt that the word was dangerous. But I was not able to veer away from—God. I wished not to cope with that thought, but there it was. It seemed stark. "God," I said aloud. Maybe I should pray. I can't not pray. Daddy didn't say so, but he meant it. It's part of integrity, isn't it? I don't think God will listen, though.

"Oh, God!" I whispered. "Do listen! I don't know what to *do*. Help me! Help! . . . Please! In the name of Jesus, please! Amen."

For a moment I felt a sort of peace. I had turned it over to God. I just sat there. Then I felt strength in the air. I didn't feel strong, but it was as though there was strength all around me. And then a voice—I knew I wasn't hearing it in my ears—a voice, small as an atom, clear as the note of tapped crystal, yet awesome in power, said: "Child, child! There is only one gateway to heaven." It was, somehow, as though a great bell had been struck, a single stroke, beautiful and terrible, inside my head.

"It meant Val," I muttered. "But what about Deirdre?" There was no answer. Had there been a voice?

My hair moved in a gusty breeze. A sheet of newspaper went tumbling across the grass. I glimpsed a headline. UNION APPEALS, it said.

Union? But that's what Richard and I have—marriage. That's what marriage *is*. The thought was like another iron stroke of that great bell. Marriage! The thought fell into the tortured confusion of my mind with a clang, and the humming note went on and on. Not just love but marriage.

But—Deirdre. Aren't we married—really married—too? Or can't we be, in our hearts? No, it is not marriage, not yet. But could it be? "No," I muttered aloud. Why did I say that? Why couldn't it be? I love her. But the No persisted. I was married to Richard—a man. A man and a woman, that was marriage. If I *feel* that No, what does it mean? Does it mean that I'm not really a lesbian? Is it just convention? What is marriage?

Marriage. Not love only, that is certain. I love Deirdre, but we are not therefore married. Marriage is intention to make a union for life: that is what the vows are. The commitment. Not till love dies but till you die. That's what I *promised* Richard.

"All right, Mary Vallance," I whispered. "You're a commitment-breaker."

My word was given. I *am* married to Richard. We built our marriage on our vows and our trust as well as love. My love for Deirdre has nothing to do with it. *Nothing!* Val and I created our marriage out of thousands of days and nights together, a thousand patiently-worked-for understandings; we built it out of pain and joy. And underlying all was the promise, each one trusting. We built our house to endure always,

274

like the hills. Oh! that's what Daddy said: built to withstand the storms. That's what this is—a storm. A storm of passion. I love her, but that's not the main thing. Val and I are *married.* We made a house with minds and hands to endure the storm, as Daddy said. Now it's come!

How do we endure the storm? There's only one answer, isn't there? But that's almost what the Voice said—"only one gateway to heaven."

I looked at the young leaves on the tree. A patch of cold remote blue had appeared in the sky. I looked at that. And I thought: It's not a question of loving Deirdre or Richard most. That's the wrong question. The question is whether the house we made shall stand or fall. The house I am committed to.

And I knew the answer to the question, now that I had asked the right one. What Richard and I had made over the years must not come to empty loss. All that unites us, with roots reaching back before wings, could be torn apart, as my arm could be torn off, but Deirdre and I could never be united by any of that. New things but not the past, which would be ruined to remember forevermore. My word has been given. My love for Deirdre does not cancel it. There is such a thing as honour. Daddy must have meant that when he said integrity. He knew. He knew I'd remember my word.

I looked at the patch of cold blue sky, and I knew what I must do. I sat there on the hard bench knowing it. Deirdre—I saw her face tear-streaked as it was that first morning—Deirdre, you and I must part.

For the first time, I completely knew what commitment was. One's truth, one's integrity, one's honour.

The knowledge of what I must do was as sure—and as cold—as the stars. I must see Deirdre once more and tell her.

Quiet and sad, I drove back to Georgetown and let myself in—Jolly had gone some place that afternoon. I sat down at Daddy's desk in the study and picked up the telephone. She would be home from the Embassy by now. I dialled the familiar number.

"Deirdre," I said, when she had answered. "I've got to talk to you. May I come over?"

"What is it, Mary?" she said. "You sound very serious. Are you—are you going back to Richard?"

"Yes," I said. "I didn't mean to tell you like this. I must go back. I love you, but I—I am committed to him. I love him, too, but it's not which one I love the most. It's—it's *commitment!* Marriage. . . . Do you understand?"

There was no reply.

Finally I said, "Are you there, Deirdre?"

"I'm here," she said in a small voice. There was another pause. Then, in a stronger voice, she said, "I've known this, Mary. I knew you would go back. I knew you wouldn't be able to break your loyalty. That's the whole thing, isn't it?"

"Yes, it is," I said. "Oh, Deirdre! I'm so *sorry!*"

Again there was a little silence. I could hear a distant siren. Then Deirdre said with a catch in her voice, "What a strange and bitter world this is! Love isn't always victorious. Mary, I . . . I don't blame you." A tiny sob came down the telephone line, and again, suddenly, I saw her as she had been that first morning, the brown eyes full of tears.

"Deirdre, darling," I said, feeling the tears on my own cheek. "I do love you. I shall always love you. But I *have* to do this. Try to forgive me."

"I do. I do!" she said. "But, Mary, please—don't come. I'll go up to Toronto tonight, where my cousin is. I don't think I could bear a meeting. Perhaps neither of us could."

"All right," I said sadly, with a sense of relief and desolation mixed. "All right . . ." I suddenly sobbed. "Deirdre? This . . . this is goodbye, isn't it?"

"Yes," she whispered. "It's all I have to give you and Richard—a goodbye. Goodbye, darling."

The line went dead.

Deirdre was gone, gone out of my life. Of course I could call her back, but I knew I wouldn't. I wiped away my tears, but more came. I thought of tears on her face. I suddenly thought of her leaving that first morning, and I knew that she had really expected that to be the end. I should have stopped then. It was my fault. Now Deirdre was weeping, there in her empty house. I wanted to run over there and kiss the tears away. I knew I wouldn't. I thought, I shall always remember her with tears on her face. Deirdre of the Sorrows.

I sat there for another quarter of an hour. Then I got out Daddy's portable and began this account. My journey to Urania. Journey to Lesbia. I would break for dinner and then go on typing into the night. Tomorrow I would send it to Richard. Tomorrow would be my birthday I remembered.

When Daddy came home, he came into the study because of the sound of typing. I ran to him and hugged him very hard.

"I'm going back to Val—if he'll have me!" I said. "Going back to my *commitment.*"

He stood back and looked at me with a little smile. Then, rather formally, he offered me his hand. We shook hands.

"Good work!" he said. "As I said before—you'll do. And if I know Val, he'll welcome you—and make it easy."

We talked only a little after dinner—I wanted to get on with my writing. I told Daddy what had happened, including the cryptic Voice—if there was a Voice—and including the importance of his own remark—the house built to withstand the storm.

"Yes," he said. "That's what marriage is. Or should be. Not a fancy house—your fancy of the moment."

I typed through part of the night and again this morning. Now it is finished, and I am twenty-four years old today—twenty-four on the twenty-fourth of April. I'll send it today. It is as true as I can make it. Richard—I'm coming home, if you'll have me. Send me a telegram.

Val—I know you will say come home. And home is where you are: I know that now, completely. I want to be there.

Val, it occurred to me this morning that I had been unfaithful to you. Unfaithful—the old word, the precise word. But then I was astonished by the sudden *feeling* that it wasn't—wasn't *quite*—unfaithfulness. It was as though the love of Deirdre and me, beautiful and passionate though it was, lacked some dimension of reality—and because of that lack, the whole thing was somehow less than unfaithfulness. I don't understand what that feeling means, but I think I should tell you. It suggests, of course, that in my feelings lesbian love-making is less real. But would that mean that it is by its *nature* less real? Or only less real for *me,* which would imply I'm not a real lesbian? Whatever the answer, you may be glad I feel so.

On another level, though, it *was* unfaithfulness. To my commitment. And the precise moment of the betrayal was in Rock Creek Park the first time—when I wouldn't pray, when I *chose* to see her again. Val, I'm sorry. That doesn't sound like enough. You can cut my head off, if you want to. Seriously, I'm truly penitent: I ask for your forgiveness. Do not send the telegram if you cannot forgive. But you will.

One thing more, Val. I love you. I never stopped loving you—that is the truth. I was caught up in the storm. I was not brave. But I knew at the back of my mind, always, that I loved you. And since I made my decision yesterday, my love for you has grown very tall.

Yours,
Mary

Journeys End

The Study, Holywell, May, 1968—Richard

The shell of silence is broken, vanished like a bubble. Mary is, in fact, singing in the other room as I open the journal and, for our future edification, begin to write the story of the days that followed the Mailing of the Manuscripts, not only on the same day but almost the same hour. My title from the Bard perhaps tells all: "Journeys end in lovers meeting."

As Mary told me to do, I read her account of the Journey to Urania or Lesbia. I've never claimed to be a speed-reader, but I fairly smoked through those pages. Then I sent her a telegram: COME HOME LOVE WITH FORGIVENESS. Then I read her journey again, the first of many re-readings.

Meanwhile, she read my immense manuscript—all the past journeys with comments and the Journey to Holywell. She read it although her decision was already made, and, she said, the rightness of her decision was confirmed a hundred times. She was most impressed—as I am myself, rather—by my conclusions about Mercia and what she called my "uncanny insight" that Miss X would be like Mercia.

In Mary's manuscript I was deeply impressed by the wisdom of her father, and wrote him a long, and very grateful, letter. Of course I was impressed, too, by the honesty and fairness of Mary's account of her thoughts and actions, and I came to understand, as well as a man can, how it had all been. I even felt a sympathy for poor Deirdre.

The past was well in hand, therefore, when we met that last Sunday in April. There was nothing we had to tell each other. All was known. We had talking to do, of course, whenever we were ready, but not telling.

There was a strangeness in meeting, there at the station. Perhaps each of us was wondering if the other would be a stranger. We did not kiss—not then. I merely took her hand and held it a moment. At the house we did kiss, almost tentatively at first—I was conscious of being a man—and then more warmly and deeply, holding each other very tightly.

Then we sat down facing each other at the kitchen table, with a pot of tea and sunlight pouring through the open window. I could hear a boy going down the street whistling. I looked at her questioningly.

"Thank you, Val," she said. "For your forgiveness, you know."

"Given gladly," I said.

"Taken gladly," she said, with a little smile. "But with thanks."

"So that's all right," I said. "It's complete. We don't need to—well, bring it up again, do we? Your father said you might make mistakes, but he thought you'd recover. He was right, as usual."

"I expect it was one of his per-found sayings," said Mary. There was a silence. Then she said, a little awkwardly, "Val, you might be wondering—well, how it seems to me . . . that is, how I feel about—well, about you being a man. Kissing you after kissing and, er, everything with a woman. . . . Are you? Wondering, I mean?"

"It did enter my mind," I admitted. "After all, I am a coarse creature by lesbian standards: I read a couple of books about it. So—how *do* you feel, old thing?"

"Right," she said. "It felt right. It seemed strange just for an instant, and then terribly *right.* . . . Er, nice, too," she added.

"Then *that's* all right," I said with a grin. "Too."

She evidently continued to think about it—after all, it was rather a key question—for she brought it up again a couple of days later. Kissing and love-making with me—with me as a man—continued to seem right to her. "But, also," she said, "it seems *real.* Right and real. I think, Val dear . . . well, you know how I've always insisted that I was a girl . . . I think I'm a *woman* now. Conrad wrote a story called "The Shadow Line" about a boy becoming a man in crisis. I've crossed my own shadow line. I am a woman. And I know with a woman's knowing that I am made for loving a man: for loving *you,* dearest Val. And for keeps."

I knew it was the truth by the look in her eyes and the tone of her voice, but I knew it also by the depth and passion of our loving. There would never again be a Deirdre, and something in me—some faint uneasiness about the future—was dispelled. Once she said with an air of discovery that it was probably much easier for women's friendship, with its charming intimacy and casual kisses, to slip over into something else than it would be for friendship between a woman and a man. There wouldn't be that little sense of being on guard with another woman.

We did talk a bit about commitment, although Mary's thoughts in Rock Creek Park had really said it all. The whole point about commitment is that it is a gift from one person to another. Its sole purpose is to give the other something to depend on. If a commitment ends when the one who gave it falls in love with somebody else, then it never meant anything in the first place. People in love stay together without commitments. Commitment is a gift requiring an act of will. We recommitted ourselves to one another, knowing exactly what we meant, for ever.

It was accepted between us that my idea of the Deirdre affair being, in some sense, a completion of Mary's childhood crush on Mercia had much truth in it. But was there some failure on our part that helped to make it possible? We considered this, remembering from our reading of the journal all that our love had been. After a good deal of talk, we decided that we had been less close in this past year, not only because of the Movement but because of taking our love for granted. And that, we agreed, was deadly danger, for a love taken for granted ceases to deepen. Eternal vigilance is necessary, not only for freedom but for love. We summed it up as Bob Dylan might have done: A love not busy bein' born is busy dyin'.

One night I said, "You know, Mary, something you said in your account of the Journey to Lesbia—or Urania—has stuck in my mind. Something important."

"Something I said?" said Mary. "What?"

"You were talking about that first morning and wanting to kiss her again," I said. "And the thing that stuck in my mind was where you said that it seemed to you that kissing her again would be right and good—remember?"

"Oh, yes!" she said. "I remember very well indeed. Right and good —and yet, at the *same* time, you know, *not* right. Incredibly confusing. And it kept on being so."

"It must have been!" I said. "Confusing, I mean. Anyway, I kept thinking about that. It seemed important somehow, but why? Then this morning I saw it. Something very simple and—I think—profound. It's this: Merely being in love with somebody is not a sanction for anything —but it *feels* like one. The very word 'sanction' suggests a sort of sacred approval—a divine okay. But being in love is *not* a sanction for the betrayal of anyone—your wife or husband, your friend, your children. It's not a sanction for breaking your word or throwing honour in the dust. Not at *all!* But what's so damned important is this: inloveness always *seems* to be a sanction. People don't expect it to. Maybe they mean to keep their vows. But, then, as you put it, it *seems* so good and right. Like a god's sanction. The sanction of Eros! But it *isn't.*"

"Oh, you're right!" said Mary, excitedly. "That's exactly it! When I wanted to kiss Deirdre so desperately, it *felt* right. Something sanctioned, as you say. The perfect word. But, Val! why isn't the world ringing with warnings about this—this false sanction? The Church, at least, should have been pointing it out."

"One would think so," I said. "Of course in this century it's often felt to be a genuine sanction. Look at modern novels and films. Of course the author usually sets it up so that whoever is betrayed more or less deserves it—but the sanction is there. If you're in love, anything goes. All's fair in love or war. Try to think of one modern novel where a character really looks at what it means to betray his vows, as you really looked in Rock Creek Park."

"I can't think of any," said Mary. "But I can think of some with that implied sanction. I shall look for it from now on."

"You do see why it's so important, don't you?" I said. "The false sanction?"

"Oh, yes!" she said. "Because nobody is aware that it will happen. So when they fall in love with someone other than their spouse, they feel overwhelmingly that *this* love is blessed or something. They don't question its rightness."

"Right you are," I said. "We're forewarned—or after-warned—now. Maybe we should write a book and warn others."

"More and more," said Mary, "I can see why Daddy lays such stress on me being an independent human being. It means questioning all the going certainties of one's own time. Like the faith in psychiatry. Or the sanction of inloveness."

Although this was an enlightening conversation, a little sense of there being a deeper question that we should be asking ourselves persisted in my mind, although I, at least, didn't know what the deeper question was. Why had she come so close to failure? Or why had we? We had won through, but would we always?

Early one Sunday morning—the first Sunday in May and a week from her homecoming—we were sitting in the kitchen with mugs of coffee laced with cream. Birds sang.

Mary took a meditative sip of coffee and said, "Val dear, do you think Deirdre happened because—well, because we've got more remote from God? Sort of cut off?"

"Ah," I said. "I've been having some vague thoughts along those lines. Of course I did have that strong sense of God's love after I turned to Him last month. You, too, in the park. But when you look at the whole year . . . Remember how we used to pray together when we were first at Oxford? And read those deep-Christian books?"

"Oh, Val!" she said. "Let's read some of them again. Right away! Let's read C. S. Lewis's *Great Divorce*—what people put ahead of God."

"Good!" I said. "We'll begin tonight—read it aloud together."

"Val," she said. "Those poems about the Movement you wrote—when I read them again, some of them seemed sort of hard and bitter. It was right after I had heard that Voice in Rock Creek Park. The poems said what we both felt, but they didn't sound very Christian . . . er, no charity."

"I *was* bitter!" I said. "Our own country! Still, you're right, of course.—Mary, do you realise we haven't made a communion since we came to America? We haven't even been in a church, except that once in New York when we heard that horrible sermon—pantheism pretending to be Christianity."

"Pantheistic humanism," she said. "Dreadful! In a Christian church, too!"

I glanced at the clock. "Look!" I said. "We've just got time. Why don't we snap into our clothes and go to early communion at—what is it, St James? No, St John's."

Half an hour later we were kneeling in St John's.

We had never really doubted that the wings had come from God. And our faith had deepened at Oxford. It had been a high and singing thing, the Christian faith—that God had dwelt in the world as the Word made flesh and had been killed by the world, yet had risen and dwelt in us and we in Him. What suddenly flashed into me there in St John's devoutly kneeling was that we had somehow fallen away from putting Christ *first*. And I saw with clarity that that falling away had something to do—perhaps everything to do—with the Deirdre thing. Nothing in our lives could be apart from God. I whispered the gist of the thoughts to Mary, and she nodded vigorously.

The priest had finished the consecration of the elements. He turned from the altar towards us, holding the Host.

He looked at us, the ten or eleven gathered there, for a moment. Then he said in a low voice: "This is the Bread of Life. This is the Gateway to Heaven."

I looked at Mary. Two startled sea-blue eyes were looking at me. Then we went up to the altar of God.

When we had come out into the sunshine of the May morning, I looked at Mary with love and said, "It is meet and right so to do. Isn't it? Let's change our clothes and drive up into the Berkshires and walk, shall we?"

We talked as we drove, talked about getting too caught up in the affairs of this world to remember the underlying reality of God. Here, too, as in keeping both love and freedom, a sort of eternal vigilance is needed. Or attention—one must *attend* to the spiritual life. And, I added, by going to church this morning we were attending to it, belatedly.

"I agree," said Mary. "Another way to put it is that you must have *active* faith. Ours hasn't been. I'm shocked at how far away we had got. I think we've been in awful peril. Not just losing each other but—well, losing our souls. When morality begins to disintegrate, you are getting pretty far from the source: God. —That looks like a nice little road. Why don't you turn down there?"

"Okay," I said, turning onto it. Then I said softly: 'Child, child! There is only one gateway to heaven.' It certainly sounds like the Holy Spirit. Just what it *would* say. Of course it might have been a trick of your, er, overheated imagination, but it sounds authentic. And then the amazing thing of the Rector's saying those same words this morning at the Eucharist. Incredible! Coincidence or inspiration, it's incredible re-enforcement, isn't it?"

"Yes," said Mary. "If ever a man seemed inspired—without knowing it at all—he did. Also, apart from the words of the Voice, there was that sense of awe-ful power all around, there in the park. I believe it. I do."

I slowed. A small track led into a wood for about ten yards. I turned into it and stopped and switched off. We climbed out and walked back to the road and continued along it in the May sunshine. The sky was deep blue, dotted with small fluffy clouds, and birds sang, full of the same springtime enthusiasm we were feeling. After walking peacefully along for a time, not talking, we spied a log at the woods edge of a meadow, and we climbed over a gate and went over and sat on it. Four or five beautiful Jersey cows looked at us for a moment with great mild eyes and then went on with the serious business of life, tearing up great mouthfuls of the long lush grass. For awhile we just sat and looked and absorbed the sunshine.

Finally I said, "The question is, what did God mean, if it was God? Isn't it?"

"Mmmm," said Mary. "At the time I thought that it meant that the only way—the gateway—was the way I was committed to: you. And it *did* mean that, I expect. But is there another level? That's what you're saying, isn't it?"

"Yes," I said. "After all, Christ is the Way—*the* Way—isn't he? So it could have been saying to be mindful of *Christ's* being the gateway to heaven. Same thing, really. Tell me again what your father said about the *other* question, when you asked him about Deirdre. What did he say about God?"

"Say 'Dee-*err*-dray'," Mary said. "And Daddy said it wasn't a question for him, whether Christ minded. What I *did* would be Daddy's answer. He said—oh, I see! He said that if God had a word to speak to me, He would speak it to *me*, not to him, Daddy."

"And the word that was spoken to you," I said, "was, 'There is only one gateway to heaven.' So, you see, that could have been the word your father meant. That is, about homosexuality. Only one way—the way of a man and a woman."

"That's three meanings, then," she said. "It could have meant I was to be true to my marriage commitment, or to follow the one way that is Christ, or to leave the lesbian way. Or maybe all three. Maybe they are all the same thing, somehow."

"Maybe," I said. "Or of course the whole thing was your imagination. Still, it's astonishing that seven words could have so many possible meanings. Leaving the Voice to one side, and our marriage, too, what do you, in fact, think about homosexuality? Your father didn't express any objections."

"He wouldn't!" said Mary. "Damn Daddy—well, not that exactly. Er, bless him. He always wants people to find their own answers. Like Socrates. Anyhow, I don't know what I think. I've always sort of assumed that love—*loving love*—is good. It is, too! It's *got* to be."

"Certainly it's good," I said. "Is that all?"

"No," she said. "It's the, er, sex. Homosex. Is that good? If the people love each other? Lots of wise Christians say homosex is wrong . . . er, sin."

"Including St Paul," I said. "What does he say about it, do you know? —What's that?" Somewhere in the distance a bell rang.

"A farm bell, I expect," said Mary. "Yes, I do know, because I looked it up while I was waiting for your telegram. I was afraid to, before. Anyway, it's in Romans I, and St Paul says that homosex—not just men; women, too—is unnatural and, therefore, degrading. 'Unnatural' is the key word. Not what we were made for, you see. Like putting grapes in your ear."

"What?!" I said, rather explosively.

"Unnatural," she said apologetically. "Eating grapes with your ears."

"Ye gods, yes!" I said, grinning. "You're an unnatural woman even to think of such a thing."

"Well, it would be unnatural, wouldn't it?" she said. "And homosex is unnatural, he says. Against nature. And I suppose the implication is— well, no babies, no fruit. Like the fig tree that got blasted."

"We could do with less fruit," I said. "The population explosion, I mean. But I suppose St Paul would say no sex, then."

"Of course," said Mary. "Look at the Catholics on birth control. Still, though, they can practice the rhythm method. That's sex without fruit. They hope. No figs."

"This world revolves around sex," I said. "Look at films and TV. Or books! 'How To Do It in 1000 New Positions!' Doesn't prove anything, of course. Real Christians have always been a tiny minority—living for the Infinite God not the Ultimate Orgasm."

"Jolly good!" said Mary, laughing. "And if your god is the Ultimate Orgasm, then of course that justifies homosex. Still, apart from St Paul, isn't it strange that *Jesus* never said a word about homosex?"

"Not really," I said. "Wouldn't you think it a bit strange if some preacher or congressman solemnly pointed out that murder wasn't a good thing? I mean, we all know that. The condemnation of murder is implicit in the society. Well, Jesus, unlike Paul, was talking to Jews—to whom homosex was an abomination."

"Oh!" she said. "I never thought of that. Deirdre was talking about how Jesus never condemned it, and I was impressed. Not so significant, after all."

"No, not very," I said. "Not at all, actually."

"There's something else," she said. "About homosex, I mean. I get the impression from things I've read, and from things Deirdre said, too, that homosexual relationships—well, don't last. Or if they do, the people aren't faithful to each other."

"My impression, too," I said. "Of course, marriage—look at the divorces! It could be just the falling away from God—moral disintegration, as you said earlier. The question is, whether two Christian people who really loved each other could have a homosexual relationship that was good in God's eyes? Or can homosex *ever,* for some people, be right? I read some book where a man was arguing that St Paul was really condemning heterosexual thrill-seekers, not real homos, or maybe condemning sex without love. I don't think *we* can answer the question of whether it may be, for *some* people—other people—right. After all,

285

remember what your father said about God not telling *him* what He had to say to *you*. If God has a word for, say, Deirdre—or any other homo— He ain't saying it to us. So we can't condemn, can we?"

"Certainly not!" said Mary. "And I agree, we cannot decide for others. But, you know, I think God has spoken to *me*—about me, I mean."

"What?" I said. "Or how? Though I think I know."

"Not just the Voice," she said. "Though that, too. But remember my feeling that the, er, thing with Deirdre wasn't *quite,* on one level, unfaithfulness?"

"Yes," I said. "It impressed me very much. Also, it made *me* feel that it wasn't, quite."

"Oh, I'm glad of that," she said. "And do you remember what I said followed from that?"

"Tell me," I said.

"One of two things," she said. "Either that homosex for *everyone* is less real or less genuine than heterosex, or that it is for *me* less so. So, you see, though we'll never know which it is, it doesn't make any difference to me: I *know* for me."

"Right you are," I say. "Quite valid. Incidentally, I think I know for myself without such thorough research." Mary uttered a small "Ahem!" and lowered her eyes, and I grinned. "It was only an approach in my case," I continued. "Still, I liked the chap then and now—he was perfectly civilised about it. Anyhow, I knew it was not for me. But there's something else. I read somewhere, while you were, er, gone, an argument that we are all bisexual—you know, able to go either way. I disagreed at the time—as you know from my account—because I couldn't find in myself any inclination to the other way. But your experience is more important, isn't it? You went the other way and, well, enjoyed it, didn't you?"

"Yes, but—" said Mary, and paused, thinking.

"Yes," I said, *"but.* But you had that feeling that it *wasn't* quite real or genuine. So, don't you see, if that feeling was valid for *you* . . ."

"I'm certain it was," she said.

"All right," I said. "Then homosex itself wasn't valid for you. And that proves that *you,* at least, aren't truly bisexual. And if *you* aren't, it can't be said that we *all* are, can it?"

"No," said Mary. "And I don't believe it for a minute."

"Let's get back to the Voice," I said.

"Look!" said Mary. "That bird—it's sitting on the cow's back! Oh, it's gone. —Yes. The Voice. And, Val, there's something else we might think about. Mercia. You know, on the beach that night. Last Sunday when I was on my way home from Daddy's I thought about what she said—or what I thought she said. She said our love was holy—and we should love each other recklessly."

"I remember," I said. "I've often thought of that—reckless love. She meant daring love, not cautious or looking out for self, don't you think? Brave love. After all, courage is the virtue on which all the rest hang, even love."

"I know it—too well!" she said. "But Val, she also said something else. She said we should offer our love to God. We never talked about that, and I don't quite know what it means, do you? But it's part of the whole thing."

"True," I said. "Your father. The Voice. Mercia. The last two possibly imaginary. But also possibly not. All sort of pointing somewhere. Where?"

"Yes, where?" said Mary. "Whither? Offer love to God and don't be selfish or cautious—that's Mercia. Hear God's word to *us*—that's Daddy. And only one gateway—that's the Voice. It all points to God, that's where."

"Putting God first," I added. "Making all choices with God in mind, open to intimations of his will."

"As I did when I galloped back to Deirdre's arms," said Mary with a wry grin. "Temptation can be, er, quite tempting. Clearly I am the awful example of what not to do. *Auwe, auwe!*"

"Cheer up, old thing!" I said. "If, through you, we both head in the right direction . . ."

"Mmmm," she said. "Anyway, you're right about putting Christ first. God has spoken His word to us in this whole thing."

"And that one way is even reckless," I said. "Faith is not knowing. It's betting your life on Christ. That's reckless, isn't it?"

"It is, it is!" said Mary. "Of course it's just as reckless if you bet the other way, even if you decide by not deciding. More reckless, really."

"Madness!" I said. "Not facing up to *that* decision." There was silence for a moment. "Well," I added. "We know our heading now, don't we?"

"We do," she said. "And, darling, we must keep each other mindful."

"You know, Mary," I said. I looked at her. "That poem of yours— 'Nocturne'—that your father had . . . the one about the, er, baby . . . it touched me very much. I read it aloud. And I've been, er, thinking about it."

"What an awful blunt way you have of not saying something!" said Mary with a smile. "If the Voice and Mercia on the beach weren't just imagination, then what about that one-minute baby a million years ago? That's what you're implying. Right?"

I smiled, too. "Something like that," I said. "And what your father said about God's eternal Now. If the past and present are all one to God, then the future, too. Not that we don't have choice—but God sees us choosing. And that, er baby . . ."

"Is what we shall have chosen?" she said. "We've never talked about children with God in mind, have we? I think we'll have to. Only, let's not talk about it now. My mind is stuffed with thoughts. It's only a very little one—my mind, I mean."

"Swiss watches are small, too," I said with a laugh. "But, as you say, later. Let's walk on now, shall we?"

We arose and walked down the road, a small breeze in our faces. I felt a sense of peace—and Mary's face was serene—because it seemed to me that, not only had we come through the storm but we were now stronger than we had been before it. The peace was like a sense of safety. No, not safety—that's dangerous. The peace came from strength and vigilance. And the right heading. I told Mary of my thought.

"The Gateway to Heaven," she murmured.

She and I walked on, hand in hand, through the Maytime.

The End